THE JUPITER GAME

Todd J. McCaffrey

A Foxxe Frey Book

THE JUPITER GAME

Copyright © 2018 Todd J. McCaffrey

Books by Todd McCaffrey

Science fiction

City of Angels

Collections

The One Tree of Luna (And Other Stories)

Dragonriders of Pern® Series

Dragon's Kin

Dragon's Fire

Dragon Harper

Dragonsblood

Dragonheart

Dragongirl

Dragon's Time

Sky Dragons

Non-fiction

Dragonholder: The Life And Times (so far) of Anne McCaffrey

Dragonwriter: A tribute to Anne McCaffrey and Pern

Books by The Winner Twins and Todd McCaffrey

Nonfiction:

The Write Path: World Building

Fantasy:

Winter Wyvern

Dedication

For Jay A. Katz—the Katz who defends dragons!

And

David A. Berger—for his kindness to strangers

CONTENTS

CHAPTER ONE

The Eurocos Spaceship *Harmonie*, near Jupiter

NIKOLAI ANATOLY ZHUKOV RAPPED THE SIDE OF HIS EMPTY WATER GLASS WITH his spoon. Silence overcame the assembled mess on the third tap. He rose with brisk, ordered movements. His blue eyes possessed a menace that was, in this instance, feigned, but nonetheless daunting. He held the silence until it seemed the tension was unbearable.

"History," he intoned in flawless French, "is no somber matter."

Unobtrusively, he flicked open his left hand. At that signal, the doors to the kitchen beyond burst open. Cooks' helpers, grinning ear to ear, raced to dispense vodka, cognac, champagne, and schnapps to the amazed crew.

"It is a drinking matter!" Smiles of relief were exchanged and glasses charged. "*Mesdames et messieurs*, Jupiter!"

Nikolai executed a precise turn to face the wallscreen displaying a view of the giant planet as seen from the command section of the ship, raised his glass, and tossed back his drink.

"Jupiter!" the crew chorused.

Zhukov turned to face them, beaming from ear to ear. The moment he did, the screen behind him dimmed, the room darkened, and the faces peering beyond him twisted with fear.

"*Merde alors!*" Karl Geister, his German first officer, exclaimed, pointing.

"*Gott im Himmel!*" his French first officer, Elodie Reynaud, agreed in counterpoint.

"What the bloody hell's that?" Peter Murray, the eccentric Englishman, demanded in his own tongue.

Nikolai allowed his eyes to follow the Englishman's bony arm to the object on the screen and felt his face drain of blood. He was at the wall intercom an instant before the ship's klaxon sounded.

"Red alert! Red alert!" Strasnoye, officer of the watch, declared. "Unidentified object on intercept course. Captain to the bridge!"

Zhukov spared time only to shout hoarsely "Stations!" before he ducked out of the mess, climbing to the angle where he jumped from the rotating crew section to the zero-gee command section. With a yell of "Make way!" he kicked off and floated out in zero-gee to the bridge.

The bridge was divided into four parts representing the key sections of operation of *Harmonie*: communications, navigation, life support, and propulsion. Everything was automated; typically, there was only the officer of the deck and a crewman to oversee all control of *Harmonie*.

Gregor Ivanovich Strasnoye was the officer on duty. He was one of the few Russian officers on *Harmonie* handpicked by Zhukov as an up-and-coming young officer, perhaps because Gregor's father was a high-ranking politico.

Gregor was in the nav quadrant. On the main screen was an overhead display of their trajectory around Jupiter. Blinking a baleful red was an object some distance from *Harmonie's* current position, but its course, marked in dotted lines, indicated a collision hazard.

By now the other officers had reached their stations. Elodie and Karl took stations just behind each of his shoulders, making Nikolai distinctly nervous.

Nikolai turned around, gave his two first officers a slight grin, and shouted across to propulsion, "Murray, stand by for evasive action!"

"Righto, Skipper!"

Zhukov turned back to Gregor. "How much will we need?"

"Not much, sir, it's just that—"

"Don't babble, man, do the burn!" Nikolai shouted. Gregor licked his lips nervously, started to say something, thought better of it, and turned back to the main nav console. "Computed. Program running."

Nikolai bent closer to the display, reading off the anticipated burn and vector, glancing first at the bright green line, which predicted their new orbit, and then to the countdown timer.

The first thrust, using reaction control jets to turn *Harmonie*, was almost imperceptible. Maneuvering rockets then fired to push *Harmonie* slightly to one side. The collision alert klaxon silenced. Finally, the Reaction Control jets turned *Harmonie* back on line with her new trajectory.

"There, that wasn't so bad, was it?" Nikolai said in a cheerful tone of congratulation. "Nothing to it, eh, Gregor?"

Then the klaxon blared again.

"Sir, its matched course with us!"

Nikolai was already racing to the comm section, programming the main console. "It's that goddamned American ship fooling around with us!"

"*Voyager?*" Murray responded. "No way; she's still on trials."

"Gregor, get a radar dish on that object and scan it," Nikolai ordered. He dialed up a broadband link on the comm console. "Unidentified ship, this is the Eurocos vessel *Harmonie*. You are on an intercept course. Please take evasive action immediately."

"I'm getting a good return now, sir," Gregor called from his seat at one of the secondary nav displays. The ensign gasped. "Length, ten kilometers—"

"What!" Elodie, Karl, and Nikolai exclaimed as one.

"Run a check on that gear, lad!" Murray added.

"It's correct," Gregor retorted. "Length, ten kilometers; width, two kilometers. It is maneuvering again." Gregor bent closer to the display.

Elodie, who had taken the main nav display, called out: "Captain Zhukov, the target has maneuvered to rendezvous." She paused. "Projecting its original course backward, the ship came from somewhere beyond Pluto."

Instantly, Zhukov triggered *Harmonie*'s distress beacon. "Who's receiving back on Earth?"

"Goldstone," Karl responded.

"Shit." Zhukov muttered. "What's the time delay?"

"One-way light speed is thirty-three minutes, one second," Elodie replied.

Zhukov hit "all hail" on the intercom beside the main comm console.

"This is the captain," he said. "We have altered course to avoid an object on intercept with us. The object itself has altered course to return to an intercept orbit." He paused. "While we may be the first manned mission to Jupiter and its moons, we are quite possibly not the first sentient visitors."

"Thirty-one minutes from now, Goldstone is going to go nuts!" Karl Geister said.

Nikolai glared at him. "First Officer Geister, you have the bridge. I shall be in my cabin."

"What's with ironpants?" Geister asked of no one in particular after the captain had departed.

Elodie gave him a sour look. "Code groups."

"Oh, to his government!"

An indistinct noise came from the vicinity of Ensign Strasnoye. Elodie glared at the young Russian. "Ensign, prepare to run a detailed analysis on the alien vessel."

"Already initiated, ma'am," the Russian said in carefully neutral tones.

"Very good," Elodie said. "Karl, why don't we see what special skills our passengers can apply to this situation?"

The crew of the *Harmonie* was mildly contemptuous of their scientist passengers. While this mission was *Harmonie*'s maiden voyage, the ship had a full slate of future missions assigned already. The passenger section consisted of seventy scientists who would remain behind in the orbiting habitat, establishing the first permanent base orbiting Jupiter. They would conduct not only a detailed scientific survey of the Jupiter system, but also an engineering evaluation to select one of Jupiter's satellites for settling.

Karl called up the passenger list on the main screen of the comm console. Elodie moved close beside him to get a better view and, also, to whisper to him, "Did you tell him? Does he know?"

Karl shook his head. Elodie hissed her displeasure.

A beep from the main comm console distracted them. Elodie glanced over at the telltale light, deftly called up a window on their main display, and pointed to the stream of numbers. "See? Code groups."

Karl glanced at them and grunted. "Going out on the data line."

Elodie stole a quick look at Strasnoye, then muttered softly, "We could decode it."

Down in his cabin, Captain Zhukov carefully replaced his code generator in its secret compartment.

There! That's done, he thought to himself. He smiled as he imagined his two first officers trying to decipher the gibberish he had sent out on the data link; his real message hidden in his verbal report to the combined Russian/European space exploration agency, Eurocos.

Thirty-three minutes from now, the message would be received by the dish antennae at Goldstone, Arizona. The Americans would copy it for their own purposes, of course, but only Ivan Petrovich, the on-site Eurocos representative, would be able to interpret the secret message. Lights would be on late at the Kremlin tonight.

*　*　*

Deep Space Network, Goldstone, Arizona

"My god!" John Ahrens, radio technician at Goldstone, exclaimed as Zhukov's voice faded into silence.

"Roger, *Harmonie*, we copy," Christopher Rogers, the unflappable station chief, responded to the stale message. "We will initiate a DSN emergency at this time. All receivers are being alerted. Good luck. Goldstone out."

Rogers pulled off his headset and turned to stare at Ahrens for a long moment. "Mr. Ahrens, in future, please keep your comments to yourself." Reprimand delivered, he continued in the same tones, "Gentleman, please ensure that all DSN stations are alerted to this emergency." He looked at Ivan Petrovich. "Mr. Petrovich, a complete downlink has been sent to Den Haag, do you need anything else?"

Ivan Petrovich nodded. "I shall need a phone presently." The beady-eyed, wiry Russian made an attempt at a smile. "And if you have any good luck charms or prayers, I think they're in order."

Ahrens guffawed but Rogers merely blinked. "Yes, of course." He gestured. "You can use the phone in my office." As soon as the door was closed, Rogers turned to the radio console. Ahrens looked on in surprise as Rogers spun the dials.

"Whitestar, Whitestar, this is Goldbird," Rogers' words rattled out. "Prepare for *flash* traffic"—he paused, turned to survey a computer console, keyed in a quick sequence, and finished—"now!" Two lights blinked on the computer console. A look of satisfaction crossed Rogers' face. "Goldbird out."

With unnatural speed, Rogers spun the radio dials and returned the station to its original frequency. He fixed a long, hard look on Ahrens.

"You saw nothing," Rogers told him in a whispered version of his usual slow bass rattle.

The office door opened before Ahrens could respond and the Russian emerged, looking relieved.

"Everything all right?" Ahrens asked.

"I have informed Eurocos." Petrovich said. "They are rather"—he paused—"excited."

* * *

The White House, Washington, DC

The vice president was dumb. There was no question about it. Following a well-established tradition in the party, the vice president had been especially chosen for his complete lack of gray matter and his boyish good looks.

"You would think," a *Times* reporter had remarked sourly over a decade ago, "that the public would catch on."

They did not, and he was elected.

It was also tradition that the vice president was given titular charge of America's space exploration program. The space program was safe with the VP, especially considering that it was, because of decades of neglect, as emasculated as the VP was brainless.

However, the previous administration had *not* followed tradition. On the contrary, it had messed up everything. For one thing, it had been a humanist administration, breaking a decades old stranglehold on the presidency. The Humanist Party had slowly coalesced out of the ashes of the long-dying Democratic Party. With such a past, it was no wonder that the Humanist Party took two decades to gain access to the White House. It was also no wonder that when it *did* get in, it proceeded to fund colossal new space exploration. That was not traditional. The Humanist Party had an intelligent vice president, which is probably why they lost the next election.

Because of that unforgiveable break in tradition, appropriately attributed to the past president's bizarre and all too public peccadilloes, the VP had inherited a vibrant, expanding space program. A well-funded space program—because it had been so well-endowed by the Humanist Administration for the new administration to strangle. Too many special interests were involved, as was traditional. Of course, the Manhattan Meteor had had something to do with the funding levels; *"Remember Manhattan!"* was an exclamation that brought tears to the eyes of most Americans.

The vice president, as might be expected given his predecessor's legacy, was not completely traditional. Ned Alquay was dumb in the acceptable manner, handsome in the acceptable manner, and fawningly respectful of the president—but he had two slight flaws: he did not realize he was dumb, and he had a penchant for espionage.

It was these two flaws that caused him to burst in upon one of the president's high-level staff meetings, one that was *not* a photo opportunity.

"Mr. President, Mr. President!" the veep cried as he burst in.

In the tense silence, the president heaved a patient sigh. "Yes, what is it?"

"A flash from Goldbird, sir," Alquay said urgently, waving the message in the air.

"Goldbird?" Brian McPhee, White House chief of staff, asked of Charles Sumner, intelligence chief.

With heavy sarcasm, Sumner responded, "I believe that is one of the vice president's own operatives."

McPhee snorted. "What's up? We're busy."

"The enemy has reported contact with a ship!" Alquay blurted. "They were on a collision course!"

"Enemy?" McPhee mouthed to the president.

"He means Eurocos," The president explained patiently. He turned back to Alquay. "So, they've met up with a ship. They're ..." he frowned. "Where are they?"

"Jupiter," Ned answered with a vigorous nod.

"Jupiter, Jupiter, I never was good with those names," the president muttered to himself. "That's the one beyond Mars, isn't it?"

"And the asteroids," McPhee corrected. Beside him, the secretary of state suddenly sat bolt upright, face white. McPhee gave him a sour glance. "Nice of you to wake up, John."

The president did not notice the exchange. The president was thinking. Astronomy was not one of his strong points. He was the "caring president" and much better at kissing babies. Something about the whole thing nagged at him. "They didn't get hit, did they, Ned?"

"Hit?" Ned asked blankly. "Uh, no, I don't think so."

"Well, so they met up with another ship. Lots of people are exploring space nowadays." The president said, "Us, the Japanese—"

"They're only interested in the Moon." Sumner quipped. The president frowned.

"—the Chinese—"

"They don't have any long-range vessels." McPhee said. The president nodded. "Except for Mars, of course."

"—India—"

"Strictly Earth orbit," Sumner said.

The president drew a blank, looked at the others for hints. "Well, who else is there?"

The secretary of state found his voice, hoarsely. "Mr. President, I think we have a very big problem."

The president groaned loudly. "Why does it always happen in an election year?" He asked the group. "So, John, what is it? Who are those people?"

"Not people, Mr. President."

The lights burned late that night in the White House.

* * *

Far Side One, the Moon

Mac waited beside the airlock as *Voyager's* flight test crew disembarked. As usual, Captain Steele was last off.

"How'd it go, Skipper?" Mac asked the tall wiry lieutenant commander in charge of the first antimatter-powered spaceship.

"Looked good from where I sat, Mac," Steele said. She paused long enough to push her curly raven hair back behind her shoulders. Then, with a gesture, she indicated for the grizzled old engineer to precede her to the control room.

John "Mac" McLaughlin was not the Navy's idea of an engineer, not even of a civilian engineer. Mac was one of the new breed of engineers: raised to space, imbued with a devil-may-care sense of independence and a damn-their-eyes dedication, these engineers were a tougher batch than the software engineers of the last century. They still persisted in dressing how they pleased, working their own hours, and torching any red tape that stood between them and the requirements of the job.

Commander Emily Steele's original disdain for the "undisciplined" and "sloppy"—her own words—engineer had changed to grudging acceptance as she noticed, after working closely with him, Mac's meticulous attention to detail and extreme dedication to the job. Mac was just as careful about the correct use of her actual rank—lieutenant commander—and her courtesy ranks—Captain in reference to her ship, "commander" when being informal—as he was with his engineering which made her even more grateful.

"Yeah, I'm careful, Captain. I live right next door to the storage tanks," Mac had said when Steele had first mentioned it. Steele's opinion had improved steadily through the tense periods leading up to *Voyager's* first flight as Mac had stomped on any brass attempting to shorten the ground test phase.

"Admiral, you can order these tests skipped," Mac had said in tones just short of violent, "but it'll be an order I won't obey." As the admiral started to make an indignant response, Mac had added: "Nor will any other of my engineers. We'll shut you down."

McLaughlin's stand had been justified; it was only during the static test that they found the startup magnetic flux transient.

"What would have happened if we hadn't found that?" Steele had asked.

"First time we fired up, the magnetic field would have let the antimatter out of the containment chamber," Mac had said. And *Voyager* would have instantaneously become the largest explosion mankind had ever created. So, Emily listened to the engineer and kept him clear of flak from her higher-ups.

"Yeah, the computers here picked up a few bugs," Mac's response now brought up Steele's eyebrows, "but none we can't stomp out in a week or two." Her face registered her dejection. "C'mon, you can't rush a baby." He knew that Steele was itching to take *Voyager* out on a real long run, something over the hour they'd managed so far.

They were in the control center, going over *Voyager's* gig list when the messenger found them. "Commander Steele, this is just in from SPACECINC."

The message was in a sealed thumb-drive container. The messenger proffered a clipboard. "Sign here, please."

Steele and McLaughlin exchanged looks before Steele bent over to sign. The messenger carefully compared Steele's signature with a duplicate, then handed the container over.

Steele looked about for an empty office, muttering absently to McLaughlin, "Excuse me."

"Sure," McLaughlin said woodenly. "Hope its good news!"

Several minutes later, Emily Steele returned with a grim look on her face. "Let's go over that gig list, Mac."

Mac barely hesitated before responding, "Sure, Skipper." Mac looked around at the busy technicians swarming around the control center. "It'll take a while to get the gang assembled. Say, twenty minutes, the conference room?"

The Naval officer shook her head. "You and me," she said, gesturing to the office she had just left, "in there. Now."

Twenty heated minutes later, Mac was shaking his head vehemently while Steele regarded him, tight-jawed and adamant. "I don't care what those damned pencil pushers want, the bird's not ready!"

"Those are the orders, Mac," Steele said, her tone icily calm. "*Voyager* is ordered for space duty immediately."

"Where?" Mac asked. Steele shook her head. "How long?" Again a shake. "What thrust?"

"Maximum."

"And just what *is* that?" Mac snapped.

The wiry commander sighed. "I was hoping," she replied as reasonably as she could, "that you would tell me."

With a visible effort, Mac collected his temper. He let out a long sigh. "The brass've got to know your stores situation. *Voyager* can't be sent out with more than thirty days' rations."

Steele shook her head. "Skeleton crew."

Mac's eyebrows arched. "How many?"

Voyager was a test ship, but the Navy had built her with a certain amount of optimism, allowing for a full crew of thirty. They hoped to make good use of the ship both for rescue and exploration. While on trials, she was normally crewed with ten men: captain, nav officer, comm officer, life support petty officer, two telemetry specialists, two engineers, and two computer engineers.

"Four—captain, nav/comm, engineer, and comp eng."

Mac shook his head. "She's still patchwork; you'll need to have at least one guy full time on telemetry and life support's gonna require an extra eye."

"I'll watch life support."

"You've got too much else to do, get another person." Mac said, shaking his head. Then he exploded, "This is all wrong! Stick with the test crew at least or you'll never make it."

Commander Steele looked at him thoughtfully. "Drop the duplicates."

"Nah, those guys'll be working their butts off. As it is, you're skirting burnout," Mac said. "It's one thing to sit a full watch for a test run, it's another to sit watch and watch for days on a system that still has kinks in it." A stray thought distracted him. "Jupiter." He looked hard at her. "It's Jupiter, isn't it?"

Commander Steele said nothing. Mac snorted. "Some goddamned stunt just 'cos Eurocos got there first!" He shook his head. "You'll have to bring some maintenance guys along; something's sure to come loose on any journey that long." He nodded, satisfied with his answer. "Twelve men."

Commander Steele agreed. "We're gonna need more scanners. I'd appreciate it if you'd make a list of what you think'll be necessary for a thorough exploration effort."

"Scanners?" Mac furrowed his brows. Then, accusingly, "So this is more than just showing the flag!"

"I need that list before close of business, Mac," she said, clear sea-green eyes meeting his deep blue ones.

"I can stay late," Mac said.

Steele shook her head. "I want to start getting that gear aboard."

Mac looked at his watch: it was nearly four. "I can get it to you by five."

* * *

The Kremlin, Moscow, Russia

The lights burned late. Things had changed a great deal since the turn of the century, but not so much that an urgent coded call from a prominent naval officer was not carefully scrutinized.

Boris Kalinsky re-read the decoded message one more time. On the opposite side of his desk Vladimir Novitsky waited in tense patience. Kalinsky thrust the paper onto his desk.

"Not Americans?"

"Who knows?" Novitsky replied. He pushed himself upright in the padded chair. "But I cannot see why the French and the Germans would go along with it."

"So, we have a spaceship no one claims to own entering orbit around Jupiter, and our captain sends us a message that his two first officers are engaged in secret activities." Kalinsky slapped the desk with his hands, pushing himself to his feet to pace the ornate Persian rug laid on the parquet floor. "This ship, could it be an elaborate ruse to defraud us of our share of the Jovian system?"

"Why would they bother?" Novitsky steepled his hands. "They could have bought us out at any time."

"Leaving them to deal with the Americans or the Japanese," Kalinsky retorted.

"That is so," Novitsky said, but his tone was dismissive. He leveled a piercing gaze on the other. "Consider this: what if the ship really *is* an alien? And the affair of the two officers something trivial?"

Kalinsky shuddered, face growing pale. "Then we are *all* in the gravest danger of immediate annihilation."

"Or in a position of great profit," Novitsky replied. He arched an eyebrow, imploring the other to consider the thought carefully. Slowly, the two began to smile.

* * *

Harmonie, Jupiter

"Well, Gregor, what have you got?" Nikolai asked, kicking off the staff briefing in *Harmonie's* briefing room.

The Russian ensign shook his head sadly. "Not a lot, I'm afraid, Captain. We have not identified the constituents of the alien's hull., We have been incapable of getting more than a simple surface analysis"—the viewscreen lit up with an image of the alien vessel— "although you can see we have learned something."

The ensign looked at his captain for permission, rose, and extended a pointer. The alien ship was shaped like a stressed ellipsoid, very much like a pumpkin seed cut in half. At the large end, where Gregor was pointing, were large openings. "This area here is more radioactive than the rest of the ship." He pointed to some large protuberances mid-ship. "These are replicated again here"—he pointed toward the pointed end of the vessel—"and here," indicating bumps symmetrically placed near the openings at the large end.

"What are they?" Murray demanded.

Gregor blinked. "I have no idea, sir!"

"Well, guess, man!" Murray barked back. Gregor looked lost. Murray heaved a deep sigh and pushed himself out of his chair. "I'll tell you what they are: they're force field blisters."

"How can you know?" Geister demanded. "They could be sensor units."

"What do the thermal images show?" Murray asked. He looked to the perplexed ensign. "You *did* take a time-lapse thermal image, didn't you?"

"Gentlemen." Nikolai Zhukov's voice was calm, controlled, and effective. All the officers turned to him. He gave them one of his famous boyish smiles complete with twinkling ice-blue eyes. "I think it is a bit premature of Dr. Murray to guess"—he held up a hand as Murray prepared a protest—"which is not to say he is right or wrong." He turned back to the ensign. "Let us hold our discussion until Mr. Strasnoye has completed his report, eh? Please continue, Ensign."

Gregor licked his lips and found his voice. "Time-lapse infrared analysis is currently being conducted by our three probes. However, as the ship has been in Jupiter's light for over an hour now, I do not hope for much useful information." He paused. "However, the temperature profile from the openings indicates that they recently have been subjected to exceptional heat—"

"Engines!" Geister said.

"Could be," Murray said. "But where's the fuel? How much fuel would this guy—" He turned to the ensign. "What's this thing's mass, anyway?"

"Our probes have not approached near enough to get good gravimetrics from the object," Gregor said. "The area of space around Jupiter is crowded with objects and it will be difficult unless we make a close pass to determine the mass of the object with any accuracy."

"Then do it, man!" Murray barked. He looked sympathetically at Zhukov. "Don't know what your service is coming to if an ensign can't take the initiative."

"I believe Ensign Strasnoye has a good reason for his caution," Zhukov said. He looked to Strasnoye for elaboration.

"Lieutenant Murray, my concern is that such a close approach might be interpreted as a hostile act," Strasnoye said.

"But how are we going to learn anything—?" Murray spluttered off as Zhukov waved down his objections.

"We shall be patient," Zhukov told him. *Yes, like Mother Russia, we shall be patient,* he thought to himself. *There is plenty of time, Nikolai Anatolovich, plenty of time for all things.* "We shall consider a list of passive devices to place on the next probe—"

"The exploration guys are not happy about using all their satellites," Karl said.

Zhukov made a slicing gesture with his arm. "I do not *care* about their feelings. This is more important." He gestured to the ensign to continue.

"What we have ascertained are accurate measurements of the ship's lengths." A three-dimensional outline of the pumpkin seed-shaped vessel appeared on the viewer. "The major axis of the ellipse shape is eleven thousand two hundred forty-three point four five meters; the minor axis is seven thousand four hundred ninety-three point four five meters—"

Murray and Geister grunted in surprise at the similarity in numbers.

"—and the thickness at the rear is three thousand two hundred forty-three point—"

"—four five meters!" Murray guessed, turning excited eyes to Geister.

Ensign Strasnoye shook his head reluctantly. "No sir, the final figures at point three five meters."

"*Was?*" Geister exclaimed *auf deutsch.*

"'Strewth!" Murray muttered.

The two reached for the free calcpad on the table; Geister pulled back his hand with a nod for Murray to take it. The engineer was soon lost in a swath of number-crunching.

Nikolai brought them both back to the present. "*That* does not concern us right now, gentlemen," he said. "We need to establish a sequence of events, a list of experiments, a procedure—"

"—we need a plan!" Elodie burst out, eyes aglow with excitement.

Nikolai ignored the outburst, turning to the exploration scientists. "We need to know where this ship came from, how it got here, why it came here, and what its intentions are."

"Does it even know we're here?" Strasnoye wondered aloud.

"It matched course with us," Murray said. Strasnoye ducked his head in chagrin.

"Did it not leave an ionization trail?" von Schliefen, the German chemist, wanted to know. Murray quirked an eyebrow at him and nodded.

"I know how to measure its mass," Elodie said.

"Good," Nikolai said to her. "Good," he added to the German chemist. "People, I give you one hour. Then I will want a detailed plan including how to outfit a special probe."

Karl looked hesitant. "Once we have all this information, what are we going to do with it?"

Nikolai shot him a look of disgust. "Analyze it, of course," the Russian responded curtly, leaving the room.

*　　*　　*

European Space Agency Headquarters,
Noordwijk aan Zee, Netherlands

"How old is this information, Toni?" Anne-Marie Foquet demanded of her secretary. Her office was a man's office: imposing cold furniture decorated it, heroic pictures adorned it. She was short with a trim girlish figure, which had fooled all too many men into believing they could manage her. Anne-Marie knew what she wanted, got what she wanted, and allowed nothing to stand in her way.

Antonio Scarli's eyes darted to his boss's face. He shrugged. "Four, maybe five hours, now."

Anne-Marie crumpled the message into a ball and threw it against the wall. "Five hours! The whole world knows about it by now! Why did we not set up our own deep space communications network?"

"Because the Americans offered us theirs and we had no reason to turn them down," Toni reminded her.

She brushed aside his reasonable response. "Prepare a press release immediately, contact the heads of government, we'll let the world know that Europe has again sailed to the new world!"

"What about the Russians?"

"Tell them, too," she said. "They may have a captain on our ship, but the ship is still *ours*." She noticed that Scarli had not rushed off. "What are you waiting for?"

"I was just thinking, maybe we should not tell the press immediately—"

"What?"

Scarli raised a hand to ward off her outburst. "What if these aliens are not peaceful? What if they destroy our ship? Why don't we wait until we have established contact with them, learned their intentions? Would that not be better?"

Anne-Marie Foquet's eyes had taken on an abstracted look as she considered his first words. Now, when he had finished, she stood locked in thought.

"You are right, Toni. We shall have to handle this carefully. Nonetheless, the information is known to too many at this time. We shall have to make an announcement. First, however, we should consult with the heads of government, including the Russians."

Sadly, she admitted, "This is nothing I can keep completely under the control of the agency."

"A wise decision," Toni replied as he turned to carry out her instructions.

"Ah, Toni! What would I do without you?" she called after him warmly, wondering if it might be sensible to seduce him again. Potentially, he was a danger to her; she wanted the security of knowing she had a firm grip on him.

Toni recognized the predator tones in her words and replied obsequiously, "I'm sure, Director, that you would perform magnificently without my miniscule aid."

* * *

The White House, Washington, DC

"Yes, Brian, what is it?" The president asked as Brian McPhee, his chief of staff, coughed politely for his attention. They were in the Oval Office, the president seated at his magnificent mahogany desk, the chief of staff standing in front of him looking out toward the White House lawn.

"Sir, I was wondering who all would be going out on *Voyager* to represent us."

The president puckered his brows. "Why not let the Navy boys sort that out?"

Brian frowned. "My sources tell me that Eurocos is doing just that with their people. I was thinking more along the diplomatic lines."

"Diplomatic?"

"Yes, sir. If these aliens aren't harmful then they're probably here to set up diplomatic relations with us."

"What if they're harmful?"

McPhee shook his head. "We'll know that thirty-three minutes after they've blown up *Harmonie*. But they're probably not, in which case we can *deal* with them."

"Deal with them?"

"Yes, sir," McPhee said. "Consider the foreign relations coup we'll get if we're the first nation to sign a treaty with aliens!"

The president's eyes widened as the thought sank in. "Will the people go for it?"

"Ten, twenty points in the polls, I'm sure of it," McPhee replied. "You'll be assured of re-election."

"Okay, send someone from State," the president decided, lowering his head to the stack of paperwork in front of him.

"Uh …" McPhee began delicately.

The president looked up again, quirking an are-you-still-here eyebrow at him. "What's the problem?"

"The mission will probably last a long time."

"So? That's what we pay them for, isn't it?"

"Yes, sir," McPhee said. "But the mission will be in zero-gee—*Voyager* isn't equipped for artificial gravity—"

"And?"

"Well, whoever goes on the mission will probably never be able to come back to Earth."

"So? Send someone expendable." The president turned back to his paperwork, rather irritated that such a simple problem continued to distract him.

"Uh, sir, do we *really* want to send someone expendable for the most important diplomatic mission ever?"

The president dropped his pen and frowned in thought. Finally, he laced his fingers and looked up at his chief of staff. "No, Brian, I suppose not. Why don't you go?"

"Me?" McPhee hadn't expected that.

"Chance of a lifetime."

McPhee laughed in astonishment. "Oh, no! Sir, you don't want that. Who would advise you? I've got kids. No, I think not. Much though—"

The president held up a silencing hand, grinning. "Okay, Brian. I just wanted to see you sweat. Who do you want?"

"Pickett."

"Pickett!" The president shot out of his chair, brows bunched together in anger as he examined his chief of staff critically. "James Earl Pickett was the biggest thorn in my thigh—"

"He's available, he'll never come back to Earth, and he's good," McPhee replied, ticking off the points on his fingers. "Besides, it'll look good politically, taking an old opponent and finding a use for him."

"What *did* happen to him, anyway? I heard some garbled account about being stranded on the Moon."

McPhee nodded. "That's it. He went up there stumping for more expenditure on space exploration, had a heart attack, and was stranded up there until his bones atrophied so bad that he couldn't return to Earth."

The president snickered. "Hoisted by his own petard! What's the old coot doing now?"

The president disregarded the fact that the "old coot" was five years younger than he was.

"Does it matter?" McPhee wondered. "You know his record. I can't think of anyone better suited for the job. Especially as he can never come home to stomp the campaign trail or partake of all the glory."

The president's eyes gleamed appreciatively. "Shrewd, shrewd." He said. "Find him and get him on *Voyager*."

"And his title?"

"Title?" The president mused, "Make him Ambassador Plenipotentiary for Alien Affairs."

As McPhee turned to carry out his instructions, a thought struck him: "What will

Congress say?"

"They'll be so happy that I solved the problem before they had it thrown on their laps that they'll form a special committee to investigate me; that'll last two years and exonerate me of any wrongdoing. You know, the usual."

McPhee grinned. "I'll get right on it, Mr. President."

"Wait a minute, Brian. What makes you think he'll do it?"

"He's lost his wife, his kids, and he's been stuck up there for five years now. Can you imagine how he feels?"

The president thought about it and suppressed a shudder.

* * *

Luna City, Near Side, the Moon

Nakatomi Tower gleamed fiercely as the first rays of Sun illuminated it. Pickett grumbled as his Photo-Finish faceplate slowly compensated for the increased light. He took another swig on the water nipple, gasped as the vodka coursed into his bloodstream, and once again cursed that he had survived another drunken week on the lunar surface.

His face tightened as an intense urge overtook him, and he growled when he found out, again, that spacesuits have no zippers in the right place. Hazy memories came back to him, and he contemplated using the suit's reeking capabilities or turning back to his underground habitat for an only slightly more dignified discharge.

I am still a Pickett! he swore through his alcoholic mist, turned back, with a rolling gait less often associated with a spacer than with a drunkard, and entered the small three-room habitat far beyond the edge of Luna City.

He rushed through the airlock, into the lunar commode, got relief, and headed back toward the airlock before he noticed his computer hailing him.

"Whaaaat?"

"You have a message," the computer informed him in soft feminine tones.

"I told you: no bills!"

"The message is from Earth."

"I'm not talking to anyone down there!" Since Helen had filed for divorce and refused to bring the kids up, there was no one on that oh-so-lovely blue pearl he had any desire to speak with.

"The Office of the President," the computer insisted.

"Oh, really?" Pickett retorted. "Which company?"

"The United States of America."

"Screw him!" The airlock door refused to close until he replenished his air supply, which reduced Pickett to inchoate spluttering, but finally the outer door opened into the glorious nothingness of space; the nothingness that so perfectly reflected his life. He took two steps out from the airlock to resume his meaningless roaming when his feet got tangled up and he fell slowly in free fall to land on the hard lunar surface. The fall, the excitement in his habitat, the argument with the computer, were all too much, and he at last got his wish: he passed out.

Chapter Two

Harmonie, Jupiter

Captain Nikolai Anatolovich Zhukov of the European ship *Harmonie* was in much better spirits. "Twenty-seven million metric tons!"

"Thereabouts," Murray agreed. "I make it twenty-six point nine five three megatons."

The captain ignored him. "Gentlemen, and ladies, you have truly delivered a magnificent amount of information on our alien friend."

Indeed, within twenty-four hours, the crew and passengers of *Harmonie* had managed miracles. They had concocted a laser drift measuring device to determine the mass of the alien ship, had calculated its albedo, and had found the end of the alien's ion trail just outside Jupiter. They knew the ship's mass, brilliance, and that it had first fired its thrusters just outside Jupiter's magnetosphere, but nothing more. There had not been one peep from the alien, not one sign of intelligence since it had first maneuvered to match *Harmonie's* orbit.

"Bah!" Karl Geister said. Zhukov shot him a quelling look but the German was unfazed. "We know nothing! Who are they? Why are they here? What do they want? What do they look like? How do we kill them?"

"Or how will they kill us, old man?" Murray threw in. "Maybe our own curiosity will do it. What if these are slow-thinking beings who take days to form one word? What if the ship is a robot?"

"It matched orbits, Paul," Elodie Reynaud reminded him. Murray nodded in recognition of her point.

There was a knock on the door, it opened and Ensign Strasnoye handed a message pad to the captain. Zhukov glanced at it, then at the others in the briefing room. "It appears we shall have to move fast: the Americans are planning to join us."

"What?" the others declared in chorus.

Zhukov nodded, referring to the message. "It appears that the antimatter ship *Voyager* is being readied for a long duration mission."

"But she's still on test flights!" Murray exclaimed.

"And now the test flight will bring her out to Jupiter," Karl corrected. "After all, the ship has long legs."

"Legs indeed, to hop out to Jupiter for a lark!" Elodie said.

"But not as pretty as yours," Zhukov said, to his horror. He was more surprised by the exchange of glances between Geister and Reynaud—did their conspiracy involve seducing him? He dropped the matter; he had other problems more pressing. His officers would obey him (and he would watch his tongue!) or they would find out just how harsh Russian military training really was.

"We now have a new deadline," he continued. "I believe that we shall have to establish communications with this alien before the Americans arrive." He glanced at the others, who all nodded in agreement. "Suggestions?"

Ney, the French physicist, raised a hand. "We could try using the standard binary sequences transmitted on the water hole frequency."

"Water hole?" Strasnoye, who should have left already, asked aloud.

"Yes, there are several frequencies we think that carbon-based life-forms might use to communicate on. One is the frequency for the water molecule, another for methane, and one for hydrogen."

"It's worth a try," Geister said.

"Very well, see that it's done," Zhukov ordered.

"We need a linguist," Murray said.

"We don't have one, Lieutenant," Zhukov said, reminding the eccentric Englishman of his rank, "but we all speak several languages and we do have software engineers aboard—"

"All they ever do is produce more bugs!" someone muttered. Zhukov chose to ignore the remark, true though it was.

"—so we should be able to figure out their language." He slapped the table and vaulted out of his chair. "Come, gentlemen, we have much work to do!"

* * *

Far Side One, the Moon

Mac presented Captain Steele with the equipment list at a quarter to five that evening. He found Steele in her office, talking in the soft controlled tones that indicated the young captain was dealing as best she could with difficult brass. Steele looked up as he entered, shrugged her shoulders apologetically, and waved him to the seat in front of her desk. Mac slid the list onto the desk before sitting down. While still listening carefully to the other end, Steele perused the equipment list, reaching for a pen to make emendations and suggestions.

Angrily, she threw her pen on the desk. "Sir, Luna City is clear on the other side of the Moon!" she shouted into the phone when she got her chance. Mac could tell by the expression on her face that the conversation suffered the usual Earth-Moon time lag.

"It will take hours—" The other end cut her off.

"Of course, sir, it can be done, but I thought this mission was—" Again she was cut off. Mac could see the veins stand out in her forehead as she fought to keep her anger in check. She let out a defeated hiss of air. "Yes, sir, of course. We'll see that it is so." She waited until she was certain the other end had heard her and had nothing more to say, then hung up. She looked at Mac searchingly for several moments. "Ever hear of a guy named Pickett?"

"'Pickett's last charge?'" Mac said.

Emily Steele nodded grimly. "The same." James Earl Pickett had made headlines when his fact-finding mission had resulted in a heart attack that had left him stranded on the Moon. "The Man-in-the-Moon's politician."

"I thought he dropped out when he found out his body had acclimated," Mac said. Life on the Moon required less cardiovascular exertion and muscle mass than life on Earth, and Pickett's lengthy enforced hospital stay had left him incapable of re-adjusting to the stronger gravity of his home planet: he could never go home again.

"He did," Steele replied. "Bought a run-down hab on the outskirts of Luna City and has been drinking himself to death." Steele pursed her lips. "He had a wife and kids; she divorced him just recently."

"So?" Mac had no sympathy for the man.

Steele made a face. "CINCSPACE just ordered me to find him and bring him along on our mission."

"A politician? From the opposition?" Mac was perplexed. "Skipper, what sort of job have you got lined up?"

She sighed. "You may as well know, as you're coming along—"

"Thanks."

"—the Europeans met up with another ship at Jupiter." She was surprised that Mac's only reaction was to nod sagely. She quirked an inquiring eyebrow at him.

Mac smiled. "What, think I can't get that sort of information whenever I want?" He shook his head at Emily's concerned look. "Not many others know, but news like that spreads mighty fast up here. I made a few calls while I was putting together the list." With a gesture, he tossed that fact off as unimportant. "So they want Pickett to dicker with these aliens? What makes them think they'll talk with us?"

"They certainly won't if we don't get there," Steele said tartly. She stood up. "I've now got to locate this Pickett character and get him to come along with us. Can I leave you here to get everything ready?"

"Sure." Mac grinned. "When do we lift?"

"As soon as I corner Pickett." Steele punched the intercom. "Yeah, this is Captain Steele. I want a hopper ready when I get there."

* * *

Luna City, Near Side, the Moon

Cold, he was so very cold. And someone was shaking him. "Mr. Pickett! Mr. Pickett, are you all right?"

Feebly, he batted at the source of the sound but it continued implacably. Gradually, he felt warmth again, realized that his skin was rubbing against soft sheets instead of the cloistering enclosure of a spacesuit. "Go 'way! Let me sleep!"

"Pickett, wake up!" The voice was commanding, authoritative. Angrily, Jim Pickett blinked open his eyes to glare at the offender. As his vision cleared, he realized that he had quite rightly categorized the tone as military; the crisp undress uniform of Navy Spacewatch filled his vision.

"Go 'way, Navy," he grumbled. A splash of cold water rolled over him. Pickett bolted out of bed, yelling, "Jesus Christ! I told you to leave!"

"Mr. Pickett, if I hadn't come you'd be dead by now."

"Dead?" Pickett's voice registered first surprise then anger. "Why didn't you leave me, then?" For the first time he picked out the other person's features in the low light of his habitat. It was a woman, tall and wiry, with a long face and trim frame. "What the hell do you want? Who are you, anyway, Navy?"

"Lieutenant Commander Emily Scout Steele, sir," the woman said, pulling herself to attention. "I've been ordered to bring you along on the *Voyager's* first flight."

Her tone included uncertainty and disbelief.

"*Voyager*? What for?"

"The Europeans at Jupiter have had an encounter," Steele replied, wondering when the politician would become aware of his naked condition.

"So?"

"The encounter was with a ship we believe to be alien."

Casually, James Pickett picked up a dry edge of a sheet and draped it around his nether regions. "What does that have to do with me?"

The change of tone in his voice was shocking: it went from slurred drunk to clinical politician in a split second.

"The president would like you to act as ambassador."

"Won't do much good—how long's it take to get to Jupiter from here, a year?"

"*Voyager* will get there in days, sir," the Navy commander responded with a touch of pride.

Pickett was impressed and, in spite of years of political training, could not help but show it. "What about the Europeans?"

"I believe our mission is to negotiate the best possible terms for the United States of America," Emily said. "However, I'm told that there is a full briefing waiting for you at Far Side Base."

"What if I don't want to go?"

"My orders made no mention of that possibility," she said, one hand dropping toward her sidearm. Pickett examined it critically, noting that it was a phased charge gun which shot a self-sealing, self-contained, electric bullet which induced paralysis the standard sidearm for both naval personnel and security officers on the Moon and in space—the press called it a "spaser"—a contraction of space-Taser.

"What's in it for me?" Pickett demanded.

Emily looked around the dimly lit habitat. It was filthy, containing mostly un-recycled vodka containers and soiled clothing. A computer blinked balefully indicating that it had been silenced prior to delivery of an urgent message. "I don't know," she replied at last, "It certainly can't be worse than this."

"Cooped up in a ship with Navy bores, flying out to meet a pack of aliens who probably have already negotiated with Eurocos, doesn't seem too attractive to me."

Emily pulled her pistol out of its holster and waved the business end at him. Then, batting her eyes prettily, she smiled and said in a little girl voice, "Please?"

Pickett glanced back between the weapon and its owner then barked a laugh. "How can I refuse such a request?"

* * *

Emily stole several glances at Pickett as she piloted the lunar hopper back toward the far side of the Moon. Pickett had cleaned up in his 'fresher somewhat and had, at Steele's prodding, even brushed his teeth so that the stench of ingrained alcohol was reduced to mere nuisance. Cleaned and vaguely sober, the once-politician looked almost presentable. His features were rugged but his eyes were a clear, penetrating blue. His hair was streaked with gray. Her eyes narrowed as she noticed the pale skin on his left ring finger.

Pickett caught her glance. "Solid gold, somewhere out in orbit I 'spect," he said, rubbing the spot. "Two kids, a nice wife, good life—doing something—all gone."

"Do you miss them?"

"Not with enough vodka!" Pickett replied, cackling. He stopped abruptly when he registered her look, remarking bitterly, "If you'd've left me out there, I wouldn't miss 'em anymore."

Steele gave him an unsympathetic look but said nothing. Sometime later she noticed by his breathing that he had fallen asleep. She switched on the autopilot and turned to gaze at him critically until the proximity beeper went off two hours later, indicating their approach to Far Side One.

Pickett woke, startled. He looked around hurriedly, caught sight of her, and schooled his expression to neutral. "Almost there?"

"LV-124, this is Far Side Control. Switch to automatic," a voice chirped over the comm unit.

"There," Emily said as she flicked the hopper to auto.

"When do we leave?"

She glanced at him out of the corner of her eyes. "As soon as the ship's ready. Tonight, with any luck."

Pickett jerked upright at that. "Wait a minute, isn't there going to be any briefing? State's certain to have instructions for me!"

Emily shrugged. "I work for the Navy. If the State Department wants to talk with you, I'm sure they'll be able to contact us en route."

"Look, lady, you hijacked me for this wild scheme, but I'll be damned if I'm going out there without knowing what authority I have!"

"They have a title for you, if that's what you mean. It is Ambassador Plenipotentiary for Alien Affairs." Pickett snarled. Commander Steele glanced at him unsympathetically.

"Between you and me," she told him confidentially, "if I had my way, I'd be running tests right now, not trying to haul a broken politician off to Jupiter."

"Tests?" Pickett echoed weakly. "Just how new is this ship of yours, Commander?"

"It's a prototype."

"Prototype?" Pickett mulled that over slowly. "That's right! *Voyager* is the prototype MAM ship." He glanced over to her. "And it's ready to hike out to Jupiter?"

"We've got enough fuel," Emily temporized, "we're laying on supplies now and getting the crew aboard."

Pickett chewed his lip. "How many hours has it flown?"

"Four."

"What's the longest time?"

"An hour."

"How many hours is it to Jupiter?"

Steele turned to him, eyes flashing. "Look, *sir*, I didn't ask for this mission, but now that I've got it I'm going to do my damnedest to make sure it goes flawlessly. How about you?"

Pickett was shocked at her vehemence and took some time to absorb it. Finally, in flat tones he told her, "Five years ago I would have jumped at this. It would have made my career: the man who brought the United States into the Interstellar Age! Now, I have no constituency, no wife, no kids, nothing."

"You can still be the man to bring us into the Interstellar Age."

Pickett nodded glumly but Emily felt a change in the atmosphere surrounding him. "So, how many hours to Jupiter?"

"Depends upon how much fuel we can carry." A beeper on the console went off. "We're landing."

Twenty minutes later, they were inside Steele's office, along with Mac and a pot of coffee. Mac's handshake had been firm. "So you're 'Space-Age' Pickett! Glad to meet you."

Pickett gave him the once over, then said, "You can call me Jim." He looked at Steele, "You too, Commander." Commander Steele's look made it clear that she was not overwhelmed by the honor. "Commander Steele tells me that you're the man who can answer this question: how long will it take to get to Jupiter?"

Mac looked questioningly to the commander who nodded that he could tell this civilian. "We've got two kilograms of antimatter in the storage rings right now. I *think* that *Voyager's* storage rings can hold that much."

"Two kilograms? Isn't that a bit small?"

Mac shook his head. "We burn 50 micrograms of antihydrogen to every one kilogram of hydrogen and that gives us thirty times the effectiveness of the Eurocos fusion engines."

"Impressive." Pickett said. "So how quickly can we get there?"

Mac held up his hand. "That's a difficult question to answer." Both Steel and Pickett gave the engineer surprised looks. "If we can guarantee that fuel will be delivered to us on orbit—"

"What else can carry antimatter?"

Mac shook his head. "We'll take all the antimatter with us. It's the hydrogen that I'm worried about. If we can get a refill, then we can get there in three weeks. Without a refill, we won't get there in under a year."

"What about aerobraking?"

"We're going to use it—the guys are already rigging the shields, Commander—otherwise we'd take six weeks to get there."

"Assume a refill," Pickett said. When Steele made ready to protest, Pickett told her, "Do you think Congress is going to leave us stranded out there?" She looked doubtful. "It's an election year; you can just bet they'll fall over backwards to help us back home." He widened his gaze to include both of them. "Now, what can *Harmonie* do in three weeks?"

* * *

Harmonie, Jupiter orbit, three weeks later

"Nothing!" Zhukov slammed the desk. He was tired and irritable. "Three whole weeks and not one peep from that vessel!"

Around the table, the officers and scientists were all tired and irritable. In fact, Zhukov had broken up four fights in the past week alone. Worse yet, his two executive officers had proved less than reliable in handling the situations themselves. Zhukov could not fathom that; both during training and the long voyage out here, Elodie Reynaud and Karl Geister had proved themselves to be exemplary officers, even if they had a trifle less militaristic manner than he preferred. And was she getting fat? Zhukov made a mental note to check her exercise log.

Only Murray was cheerful. The reason for his cheerfulness was cause for irritation among the others. It orbited not two kilometers away from their large ungainly ship. "Isn't she beautiful?" Murray chuckled, examining the sleek *Voyager* on his viewscreen. "Three weeks! Imagine! Just three weeks! It took us over two and a half years to get out here and they did it in—"

"Shut *up*, Lieutenant!" Geister growled at the Englishman. It was a particularly sore point for the German, as it was their fusion drive which powered the slower-moving *Harmonie*. "It's just a—how would you say?—a yacht, a dinghy! A little putt-putt. *Harmonie* is much more than that."

"Oh, I don't know," Murray responded offhandedly. "It reminds me of little *Turbinia* steaming through the Grand Fleet."

"But they used aerobraking!"

"And they've got no fuel," Elodie added, looking at the empty bladder tanks which surrounded the aft end of the trim American ship.

Murray bit off a response, reminding himself that some of his information was not common knowledge.

Strasnoye hailed them from the bridge. "Sir, the Americans are hailing us!"

Zhukov expected no less; the American vessel had just completed its final orbital correction a few minutes ago. A low growl filled the room. Zhukov waved the others to silence. "Send it down here."

"It's visual," Strasnoye responded. "I'll send it on channel two."

Zhukov deftly switched the main view screen controls.

"*Harmonie*, this is *Voyager*. Over." The face on the screen was female who bore the rank of a lieutenant commander. Zhukov recognized her from one of the many briefings they had had in the last three weeks.

"Lieutenant Commander Steele, this is Captain Nikolai Anatolovich Zhukov," Zhukov said. The disparate use of rank was not lost on the American commander, who dimpled at the slight.

"Captain Zhukov, as commander of the first antimatter ship in commission,"—Zhukov winced at her deft riposte—"and on behalf of the United States of America, I should like to put my ship, my crew, and my passenger at your disposal in the current tense situation we find here."

"On behalf of Eurocos, the consortium of the European Space Agency and the Russian people, I must thank you and your nation for its kind offer but—" His carefully prepared speech was interrupted by pandemonium from his bridge and behind the American commander.

"Sir, the alien ship!" Elodie said, pointing at the display.

In the ensuing silence, Zhukov could plainly see the ship's blisters opening up.

* * *

Voyager

"Geez!" Mac said. He turned to Steele. "Skipper, I'm picking up all sorts of heat signatures from that thing—she's warming up a reactor or something!"

"Weapons?" Pickett asked.

"Can't tell yet."

"What's Zhukov doing?" Steele asked.

"He's brought his reactors online," Mac said after scanning the other Earth ship. "Maybe he's going to run for it."

"Getting heating on the pods!" Jenkins, one of the techs, called out.

"How soon can we get ourselves outta here?" Pickett asked Steele.

Mac snorted, shaking his head. "No fuel!"

Pickett absorbed this with widening eyes. Captain Steele frowned, turning to Mac, "What happened? *Harmonie* hasn't gotten a peep out of that ship in three weeks, and the first time we talk, the aliens fire up a reactor!" She shook her head. "That doesn't make sense."

"Well, *Harmonie* was using the waterhole and we were communicating on visual—" Mac stopped abruptly, mouth agape. Steele and he had the same thought at the same time.

"They're listening on VHF!" both said in unison. Mac sprinted to the comm console and spun the dials. "Got it!"

Steele and Pickett crowded him from either side as he analyzed the incoming signal. After a while, Mac sighed. "I don't know, Skipper."

Jenkins, who had been watching from a distance, piped up: "It looks like old style TV signals."

"Old style?" Pickett said.

"Sure. Five hundred twenty-five lines, you remember," Jenkins said. "They used to broadcast like that back in the old days."

"Yes!" Mac yelped exultantly. "Jenkins, you're a genius! Now what was the signal format?"

"Try the oldest first," Pickett said. Steele gave him a stormy, I'm-in-command look, so the politician expanded: "They've been receiving for the last hundred years or so."

"Mac, get to it," Steele said. She turned to Jenkins, "Can you rig up a program to convert our signals to the old format?" The tech pursed his lips thoughtfully then nodded. "Good, get to it."

Fifteen minutes later, Mac proudly presented the first decoded signals from an alien race.

The image was fuzzy, something which Mac quickly corrected, but there was no sound which caused a great deal of conversation. "Maybe they can't hear!"

"What makes you think they ever decoded the side frequencies?" Captain Steele asked.

"If I may," Jenkins said, "I think they probably never detected the sidebands that carry sound."

"Oh!"

"What is it?" Steele demanded of no one in particular. Here she was, the first captain in history to receive a communication from an alien race, and she could not make it out. It disturbed her.

"Look! It's changing!" Indeed, the signal had been replaced by a face.

"What is it?"

"Is that one of *them*?"

Suddenly, Mac let out a loud, inarticulate groan which silenced everyone in the crammed cabin. Wordlessly, they all waited for him to recover. "I remember that! It's *Howdy Doody*!"

In the shocked silence that descended, Pickett chuckled. "My god, wait until we tell the president!"

"Never mind him, how do we respond to the aliens?" Steele said.

"Well," Mac said, "We've got at least twenty minutes until the show ends." He frowned. "We need to figure out which version of *Howdy Doody* this is; which broadcast."

"Why isn't it the first?" Steele asked.

Mac shrugged. "It could be, for all I know, but it's just as possible that the aliens did not detect our broadcasts as intelligent"—he changed his inflection as Buffalo Bob did a pratfall—"transmissions for quite some time."

"I see your point," Steele said. "However, why should we figure out which version we're watching?"

"So that we can reply," Mac answered with a hint of exasperation.

"That I see … but I wonder if perhaps we need to find out what comes after *Howdy Doody*," Steele said.

"Mac, are you hoping to start communications by swapping TV episodes?" James Pickett asked in disbelief.

Mac nodded. Pickett groaned. Steele shrugged. "It makes perfect sense to me." Pickett raised an eyebrow. She explained, "They've been watching these for a certain period of time, so they must have drawn some conclusions—"

"What? What conclusions could an *alien* race draw from that?" Pickett asked, jabbing a finger at the display.

"Well, judging by Buffalo Bob's expression, I suspect they might come to the conclusion that we don't take too kindly to having pies shoved in our faces," Mac said.

The United States' ambassador vented his ire in a hiss.

Emily spread her hands in a placating gesture. "There are a lot of things to be learned. Remember that children learn most everything from television nowadays"—Mac grunted his opinion of the upcoming generation—"and deaf children have learned directly from television."

Pickett fumed. "Commander, what makes you think they understand them?"

"They're broadcasting," Commander Steele said. "They started broadcasting in response to our use of VHF signals. Clearly they expect a response and hope to communicate."

Pickett bit his lip. "Yeah, I suppose you're right."

Mac gave Steele a quizzical look, gesturing at Pickett's behavior, but Emily deflected it with a shake of her head.

Pickett noticed it but pretended to ignore it. "Okay, how do we get all these TV episodes?" He turned to Mac. "Do we have them in the ship's library?"

Mac laughed. "Mr. Ambassador, aside from the few books I brought and the girlie mags Jenkins smuggled aboard"—he wagged his head at the red-faced tech— "we don't *have* a library."

Pickett took in the information with a sigh, turning to Steele, "Commander, how much storage do we have spare?" Before she could reply, he added out of the side of his mouth, "And I'll want to see those mags, Jenkins." Emily raised a brow. Pickett coughed. "Well—uh, they might be useful in our negotiations." Commander Steele nodded in feigned comprehension. "Storage?" Pickett prompted again, ignoring Mac's quiet chuckling.

"The ship has—oh, about two terabytes of data storage," Steele said, running a hand through her hair without realizing it.

"What about *Harmonie*?"

"She's got loads—" Danni McElroy, *Voyager's* communications officer, volunteered, using the opportunity to remind her captain, "Uh, *Harmonie's* is still online."

"Oh, shit!" Emily swore, turning towards the pickup. "Captain Zhukov, are you still there?"

In the crowded cockpit, the crew of *Voyager* listened intently to the speaker for a reply. Finally: "Yes, *Voyager*, *Harmonie* is still with you."

Emily could see him on screen. She placed him at the communications console. By the way he kept glancing off to his right, she guessed that he had just come from the navigation console and was keeping an eye on it. Behind him, she could make out the German first officer, Geister. In a display of stern control which fooled her not one bit, the German was standing erect with arms clasped behind his back in parade rest.

"That's good, we thought you might have lit out on us," Mac drawled from behind *Voyager's* captain.

Zhukov's nostrils flared. He shook his head. "We have started our main engines to obtain extra power for our transmissions."

Behind her, Commander Steele could hear Pickett tap Mac questioningly and Mac's response: "Probably wet his pants."

Harmonie's speakers were good, or McElroy had the mike turned up, because Zhukov jerked upright at the remark. "Captain, *who* is that man behind you?"

Emily signaled Pickett with a hand behind her back.

Pickett moved forward, subtly blocking Zhukov's view of Mac. "James Earl Pickett, sir, at your service, sir."

Emily gave him a startled look, and even Jim had to admit it was a surprise how quickly his glad-handing skills returned to him.

"I have been appointed by the president of the United States of America to act as ambassador," Pickett continued smoothly, hoping that Zhukov would not think to ask what his embassy was or about the full extent of his powers. "I must say that I would like to congratulate you and your gallant crew on both their audacious journey and the amazing discovery you have found at the end of it." He bent his head in an abbreviated bow.

Quick, Jimmy, don't let them remember that you got here in three weeks!

"I am sure that these times have proved quite taxing for you and your crew, expecting, as it was, only to conduct a scientific survey of lifeless planets, to instead encounter a totally new race of beings. I can only say that, as our ambassador"—*Good! Be vague!*—"I believe that you have all done splendid work. I am sure that you will be relieved now that we have established communications with the aliens to allow us to continue with diplomatic matters whilst you continue on your historic mission." Zhukov's eyes narrowed. *Damn! He's not buying it!*

Karl Geister reacted first, stepping squarely into view. *"Who is this man?"*

"Sir," Pickett responded with an easy grin, "as I explained, I am the ambassador." He turned back to Captain Zhukov. "I'm certain, Captain, that if you would like to assist us in our negotiations we would be most grateful. I am assured that a resupply ship will be arriving in due time. We could certainly make good any supplies you expend on behalf of the human race."

Now Emily turned to stare at him. From the view of the camera, Pickett did not react but, below its view, he nudged her foot with his. *Don't screw me up, lady!*

"Although, I'm sure you have other important matters to investigate, Captain," Emily said. "Still, your personnel would be very useful and clearly of benefit to all mankind."

Geister let out a roar. "I'll bet! I'll just bet!" He turned to stare full in the screen. His accent grew thick. "Who told you zat you vere in charge here, eh? Who told you, Mr. Ambassador? Ve vere here first und ve—" His face took on a pained expression and he floated away from the camera.

Captain Zhukov returned to view. "I must apologize for my first officer." His eyes blazed in barely controlled rage. "He has been under a lot of pressure—as have we all—and I am afraid that he thinks you are pulling a—how do you say?—a 'fast one' on us."

Pickett drew breath for a glib reply but Emily beat him to it. "Captain Zhukov, you must realize what a very delicate situation we have here."

"Yes."

"It does not even bear mentioning that the fate of the world is at stake," Pickett added.

Zhukov glared at him. "I am aware of that, Mr. Ambassador, and have been for quite some more time than you."

Pickett jerked as the point scored home. "Yes, sir, I'm sure you are. So I'm sure you can see why we should work together on this in a spirit of self-preservation."

"What I *see*, Mr. Ambassador," Zhukov responded coldly, "is a noisy politician and greedy latecomers who appear to be trying to give me and *my* officers orders!"

Pickett looked hurt and heaved a wounded sigh. "Captain Zhukov—" He stopped, grimacing. "No, to hell with that!" He said. "Look, mister, I'm here because I've been dragged off the Moon so that I can maybe—*maybe*—save our collective asses from getting blown to kingdom come.

"Yes, I'm a politician. And I was a damned good one, too. But I was the 'Spaceman's friend,' the guy who stuck his neck on the line trying to get more for space development. This ship I'm in is *mine*. I fought for it, I sweated for it, and when I had to, I lied to get it funded."

He drew a breath and waved a hand in the direction of the alien ship. "Those guys out there, they may have just stopped in for a visit, or they may be the local exterminators. It's my job to deal with them. I've been politicking, and that means *dealing* with people, for a damn long time. Your job is to command a spaceship, my job is to *lead* people and get them to work together for the greater common good." He glanced at Zhukov's expression and shook his head. "Look, which of the two of us do you think is better at *negotiating* with people?"

Nikolai grew thoughtful. "A politician ... no, I would prefer a lawyer."

Pickett grinned. "Then you're in luck, I'm a lawyer, too. My specialty is space law."

A fleeting look, hopeful, crossed Zhukov's face before he could school himself. He nodded curtly. "I shall have to consult with Eurocos and they shall have to consult with their governments."

"We haven't got the time!" Pickett said. "They're transmitting now! We need to pick up an uplink, we'll need your satellite dish and we'll need the DSN." Behind him, Mac stirred uncomfortably.

"Dee Iss Enn?" Zhukov repeated blankly.

"Deep Space Network."

"Oh!" Comprehension dawned. "Day Ess Enn! You pronounce letters differently, I forget," Zhukov explained with some relief. "But the time delay! If you need it now, you are over an hour too late!"

Pickett thought that through: because light or radio waves took over thirty-three minutes to get to Earth it would take over an hour to get the first feed of old TV episodes.

"Which is why we need it immediately!" Commander Steele broke in, moving Pickett to the side. "We need to broadcast the information we have back to Earth, and we need your help."

Zhukov mulled it over. "Send me your information and I'll piggyback it on my transmission." He noticed Steele's frown. "*Harmonie* has the larger antenna and greater power, Commander."

"Very well," Emily agreed. She turned to McElroy, her communications officer. "Danni, send it over." She turned back to Zhukov. "I'm going to have to sign off to make room."

"Yes, I understand." Zhukov said. "It is a pity your experimental ship has but the one antenna. Captain Zhukov out." The display filled with static.

Instantly, Steele turned around. "Mac, get Harry and Willy checked out for EVA. We're going to set up the big dish."

Danni McElroy looked back from her position on the communications console. "What about Deep Ear?"

Steele looked pained and the young comm officer winced. Pickett looked between the two and grinned. "You mean the two-hundred-meter dish on Far Side, right?"

Emily controlled her shock. "Well, maybe Mac *didn't* know! That thing's classified, after all!"

Mac shouted back from down the corridor where he was helping the two men into spacesuits. "Sure I knew, Skipper! I figured you were going to get to use it on the final test run."

Steele sighed, shaking her head despairingly. "Just don't *you two* tell anyone else, okay?" She looked at Jenkins. "And that goes for you, too!"

"Sure thing, Skipper," Jenkins said.

"Mac?"

"Righto, Commander," Mac called back. "Say, should we bring out both dishes?"

"You brought *two?*"

"Of course, one for Earth, one for the aliens, and the li'l itty bitty one for *Harmonie* if we ever want to talk to them again," Mac said, grinning. Then he sobered up and admitted, "Actually, the second was a spare in case we had trouble."

"Worry about one first, then see if we can find a nice place for the second," Steele called back.

"A nice place?" Pickett echoed. "Like a place where *Harmonie* won't notice?"

Emily nodded. Then she looked at him carefully. "Are you okay?"

Pickett held up a hand; it was shaking. "I need a drink."

Chapter Three

Voyager

"My cabin, now," Emily said to the person who would be responsible for the first ever negotiations with aliens.

Pickett shuffled off ahead of her, looking slightly green. Emily turned back to her comm officer. "You have the conn, Danni. Get a list of what programs we'll need and send it off to CINCSPACE ASAP."

"Aye, sir," Danni McElroy responded with ingrained training, adding considerately, "Should I send Louise along?"

Emily shook her head. "Not yet." She leaned closer to the worried lieutenant. "And Danni, not a word to the others. If they ask, we're having a powwow."

Wide-eyed, McElroy nodded. Emily gave her a friendly pat on the shoulder and pushed off down the corridor to her cabin. She found Pickett stooped over, leaning from one end of the cabin to peer at the vid display on her cabin wall. She had left it set in portal mode; it showed the view of space as it would be seen from her cabin. Jupiter loomed large in the view.

"It's fake," she told him as she stepped in, firmly planting her feet on the Velcro floor. The door slung shut behind her. With two in the cabin, the room showed its true dimensions—claustrophobic, even with the 3D effects of weightlessness.

Pickett fiddled with the dials on the desk below; the view changed to a close-up of the alien ship. "I know."

Steele reddened. Pickett's cabin was catty-corner from hers and identical. In three weeks, he would obviously have figured that out.

In fact, she reminded herself, Pickett had proved very useful on the journey out.

Voyager had proved just as tough to handle as Mac had predicted, requiring constant minor maintenance and continual oversight which stretched her crew to the limits.

Pickett had been quick to realize this, and he volunteered to help long before Commander Steele had thought to draft him. He proved to be a quick learner with a degree of knowledge in all the fields of *Voyager's* operation that had left the crew pleasantly surprised. Adding him to the crew roster enabled Emily to set up three watches and leave herself free for emergencies. It had also meant that tempers, so often apt to flare in tight quarters—and *Voyager's* were ridiculously tight—were kept in better check as the crew enjoyed more sleep and greater leisure time. But while Pickett had seemed all right at the start of the voyage, he had grown increasingly nervous as it progressed and additional State Department directives were shot at him.

Steele blew a sigh. "What is it? The DTs?"

Pickett turned up from the vid at that, a probing look in his eyes. He snorted. "You're serious!"

"Six months drinking vodka, you're hooked," Emily continued, with an understanding nod. "We've got stuff in the medkit. We'll call back to Earth. *Harmonie's* certain to have someone onboard—"

Pickett made a chopping motion with his arm. "That's *not* it!" When the captain continued to look at him, he said, "Jeez, don't you see?"

Steele shook her head.

"Those aliens!"

Emily pursed her lips, examining the man as she would any subordinate. Pickett was going gray around the temples, his hair long and listless; crow's feet lined the sides of his eyes; the skin of his face was beginning to sag with age. His eyes were clear, though, clear with a frightening vision. Unconsciously, her hand went out to him. She drew it back as soon as she became aware of the motion.

He turned to face her, dragging his feet free of the Velcro and planting them with irritated, exaggerated movements. "Have you ever," he asked, "gotten what you wished for?"

Emily nodded, waving her hand to indicate *Voyager*.

Jim shook his head and a ghostly grin crossed his face. "*This* isn't what you want."

Emily groped. "There're people on *Harmonie*—maybe they can—"

Pickett growled. "There's only one politician up here, lady, and you're looking at him." He shook his head. "No, the crews back at ESA and in the Kremlin are going to be all too glad to leave this one with me." Dubious, Steele tilted her head and gave him a look from the corner of her eyes.

"They don't realize the stakes! They're still thinking about popularity polls, the next election, their image!" Pickett's voice took on a tone that worried the commander. He shook his head and looked at her with surprisingly clear eyes. "Three weeks ago, I was playing Russian roulette with vodka and the Moon." He winced in self-recrimination, shook his head. "Now, Captain, I am going to be playing a game whose rules I don't know, with stakes …" His voice drifted off, his eyes closed in pain.

This man has nothing *to live for!* While that realization sank into her, Pickett's expression changed.

"Why TV?" he wondered aloud.

"Well …" her voice trailed off, any glib explanation dying before it could pass her lips. Irritated, she shook her head, dropping the question. "That's not the issue, the issue is whether—"

"The issue is whether I can handle this," Pickett finished for her. He heaved a sigh and shook his head. "I don't know," he said frankly. "But I'll tell you this: every time I stood in front of an audience, every time I made a speech, every time I made *any* public appearance, I was as nervous as a kitten. And after sessions like … like *those*," he pointed back towards the galley and his interview with Zhukov, "I'd take a good stiff belt to calm my nerves."

"Why?"

"Lady," Pickett began harshly, then took a second look at her. "You don't understand, do you?" He shook his head. "I went up *cold* against that guy, I knew *nothing* about him aside from his dossier, and I had to win him over." Pickett grimaced. "I don't think I did but I could be wrong, it's hard to tell with his type. But I feel like I've been through the wringer; I put everything I had into reading him, into trying to sway him."

The intercom burst into life as Mac called: "Skipper, I think you'd better get up here."

"What's up, Mac?"

"We just ran out of time." Mac responded. "They're rolling credits now."

"Were there any commercials?" Pickett demanded.

At the other end, Mac spluttered, "Commercials? Hell, I didn't stick around to watch!"

"I did!" Jenkins burst in. "There were commercials. We've got the whole thing on tape."

"Well, when they stop, can you send out a test pattern?" Pickett asked, giving Steele a reassuring gesture.

"Think so." Jenkins replied. "I suspect they aren't much different from the ones nowadays."

"Probably," Pickett replied, shrugging his shoulders visibly for Steele's benefit. "Hey! And when you're done, Jenkins, get an inventory of what video we brought along—and include any X-rated stuff you might have packed along with those girlie mags of yours."

Steele frowned at him. Pickett explained *sotto voce*, "Might be useful for biology." A new thought struck him. "Say, Jenkins, have they finished with the credits?"

"Sure. The screen's gone to static now. I think they're waiting."

"We'll have a dish online in about three minutes, Skipper," Mac added.

"Hmm." Emily nodded to herself. "That means we'll have one for Earth reception, and one for the aliens."

"If we could warp alongside *Harmonie*, we could rig a cable feed directly to one of their dishes," Mac pointed out.

"Warp?" Pickett asked the captain in an astonished whisper.

Commander Steele shook her head. "Not the warp you're thinking of—it's nautical and means to pull a ship with cables."

"Oh." Pickett was educated, if not enlightened.

"I'll be up in a moment," Steele told Mac, breaking the connection. She turned back to Pickett and sighed. "Okay, Mr. Pickett, I guess I'll just have to keep my eye on you and hope things work out for the best."

Pickett smiled at her. "Thanks."

She turned, opened the door, and gestured for him to precede her.

"But, Commander, just so that you don't get confused, please remember that, as ambassador, *I* am in charge of this mission, not you."

Emily's jaw dropped. She shook her head in amazement. "Well, Mr. Ambassador, you certainly *do* know how to lay on the charm!"

"Look, this could get awfully squirrely," he told her, "and I don't want to thrash this out *then*."

Emily absorbed that with a slow nod. "I understand," she said at length, "and I understand the importance of this mission. So I'll tell you squarely: if I think you're losing it, I'll pull you out of the loop."

Jim Pickett shook his head. "Uh-uh. If you think I'm losing it, you talk to me first, then you whistle up the boys in State, *then* maybe you pull me."

"Well, it probably doesn't matter anyway. The Euros'll appoint an ambassador of their own and the two of you will keep tabs on each other," Emily said, waving the argument aside.

"I don't think so." Jim responded. "In fact, I'm going to do my damnedest to make sure it doesn't happen."

"Why?" Emily asked, "Do you want all the credit?"

"No," Pickett said, "I want the States to have all the credit."

Emily shrugged and irritably waved the politician out of the small cabin.

* * *

The Bridge, aboard *Harmonie*

Zhukov held the briefing on the ceiling. It was a perfectly excellent place to hold a briefing: out of earshot from the rest of the crew but within sight. The two first officers and all the lieutenants were collected. All of them had tablets which were currently displaying the new duty roster.

"Now," Zhukov said to First Officer Geister, "if there are no more changes to the divisions, you may dismiss the watch below."

Karl Geister looked over the list that comprised his half of the crew. He was unhappy with the captain's orders to go watch-on-watch but understood that, in the current state of emergency, the grueling twelve-hour shifts were absolutely necessary.

As usual, when switching from one duty cycle to another, many people would have to take their first watch without sleep—it was impossible to switch from the easygoing four six-hour watches *Harmonie* had been using to two twelve-hour watches without some sacrifices.

As senior officer of the late watch, Geister was guaranteed only snatches of sleep just as Elodie—Lieutenant Reynaud—would. He glanced at her anxiously then noticed the captain's look. "No, sir," he replied, shaking his head, "I'll relieve them immediately."

Zhukov held up a hand. "Once we've finished our meeting." He looked at the others. "We still have twenty minutes before we can expect a response from Earth. We must be ready for every contingency." He glanced at Lieutenant Ives, the communications officer "Have your men had any luck with the linguistics?"

Ives shook his head ruefully. "We will continue working, of course. I have instructed your ensign"—the Frenchman Ives insisted on referring to his second-in-command, Ensign Strasnoye, in such a manner rather than as *his* subordinate—"and he will continue to monitor the efforts when his watch comes back on."

"Very well." Zhukov sighed, both at the lack of progress and at the Frenchman's gall. "I suppose it was to be expected that they would monitor American television." He glanced below him to the screen that continued to display the antics of *Howdy Doody*. "I shudder to think how they have interpreted this."

"Could have been worse," Murray muttered. "If it had been 'Jackanory,' they would have *vaporized* us!"

Geister shuddered in agreement. "I have seen that show."

Zhukov redirected them to matters at hand. "Commander Reynaud, I will expect you to produce a plan for interfacing our ship with the Americans'. Commander Geister, when your watch comes on duty, I will expect you to review that plan and prepare one of your own for the deployment of the exploration team."

Elodie Reynaud nodded her acknowledgement, but Karl Geister was confused. "You mean deploy the scientists *here*?"

Zhukov raised an eyebrow. "That is one option you will explore, yes."

"Interfacing to the Yanks is going to be a bloody nightmare!" Murray muttered, shaking his head.

"Does that mean, Captain, that you think we will be forced to work with the Americans?" Lieutenant Milano, *Harmonie's* navigation officer asked. "They will steal all the honor for themselves!"

His statement provoked a rash of similar outbursts from the others. "It is the honor of France!" "We don't need the Yanks!" "The glory should go to Europe!" "They come late and demand to be first!"

Zhukov quelled them with an icy gaze. "The choice is not theirs," he said. "It is not ours, nor even for those back home." He gestured to Murray. "Even you, Lieutenant, know that there is a difference between British humor and American humor. If the aliens have only seen the Yanks' broadcasts, would *you* feel safe communicating with them?" His officers digested this. "It will be dangerous enough, trying to communicate with the aliens, but to attempt communications without understanding the culture behind the symbols they use—that is madness!"

"Sir," Elodie wondered, "why do you feel the Americans will be any better?"

Zhukov made a sour face. "Much though I hate to admit it, I believe that that American *politician* has the best grasp of his American culture. I think that *he* will be able to do it." A sly grin spread across his face. "However, we *will* arrange it so that he will not forget who met these aliens first."

"And if he should fail?" Geister demanded.

"In that case," Zhukov replied with a broad smile, "I am sure that we will be able to explain to those back home how we deferred to the Americans because they demanded it."

"So, you are predicting what Eurocos will do, sir?" Lieutenant Immelman, *Harmonie's* life support officer, asked.

Captain Zhukov was not happy with the officer's question, and his expression showed it. "I do not see how they can do otherwise."

"He's right, you know," Murray quipped. "But what if they *do* decide differently?"

"I doubt they will. However, we shall have our answer soon enough."

"Provided the *Amis* continue to let us use their Deep Space Network," Lieutenant Ives remarked. The others stared at him in astonishment.

*   *   *

Deep Space Network, Goldstone, Arizona

"*Howdy Doody!*" John Ahrens exclaimed, shaking his head and clutching his sides with laughter. "The boys in SETI are going to spit bullets!"

"Mr. Ahrens," the strait-laced station chief, Christopher Rogers, intoned distinctly, "now is not the time for jest. Have you completed decoding the messages?"

"Oh, sure," Ahrens responded easily, indicating a stack of displays, "*Voyager's* stuff is on the top one and *Harmonie's* is on the next one down." He shook his head. "I don't know why *both* of them bothered!"

Rogers turned to the other person in the room. "I assume that you will want to relay this immediately?"

The ESA representative, Russian Ivan Petrovich, had grown frenetic in the three weeks since *Harmonie's* historic contact, and now, with darting looks and red-rimmed beady eyes, called images of the actor Peter Lorre to Ahrens' mind. Petrovich licked his lips before replying, "Oh yes, indeed! Our operatives will be eager to see this."

Wordlessly, Rogers handed the nervous Russian a disc copy of the transmission. "We will relay it immediately via satellite link but you may wish to use my office—"

"Oh, no! That is not necessary!" The Russian pulled a portable phone out of his jacket pocket and proceeded to dial. He looked nervously at the other two, turned away and proceeded to speak quickly into the handset in Russian.

Angrily, Rogers frowned, then snapped to Ahrens, "I'll be in my office!"

"Is it okay if I start getting the stuff together?" Ahrens called after him.

"Stuff?"

"Yeah," the easygoing technician returned, "I know a couple of guys at JPL and in Hollywood. I figure we can get a good compression code, get all the tapes running, and have stuff ready to send back in the next half hour."

Consternation warred with relief on the station chief's face. Finally, he growled, "Do it."

Ahrens turned to his computer, muttering under his breath, "Sheesh! Nice of you to thank me!"

"This is Goldbird." Rogers was furious that the Russian's good-nature had reduced him to using a telephone. So, judging by the deepening expression on Rogers' face, was Whitestar. "I'm sorry but the other channels were compromised," Rogers explained. He continued in grimmer tones, "I have news on Satanspawn."

* * *

The White House, Washington, DC

"So, Annie, what's this tell us?" President Merritt asked his press secretary as he perused the latest opinion polls. They were in the Oval Office.

Anne Byrne was the only woman in the president's inner circle; an awkward position, particularly in these times. In the past three weeks, public opinion had oscillated widely over the "Alien Encounter," as the media called it. For the first week the public had been wildly supportive of the president's reaction, then strange things started happening: the more lunatic fringe of the Religious Right, particularly the "Church of Jesus the Judgmental"— which had predicted that Jesus would return at the millennium to kick off Armageddon and continued to survive only by revising its readings of the scriptures to show that this year was *the* year—demanded that the president not kowtow to the aliens who were almost certainly soulless and therefore spawn of the Devil. The president's continual efforts at damage control with that group discontented the less pious, so he started losing popularity on both sides.

Congress had a fit over the problem and assaulted him for not consulting them over the choice of ambassador, for dispatching *Voyager*, for not dispatching *Voyager* sooner, for not disclosing fully every development as it occurred (ignoring that for the past three weeks there *were* no developments), for not making *Voyager* go faster, and even proposed a bill of impeachment because he had not established a defense policy against alien attack. With all this heat, the president did the only wise thing: he let his press secretary handle it.

"It's early days, yet, sir," Annie temporized. "The media is having a field day with it or the public would have lost interest by now." She frowned. "Except the loony right, of course."

"I wish it *was* the *loony* right: on the Moon and out of my hair," the president said. "What can we do?"

"I don't see much that we *can* do," Byrne said. "We're at the mercy of a thirty minute time lag and we haven't figured out how talk to the aliens yet. We don't even know what they want."

"What do they want?" the president asked. Byrne blinked at him. "I mean, what does the public think they want?"

Annie shrugged. "Depends upon who you ask: the Judgmental Jesus followers think they're going to destroy us and they're just waiting to increase the agony; the liberals think that they're here to lead us into a galactic confederation and are merely putting the finishing touches on the announcement or are programming their factory machinery to build us a Utopian society; the white supremacists think that they're building some chemicals that'll purify the planet; the black extremists think the same only in reverse; the scientists think they're studying us and the sci-fi guys think—"

She stopped as Brian McPhee rushed into the room. He was sweating and breathing hard. "The aliens are talking!"

"What?" the president and the press secretary cried in unison.

"Well, not exactly talking, but when *Voyager's* captain sent a message to *Harmonie's* captain the aliens responded on the same frequency," McPhee explained.

"What'd they say?"

The chief of staff realized that perhaps he had overstated the situation. "They didn't exactly *say* anything, they, uh—" He licked his lips. "Well, apparently they picked up some of our transmissions and, uh—"

"Spit it out, man! Spit it out!" Byrne cried in exasperation.

"They sent us a clip of *Howdy Doody*." McPhee said.

The president groaned. Byrne frowned. "What's *Howdy Doody*?"

The two men looked at her in astonishment. "Didn't you ever watch the Children's Channel? The Kiddie Khannel? The Bouncing Baby Broadcast Network?" Anne Byrne shook her head three times.

"Well," the president concluded, "it's an old, old children's show."

"Oh, god!" Byrne cried, putting her head in her hands. "Can you imagine the press conference?"

McPhee blanched. The president guessed, "'And what were the aliens' first words, Mr. President?' 'Well, Walter, the aliens' first words were: *What time is it? It's Howdy Doody time!*'" He looked at Byrne. "*You* give the press conference!"

"You know," McPhee said, "this might not be so bad."

The two gave him inquiring looks. Anne Byrne's was tinged with the anticipated press conference/disaster.

"Well," the chief of staff said, "if they played *Howdy Doody*, then they've been receiving our transmissions, possibly for over a century, and so they'll know," his voice dropped as realization struck, "all about us.…"

"What if they haven't been receiving all those years?" Merritt said. In the past three weeks he had done a little bit of research on the problem and had the bright boys present him with an intelligence evaluation. "You know, they could live light-years away from us. If that's so, they could only *just* have picked up our messages and dropped in immediately."

"I fail to see the point," McPhee said.

"Think about the *news* broadcasts back then," the president said. McPhee frowned and shook his head to show that he still did not understand. "Do you remember your history? The Cold War? Atom bomb testing? The Iron Curtain?"

"Oh, yeah," McPhee said, frowning as he recalled history. Then his eyes widened.

"Oh, my god!"

Byrne stifled an exasperated sigh. "Isn't it possible, Mr. President," she asked as sweetly as she could, "that the aliens would fail to comprehend the difference between a regular television show and a news broadcast?"

The president thought it over. Shrugged. "Heck, half the public can't figure out the difference!" He shook his head, dismissing the issue. "What's the next step, Brian?"

"That's the *real* problem, Mr. President," McPhee said. "*Voyager* wants over two decades of television images as soon as they can and any linguistic AI programs we can send them."

The president chuckled. "They plan to communicate via TV shows?"

"Seems likely," the chief of staff said.

"Right," the president said. "We'll exchange snatches of *Leave it to Beaver* against *The Honeymooners*!" He shook his head. "Well, do it."

McPhee coughed. "There's a problem, sir." The President gave him an isn't-that-what-I-pay-you-for? look. "Well sir, even with six-to-one compression we'll have a heck of a time sending up two decades' worth of broadcasts. Also, we'll have to pre-empt not only our own transmissions but Eurocos' as well."

"Hmm. They're not going to like that, are they?" The president thought it over, then thumbed his intercom, "Get State in here. Oh, and Navy, too!" A second later he jabbed it again: "Make that Briefing!"

As they walked to the Briefing Room, the president asked his press secretary, "What can we do to get a better rating?"

"Two things," Anne Byrne began in reply, ticking the items off on her fingers, "one: take a positive stance one way or the other and two—"

"Gee, Mr. President, is there a meeting or something?" the vice president asked as he bounced up the corridor.

Anne Byrne locked eyes with the president. "*That's* two!" *Sotto voce*, she continued, "He's half the negative points we've seen to date."

"I don't know what we can do," the president said. "We have to keep him around and he draws flak for me."

"If only we could send him somewhere far away—" Anne Byrne murmured just before the veep came into earshot.

"Yeah, like the Moon!" McPhee, whose ears were specifically attuned to any *sotto voce* speech, quipped. He and the president both exchanged surprised looks as they reflected upon his egregious suggestion: "Deep Ear!"

"Perfect!" President Merritt declared. "For the national interest, keeping up the spirits on far outposts—"

"Deep Ear?" Byrne asked.

"No need to know," McPhee said.

"This one's no big secret, Brian," the president said. He turned to his press secretary.

"Deep Ear is a special antenna we put up on the Moon for advanced deep space work."

"Near Side or Far Side?" She wanted to know.

"Far Side."

Byrne let out a relieved sigh. "That would be perfect. With him there, we could play up his role as space father while keeping him far away from the press."

"What about the dangers?" McPhee asked.

"Of space travel or of keeping him here?" Byrne retorted.

McPhee mulled it over, then nodded. He turned to the vice president. "Ned, how would you like to go to Far Side?"

The vice president flashed a smile at his boss as they entered the Briefing Room. "Gee, Mr. President, could I?"

For easily the hundredth time, President Greg Merritt forced himself to remember that Vice President Ned Alquay had been essential in getting the Religious Right vote he needed to swing his election. And, to be fair, the vice president was personable and presentable and followed orders well. "Sorta like a talking dog," as one astute reporter had noted.

"Certainly, Ned," Merritt replied with an ingratiating smile. "In fact, I want you to arrange for it immediately." He looked up as Elijah Wood, Secretary of the Navy, and Admiral Kinnock, Chairman of the Joint Chiefs, took their seats. "Harry, I was just telling Ned here that I thought now was an excellent time for him to take a tour of the bases on Far Side," he said to the admiral.

Kinnock turned away to regain his composure, then turned back to argue, "Mr. President, given the circumstances, are you certain it is wise to—"

"We've talked it over already, Harry," McPhee cut him off. "It's absolutely vital that this administration show its continued support of Skywatch and the people on the Far Side of the Moon. And," he continued, turning to smile at the beaming vice president, "I can't think of a better spokesman."

"Absolutely!" Wood chimed in, as if on cue. "Come on, Harry, you've been saying now for a while that the administration should show more interest in the latest space developments, particularly since what's-his-name—Pickett —has left the scene."

Admiral Kinnock's shoulders slumped. "Well, I just am worried that—"

"What, Harry, aren't your ships *safe?*" demanded Secretary of State Ellington, who had arrived halfway through the proceedings.

Kinnock spluttered at the implication, looked around the table, realized that he was defeated, and gave in graciously. "Not that at all, Mr. Secretary. It's just that I'm afraid the vice president might not be aware of the discomforts he'll have to bear on the trip—"

"Anything to help the troops!" Alquay proclaimed with a beaming smile.

"Excellent!" the president said, rapping a hand on the table like an auctioneer closing a bid. "Get started immediately, Ned. You can skip this meeting. I want you up there as soon as possible."

A troubled look crossed the vice president's placid features. "But Mr. President, I have to report—"

Merritt held up a restraining hand, shaking his head. "No, really, Ned, there's no reason to stick around. We can handle everything here. You just get out and get ready. I want to see you on the Moon as soon as possible."

"But I got a message from Goldbird!" he protested, looking around the room petulantly.

"I'm sure we'll cover that in the briefing, Ned," Merritt said. "You just get along."

Alquay blinked, rose, and with a final gesture of encouragement from the president, left the room.

"Whew!" The exclamation was universal.

"Okay, what have we got?" The president demanded, bringing the meeting to order.

They reviewed *Voyager's* dispatch, including the captain's request that all available television programs be sent out to Jupiter in sequence to allow the U.S. ship to establish communications with the aliens, or at least make the attempt. Therein followed a lengthy discussion of the best way to get the information out to *Voyager*. They called in Ron Grimminger, the White House science adviser, to get more details on how fast they could radio the information to Jupiter.

"How fast we can get them the information depends upon a number of things," the science adviser told them, ticking off on his fingers: "the frequency we transmit on—the higher the better—the power we transmit with, again higher is better, the size of the transmitting antenna, and the receiving antenna, and here again, bigger is better. We also could possibly compress the signals using some digital transforms and get much more information out there in the same time." As he spoke, he fiddled with his tablet, working a spreadsheet. "With *Voyager's* ten-meter dish, we can only transfer at a two to one rate—"

"Two to one?" The president was confused.

"Well, sir, that means we could transfer two hours of real time in one hour," Grimminger explained. "That would mean that in order to transmit all three networks' broadcasts for a week up to *Voyager* would require a week and a half." He frowned.

"Isn't that good enough?" McPhee asked.

Grimminger shook his head. "No, I don't think so. Granted we don't know what these aliens will do or how they'll react, but I think that we must provide the people at Jupiter with as much as we possibly can."

"So, what do you suggest?" the president asked.

"The European ship has a hundred-meter dish—" Grimminger began.

"They'd never let us use it!" Admiral Kinnock burst out.

"Well," the president drawled, "if they did, there'd be a *price*."

Grimminger disagreed. "If we do anything we're going to have to use the Deep Space Network, effectively cutting the Europeans off anyway."

"They're not going to like that one iota," Ellington of State said. The United States was notorious worldwide for its poor treatment of other nations' space interests.

"We could send up disks with Alquay to Deep Ear," Wood of the Navy suggested.

McPhee pursed his lips. "Too late. It'll take at least three days to get there."

"They need that information *right away*," Grimminger agreed. "If we could use the hundred-meter dish on *Harmonie*, we could transfer," he paused, checking the numbers, "a whole week's broadcast of all three networks in just about a day." He looked over at Admiral Kinnock, "With Deep Ear that goes down to just an hour."

"We can't tell them about Deep Ear!" Kinnock growled.

"Admiral," Grimminger asked, "what will the American people say if they find out that we haven't done everything possible to communicate with those aliens?"

"Some of them will bless us," Byrne muttered under her breath.

"There's a half-hour delay from here to there," Grimminger added ominously.

"What are we doing now?" the president asked.

"One of the guys out at Goldstone is already on it, sir. He's contacted JPL and Hollywood. The networks are falling over backwards to do what they can, but this sort of effort has never been envisioned before."

"Well, nobody ever thought that aliens would listen to that *junk*," Kinnock muttered.

"I know," the president said, "and it worries me." He sighed, looking around the table at all the expectant faces. "Very well, I declare a Deep Space Emergency, pre-empt the DSN for *Voyager*."

"I'm afraid the Europeans have already declared an emergency, sir," Grimminger corrected. "And sending the information to *Voyager* would be too little, too late."

"What do you suggest?" McPhee said.

"Send the information to *Harmonie*. Talk to Eurocos, tell them what we're doing and why."

"They'll go nuts!" Ellington said.

"Time is precious," Grimminger urged the president.

Greg Merritt looked at the faces around the table. He sighed. "Very well. Do it," he told Grimminger. He turned to Ellington of State. "Talk to Eurocos—"

"But that's Navy's job!" Ellington pointed out.

"Oh, I think in this instance, John, I'll be willing to let you do it," the secretary of the Navy allowed drolly.

"How soon will it be on its way, Ron?" Anne Byrne asked.

"When I spoke to him, the guy at DSN said he'd have the first lot ready to go in about an hour, and that was twenty minutes ago," Grimminger said.

"Why, thinking of making a press statement?" the president said.

"The people will be glad to hear that we're finally getting somewhere," Sumner of intelligence predicted.

"Well," Byrne said, "some of them!"

* * *

European Space Agency Headquarters

They met in the central briefing room. Toni Scarli and Anne-Marie Foquet had arrived together, Werner Ulke had scurried in not much later, and the video link was established with Moscow five minutes later.

"You have the latest transmission?" Anne-Marie began without preamble.

"Yes, we have it," Vladimir Novitsky said. He made a face. "*Howdy Doody*—is it as bad as we believe?"

Madame Foquet nodded. "Worse. However, the ramifications are our concern."

"*Can it be worse than* Wanderly Wagon?" Boris Kalinsky, Russia's minister of science and technology, wondered in Russian.

"*No, nothing is that bad!*" Werner Ulke, ESA's chief science adviser replied in the same language.

"Ah, *danke schön*," the minister, not to be outdone, returned in serviceable German.

"*Wanderly Wagon?*" Antonio Scarli asked.

"We bought it from the Irish long ago when they were the only ones being nice to us," Kalinsky said. He shuddered. "After that, we explained that our transmission signals were different from theirs and we could only show their products after extensive re-engineering." He shrugged. "We bought their butter instead."

Administrator Foquet's lips had drawn to a tight, thin line. Vladimir Novitsky noticed and asked, "Madame Foquet, how does the European Space Agency feel about the Americans' request?"

"I don't know how much longer my organization can keep this from becoming political," Anne-Marie said. *Of course,* she admitted to herself, *it already* was *political.* She had had to fend off daily inquiries from the president of the European Community, the president of France, the president of Germany, and the prime ministers of countless other member countries in their efforts to obtain some reassurance that *their* team members on *Harmonie* were invaluable to the alien encounter. Not that that mattered to her. What mattered was expanding her control over the growing European space empire. This conversation with the Russians was merely another step in a sequence of "glad-handing" (as the Americans so aptly put it) the members of her Eurocos organization. "Already, I have received a lot of pressure to yield control to a special EC committee."

"We, too, have received such pressures," Novitsky said, avoiding a glance at the minister seated beside him. "I would not be surprised if you find your continued freedom of action constrained by your current successes as we do here."

Such an oblique way of turning the knife you have, Anne-Marie thought bitterly to herself. "Of course. And now with this request from the Americans …" She trailed off, hoping to draw the Russians into revealing their opinion.

Kalinsky was too quick, however. "Ah, yes! How does ESA feel about this request?"

Toni Scarli noted how Madame Foquet's eyes narrowed in anger, but doubted that any of the others knew how to interpret it.

"ESA," the administrator said, "would like to have the opinion of our Russian partners in this venture."

Kalinsky made a show of thinking the request over. "Our cosmonaut captain indicated in the report that there was little alternative," he said at last. "However, it does put the Americans at the center of world attention."

And you don't like that anymore than I, Anne-Marie thought sourly. "True," she admitted, "but only at our indulgence, a fact which we can make available to the world."

"And *Harmonie* is the more capable ship," Ulke said. Kalinsky and Foquet were both irked at his interjection. The chief science advisor continued, unperturbed, "She has more room, a larger crew, a surfeit of scientists, larger and faster computers—the Americans will need all these when negotiations commence."

"Negotiations?" Kalinsky's question was veiled in neutral tones.

"We could insist that the Americans merely establish communications and allow us to start negotiations," Anne-Marie said.

"Captain Zhukov stated that he was certain we would be at a disadvantage attempting negotiations with aliens used to talking *American*," Boris Novitsky felt compelled to say.

"And if the Americans fail in their attempt—" Antonio Scarli began, but Kalinsky cut him off.

"We have no guarantee that if the negotiations fail there *will* be a further position," the Russian minister said bluntly.

"Clever of the Yanks to send out a politician," Ulke said.

"Could we send out a politician of our own?" Kalinsky asked.

"To what purpose?" Anne-Marie asked, her expression making it clear that her question had more than a few political ramifications.

"In the past," Kalinsky replied coolly, "we have managed to communicate with people who do not speak our language."

"Yes," Foquet said, "but I believe in the cases you refer to, it was always from a position of strength." She paused dramatically. "Please recall that their ship is over eleven kilometers in length."

Minister Kalinsky nodded. "So we let the Americans run the show."

"For now," the ESA administrator agreed.

"You know, they could just *take* their network from us," Ulke said.

"They could, but they would lose our cooperation on any future projects," Foquet said. "No, they will ask and we will agree … but only after we have wrung concessions from them."

"And their ambassador?" Kalinsky asked, stressing the last word.

"I believe that we have little choice in letting their politician open communications with the aliens," Anne-Marie said. "However, it took three weeks to get any response from the aliens—"

"Only because we used the wrong approach!" Ulke snapped.

Administrator Foquet's eyes narrowed to thin points as she glared at the ESA scientist, but she continued as though he had not spoken, "—and it may take even longer to establish good communications. In that length of time, many *ambassadors* could be sent to Jupiter."

"But, Madame," Novitsky protested faintly, "the only ship capable of such a journey is *Harmonie!*"

"We could deploy the settlements and have *Harmonie* return on a high-speed orbit," Werner Ulke volunteered.

"So, Minister Kalinsky, are we agreed that the Americans can have back their communications network?" Anne-Marie asked, ignoring her scientist's outbursts.

Kalinsky pursed his lips and nodded slowly. "I trust, Madame, that you will make the Americans fully aware of our graciousness in this matter?"

"I am certain that they will be quite ready to acknowledge our generosity in this instance," Foquet agreed, answering the hidden question of whether the Americans would be made to pay in the future with some return favor.

Vladimir Novitsky was amused at the prospect. "Do you mean we will get the *Amis* -- your friends -- to pay for use of their own communications network?"

Antonio Scarli took one look at the gleam in his boss's eyes and responded, "As I believe the Americans say, 'in spades.'"

* * *

The White House, Washington, DC

"They agreed!" Secretary of State Ellington reported to the president two hours later. He turned to the secretary of defense. "George, you can tell Elijah or Kinnock to go ahead."

"Heck, they've been running that information up for over an hour," Charles Sumner of intelligence said.

"Have they?" George Morgan asked. "It wasn't sanctioned, you know."

"Oh, I don't think it was official," Sumner said. "But that Ahrens out there started sending as soon as he got the first bits in from Hollywood."

"Well, I'd better tell Elijah," Morgan said. "I know there's some old NASA fossils out there who won't spit without authorization."

"Yeah, Navy inherited a pretty odd bunch when they got the Skywatch job after the Manhattan Meteor," Ellington said.

* * *

Deep Space Network, Goldstone, Arizona

"Got a message in from headquarters," John Ahrens remarked absently to the station chief, as he watched the progress of his transmission up to *Harmonie* orbiting Jupiter.

Rogers took the proffered disc from Ahrens with ill-disguised outrage. He decoded it and read it quickly on his tablet. "We are instructed," the station chief announced with emphasis on the last word, "to transmit compressed television signals to the Europeans so that *they* can send them to the alien ship."

"Heck, I've been doing that for an hour now," Ahrens piped up, turning to catch the station chief's response. Rogers was an odd bird but Ahrens still valued his praise.

Rogers' eyes bulged in outrage. "*You* have been transmitting all this time?"

"Yeah, well, sure, if we're going to talk to those eetees up there, then we have to act fast," John said.

"I have not heard from Whitestar," Rogers muttered to himself, eyes searching out some unseen horizon. "Orders to communicate with the soulless ones, the Satanspawn."

"Mr. Rogers?" Ahrens asked. "Are you okay?"

Christopher Rogers did not respond to his question. Instead, he turned swiftly and marched into his office, lips working soundlessly.

"Your superior seems distraught," said Ivan Petrovich, who had watched the whole affair seated at another console.

"Yeah," Ahrens agreed, "he gets that way sometimes." He turned back to his console. "Hey, wait a minute! We've stopped transmitting!"

"What has happened?" Petrovich demanded, coming over to the technician's console.

"I don't know, all the sudden we just stopped transmitting." He called up a display, shook his head. "We're not past the terminator. We've got carrier but nothing's going over it." He switched to another display. "The booster station's getting carrier only."

He continued tracing but was interrupted as Rogers burst out from his office.

"Hah!" he shouted. "I've done it! The spawn of Satan shall never succor us with honey-sweet phrases! I have saved us all!" Spittle foamed at the corners of his mouth as he looked heavenwards in rapture. "The day of judgement shall come at last and find me ready!"

"Oh, shit!" John Ahrens said. He grabbed for the Russian's portable phone.

*　*　*

The White House, Washington, DC

"What is it?" President Merritt rasped into the telephone as he blearily tried to make out the time displayed on his bedside clock. Beside him, his wife turned over wearily.

It was Elijah Wood, Secretary of the Navy. "Mr. President, we have a problem!"

"What?"

There was a pause on the other end. Finally, "The Deep Space Network's gone down."

"Down? I thought it was a whole bunch of antennas all over the world."

"Yes, sir, it is," Wood agreed, "but the controlling software is coordinated. That software has locked the network."

"What happened?"

"Apparently, the station chief at Goldstone ran amok. He sent out a software virus that's brought the whole system down."

"Jesus! What was his problem?"

"Apparently, this man was a recent convert to the Church of Jesus the Judgmental, you know—"

"Yes, yes, the apocalypse tomorrow loonies," the president said. "Ned was just out at one of their rallies a couple weeks ago."

"The vice president, sir?" Wood's words were anxious. "You don't suppose—where is he now, sir?"

"Huh?" President Merritt thought for a moment. "Oh, he's over at Far Side by now." He brightened. "He's got a backup of the data; we can send it out there."

"That's *great*, sir! Why, with the vice president there, we'll be sure to have no tampering."

"Yeah, it was lucky I sent him," the president said, thinking how odd the veep had been acting in the past week.

"Sir," Wood's asked anxiously, "you don't suppose, I mean, he attended a Judgmental rally?"

"So? I mean, what's the worst that could happen? He could be converted—oh, no!"

* * *

The Naval Deep Ear Installation, Far Side, the Moon

"Mr. Vice President, sir, are you sure that these disks are supposed to be executed? Aren't they data disks?" the base commander asked with as much respect as he could for someone who did not understand that a vacuum meant that there was no air to breath.

"Oh, sure," the vice president replied with a boyish grin. He held up another stack of discs. "*These* are the data discs. Mr. Rogers was absolutely certain that I'd want to have you run the program on those discs."

"Very well, sir," the commander said. He nodded to the nervous rating at the computer console. "Did he say what the program was supposed to do?" the commander asked as the program ran.

The vice president made a face. "Well, Commander, I'm not a technical sort of person. Mr. Rogers assured me that the program would do what we want it to."

"Ah! A data compression program, no doubt." The commander frowned, recalling that the data was supposed to be compressed in standard Huffman encoding; that would not require a special program.

The vice president shook his head. "No, I don't think that was it. He said it would lead us to salvation."

"Lead us to salvation?" the base commander repeated worriedly.

"Sir!" a rating called. "The frequency modulation unit has just failed—we're only sending carrier!"

The vice president brightened. "That's right! That's what is supposed to happen! Now those spawns of Satan will never send their message of deceit to us." He frowned momentarily. "Pity about the folks aboard *Voyager*."

Beside him, Base Commander Smith turned a very pale shade.

CHAPTER FOUR

Voyager

"VERY WELL," CAPTAIN STEELE COMPLETED HER ADDRESS TO THE COLLECTED crew, "Lorie, you have the watch."

"Aye, ma'am," Ensign Lorie Dubauer replied crisply. She gestured to Bill Pusser, and the two floated off to *Voyager's* cockpit.

"The rest of you, get some sleep if you can." They were in *Voyager's* mess room, seated at or floating near the eight-place table. Every ship had a natural congregation point: in the old navy, on the seagoing aircraft carriers, it was the Combat Information Center (CIC); in older battleships, it was the bridge; on *Voyager*, it was the galley. The reason for that was the collection of displays which were hung above the eight seats at the dining table. A crewman with his individual infrared keypad and combined headset—called a Crewmember Communication Unit or CCU in Navy—could interface with any free display to work, watch, play, or simply talk to another crewman.

All of the functions of *Voyager* could be accessed through any of the ship's displays. A CCU was distinctly identified so that a crewman could go from the cockpit all the way back to engineering and have his display follow him from screen to screen along the way.

Emily glanced sourly towards Jenkins and Lieutenant McElroy. Both were deeply engrossed with their individual displays and showed not the slightest inclination toward sleep.

"*One* of you, get out of here!" Emily growled at them with equal parts admiration and annoyance.

Danni McElroy glanced up then elbowed Jenkins, who was still immersed in his programming. "Huh? Did they come in?"

"No, skipper says for you to get sleep," Danni told him. Jenkins turned to Steele, back to Danni, and waved at his screen.

"I'm hot on this! Skipper—"

"Danni, get," Emily said in a soft firm voice.

"Aye aye," Danni said, floating up out of her chair and kicking off down to her cabin.

Emily glanced at Jenkins, considering whether to order him, too, but decided she had more pressing matters to contend with. She had split the group into four watches, composed of two primary watch standers and an emergency 'stander. With *Voyager* safely in orbit, all she required was observation of the life support and power systems but, with an alien vessel over fifty times their size floating nearby, it was prudent to keep a watchful eye. Things would get hot enough when the signals arrived from Earth.

"*Voyager*, this is *Harmonie*," a voice called.

"Skipper?" Lorie Dubauer called questioningly from the cockpit.

"Take it," Emily called back, mentally deducting points from her opinion of the young ensign and then correcting herself, Lorie was only acting courteously. "I'll monitor."

She punched up the signal on her display. Behind her, Mac and Pickett crouched down to get a look.

"This is Commander Reynaud of *Harmonie*," the voice identified itself. Emily punched a request on her keyboard and a window popped up in the display listing the vital statistics on Elodie Reynaud, *Harmonie's* French first officer.

"Ensign Dubauer, officer of the watch," Lorie replied.

"Ensign, I have been ordered to produce a plan in case it is desired to interface our two ships together—"

"Just what sort of interface are we talking about here, Commander?" Lorie asked.

"I believe that will depend upon the situation as it develops," Elodie said. "I would like to produce plans for varying levels of interface, from complete physical connection to simple data exchange. Will you assist me?"

Lorie glanced at her captain, who nodded an affirmative. "Yes, I believe that is possible."

Jenkins looked up from his programming, saw the display and hissed, "Ask her if they've had anything from Earth." Emily raised an eyebrow. "They might have sent the stuff to *Harmonie*—better bandwidth."

"Lorie?" Emily called over her headset. The central computer directed the request to the ensign. "Check if *Harmonie's* had anything in from Earth yet."

"Commander, have you had any transmissions from Earth?" Lorie relayed. On the screen, they saw Reynaud turn and converse silently with another officer. *Voyager's* computer identified the second person as Ensign Gregor Strasnoye. The ensign shook his head.

"Thank you," Lorie said in response to the ensign's negative. "Would you let us know if anything comes in?"

"Of course," Elodie replied. "Now, about your power subsystem …" She started into the detailed technical discussion of how to mate *Voyager* with *Harmonie*.

Voyager was constructed in two parts: A Personnel Module, which followed the Navy standard for a courier, and a Propulsion Module, which consisted of the prototype MAM engines, a radio-thermal generator for electricity, and maneuvering jets large enough to shove the combined mass of Personnel and Propulsion Modules around. All the life support, computers, major controls, and living area were contained in the Personnel Module.

Partway through the discussion, Emily staged a very loud yawn and proclaimed, "Well, I'm off for some rest." She looked at Mac and Pickett. "You two should go as well."

"I'm on standby," Mac said.

"So? Lorie knows where you sleep."

"But I want to stay and …" Mac's protest faded away as Captain Steele glared at him. "Well, yes, forty winks wouldn't hurt."

Up in the cockpit, Lorie Dubauer did not notice their departure as she explored possible connections between *Voyager* and *Harmonie* with Commander Reynaud. They whittled the list down to five options: no change, close proximity for speedier data exchange, physical connection of data feeds, physical networking of computer systems, and physical connection of the two ships.

"We would have to deploy the Science Module for either networking or connection," Commander Reynaud said.

"Your ship's five hundred meters long? How 'hot' is your tail?" Lorie asked, adding, "We'd certainly have to separate our Propulsion Module for any close in work."

"Is that difficult?" Elodie asked. She pursed her lips. "I thought—" She broke off, interrupted by the ensign on communications. They spoke for several moments before Elodie returned to screen. "We are receiving a signal from Earth."

Back on *Voyager*, in the galley, Jenkins looked up from his programming. "They're receiving?" He brought up a display linked to Dubauer's and listened in.

"Is there anything for us, Commander?" Ensign Dubauer asked, hearing Jenkins' question faintly from the galley. Cautiously, she checked *Voyager's* thirty-meter dishes but heard nothing from Earth.

"We have not broken it down, yet," Elodie said. Typically, transmissions from Earth included multiple channels of voice and data. "They are transmitting a lot of data."

Jenkins broke in, "Commander, could I get a feed, please?"

"Who is that?" Elodie asked, peering into the display focused on Ensign Dubauer.

"Jenkins, ma'am. I was listening in; I hope you don't mind," he said. "I was the one who first decoded the alien transmission. You could piggyback it on this frequency, I'll break it out here." Jenkins watched her carefully in the display, adding when it looked like she would turn him down, "We've been transmitting station identification for over a half hour now. The aliens are probably getting impatient." He persisted, "Please, I'm familiar with the DSN formats! I'll just let you know how the data's been sent."

"I am sure that my own—" She broke off as her comm officer approached, grim-faced. "Excuse me." She slipped out of hearing but not out of view as she spoke with the young ensign. Her face clearly showed that she was not pleased with what he told her. The young ensign left, looking miserable. Reynaud straightened her uniform with a sigh and returned to the microphone. "Perhaps that is a good idea. My ensign will begin transmission on your mark."

Jenkins suppressed a grin. "Thank you," he told her. To Dubauer, he said, "Ensign, is this all right with you?"

"Certainly."

"Good." Jenkins set up a program to capture the incoming data, started it and called: "Ready for my mark. Five … four … three … two … mark!" He put the incoming transmission on another display and started analyzing it. Five minutes later he announced, "What you've got, *Harmonie*, is 800 MHz of data—100 Megabytes a second—most of it consisting of compressed TV signals. There's a spare 8 MHz of data that they've filled with—hmm, looks like they've got several things there." Jenkins fiddled with his keyboard. "Okay, one's a code for *Harmonie* and I'll bounce it back to you, the other's a quick decompress program for the data—have you been storing this?"

"Of course!" Elodie responded.

From the cockpit, Lorie hailed the captain "*Harmonie's* receiving from Earth."

"On my way." Emily paused only to rap on the cabins of Mac and Pickett before floating up to the galley. "Signal from Earth!"

In the galley, she found Jenkins working feverishly. "I'm comparing the very first *Howdy Doody* with what the aliens sent, Skipper." Jenkins glanced up to the display on his right and grimaced. "They aren't the same."

"We don't want it; we want the program that followed it." Pickett pointed out then slapped his head in shame. "Never mind! You have to find *that* episode before you'll find the program that follows it." He looked around the galley, swam over to the stove, and pumped out a cup of coffee. "Anybody else need to jumpstart their brains?"

Emily glanced at the patterns working across the display. "How fast is this stuff coming in?"

"Twenty-two to one." Jenkins replied, his expression grim.

"At that rate we'll get a week's programming in eight hours!"

"They had three channels back then," Pickett corrected, "it'll take a whole day."

"Are they transmitting all three networks sequentially or in parallel?" Mac asked Jenkins.

"Sequentially. I'm getting NBC." Jenkins glanced at the display directly above him. "They encoded some information about transmission times and dates: the first *Howdy Doody* went out August 15, 1948. Prior to that it was called something else." His fingers flicked over the keyboard of his CCU. "On the left screen I'm running a comparison program." He glanced up at the center screen. "We should get the next day in ten minutes."

"Ten minutes? Isn't that fast?" Mac said.

Jenkins shook his head. "They were only transmitting eight hours a day back then." He ran his fingers over his keyboard again. "I've got the old NBC station identification. Why don't I replace the one we cobbled up? That should at least alert them."

"Sounds good." Emily said.

"They've probably picked up the transmission from Earth," Pickett said.

"Maybe," Mac said. "Perhaps not. The only frequency we *know* they are receiving is the TV frequency. Also, they'd have to break out the data, figure out which is the compression program, *then* figure out what that program means and, since it was built for our computers here on *Voyager*, I doubt their computers—if they have any—could run it."

"Oh," Pickett replied abashedly, pointedly taking a long swig of his coffee. "Is anyone hungry? How about I make some breakfast?"

"I'll take a cup of coffee and some pancakes," Jenkins called out. Mac and Emily seconded the motion.

"Hey, in the cockpit! Need nourishment?" Pickett yelled.

"Coffee!" Bill Pusser called back from the cockpit.

"I'll get it," Mac said.

Pickett was still working on the pancakes, a difficult task in zero-gee, when they received the next episode of *Howdy Doody*.

"That's not it, either," Jenkins said, adding with a sigh, "Another ten minutes."

When he gave the same report ten minutes later, Captain Steele tried to cheer him up. "It's okay Jenkins, it was unlikely we'd hit pay dirt this quickly."

Jenkins nodded. "I just hope we're not off by a year or we'll be waiting for months!"

"If that happens, we'll get them to send it on Deep Ear," Pickett said.

"I don't know," Emily said, "that'd mean letting Eurocos know about it."

Pickett shook his head. "I don't think that would be a prob—" He broke off as the center screen went white with static.

"*Harmonie*, what happened?" Jenkins called.

"*Voyager*, this is Ensign Strasnoye, we've lost signal from DSN."

"Lost it?" The words were chorused by everyone in the galley. "Are you coming up on LOS?" Jenkins asked, bringing up a display of *Harmonie's* position relative to Earth and Jupiter. It was obvious that the Eurocos ship had several hours before it would pass into the shadow of Jupiter and out of radio contact with Earth. "Have you checked your alignment?"

"Yes," Gregor responded. "We're still getting carrier but no signal."

"Could be a glitch," Jenkins muttered. "Give 'em a couple of minutes, maybe they'll get it sorted out." Five minutes later, Jenkins swore and slapped the table. "Skipper, I think we've got a problem."

Emily was not worried. "What's the problem, Jenkins? Earthside's got a glitch; we wait until they fix it and continue with the transmission."

"I wish it were that easy," Jenkins said. "But it looks like the transmission broke off because someone introduced a virus into the DSN system—"

"How can you tell?" Pickett asked.

"Because the same virus was the last thing they transmitted."

"You've isolated it?" Captain Steele asked.

Jenkins shook his head.

"Any idea what it does?"

He nodded. "I suspect it reprograms any signal modulator or demodulator that works on the Ku or Ka band to shunt signal to ground."

"Sabotage! The Europeans sabotaged us!" Lorie Dubauer swore from the cockpit.

"It wasn't the Europeans. They use the same hardware."

"So they're already dead," Mac noted. Jenkins nodded. "Can you dig out the virus, kill it?"

"In time," Jenkins said. "*Harmonie* must have programmers in her crew that could do this."

"How long is it going to take?" Pickett asked, looking up at the displays.

"Days, maybe two weeks, tops," Jenkins replied.

"Well, that's no problem, the aliens waited three weeks before they started talking to us." Mac said.

"I think they've gotten impatient," Jenkins said, pointing to the left-hand display. The display showed the station identification that Jenkins had just sent.

"I'd say you're right." Pickett agreed. He turned to the captain. "So, what do we do now?"

"I'm open to suggestions." Emily said. "*Harmonie*, are you still listening?"

"Yes," Commander Reynaud said. "I have called our captain to the bridge."

"Do you have any suggestions?"

"No," Elodie replied. "However, I have assigned programmers to investigate the virus your technician discovered."

"Good," Emily said. She turned back to Jenkins. "Do you want some help from Lieutenant McElroy?"

"It's your pigeon, Chris," Mac told the technician.

"Great," Jenkins groaned. He glanced up again at the incoming alien signal, dropped his head, and slumped his shoulders.

"We've got two hours to LOS," Ensign Dubauer called back from the cockpit.

"Thanks, Lorie," Jenkins muttered.

Pickett looked at Mac. "LOS?"

"Loss of signal—we'll be in Jupiter's shadow, hidden from Earth."

"If *Harmonie* deployed their science labs, they could orbit some TDRS," Lorie called out.

"Tracking and Data Relay Satellites," Mac translated in response to Pickett's strained look. Pickett nodded in thanks.

"Good point," Captain Steele said. She looked at Pickett. "How do you think the aliens would react to that?"

"To what?"

"If *Harmonie* deploys the science labs." Emily called up a display on the leftmost screen, one that Jenkins had not yet appropriated. "That's *Harmonie* with the science labs"—a section at the nose of the European ship turned red—"those are the science labs. They deploy"—the sequence animated, showing the four modules separate from the sides at the front of *Harmonie*, resolve themselves into four cylinders, then float forward and spread apart and start spinning about a common axis—"like that."

"Why wouldn't the aliens assume that to be a hostile act?" Pickett asked rhetorically. He gestured to the other side of the table. "Come over here, I've been thinking about these aliens and aliens in general and I want to bounce my conclusions off someone." Emily followed him to the other side of the table. Pickett seated himself nearest the cockpit.

"Actually, I've been thinking about life itself."

"Isn't that getting a bit vague, Ambassador?"

"Just listen," Jim said. "If you look at life from the point of view of thermodynamics—"

"I didn't think thermodynamics was something you'd studied!" Emily burst out.

Pickett shrugged modestly. "In politics, particularly space politics, you get around," he said. "Anyway, from a thermodynamic point of view, life requires a temperature difference in order to extract energy. You can go further than that; life requires that the acquired energy must be greater than the energy expended to acquire it—"

"Why not equal?"

"Several reasons, first of which is that organisms aren't perfectly efficient. A biologist would recognize this as 'survival of the fittest.' I think it can be expanded to biomes and to intelligent life."

"Biomes?"

"Whole ecological systems," Pickett said. "If the ecosystem of these aliens is older and more evolved than our ecosystem, then they would have absolutely no problem in supplanting our ecosystem with theirs." He waved a hand. "Of course, they would have to be compatible with our ecosystem; oxygen breathers, at least."

"So, you think they're going to invade us?"

"It's a possibility," Pickett admitted with a shrug, "but I don't think it's very likely. First of all, if they are rational beings, then in order for them to consider an invasion or an ecological plantation, they would have to believe it to be energy efficient, economical."

Steele raised a brow. "Economical?"

Pickett nodded. "Sure. Of course, I'm using economics in a purer sense than we are accustomed to." He noticed Steele's inquiring look and explained, "Let's assume that economics can be related to energy transactions. If that's the case, then the aliens would have to perceive that the energy they expend to conquer us would be less than the energy they could recoup in a suitable period of time."

"Acquiring a whole solar system's worth of energy is nothing to be sneezed at!"

Pickett nodded. "True, but only if the cost of colonizing a system and the benefits of the system work with the alien economics. They might consider the initial cost too high for the return."

Steele frowned. "Particularly if we can show them that the price will be higher than they bargained on."

"I don't think that will be necessary," Jim Pickett said. "Let's consider cost some more: for every transaction at a distance from their home base, the aliens would have to include the cost of transportation."

"Against a solar system that cost has to be negligible!" Emily protested loudly. Guiltily she looked over at Jenkins, but he continued to work obliviously.

"That presupposes that the aliens are more advanced than we are."

Emily waved in the direction of the aliens. "They've got a starship, haven't they?"

"But how much of a technological leap is a starship from where we are now?"

"Neither of us knows," Emily said. "They could be thousands of years more advanced or just a decade ahead of us, what does it matter?"

Jenkins interrupted them. "Skipper, I think we've got it."

Emily gave Pickett an apologetic look and moved over to Jenkins. Pickett followed her. "Let's see," Emily said to the young technician.

"Well, I started by asking myself about how the aliens found that signal," Jenkins began. "They probably noticed the sync pulse first—"

"Sync pulse?" Pickett asked hoarsely.

Jenkins looked over to him. "Do you know how television works?"

"No."

"Well, a television receiver, your basic TV set, receives a frequency modulated signal—one whose frequency varies slightly—and decodes it into a sound signal and a video signal," Jenkins explained. "The video signal itself is complex. It—" Jenkins halted, noting that Pickett had taken on a glazed look. "Let me show you."

He started a new screen on the display. It showed a triangular wave rising from left to right; the wave itself had smaller waves in it. "That is how a single line of a television screen is transmitted. The large saw-tooth wave forces the beam, which draws the image, to move from left to right, while the smaller waves contain the intensity of the light the beam is to use."

He flicked fingers over his CCU and the image changed to show a whole series of saw-tooth waves each starting from the end of the other and climbing up on the screen. The last saw-tooth wave fell back down to the level of the first wave. "Those smaller drops in the wave are the vertical synchronization pulse—it forces the beam back to the left, but, as you can see, there is extra signal which moves the beam further down the screen. The large drop at the end forces the beam all the way back up to the top of the screen and starts the process over again." His fingers flew over his keyboard again and the image grew smaller, showing another complete wave.

"That one's different," Pickett said.

"Yes," Jenkins agreed. "That's because of the way the screen is drawn; television images are interlaced—that is, the odd screen lines are drawn first and then the even screen lines. The reason is to ensure the image does not flicker."

Pickett frowned thoughtfully. "So what you're saying is that's what the aliens are seeing?"

"I don't know what they're *seeing*," Jenkins replied. "I don't even know if they *look* at these signals."

"They're certainly receiving them, and they know that the signals are intelligent," Pickett said.

"Yes. And they can probably make some inferences from the way the signals are sent," Jenkins said. "They probably realize that the two horizontal sync pulses constitute a complete data frame and that the data impressed upon the saw-tooth waves is sequential in some fashion—"

"Jenkins," Emily broke in, "get to the point."

"Sure," Jenkins said. "What I propose to do is to use two scan lines and encode basic binary information." His fingers worked the CCU, putting his words into motion. "We'll send them a blank screen followed by a series of pixels representing numbers."

"What numbers?"

"Binary," Jenkins said. "I figure that the difference between something and nothing— on and off—has got to be a universal. I'll count in binary *here*"—the screen displayed a series of black dots growing from the center of the screen toward the right-hand side—"and I'll have room for negative numbers, increased powers, and fractions."

"Will the aliens understand it?" Pickett asked.

Jenkins shrugged. "If not, we'll try something else. But I figure that if I count to eight, they should probably count to fifteen and then we'll know they understand. After that we'll show them some of our mathematics—"

"I want to *talk* to them, not trade numbers!" Pickett said.

"You can't run before you walk," Jenkins said. "Once we get mathematical references, my AI program will take over."

"And then we'll be able to talk?"

"Maybe."

Emily Steele ruminated. "Why left to right? We normally write numbers out right to left."

"Because the saw-tooth is already increasing in that direction," Jenkins said. "It makes sense to imply that greater quantities follow the saw-tooth representation."

Emily glanced at Pickett. "Sounds all right to me."

"We should tell *Harmonie* what we're doing," Jim said.

"Agreed," Emily said, she hailed the European fusion ship. "*Harmonie*, this is *Voyager*." She had to wait for a reply. "Go ahead, *Voyager*. This is Captain Zhukov."

"Captain, we are going to send a binary pattern to the alien to open communications."

"And you think they will recognize it?"

Emily shrugged. "We have no reason to believe one way or the other. It certainly seems logical, more so than believing the aliens could decode and comprehend *Howdy Doody*."

"Well, maybe no less preposterous than that notion," Zhukov allowed. "Very well, thank you for telling me, and please keep us informed." He glanced off screen. "Oh, our programmers estimate that it will be several hours before they hope to break that virus. My engineers are working up an alternative to the sabotaged modulating unit."

"Very good," Emily said. "Would you inform my government of our actions when you regain contact?"

Zhukov nodded. "Of course."

"Thank you. *Voyager* out." Steele broke the connection. She turned to Jenkins. "Okay, do it."

Jenkins nodded. "The center screen is what we're transmitting, only slowed down so that we can track the changes; the right screen will be what we receive. We'll start with a blank screen." He started the program. His screen started black, then a white dot appeared in the center, moved right, a second dot joined it, then both were replaced with a new dot further right, a dot in the first spot joined the other dot, all three dots glowed and were replaced by a dot three spaces to the right. "Transmitted." They looked expectantly at the return screen. The screen went white, then a black dot appeared in the center and Jenkin's sequence was repeated, with the aliens continuing it to the next space. Jenkins let out a *yelp!* of excitement. "They did it!"

"But their screen was white!"

"Yes! Isn't it great?" Jenkins said. "That shows that they realize that the *dots* are what are important!" His fingers flew over his keyboard.

"Now"—a series of images moved across his screen—"we'll show subtraction." The bottom half of the screen went white. "The bottom half will be negative numbers. Let's see … we'll start with five and subtract two and show the answer."

He sent the patterns across: the binary number five (**101**) in the top half of the screen; a screen with both five (**101**) and two (**010**) in the bottom half of the screen; followed by three (**011**) in the top half of the screen. The alien response was startling: a screen with five (**101**) in the top half; a screen with two (**010**) in the top half; a screen with an all-white top half and an all-black bottom half; then a final screen with (**111**) in the top half. "What …?"

"Addition!" Mac exclaimed. "They sent you back addition; they used a screen to represent each number. The screen flash when they reversed the colors, was to show the addition."

"That makes more sense than your technique," Emily added.

Jenkins mulled it over. "I dunno, let's see if you're right." He sent back three screens— all ones (**001**), a flash and the sum of the three numbers: three (**011**). The aliens sent back a screen of three (**011**), a screen of one (**001**), two flash screens and a screen of three (**011**).

"Multiplication?" Steele suggested.

Jenkins pursed his lips. "Let's see." He sent them back 3 x 5 = 15 and they sent 5 x 7 = 35. "Let's see if we can agree on division, then I should be able to hand this over to the AI program."

"Try reversing the second flash," Pickett suggested.

"Sure," Jenkins agreed. "I'm sending thirty-five, seven, flash, reverse flash and five." The aliens responded with 15 / 5 = 3.

"Looks like they understood division," Mac commented.

"Uh-huh," Jenkins agreed as his fingers played over his CCU's keyboard. "The AI program's been watching; let's see what it wants to do next." The AI program wanted to try

13 / 2 = 6.5, using the first dot left of center to indicate 1/2. Jenkins let the program run. The aliens responded with 2 X 1/2 = 1.

"I vote we let the AI program continue," Jenkins said, looking up at the others.

"Do it," Emily ordered.

"The AI program is taking over …" Jenkins' fingers played across his keyboard: "… now!"

"How long will it take before we can start communicating?" Pickett asked.

Chris Jenkins shrugged. "I don't know. The AI program has been instructed to work toward abstract symbols, the periodic table and things like that. It'll let us know when it thinks it has a suitable syntax down." He yawned, stretching his arms up above his head. "The way the aliens set it up, it'll take a bit longer as we're only exchanging thirty frames a second; I was hoping to exchange thirty ideograms a second."

"Ideograms?"

"Yeah, like three times five equals fifteen or six minus four equals two." Jenkins said. "As it is, we take longer to communicate one complete thought because we send part of an ideogram each frame."

"And larger concepts will take more frames to express," Mac added.

"Exactly," Jenkins said. He turned to Pickett. "My guess is that it'll take a couple of days before we get to abstract communication."

"Days?" Pickett was crestfallen.

"Yeah, probably," Jenkins responded with a shrug. He looked at Captain Steele. "Captain, I'm pretty tired and I have a watch—"

Steele cut him off with a nod. "Okay, Jenkins, get some sleep."

"What if something goes wrong?" Pickett asked as Jenkins floated down to the cabins.

Jenkins twisted deftly to face the politician. "Nothing should go wrong. But if it does, the program will sound a beeper and halt."

Emily waved Jenkins away to sleep and turned back to Pickett. "Not too long from now, the aliens will be able to communicate with us; what are we going to say?" Mac moved in to hear Pickett's response.

"I don't know," Pickett answered. Mac jerked his head up to stare closely at the politician. "It depends upon whether they speak first and what they say." He jerked a thumb towards the flickering screen where Jenkins' AI program was communicating with the alien ship. "It also depends upon how much that AI program teaches them."

"Wouldn't it be smart of them to play dumb and learn everything they can from the AI program?" Mac said.

Pickett nodded. "That's what I would do."

Emily was glum. "So then the aliens would know everything about us and we would know nothing about them."

Pickett shook his head. "I don't think that Jenkins' program is capable of sending technical data—it works in mathematical constants."

"So the aliens would only have an understanding of our mathematical knowledge," Mac observed. He looked at Captain Steele. "Would that be enough?"

Abruptly a loud beeping emitted from the screen above them. "Jenkins! Your program's broken!" Steele shouted down the corridor.

"I don't think so," Pickett corrected, pointing to the screen. There, in plain letters was: DO YOU SPEAK ENGLISH?

Chapter Five

Jenkins was incredulous. "That's impossible! There's no way they could have gone from the code to written words!"

"Forty columns, twenty-five rows," Mac noted to himself. "The maximum capability you can get with that particular signal."

"English," Emily muttered to herself.

"Jenkins," Pickett attracted the young tech's gaze, "can you rig up to transmit the same way?"

Jenkins shook himself out of his daze. "Uh, sure." He fiddled with the keyboard of his CCU. "There."

"May I?" Pickett held out a hand for the keyboard. Jenkins jerked his keyboard out of Pickett's reach.

"You can use yours," the tech told him with a trace of apology in his voice.

"Oh." Pickett tapped his keyboard and scanned the screen. "Hmm. When do we transmit?"

"Press your 'Print Screen' key."

Pickett nodded to indicate that he had heard the tech and eyed the screen overhead. He typed, YES—and added—HOW DID YOU LEARN TO SPEAK ENGLISH?

SESAME STREET.

Ah! That explains it! Pickett replied, adding under his breath, "Particularly the damned typeface."

GOOD. WE WELCOME YOU TO THE FEDERATION OF SENTIENT WORLDS.

"The Federation of Sentient Worlds?" Emily Steele echoed in the background.

"*Harmonie*, are you getting this?" Pickett asked, calling up another screen.

"This is Captain Zhukov of the *Harmonie*. Yes, we are receiving this." The Russian's face showed signs of strain.

"Say, Captain, how goes the work on that software bug?" Jenkins asked.

"Our people are looking at deploying a different modulator on our main antenna while our software personnel continue to work on the virus," Zhukov responded stiffly.

"That's excellent, Captain!" Pickett replied. "As soon as you can, please relay our historic breakthrough back to Earth." Adding to remove any sting, "This is a great moment for all of us."

"Ambassador, can you find out as soon as possible if we can deploy our science modules and investigate the alien ship?" Zhukov asked.

"Certainly, Captain," Pickett said with a nod. "I understand that at that point we might consider linking *Voyager* to *Harmonie*."

"It is possible."

"We may be here for a long time and I would take it as a favor if you could extend the use of your gravity section to the crew of this vessel." Jim said. "Now, if you'll please forgive me, I think I cannot keep our new acquaintances waiting."

"Indeed."

Pickett turned back to the center screen. Federation of Sentient Worlds? He typed. Could you explain?

"I don't know why you bother asking," Mac grumbled behind him, "Federation of Sentient Worlds is just about what everyone expected to find."

"Why?" Pickett wondered. "Particularly, why if the aliens know our language and have been receiving our television signals all these years?"

Mac's brows narrowed perplexedly, but Emily saw where the politician was heading. "You mean that they could have used that phrase to fool us?"

Pickett shrugged. "It's possible, or it's possible that they are who they claim to be. Let's find out."

The Federation is a peaceful organization of aliens who trade with each other for mutual gain.

Jenkins' heartfelt "Wow!" reflected the relief of everyone aboard *Voyager*.

You are here to offer us membership in this Federation? Pickett responded.

Membership is automatic for any race which achieves faster-than-light travel.

"Faster-than-light travel?" Pickett echoed, looking around to both Steele and McLaughlin. "Is there something I should know?"

"Nothing that *I've* heard of!" Commander Steele swore, hands raised in a warding gesture.

Pickett turned to the display of Captain Zhukov onboard *Harmonie*. "Captain, do you know of any FTL effort by Eurocos? Or ESA?"

Zhukov shook his head. "No, nothing at all."

Pickett sighed and composed a reply. When did you detect our Faster-than-Light travel?

Some four of your weeks ago.

We are aware of no faster-than-light travel by any Earth vessel. Pickett responded.

We clearly traced it here.

"Ask them how they traced it." Jenkins said.

Pickett did and the aliens replied: We need to use a better method of communication if we are to show you our methods.

"Jenkins, sounds like your bailiwick" Pickett said. The young tech shrugged and took over.

The watch ended before Jenkins managed to get it sorted out. Mac stayed with him.

As the final set of images flicked by, Jenkins turned to him and asked, "What do you make of that?"

Mac frowned. "Wellll"—he pointed to the screen,—"that looks like a trace of our exhaust signature, mostly the high-energy particles...." He sighed. "Send them the rough schematics for our drive and for *Harmonie's* fusion drive and ask them if somehow that's what they tracked."

"Huh?"

"Let me." Mac motioned for Jenkins' keyboard. The young tech relinquished it, watching the display with growing understanding as McLaughlin phrased his question.

Apparently so did the aliens: Ooops...

"Ooops?" Jenkins echoed. "Aliens go 'ooops'?"

Mac shrugged. "These do." He went on, "It seems that from their distance, they got the high-energy signature from our engines and from *Harmonie's* fusion drive mixed together; that mixed high-energy signature looks exactly like the signature of their FTL drive."

Pickett, who had been dozing at the far end of the galley, pushed himself over to the mess table. "Mac, could we make an FTL drive with that information?"

Mac snorted. "Not likely. That's like making a car engine by analyzing the exhaust fumes."

Pickett made a rueful face, shrugged. "I wonder what they'll do now."

"They could leave." Emily suggested.

Pickett nodded. "They could. I wonder if they will ..."

"Why did they say 'ooops'?" Jenkins repeated. The others looked at him. "I just can't imagine them learning 'ooops' without *hearing* it somewhere."

Mac shook his head dismissively. Captain Steele shrugged in a manner which showed that she felt it was not important, but Pickett looked thoughtful. Finally, he looked at Jenkins. "Chris, can we get a *regular* screen going with those guys—no more of that damned *Sesame Street* typeface?"

"Sure, I suppose."

"They might not understand it," Mac pointed out.

"Try it, Chris," Pickett said to the technician.

Five minutes later, Jenkins announced, "There ya go. And we've agreed on a graphical interchange system."

Pickett motioned for the keyboard, Jenkins passed it over. He paused reflectively, fingers poised over the keys. **Are there rules against contacting non-spacefaring races?**

Yes.

Are there any records of contacts with non-spacefaring races? Pickett typed.

Yes. They ended rather... tragically.

We had, in our writings, proposed that a non-spacefaring race would be so overwhelmed by such contact that it would destroy itself, Pickett wrote.

That has happened.

"Well, that's that," Jenkins muttered. Emily shushed him.

Pickett frowned, typing: **Every time?**

No.

"Whew! Maybe there's hope after all," Jenkins said.

"At least we know that FTL is possible," Steele said.

"But that's *all* we know," Mac pointed out. Emily's eyes flashed as she prepared to protest, but Mac continued, "Without more data, we've no way of knowing how they manage it."

Pickett paid no attention to the conversation going on around him. **We believe that we will not succumb to such despair and will develop interstellar travel on our own.... However, we are concerned that you will suffer hardships for having accidentally revealed yourselves to us....**

"What are you saying?" Emily demanded from behind him.

Pickett paid her no mind, continuing: **Is there perhaps a way we could help you? If you could forget this meeting—**

Jim interrupted them. **I am afraid that our entire world knows of this meeting already... is there some other way?**

Do you have a suggestion?

You have evidence indicating that we had FTL drive prior to your contacting us... could we not trade for a "better" FTL drive? Jim typed back.

Uh... that would be highly irregular.

I agree. However, would it not, Jim typed, **in the spirit of trade your Federation supports, be mutually beneficial and obviate a rather delicate situation?**

I must consult with my superiors.

Please do. In the meantime, Pickett typed, **assuming that they agree, what can we do to speed the process up?**

Well, we would need to see some of your trade good, the alien replied.

Could we also see some of yours? Pickett responded. **It would be helpful in determining the types of goods you prefer.**

I shall ask.

"Well, that's that." Pickett said, sitting back in his chair.

"*Harmonie*, did you get that?" Emily asked on the other comm link.

Captain Zhukov's lean features faced her. "We did," the Russian captain said. "I must admit that I am curious—Mr. Ambassador, what do you expect to trade with the aliens?"

Pickett slipped out of his chair and entered into view of the pickup. "Captain, I expect that there will be certain artifacts of ours that the aliens will find of value; probably things we ourselves have no use for. Also, some of our technology might be useful—"

"What could these aliens want of our technology?" Karl Geister asked, peering from behind Zhukov with a surly expression.

"Lots of things," Mac jumped in. "It is entirely possible that some of our techniques are totally unimagined by the aliens because they did not evolve on a planet with the same resources as ours. New planets more similar to ours would be best exploited using the technology we've developed."

"They could just take it from us," Geister said.

"True," Mac agreed, "but there are a thousand little questions between the knowledge of a technology and its application—in such cases it is easier to have the experts explain their solutions than to use trial and error."

Across the vidlink, Geister grunted in agreement.

Behind Zhukov, another figure came into view. "Captain, LOS in two minutes."

"We're about three minutes behind them," Jenkins added.

"How long is our loss of signal with Earth?" Jim Pickett asked.

"A little more than two hours."

Emily pursed her lips. "Plenty of time for them to jump us."

"Or gobble us up," Mac said.

"We've been through three LOSs already," Captain Zhukov pointed out.

"But that was when they thought they were still dealing with a race equipped with FTL drives," Karl Geister said.

"LOS," the crewman on *Harmonie* announced.

Pickett turned to Emily. "Your earlier arguments about whether the aliens would want to overrun us—I think that depends also on their lifespan."

Emily quirked an eyebrow.

"The economics are different for a long-lived species. To them, a project of fifty to a hundred years might seem quite economical, whereas to us those projects are deemed uneconomical."

"You are basing all your thinking on a thermodynamic approach to life?" Zhukov asked across the vidlink.

Pickett turned to face the display in surprise. "I hadn't realized you were listening in but—yes, I am."

"What happens if they live on a world of greater extremes than ours, or a hotter world?" Emily asked. "They could think faster than us."

"Yes, but their lifespan would be less and the project no more profitable to them than to us," Pickett said. He pulled his lip. "In fact, I suspect that you could derive a constant from lifespan and speed of thought. If that's the case, then because the concept is unprofitable to us, the concept is probably unprofitable to all aliens no matter how long their lifespan."

"A constant?" Mac repeated.

"Yes," Zhukov said, "that the relationship between lifespan and speed of thought is constant: the longer the lifespan, the longer the thought processes; the shorter the lifespan, the faster the thinking. That is: speed of thought is inversely proportional to lifespan."

Emily looked at Pickett. "Your theory is tenuous. Besides, what if their capabilities are far greater than ours?"

"Then why contact us at all?" Zhukov asked. "Why not merely take over the planet without announcing their intentions? Indeed, they could have destroyed *Harmonie* long before we knew of their presence. *That* would have concentrated Earth's attention here, at Jupiter, and make their assault that much easier."

"Consider the speed of their offer to join their Federation," Pickett said. "If they were long-lived, they certainly would have spent more time analyzing their data before approaching us."

"So you've ruled out their long lifespan two different ways," Emily said, "but neither is conclusive." She mulled the situation over. "Captain Zhukov, would you do me a favor? Would you apply your experience and imagination to describe to me how the aliens came to initiate this contact?"

Zhukov raised an eyebrow at the suggestion. "From the beginning?"

Emily nodded. "I think it might be useful."

"Very well," Zhukov said. He bowed his head, stroking his chin thoughtfully. "The aliens said that they started the contact when they picked up the combined signals of our two ships and mistook them for the signature of a faster-than-light drive."

"How come they didn't detect that the signals were coming from two discreet sources?" Emily asked.

"They must have been far so away that they could not resolve the two signals at the distance," Commander Geister said over the vidlink.

Mac called up a calculator on another monitor and rapidly punched in numbers. "That would have put them nearly thirteen thousand light-years away."

Geister raised his brows. "How did you get that figure?"

"I used the distance between Earth and Jupiter in light-years and the assumption that the aliens' resolving capability at distance is no greater than the best we have—one one-thousandth of an arc-second." Mac explained. Commander Geister nodded in reluctant acceptance of the process.

Jim Pickett narrowed his eyes. "Isn't that odd? Thirteen thousand light-years?" The others on *Voyager* looked at him in confusion. Across the vidlink, Geister gave an exaggerated sigh, indicating his poor opinion of Pickett's mental abilities. But Pickett persisted. "If they received the signal thirteen thousand light-years from here, where would that put them?"

"Thirteen thousand light-years away," Geister growled.

"No!" Mac exclaimed, turning to nod approvingly at the ambassador, "It would put them thirteen thousand years into the future!" A moment later, he added, "Or the past."

Emily's eyes widened as she digested the concept. Across the vidlink, Captain Zhukov gave Pickett a long penetrating look. After a moment, he said, "Of course faster-than-light travel could quite possibly include time travel."

"But if it does, why bother traveling *back* in time? If we had developed FTL thirteen thousand years before they noticed it, why had not they contacted the Earth of that future?"

Mac protested.

"Maybe they were not tracking signals that moved at light speed," Geister said.

Mac nodded. "You're suggesting that they tracked *tachyons*? If that's the case, then my earlier calculations are probably in error." He frowned. "But that would raise the question again of why they did not notice that our two signals were separate."

"Perhaps our signals propagated in exactly the correct manner," Geister said. "Or maybe they traveled at such a great speed that the difference in distance was indistinguishable."

"I like your second proposal better," Emily said. She looked at Zhukov's image in the vidlink. "Let us continue with the exercise, Captain. Given that they detected the signal, what then?"

Zhukov shrugged. "They would triangulate to get an accurate fix."

"And why wouldn't they have noticed the distance in signals then?" Mac asked.

"For the same reasons as before," Commander Geister said. Mac passed on that with a shrug.

Zhukov had followed the exchange closely. "After they triangulated, they would jump closer to our system and listen in."

"Yes, go on," Emily said. "What then?"

"They picked up television signals because the horizontal sync pulse was the most obvious indication of an intelligent control, and we've been broadcasting for over a hundred years now. And then they came here."

"Why not midway between the two signals?" Pickett asked.

Karl grunted. "Perhaps because the FTL signals have direction and point to the destination of the spacecraft."

Pickett made a sour face. "It stinks."

"Why do you say that, Ambassador?" Captain Zhukov asked.

"Too many *ifs* and *maybes* in all this," Jim replied. "*If* our signals just happened to look like an FTL drive, *if* they couldn't resolve the two targets, *if* the signals point in some direction, *if* they picked up our television signals, then *maybe* they'd come here."

Karl Geister glared at him disparagingly through the vidlink. "You're a politician, you can't trust anyone by your very nature."

Jim caught his eye across the vidlink and smiled at him, teeth bared. "Yeah, I'm paid to be paranoid."

Chapter Six

It was huge. And dark. Even with the light of Jupiter, the ship was only discernible as a lighter shade of dark against the black of space. A distended prolate spheroid—the shape of a pumpkin seed—it measured 20444 *xlernen* in length, 13624 *xlernen* in width, and was 5898 *xlernen* thick at its greatest section toward the rear (although the crew were told that it was 6000 *xlernen*). Its crew of two hundred had more than enough room for themselves, their cargoes, and fuel—the ship required *lots* of fuel.

If asked, and depending upon who did the asking, the crew of the *Xythir* would say that they were proud of their ship and their mission. Certainly Nexl, its captain, was proud. Nexl was also rather nervous. Currently, Nexl was covering this nervousness by relaxing in its quarters. Nexl was listening to an amusing Earth broadcast when a knock at the entrance interrupted. Of course it was dubbed, as the Xlernen don't hear—or talk—the same way as the humans.

\>\>**Yes?**\<\< Nexl rapped. The communications officer—Exern—appeared in the entrance. \>\>**Well?** \<\<

\>\>**The Earthlings want to trade.**\<\<

\>\>**Good!**\<\< Nexl was encouraged. \>\>**That should solve a lot of problems.**\<\<

\>\>**Indeed,**\<\< the comm officer agreed. Nexl detected a certain lack of enthusiasm in the response.

\>\>**What's the worry? You will ask them to let us examine their technology files so that we may see what is worth trading.**\<\<

\>\>**They have already suggested trade goods,**\<\< Exern replied. \>\>**It may be difficult.**\<\<

\>\>**Try,**\<\< Nexl suggested. \>\>**And if not, send them some garbage. Let's see what they make of it.**\<\<

Exern seemed relieved. \>\>**Very well. I had hoped that would be your answer.**\<\<

Nexl waved him out. \>\>**I'll be here if you need me.**\<\< In the background, an Earthling voice rapped in the accent that was known as American, *"... and we'll be saying a big hello to all intelligent life-forms everywhere... and to everyone else out there, the secret is to bang the rocks together, guys!"*

The captain of the alien ship *Xythir* clucked ironically. "Ha, ha!"

* * *

It was definitely a lash-up job: a plastic bucket resting in a wire cage from which sprang several mangy ears of aluminum foil. It wobbled and spun as it made its way slowly from *Voyager* to the alien ship. In contrast, behind it in the distance, the Eurocos ship *Harmonie* opened like a blossoming flower as it detached the science modules from its command section.

Small bursts of flame indicated where the European crew flitted about to oversee the extension of the four individual science modules on their supports to form a great square. Larger flames indicated that, having succeeded in extending the structure, the Europeans were now spinning the science modules about their common center to produce artificial gravity.

Sometime later a compact shiny object sped from the Eurocos ship to the alien ship. Shortly afterwards the aliens sent a craft of their own aimed precisely between the two human spacecraft.

"We've got contact!" Ensign Dubauer reported from one of *Voyager's* two shuttle craft. The craft were little more than propellant tanks and strap-in seats; life support was provided by spacesuits. "Radar return is strong—I estimate it to be ten thousand klicks and closing." Lorie worked her suit computer and sighed. "It'll take several hours at its present speed to reach this position—more than our oxygen reserves."

Back on *Voyager*, Captain Steele turned to Lieutenant Cohen. "Alan, get your crew ready on Shuttle Two."

"Righto, Skipper," Cohen responded cheerfully. "Resupply or relief?"

"You'll relieve them," Emily decided. "I don't want people falling asleep out there."

Cohen nodded and turned away. "C'mon, Harry, let's get our gear on," he said to Chief Long, the other crewmember of Shuttle Two.

Up in the cockpit a comm line crackled to life. "*Voyager*, this is *Harmonie*. We are ready to assist," the voice of Elodie Reynaud, French first officer on the Eurocos ship, informed them.

"Thank you, *Harmonie*, but we'll get the package, no problem," Emily Steele responded from the galley. "How go the modifications?"

"We should have them completed in the next two hours," Elodie said. "Will you be ready to dock with us at that time?"

Emily turned to Mac, who frowned, considering, then nodded. "It'll be nip and tuck with the crew spread so thin, but I think we'll be able to undock the MAM unit in that time," he told her. He glanced critically at Pickett, who was miserably attempting to squeeze himself into a spacesuit. "I don't know how long the ambassador'll last, however."

"Don't worry about me!" Pickett said, flailing his arms into the suit's sleeves. "Just get whatever the aliens sent us!"

Elodie overheard the exchange and a smile lit her face. "We could send some of our crew over, if you wish."

Emily shook her head hastily. "No, no, that won't be necessary!"

"The MAM unit's still classified!" Mac muttered under his breath.

Several hours later, *Voyager* broke in two as it separated the command module from the propulsion module. The MAM propulsion module, with its power supply and exhausted, shriveled fuel bladders, remained parked in the previous orbit while the command module was slowly nudged by *Harmonie's* small fleet of space shuttles to a prearranged position forward of the Eurocos ship's rotating section. The command module was dwarfed beside the larger Eurocos ship. A makeshift docking collar was attached between the central airlock of *Voyager's* three and one of *Harmonie's* side airlocks.

Moments later, Captain Zhukov was the first Eurocos officer to step aboard the US vessel. He snapped a curt salute. "Permission to come aboard?"

"Fine by me," said the man at the airlock door.

Zhukov gave him a startled. "Oh, you are the one they call Mac."

Mac smiled and extended a hand. "Pleasure to meet you, Captain."

"Where is your captain?"

"Captain Steele's up in the galley overseeing the rendezvous," Mac said, gesturing for Captain Zhukov to precede him. "We're a little cramped here. Because the galley's well-equipped, it has become our conference room and bridge." He waved a hand. "She'll meet us at the interdeck transfer."

Zhukov raised a brow. "Interdeck transfer?"

Mac sighed. "It's a long-winded way of indicating the gap in the upper deck flooring where you can transfer to this deck. The cockpit's just above us, and the galley's to the right of the interdeck transfer."

They arrived at the interdeck transfer—just a short distance from the forward airlocks—and Mac jumped lightly up to the next level. Zhukov emulated him with the ease of an experienced spaceman.

Captain Steele was directly in front of them, her head turned away as she said, "Make sure they bring it to *Harmonie's* airlock, not ours."

"They'd have a hell of time docking with us anyway, Skipper," Mac said.

The woman whipped her head around to face them. Captain Zhukov had a vision of jet-black hair floating around a long oval face with high cheekbones and piercing blue eyes. Freckles flecked the bridge of a long, straight nose on an otherwise snow white visage. Nikolai Anatolovich Zhukov was speechless.

"Lieutenant Commander Emily Steele, United States Navy, Captain of XSS-1 *Voyager*," Emily said herself, extending a hand.

Zhukov took it firmly and shook it briefly. "A pleasure," the Russian said, a grin breaking out on his face. "Your people handle this ship commendably."

In spite of herself, Emily dimpled. "Thank you, Captain." Such a compliment, one captain to another, was praise indeed. "I look forward to touring your beautiful ship."

Zhukov, in his turn, flushed appreciably. He found his way onto the galley's flooring and clicked his heels together—no mean feat in zero gravity. "She is unique. It is an honor to command her."

"Captain, we've established comm links with *Harmonie*," Cohen reported from the inbound shuttle. His voice echoed oddly as it was relayed both by *Voyager's* ship-to-ship comm link and the pass-through link with *Harmonie*.

"I have made arrangements for your people to bunk in our spinning section and have laid out a meal," Zhukov informed Captain Steele politely. "After the work your crew has had these past three weeks, I felt that they would appreciate a rest in lunar gravity conditions."

Emily nodded. "Thank you, Captain, I appreciate it."

"It'll be nice to eat without slurping," Jim Pickett muttered from behind her.

"You could establish your command aboard *Harmonie* and leave a team on watch on this ship," Zhukov suggested.

Emily was dubious. "I shall have to consult with my superiors."

"We have re-established communications with Earth," Zhukov told her, his tone apologetic for not having mentioned it earlier. "My communications people have arranged a pass-through link for all radio traffic."

"Thank you!" Emily said.

"Now, Captain, would you care to board my ship?" Zhukov asked. He grinned. "I shall be delighted to guide you on a tour."

"Does it include a tour of the galley?" Emily asked wistfully. Even for her, three weeks of weightless rations had grown monotonous.

Zhukov again performed the amazing feat of clicking his heels together in zero-gee. "First stop."

"I'd love it!"

From behind her, Jim Pickett asked, "May I tag along? I can't purvey the galley if it sports full-gee, but I would appreciate a bite at lunar levels."

Zhukov frowned. "Oh! I am sorry, Mr. Pickett! I had forgotten about the unhappy circumstances which had left you stranded on the Moon." Pickett raised an eyebrow in surprise. Zhukov shrugged expansively. "I found it intriguing to learn more about the man chosen to represent the United States in its first alien contact."

Pickett snorted. "*They* sent my dossier up?"

Zhukov agreed with a tilt of his head. "It was interesting to read no matter its origin. *And,* you will be pleased to note, I've made arrangements for you to eat in a lunar gravity environment."

"Thank you, Captain, thank you very much!"

On *Harmonie's* side, the airlock adjoined the protective water blanket around the bridge. A small shaft pierced that blanket and opened directly onto the bridge itself. Captain Zhukov guided them hastily around the bridge and introduced them to the officers on watch.

"This is Commander Elodie Reynaud, my French first officer." Zhukov said as he introduced the dark-haired, dark-eyed diminutive Frenchwoman. Elodie shook hands gladly with Pickett, but Emily cocked her head at the officer and nodded at her.

"My thanks for your excellent work. I hope you did not find it too stressful," she said to her. Elodie nodded, her wide eyes solemn.

Elodie politely followed them as they continued their tour around the bridge. From time to time, Jim caught Steele glancing surreptitiously at the woman. As they paused at the communications section, Pickett asked, "What sort of communications have you been getting from Earth?"

Zhukov frowned. "They seem to have put together a list of cogent suggestions—"

"All of which are over an hour out of date, I'm certain," Pickett injected drolly. "I wonder if anyone has done a study on how long a time lag must be before long-range meddling becomes completely useless."

Zhukov chuckled. "Certainly not Eurocos!"

Pickett nodded in understanding. He looked from one captain to the other. "I don't suppose there's much chance of getting a secure line back to Earth myself, is there?"

The two captains exchanged looks then assured him, "Why, of course!"

Pickett glanced at them craftily then snorted. "Thought as much."

"Do you wish to do it now?" Lieutenant Ives asked solicitously, lips pursed as he mentally prepared to open another channel with Earth.

"No, it can wait, I'm sure," Pickett said. With a quick grin, he added, "Your captain has promised us some real food!"

Lunch was all that the two from *Voyager* could hope for; Captain Steele had to remind Pickett (and herself) to go easy in their first lunar gravity meal. But she could not restrain herself when the steward arrived with a pleasant-smelling tray of steaming mugs at the end of the meal.

"Coffee!" She passed a cup on to Pickett and happily gulped from her own mug. "Gods, that's good!" She turned to Captain Zhukov, who spent the moment appreciating her reaction. "It's such a relief not to have to *suck* the damned stuff all the time!" she explained, joyfully warming her hands on the sides of the mug.

"I am delighted that my ship can provide you with such pleasures, Captain," Zhukov said with a twinkle in his eyes.

"Indeed, you are very kind," Pickett told him, placing his empty cup on the tray. "Your people must have gone to a great deal of difficulty to prepare this room."

Zhukov waved a hand dismissingly. "It was nothing. These rooms were freed up as our scientists transferred to their habitat. All the rooms on the rotating section are soft-configurable, with partitions which can easily be moved about."

"All the same, we appreciate it," Emily told him. "My crew will be exceedingly thankful."

They returned to *Harmonie's* bridge. There they met Karl Geister, who had relieved Elodie Reynaud of the watch.

"The Americans have brought the alien container to the space habitat as ordered," Geister said to Captain Zhukov. He glanced at Steele and Pickett then away again, dismissing them from his universe. Steele frowned. Beside her, Jim caught her look and nodded imperceptibly to himself.

Emily started toward the airlock connecting the ships, but Zhukov forestalled her.

"If you wish to oversee the analysis of the alien container, Commander, you would be well-advised to remain here," he said. Emily paused, glancing back to Pickett. Zhukov continued hastily, "Of course, if you have other duties aboard your ship …"

"The shuttle is returning," Emily told them.

"I'm sure your crew can handle that, Captain," said. "However …"

"They have been ordered to let me know of anything out of the ordinary," Emily said by way of agreement. "But …"

Zhukov smiled and waved her off. "I understand, Captain. It is *your* ship, your command."

As Emily gratefully crossed to the airlock, Zhukov said to Pickett, "I plan to retire to my officer's briefing room and follow the investigations from there. If you would care to join me?"

"Certainly, Captain."

As they settled in the briefing room, Captain Zhukov partitioned the large wall display into three sections: two displayed space views of the recovery of the alien offering; the third he used to produce a schematic of *Harmonie's* status.

A beep indicated an incoming message. Zhukov punched a button on the display and they heard Lieutenant Ives say, "The Americans are requesting a link with Mr. Pickett."

Zhukov shrugged, shrank the ship schematic display, and indicated a nearby control panel to Pickett. The American eyed it with a frown but soon discovered that the workings were very similar to those of the keyboards on *Voyager*.

"Pickett," he said into the mike.

The display crackled to life, showing *Voyager's* familiar galley. McLaughlin stared back at him. "Mr. Ambassador, we've detected a transmission from Earth—"

"Yeah, we're getting the feed down here."

"—also, we've got some preliminary observations on the alien probe," Mac paused, examining a separate screen. "The radar return from their reflector was 80% better than ours even though it has 20% less surface area."

"Good, huh?"

Mac pursed his lips. "Maybe. I've asked the Frenchies if they'll let Jenkins inspect it."

"Why?" Zhukov asked.

"Well, the radar return off your probe was worse than ours. I've no doubt that your crew also had to do a lash-up and wouldn't be surprised if they used some equipment that's similar to our data probes. All things considered, you'd expect the aliens to do the same sort of thing—"

"Maybe their technology is better than ours," Pickett said.

"Sure. They've got a star drive and we don't," Mac agreed easily. "But there are only so many ways to lash-up a good passive radar reflector."

"I don't see your point."

"It's this: if the aliens haven't used something exotic that we've never seen before, then either they were using an active radar source—which is unlikely—or they carry these sort of radar reflectors all the time."

Zhukov took on a thoughtful look. "Why would they carry purpose-built radar reflectors?"

"Why not? Aren't they good for rescue operations?" Pickett asked.

Zhukov shook his head, a movement mirrored by McLaughlin in his display. "Radio is better; radar's only good at relatively short distances in interstellar work," Mac said.

"Yes, Mr. McLaughlin, I believe that an investigation of that reflector would prove interesting," Captain Zhukov decided. "You have my authorization."

"Thank you, sir. I'll put Jenkins on it immediately."

Mac moved to break the comm-link but Pickett forestalled him: "May as well leave it open, Mac."

They turned their attention to the incoming communications from Earth. In a matter of seconds, they agreed that it was useless, merely a repeated statement that their communications had been restored and would either *Harmonie* or *Voyager* please respond.

"The pucker factor must be pretty high back there," Pickett said, shaking his head.

Captain Zhukov nodded in agreement then stopped. "Would your government have realized that our antenna would also be incapacitated?"

Pickett shrugged. "I suspect that there's a lot of confusion back there right now. However, once they've isolated their failure, they'll be quick to realize that it will affect *Voyager* and hopefully your people will point out that it also would affect your ship."

The display screen rippled as a new image appeared. It was a close up of a mustached face inside a spacesuit.

"Captain, we have separated the alien craft from its reflector," Dr. Ney reported. "Our people are ready to open up the container."

"Very well, proceed," Zhukov said. "Let the Americans have the reflector for analysis."

"How do you enjoy suit work, Doctor?" Pickett asked the Frenchman politely.

An eyebrow arched in response. "It is very… constricting."

"As soon as you have verified the individual articles as not harmful to human life, you may bring them aboard your science module," Zhukov said.

"I look forward to that."

A few minutes later, the alien artefacts were safely deposited in the science module's external laboratory. The aliens had sent ten different items, all individually wrapped. In twenty minutes of hasty work, the scientists had separated the items, re-pressurized the lab, and unwrapped the items from what looked to be nothing more than simple plastic bubble-wrap.

"What, is bubble-wrap universal?" Pickett wondered in disgust when the nature of the packing was revealed.

"Well, it may not be a plastic as we know it," Dr. Ney conceded, "but there is much to recommend an insulated wrapper for the packaging of articles to be subjected to a vacuum."

The German chief chemist, Dr. von Schliefen said, "There is a complete lack of uniformity in what they sent."

"And what did you send?" Pickett asked, turning to Captain Zhukov.

"Well, naturally we were unprepared for this exchange," Zhukov temporized. Pickett raised an eyebrow. Zhukov frowned, tapped on his console and turned it toward Pickett. "And what, Mr. Ambassador, did our American... allies... send in this first contact?"

Pickett pretended to be engrossed in the *Harmonie's* list. Really, there wasn't much remarkable in it, except maybe the Rembrandt reproduction, the rest was pretty much as could be expected. "I'm not sure I would have recommended that," Pickett said, pointing to the screen.

Zhukov's lips twitched. "I'm given to understand that the dubbing in French made Mr. Lewis' performance quite memorable."

"I wouldn't be surprised if they just sent us junk to confuse us," Pickett said.

"And what did your crew send?" Zhukov repeated.

Pickett pulled a piece of paper from his pocket and passed it over to the Eurocos captain. He rather enjoyed the way the Russian's eyebrows rose and rose and rose further with each new entry.

"I see that Jerry Lewis is a popular choice," Captain Zhukov said, pointing to the final item on the American list.

"It was the only thing Jenkins was willing to part with," Pickett said. He raised his eyebrow as he added, "The boy has quite a collection of pornographic material."

"Oh, I wouldn't be at all surprised if we find some interesting trades occurring between our crews," Captain Zhukov allowed drolly. Wordlessly, Pickett pulled another piece of paper from his pocket and passed it over. The Eurocos captain perused it for a moment and then quietly slid it into his pocket.

"You'll note that Jenkins was wide-ranging in his collection," Pickett noted.

"It would be best if he traded with Ensign Strasnoye who seems to have similar... um... commercial inclinations," Captain Zhukov said.

Pickett said nothing; he was not surprised that the Russian captain had ensured that the best man for contraband on his crew was also a Russian. *Thinking ahead, no doubt.*

"You're not worried that the aliens might be offended with your ship's rather... ah... non-functional offer?" Captain Zhukov continued, unaware of Pickett's thoughts.

"I suspect that between our two offerings, they'll find something of interest," Pickett replied. "Although I sincerely hope that we won't be called upon to trade the complete works of Jerry Lewis—either in French or English."

"*Chacun à son gout*, as they say," Zhukov replied in perfect French. Pickett affected not to understand, so the captain politely translated, "Each to his own taste."

"Ah!" Pickett said, leaning back in his seat. "I see."

"Well, now, I suppose we've got nothing more to do than wait," Captain Zhukov said, moving to end the conversation.

"Indeed," Pickett said, rising with him. "I think I'll return to *Voyager*, as I don't want to be underfoot."

"You're quite welcome to—"

"To be honest, I need some rest," Pickett cut him off with a placating wave of his hand. "There's no telling when things will heat up and I'll need to be on my toes."

"That is quite wise. I agree."

Pickett rewarded him with a quick smile and then moved back toward *Voyager*.

Back in the courier ship, Pickett found that Jenkins was the only one on watch.

"I've been told that Ensign Strasnoye is your opposite number on the *Harmonie*, in matters of trade, that is," Pickett told him quietly.

"Yes, sir, I've already had a chat with him," Jenkins said, not quite keeping a smug look off his face.

"Just remember, if we're out here long enough, we'll be asking to eat their stores," Pickett said. "I'd like to keep any complications to a minimum."

"The captain had the same talk with me already," Jenkins replied with a rueful look.

"Which captain?"

"Ours."

"Good enough," Pickett said. He clapped the younger man on the shoulder. "Don't be surprised if you hear from the other captain, too."

"What if one says the opposite of the other?"

"Use your best judgment," Pickett said. "I'll be in my cabin if anyone needs me."

"Uh …" Jenkins said. Pickett raised an eyebrow. "I don't think the captain's quite thought this watch thing through… I've got no relief right now."

"Need to use the can?"

"The head," Jenkins corrected him automatically.

Pickett gestured to the controls and said, "Show me what I need to watch for and I'll spell you."

"Oh, thank you, sir!" Jenkins said. Quickly he pointed at three active panels and gave Pickett the rundown.

"If any other ones light up, what then?"

"Pray," Jenkins said with a wave as he floated off toward the ship's head.

* * *

The White House, Washington, DC

"Christ, now the Chinese want in on the act!" President Merritt swore as he plopped himself into the plush seat at his desk in the Oval Office. Others of his staff sat themselves in the two couches that were positioned in the center of the room.

"And we've got a number one diplomatic and political crisis on our hands with that idiot Alquay," Brian McPhee grumbled.

"What's the word on him?"

"He's under sedation at Deep Ear," Secretary Wood replied with a sour grimace. "We've got the DSN and Deep Ear back online but we've lost hours—"

"We could have lost everything," Morgan, the secretary of defense, reminded him.

"Yeah, it seems like Pickett was lucky," Merritt said, shaking his head in disgust. "I'm just glad that he'll never be able to come back home."

"We'll have that captain, Steele, take the victory lap for him," Anne Byrne, the president's press secretary, suggested.

"First we've got to get the victory," Morgan muttered.

"The Chinese—" the secretary of state prompted.

"What's their price?" Brian McPhee asked. He turned his eyes toward the president for confirmation of his taking the lead. The president nodded, blowing out a weary sigh. This was not the presidency he had campaigned for.

"I'm not sure—" Ellington of state began angrily.

"Oh, come on, John!" The president said. "We've agreed with the Europeans, with the Russians, with the Japanese, what price do the Chinese have?"

"They want pretty much the same as everyone else," John Ellington replied with a sour look. "They want their share of whatever we get in trade with these aliens and assurances that we'll take the fall if anything goes south."

President Merritt absorbed this with a nod, then said, "And what else?"

"Sir?"

"Oh, come on, John! Don't pussyfoot around with me!" the president shot back. "If it were that simple, you'd have an agreement in hand."

Ellington puffed out a sigh and in a low voice said, "They want Taiwan."

President Merritt swiveled his gaze to George Morgan, Secretary of Defense. "How's Korea?"

Morgan jerked in surprise at the question and then slowly smiled. "Not a peep, sir."

President Merritt waved a hand toward the secretary of state. "They're bluffing, or they'd have North Korea rattling nukes at us."

Brian McPhee shook his head. "They must want something else and Taiwan is their opening bid."

"Yeah," the president said, sitting back in his chair. He waved a hand to Ellington of state. "Find out what it is. We need this deal closed yesterday."

John Ellington nodded and pulled out his cellphone. He spoke into it quickly. "I've got someone on it, sir."

"Good," the president said, leaning back in his chair and bringing a hand to eyes. When he took it away he sat straight up, his eyes on the secretary of the Navy.

"So, Elijah, what are our options?" he said in a very soft, dangerous voice.

"If the aliens turn hostile, sir?" Wood asked. When the president nodded, the secretary of the Navy glanced to his direct boss, the secretary of defense, who nodded grimly. "Sir, unless they really mean to deal with us, we're probably screwed."

"Yeah, I knew that," the president said. "I want to know what our options are."

Elijah Wood turned to Admiral Kinnock and gave him a reluctant nod.

"Obviously," Admiral Kinnock said in preamble, "this must not leave this room."

Everyone nodded, some snorted derisively. It was nothing they hadn't heard before.

"I'll get with you later to give you the list of leaks," the President said to his press secretary.

"Actually, sir, that brings up an important point," Anne Byrne said. The president motioned her to continue, despite the agitated posture of Admiral Kinnock. "Well, sir, so far the news has held. The people in the DSN have been marvelous and they're the gatekeepers to all our communications. Eurocos and the Russians have been just as good but—"

"There's money riding on this," the president guessed.

"Trillions," Brian McPhee agreed. "What this will do to the markets—"

"Particularly the defense industry," George Morgan added.

"Anyway, we should be considering damage control, too, sir," Anne Byrne finished, sitting back on the couch to relinquish the spotlight back to the admiral.

"Ms. Byrne has an excellent point, sir," Admiral Kinnock said, giving her a tight smile, "but we have to consider the negative prospects as well."

"What's the best case?" Brian McPhee asked.

"Best case?" Admiral Kinnock repeated, crossing his hands over his crossed legs. "Best case is we establish mutually beneficial trade and discover that we have a significant military advantage over the eetees."

"I doubt that will happen," Charlie Sumner of the NSA said with a frown. "They're the ones on our doorstep, not the other way around."

"I said best case," Kinnock replied. He dismissed the NSA chief with a flick of his hand and returned his attention to the president. "Worst case... well, that's obvious: they blow us back to the Stone Age or just wipe us out entirely."

"If they'd wanted to do that, they wouldn't have stopped at Jupiter," Sumner countered. The president glanced at him. "Sir, if these aliens were hostile, they wouldn't have made contact—"

"Except with nukes," George Morgan quipped.

"That's my opinion, too," John Ellington said, leaning forward in his seat and steepling his fingers on his crossed knees.

"And if we're wrong?" Admiral Kinnock asked, glancing around the room. There was silence.

Finally, the president said, "Okay, Harry, tell us what we do if we're wrong?"

"*Voyager's* MAM holds a good kilogram of antimatter," Admiral Kinnock replied. "We ram the propulsion unit into the alien ship and see how they handle *that*."

There was a moment's silence.

"What about our people?" The president asked after a moment.

"Navy, sir," Kinnock replied with a touch of pride in his voice. "They knew what they signed up for."

"And the Europeans?" Ellington asked. "Assuming we're lucky and that antimatter destroys the alien, it'll probably take out everything else nearby—that's not just our ship, but the *Harmonie* as well."

"I'm sure they'll understand under the circumstances," Admiral Kinnock said.

"I'm not even sure our own people would understand," Secretary Wood objected.

"Well, sir," Admiral Kinnock replied with a vulpine smile, "that's the beauty of remote programming."

"You mean you can program it from here?" George Morgan exclaimed.

"Yes, sir," the admiral said. "In fact, we've already uploaded the base package." He paused. "All that's needed is the order."

The president sat bolt upright in his chair. "Do you mean to tell me, Admiral, that you've already programmed *Voyager* to self-destruct?"

"The activation code is still required, sir," Kinnock said defensively.

"Admiral," the president continued in a slow, deadly drawl, "could this code be transmitted from Deep Ear?" He didn't wait for the other's brain to catch up with him. "From the place where the vice president is currently locked up?"

"He's secure, sir," Admiral Kinnock assured him.

"Elijah, Admiral Kinnock has just tendered his resignation," President Greg Merritt said. "Take his badge and get his replacement here right after you rescind those damned codes!"

"But sir—!" Admiral Kinnock protested.

"Elijah, I thought I was the only one who allowed himself to be saddled with damned fools," the president swore. To the admiral, he said, "And how do you know, Admiral, that the vice president isn't right now arranging his own escape?"

"But he's insane!" Admiral Kinnock said. "He's aligned with that lunatic Satanspawn fringe."

"And how many other Satanspawn people are there at Deep Ear?" the president asked. "I'll be damned sure you don't know." He waved to the secretary of the Navy. "You've got work to do." He nodded to Kinnock. "Here's the good news, Admiral. You're going to spend a lot more time with your family."

Two Secret Service men entered the room and glanced significantly at the admiral who sighed and rose from his chair. He paused long enough to say to the president, "I'm sorry to have let you down, sir."

"Yeah, yeah," the president said, waving him away. When he was gone, he speared Morgan of defense with a fierce look. "You get your goons in order, John, and make sure we pull this one out of the fire."

"Do you really think Alquay would destroy *Voyager*, sir?"

The president thought for a moment and shook his head. "Hell, I doubt Ned Alquay takes a crap without someone to remind him! Trouble is, there's quite likely to be someone up there to remind him. There certainly was someone who sent him on his way."

One door burst open and a Navy commander rushed in. He looked for the admiral, then the secretary of the Navy, then stopped in confusion.

"How about you give it here, son," President Merritt said to him, pointing to his desk. The commander's eyes widened and he started to salute, thought better of it, and handed the dispatch to his commander-in-chief directly.

"What's it say, Greg?" Brian McPhee said, rising from his chair in hopes of reading the message upside down.

"Well, I'll be …" the president muttered to himself. He picked up the dispatch and brought it close to his eyes—and away from his chief of staff—and read it again. "That damned Jim Pickett!"

"Sir?" John Ellington asked.

"It seems we are in communication with the aliens," the president said, sliding the dispatch over the desk where Brian McPhee hastily snatched it; Anne Byrne moving to read over his shoulder. "They speak English."

"What?"

"We've even exchanged goods," the president added. "In fact, both we and the Eurocos each sent them ten items and we got ten items in response."

"What are they?"

"No one knows," the president said. "But apparently we'd best hope the aliens like Jerry Lewis."

Everyone rose and rushed to read the dispatch, which McPhee relinquished as soon as he was done. Anne Byrne returned to her seat, trying to comprehend the events that had transpired over an hour ago at Jupiter. She was still thinking when a silence fell in the room and someone nudged her knee. She looked up. It was Scott Murphy, her secretary. He had a note.

"Annie?" the president said as he caught her look.

"It seems, sir," Anne Byrne said in a small voice, "that we're going to need a press conference soon." She rose and handed the note to the president.

"Holy shit!" President Merritt said as he finished. He looked up to Anne Byrne. "Schedule an emergency conference in twenty minutes." He glanced over to Brian McPhee. "Radio Free Luna has just announced that it has destroyed the Satanspawn, the aliens who are attempting to take over our world and 'force us to denounce Jesus Christ, Our Lord.'"

* * *

Voyager

"Jenkins!" Pickett yelled as soon as he noticed the red light blinking on one of the "other" boards. "I've got a red light and it's not on your boards!"

Nothing. It was a long way from the bridge to the head.

"Jenkins!" Pickett shouted. Then he punched up *Harmonie*. "I need to speak to McLaughlin, it's an emergency."

A moment later, he heard, "McLaughlin."

"Mac? This is Pickett. Jenkins is taking a dump and there's a red light just flashing on the communications panel."

"Red light?" Mac said. "Is it the one right above auxiliary communications?"

"Yeah, that's it," Pickett replied. "What should I do?"

"Nothing."

"Nothing?"

"Yeah, it's just some moron from Earth trying to blow up our ship," Mac replied.

"Mac?"

McLaughlin sighed. "I'd better come over. I'll bring the skipper."

"Sure." Pickett said. "Is there anything I should do?"

"Yeah," Mac said. "Don't touch *anything*. And don't let Jenkins touch anything either."

It seemed forever before Jenkins came back. Pickett refused to relinquish the chair to him, explaining that McLaughlin and the skipper were on their way.

"Okay, Mac," Emily Steele's voice bounced into the bridge ahead of her, "this better be good."

"It'll make you want to resign your commission," Mac said, his voice closer. In a moment he was in the bridge. To Pickett he said, "I've got it, sir."

Pickett was reluctant to relinquish the control seat even to Mac but forced himself, recalling that MacLaughlin knew more about the MAM drive than just about anybody.

"See this, Skipper?" Mac said, pointing to the flashing light. He typed some commands on the main control unit and grunted as a new display appeared. "This is what you call a dead man's switch."

"Mac?" Emily said, prompting him to explain.

"Hang on a sec," Mac said, scrolling through information and shunting it to another screen. "Shit!"

"What is it, Mac?" Emily demanded.

"See that line of code there, Skipper?" Mac said, pointing to a line on the second screen.

"Shit," Emily said as she read it. "Is that what I think it is?"

"If you think it's a self-destruct code for our MAM engine, it is," Mac replied.

"Self-destruct?" Jenkins repeated. Pickett could tell from his voice alone that the young man was as white as a sheet.

"See this line here, Skip? That's the one that should cause you to resign," Mac said.

"Wait a minute," Emily said, motioning for Mac to move aside. He let her have the control seat and muttered appreciatively as she dove into the code on the screen. "What's this subroutine here, Mac?"

"Thought you might like that one particularly, ma'am," Mac said. He leaned closer so that he was pointing over her shoulder. "That subroutine is a selective homing routine. The idea is that it can target the command module, *Harmonie*, or our alien friend."

"And what's it set for?"

"Why right now, if this code were functional, our MAM would be ramming the alien and blowing itself to bits."

"Captain Steele?" Captain Zhukov's voice carried up the corridor. "Is there a problem?"

Emily started to reply but stopped as she felt Pickett's hand clasp her shoulder.

"Tell him the truth, Captain," Pickett ordered. Emily turned, her eyes flashing at him but Pickett's eyes were hard. "Politics, Captain, are built on trust."

"If this is some internal affair—" Captain Zhukov began placatingly.

"No, sir," Emily said. She motioned for Mac to step aside and gestured Captain Zhukov to take his place. "Apparently, someone from Earth embedded some secret code in our computers."

Zhukov's eyebrows rose.

"The code is a self-destruct sequence designed to have our MAM propulsion unit ram one of three targets," Emily said. Her lips drew so thin they disappeared. "Target one was our own command module. Target two was your *Harmonie*."

"And target three?"

"Target three was the alien space ship."

"They are insane!"

"Oh, I completely agree," Pickett said. "And, I suspect from the look of our captain, here, so does she."

"Yeah," Emily said in a small voice. She turned to Mac. "So, what's this red light, Mac?"

"Oh, that," Mac said with a negligent shrug. "That lights up when the destruct sequence has been sent."

"And yet we're all still here," Captain Zhukov noticed. He turned to Mac. "May I assume, Mr. McLaughlin, that you somehow disabled this particular order?"

"Damn straight," Mac said fiercely. "Ain't no damned REMF puke gonna blow up my ship!"

"By which," Emily said slowly, "I take it that this sequence is still functional?"

"Yeah, Skipper," Mac said. "You hit the override and the damned thing goes off."

"I will like hell," Emily swore hotly. "Can you rip this fucking code out of my ship, Mac?"

Mac smiled and pointed to a small screen. "Just push that button there, Skipper, and the bastards won't be able to touch us."

Emily pushed the button.

"Captain Zhukov," Pickett said as soon as they'd all collected their breaths.

"Yes?"

"If you don't mind, I think it would be a good idea if we have someone conduct a search in your ship's programs for any similarly misguided remote efforts," Pickett said.

"I don't think—"

"Nor did I," Emily cut across him. "Sir."

Zhukov pursed his lips. "I suspect that the code for *Harmonie* is much greater than that for your *Voyager*."

"So, the sooner the better," Pickett said. "We were lucky this time." He paused. "How long will it take us to delouse all your ship's code?"

"Actually, Mr. Pickett, the smartest move would be to filter any incoming transmissions," Mac said. "We'll still want to audit *Harmonie's* code but if we can catch any, er, miscommunications before they come in, that will be the quickest way to ensure safety."

"I'll leave it to you all," Pickett said with a wave of his hand. "I think the other matter—that is, who exactly and why exactly our ship was supposed to start an interstellar or intergalactic—"

"Skipper, we've got incoming traffic!" Jenkins said, pointing to a green blinking light on the communications panel. Emily turned and called up the appropriate screen.

"Flash traffic," she said.

"If we're lucky, we'll get some answers," Pickett muttered.

"Or something," Emily said. She swore to herself. "It's in code."

"Bring it up here, Commander," Pickett ordered. He turned to Zhukov. "I think *we* need to be beyond secrets."

"Yes," Captain Zhukov agreed. Emily frowned but said nothing as she typed in the password to decode the flash traffic.

"The idiots shouldn't be encrypting in the first place," Mac muttered.

"No …" Pickett said, his brows furrowing, "there are still people who should not be able to read our mail."

"The aliens?" Mac snorted derisively. "Who says they can't decrypt everything?"

"I wasn't thinking about the aliens," Pickett said. He gestured to the no-longer-blinking red light. "I was thinking about those who sent us *that* little message."

"Oh," Mac said, mollified.

"Well, that's useful!" Emily said sarcastically as the clean text message scrolled on the screen. "We're to be aware that certain factions on Earth are inimical to our communications with the aliens and may try anything—including our destruction—to prevent them. We're to take all necessary precautions."

"Who signed that?" Pickett snapped.

"CINC," Emily replied in a small voice. She turned to Pickett. "Why?"

"The commander in chief," Zhukov translated for himself. "That's your president, right?"

"Yes, sir," Jim Pickett said with a smile. "That is indeed our president, Greg Merritt himself." He turned to Emily. "You know what this means, right?"

"It means that you're gonna do whatever the hell you want, doesn't it?" Emily Steele said, her eyes glowing with delight.

"Yup."

"So, Mr. Ambassador, what are your orders?" Emily said.

"Clear out that muck, help *Harmonie* to get rid of the same, and see what we got from our alien friends," Pickett said, "and call me when you get something."

"Where are you going?"

"To get a nap," Pickett replied, moving down the corridor. "Oh, and set up a two-man watch."

"We don't have enough people," Emily reminded him.

"Cross-train the *Harmonie* people," Pickett said airily. He turned back, floating backwards long enough to say to Zhukov, "If that's acceptable to you, sir."

"I think, given all that we've encountered so far," Captain Zhukov said, "that is an excellent idea."

"But *Voyager* is still classified!" Emily protested.

Pickett pointed toward where the alien ship lay in orbit. "Really, Captain?"

Emily groaned as she caught his point. "Yes," she said, "you're right. The sooner we start cross-training our people, the better." She looked at the Russian captain. "Although, to be honest, aside from the MAM propulsion unit, *Voyager* is pretty much a stock courier ship."

"Include the MAM," Pickett said. Emily gave him a pained look. "Captain Steele, we've no idea what we're dealing with over there. We're going to need people who are adaptable. If Captain Zhukov is willing to train your people on their fusion drive, you need to be willing to train his people on our MAM drive." With a smirk, he added, "If we're lucky, we'll have something even better to work with in a short while."

"Do you really think they'll trade us their FTL drive?" Captain Zhukov asked.

"They seem to be just about falling all over themselves to do just that," Jim Pickett said. His expression tightened for a moment, but he let whatever had passed through his mind go with a shrug. "I don't know about Russia, but in the States we have a saying about not looking gift horses in the mouth."

"We do, too," Captain Zhukov said.

"Anyway, if you'll forgive me, I really need some rest," Pickett said with a weary sigh.

"Indeed, Mr. Ambassador," Emily said. To Zhukov she said, "Perhaps we should arrange our watches and this training?"

"My bridge, perhaps?" Zhukov suggested. "Or the galley, where we've got gravity?"

"Oh, the galley!" Emily replied with undisguised longing. As she started to push off, she turned back to Jenkins. "Will you be okay?"

"I'll sit with him for a bit, Skipper," Mac said, moving toward the second control seat in the crowded bridge. "I can keep up with the examinations well enough from here."

CHAPTER SEVEN

Xythir

NEXL WAS WITH EXERN WHEN NOXOR TROMPED IN, UPPER LIMBS AGITATING wildly over its head. The Xlern were hermaphroditic but in their thinking tended to refer to themselves with what humans would consider male pronouns.

>>**They were going to blow us up!**<< Noxor chittered angrily. >>**I have the energy cannon on standby, Captain!**<<

>>**That won't be necessary,**<< Nexl replied with a languid set of waves.

Beside him, Exern's limbs were frozen in place. >>**Noxor, really? Could they have hurt us?**<<

>>**With a kilogram of antimatter? Of course!**<< Noxor replied, two of his uppers striking upward in emphasis.

>>**Would you have let them?**<< Nexl asked, waving one limb languidly in a smooth motion, similar to that used with Xlerna just crawling on shore for the first time.

>>**Well ... no,**<< Noxor admitted, bobbing up and down on his lowers just like a Xlerna who had been caught self-impregnating.

>>**So there's really no point in this, except perhaps to assure me that you had firm grips on everything,**<< Nexl replied, waving two limbs now in a sinuous motion that implied respect coupled with a certain amount of boredom. Doubtless that was the root cause of Noxor's theatrics: the security officer was bored. Nexl swiveled his attention to his communications officer. >>**And what can you tell us about this aborted operation?**

>>**Not extraordinary, sir,**<< Exern replied with a diffident set of waves. >>**Contacting an un-integrated species normally entails certain risks, particularly with those inclined toward over-limbing a situation.**<< The Communications Officer, the captain noted, was very careful not to wave a limb in the direction of the security officer.

Nexl suppressed a shudder, knowing that his irritation with his two subordinates would merely start them bickering and pinching out of his proximity. They'd been together for a number of missions. One would have hoped to see more signs of clanning amongst them. Apparently Nexl would have to make his "we are tribe *Xythir*" speech yet again. If the two weren't so competent in their individual assignments and, Nexl admitted with a twinge in his gut, if it weren't so much trouble to intertwine new crewmembers into the existing tribe, he would have gotten rid of them long before.

But there was profit to be turned, new shores to be sown. Nexl could not quite imagine sharing a tribe with either of the two but, perhaps, in time this view would change. Stranger things had occurred.

>>**What other weaponry have they available?**<< Nexl said now to Noxor.

>>**Nothing!**<< Noxor said with a derisive twitch of his forelimbs. >>**They could try to ram us, I suppose, but that would be more than futile.**<<

>>**The antimatter was not a true weapon,**<< Exern noted, swiveling to include the security officer in its statement.

Noxor flicked a limb dismissively.

>>**So, from our point of view, they're now totally defenseless?**<< the captain persisted.

>>**As if they were still back in the sea,**<< Noxor replied, its limbs moving into attack position.

>>**Good,**<< the captain clicked. >>**I wonder if they realize it?**<<

>>**That they're negotiating from a position of weakness?**<< Noxor rapped with a derisive twist of its forelimbs. Its body shook in quick negation.

>>**Oh, no, Security Officer!**<< Exern felt compelled to object. >>**If they even knew that we detected their attempt.**<<

>>**We will do everything to ensure that they never find out, Communications Officer,**<< Captain Nexl reminded him firmly.

Exern raised its limbs in salute. >>**Of course, Captain!**<<

>>**If we're not going to destroy them, what's our next step?**<< Noxor asked, just barely avoiding a belligerent stance.

>>**Our next step is to practice waiting,**<< the captain rapped.

>>**I hate waiting,**<< Noxor returned in a redundant statement.

An admittance light chimed outside the captain's quarters.

>>**Enter!**<< Captain Nexl clacked, wondering what new challenge would present itself.

>>**Captain, Captain!**<< It was Ixxie, the trade officer. Ixxie's limbs were all askew as if the Xlern had bounced its way to the captain's quarters—being far too excited to coordinate its lower limbs.

>>**Yes?**<<

>>**We've decontaminated the trade goods,**<< Ixxie reported, limbs moving in near ecstasy. >>**They sent us *two* recordings of Jerry Lewis!**<<

>>***Now* can I destroy them?**<< Noxor begged.

*   *   *

"You know, I'm beginning to think that most of this is junk," Jean-Paul Ney said as he set aside the ninth alien artifact.

"We don't even know what it is," Heinz von Schlieffen reminded him. "It could be valuable jewelry for all we know."

"Or Jerry Lewis," Jean-Paul replied with a scowl. Unlike most of his compatriots, he had first heard Jerry Lewis' works in the original English and had no respect for them at all. Jean-Paul held up one object in his gloved hand, saying, "Take this for example."

"Yes?"

"Well, there's a definite tear in the central filament but no signs of collectors," Jean-Paul said, pointing to a screen which held a close-up image of the object in question. "It's about 3 centimeters in length and made of some flexible transparent material—some simple polymer, really—so it could be some form of light bulb … except that it's broken."

"Ah," Heinz said. He frowned at the screen for a moment, nodded to Jean-Paul for permission, and brought up a new image. "This is what I've been examining."

On the screen Jean-Paul saw something that appeared metallic, thin, and cylindrical—except for a bulge in the middle.

"I've taken an ultrasound and this is what I get," Heinz said, flicking up a new image.

"Is the center smashed?"

"So it would appear," Heinz replied. "In fact, the exterior seems to be nothing more than mild steel. Admittedly there are some impurities that aren't normal, but for all intents and purposes—it's steel."

"And?"

"If I had to guess, it's some sort of piping," Heinz replied. "Perhaps part of a pneumatic or other low pressure system."

"Low pressure?"

"Mild steel," Heinz said in explanation. "Not built for high pressure or excessive heat." He pointed at the ends. "What interests me most is that these ends seem to have been connected to something before—I've traces of organic compounds, maybe a gasket—but they were easily separated."

"Hnh."

"However, *this*," Heinz von Schlieffen brought up a new image, "is certainly a paraboloid antenna."

"Really?" Jean-Paul said, brows rising.

"It suffers some embrittlement by which I guess that it served as an exterior antenna."

"Or an interior antenna in an intense environment," Jean-Paul suggested.

"Either way, what are we going to tell our captain?"

* * *

"It's junk," McLaughlin's voice was sour. He gestured to the other scientists gathered in various screens on the *Harmonie*'s bridge. "As near as we can tell, it's all junk."

"Have you identified it all?" Captain Zhukov asked, his eyes going to the two senior Eurocos scientists.

"*Non,*" Jean-Paul replied quickly.

"But we've identified enough to be reasonably sure of the conclusion," Heinz added.

"Where does that leave us, then?" Lieutenant Commander Reynaud asked.

"What about the biological hazards?" Jim Pickett asked, glancing to the two scientists on the screens.

"We used standard clean-room technique," Heinz von Schlieffen answered.

"And our instruments have detected nothing," Jean-Paul Ney added.

"All the same, gentlemen, your science modules will remain where they are," Captain Zhukov declared.

"Absolutely," Jean-Paul Ney agreed. "We've just finished establishing our operations; we can commence our science mission immediately."

"Wouldn't you prefer to modify the mission?" Captain Steele asked, waving a hand in the general direction of the alien ship.

"*Capitaine* Steele, we prepared to study *Jupiter*!" Jean-Paul Ney exclaimed in affronted tones.

"And, to be truthful, Captain, our team is not equipped to take on this additional mission," Heinz von Schlieffen added. "We are prepared to study the moons of Jupiter and the planet itself. Most of us have spent our lives learning all we can about Jove in preparation for this one mission."

"Do I understand you?" Jim Pickett chimed in. "Are you saying that the greatest single scientific discovery to occur in all our history is an *inconvenience* to you?"

The two scientists had the grace to look abashed.

"And weren't you planning on looking for signs of life on Europa?" Commander Geister asked them.

"Of course! But that was different!" Jean-Paul Ney protested.

"How so?" Emily Steele wondered.

Before the scientists could frame a response, Pickett cut them off. "Gentlemen, you can consider your original mission suspended until the successful conclusion of our negotiations with these aliens."

"But—!" the two scientists spluttered in insulted unison.

"Nobel Prize," Captain Zhukov said, raising his voice above theirs. He was rewarded with an instant silence. "In fact, I wouldn't be surprised if there were more prizes to come out of this than you have staff."

"I can coordinate with Eurocos headquarters to redesign our mission," Commander Geister offered. Captain Zhukov nodded absently in his direction.

"What do we do next?" Captain Zhukov said, turning his gaze to Jim Pickett.

"We thank them for their samples and tell them that we have no interest in trading at this time," Pickett replied calmly.

"What?" Zhukov and Steele cried in unison. "Are you insane?"

"And we need to tell them before they tell us," Pickett continued with no sign of the slightest perturbation over their outburst. He glanced between the two captains and then asked with a hint of exasperation, "Haven't either of you ever tried to sell used cars?"

* * *

Xythir

>>**Yes, Exern, what is it**?<< Captain Nexl clicked calmly when the alert came in from the communications officer.

>>**I have received a response from the humans,**<< Exern replied.

>>**I would imagine,**<< Captain Nexl responded breezily. He waited for a moment, then prompted, >>**And?**<<

Exern was a moment in replying. >>**They thank us for our samples but say that they have no desire to trade at this time.**<<

>>**What?**<< Nexl's limbs went taught with surprise. An inhalation expanded his body. It required effort to release it again, so great was its surprise. >>**Get Ixxie.**<<

>>**It shall be done,**<< Exern responded needlessly. A moment later, Ixxie entered the connection.

>>**Has our communications officer explained the situation?**<<

>>**Indeed,**<< Ixxie responded. There was a moment of thoughtful silence. >>**This is unexpected.**<<

>>**I was not aware that you were prone to understatements, Trade Officer,**<< Captain Nexl responded brittlely.

>>**I'm just thrashing out my thoughts, Captain,**<< Ixxie responded, apologetically.

Nexl wondered if perhaps the trade officer was confusing itself with the Yon, for which such statements could be taken literally. That thought led the captain to wonder if the trade officer wasn't considering bathing at different shores—perhaps even alien ones.

Nexl sighed. It *had* always been part of the greater plan because the Yon were just as guilty as the Xlern, but Captain Nexl had always hoped that he and those on *Xythir* could handle the four-limbs by themselves.

Ixxie had gathered its thoughts and now clicked, >>**I believe, Captain, that the humans are bluffing.**<<

>>**What do you suggest?**<< Nexl asked, feeling like he'd ingested too heavily.

>>**We should up the ante and then call it,**<< Ixxie rapped simply.

>>**Very well,**<< Nexl responded. To Exern he clicked, >>**Fire up the hyper-transmitter and let our friends know we want them to come in.**<<

>>**As you command!**<< Exern replied promptly.

Let's see how the two-legs respond to this, Captain Nexl thought to himself, rubbing his upper limbs together with glee.

* * *

"You know, Mr. Pickett, there's something about all this that bothers me," John McLaughlin said as he finished examining the latest data from the scientists of the Eurocos mission.

"Just something?" Pickett asked, his lips twitching upwards.

McLaughlin raised an eyebrow. "You're not worried, are you, Mr. Ambassador?"

"Oh, no, Mac, not at all," Pickett said, barking a laugh. He forced his mouth closed, then opened it again when he had himself under control. "What bothers you, Mac?"

"Well, first, there's that whole parallax issue," Mac said. "If the aliens could detect us thirteen thousand light-years away, how come they didn't notice that what they thought was an FTL drive signature was really two *separate* propulsion units nearly half a solar system apart?"

Pickett waved for him to go on.

"I mean they must have popped up closer to monitor our communications. They talked to us in TV signals—signals that were only sent out for a short period of time before we switched types and went to cable."

"So?"

"So why couldn't they have looked for our signals again? At the closer distance, they would have seen their error."

"How could they? We didn't have our ships back when we were transmitting *Howdy Doody*."

"And then there's their ion trail," Mac added. Pickett smiled and Mac's eyebrows twitched. "What's so funny?"

"I was wondering when you'd get there," Pickett said. "What do you know?"

"Mr. Pickett?" Mac said, completely baffled.

"Have you managed to get a copy of *Harmonie's* sensor data?" Jim Pickett asked. "We've got a mass estimate for the alien, right?"

Mac nodded slowly, a look of suspicion growing on his face.

"And we've got an idea of the strength of the ion trail, right?" Pickett guessed. Mac nodded slowly, challengingly. Pickett laughed. "Mac, you might not remember it but I was once called 'the Spaceman's Senator.'"

"I remember," Mac said gruffly.

"So, I know a bit about propulsion systems," Jim Pickett told him. "I know that ion drives are efficient but they don't have a great deal of thrust. So, from what you got, did you conclude that our alien friends couldn't have used an ion drive to get the accelerations they showed us?"

Mac nodded. "How long have you known, sir?"

"Known?" Pickett shook his head. "Not until you told me just now. Guessed? For a while now." He paused, his expression intense. "Our new friends are scamming us, Mac."

"Scamming us?"

"Yeah," Pickett replied, "and I've got to wonder why."

"Mr. Pickett," Mac began, licking his lips and choosing his words with care, "you're saying that—"

A loud klaxon on the command panel cut across his words and the navigation screen was suddenly full of bright red indicators.

"Contact!" Mac said, his whole manner converting in an instant to the calm, perfect professional. He punched a communication button. "*Harmonie*, this is *Voyager*. I show a second contact, orbit unknown, just beyond the alien ship."

"This is *Harmonie*, we concur with your readings, stand by," young Ensign Strasnoye's voice came back in the same precise, unflappable tones Mac had used.

"Yup," Jim said, his eyes twinkling, "just about what I expected."

"What?" Mac barked in surprise.

"They're upping the ante," Pickett replied calmly. "They've called our bluff."

"It seems to me they hold all the cards," Mac said, as he scanned the incoming data on the new ship. Already he could see that it was shaped entirely different from the first alien ship.

"If they did, why would they bother playing with us?"

Mac was ready with a sharp reply but it died on his lips. Why, indeed? "So, what do you think is up, sir?"

"I think they want something from us; they're trying to spook us into giving it to them," Pickett said. He turned his eyes to the engineer. "Did you ever study U.S.-Soviet relations?"

Mac shook his head.

"This reminds me a lot of Nikita Khrushchev and his famous, 'We will bury you.'" Mac's eyes widened. "The Soviet Union spent over forty years running the world's biggest bluff."

"They're bluffing?" Mac spluttered, gesturing to the two alien ships, which each dwarfed the combined mass of *Harmonie* and *Voyager*. "Interstellar faster-than-light traveling aliens are *bluffing*?"

"It sure looks like it."

* * *

"This ship is nothing like the first one," Dr. von Schlieffen said over the comm link to *Harmonie*. "Thanks to Ensign Strasnoye, we have dimensions and mass." He paused to nod acknowledgement to the Russian officer. "The ship is roughly pyramidal in shape with the dimensions in the proportions of 9:4:2. It is about eleven point two-five kilometers in length and masses over twenty-three million tons."

"And it just *appeared*!" Karl Geister exclaimed, still in shock over its sudden presence.

"Have we had any communications from it?" Captain Zhukov asked, turning his attention back to Ensign Strasnoye and then to the comm link to *Voyager's* command bridge.

"Nope, not a peep," Lieutenant McElroy, *Voyager's* communications officer and officer of the watch, replied. At the conference table, Ensign Strasnoye nodded in agreement.

Captain Zhukov sighed and turned to Captain Steele and then to Ambassador Pickett. "What do you recommend?"

Emily Steele had the impression that the question was really directed to Pickett and shrugged, gesturing to him.

"We wait," Pickett said. "We send all this back to Earth, so that they know."

"That's all?" Karl Geister said, moving agitatedly in his chair. "You wish us to just wait?"

"We don't know anything about this second ship," Pickett said, opening his hands in a helpless gesture. "Until we do, I think we should wait and see what happens."

"Captain Steele?" Caption Zhukov said, soliciting the American captain's opinion.

Emily was silent for a long moment. Finally, she sighed. "I'm willing to go with Mr. Pickett's suggestion."

"For how long?" Karl Geister demanded, glancing around the conference table with ill-concealed disgust.

"What would you recommend, Mr. Geister?" Captain Zhukov inquired in a deceptively mild tone.

Karl's jaw tightened, and he glanced quickly toward Commander Reynaud before swallowing visibly and shaking his head. "I'm sorry, Captain. I suppose I was hoping for a better choice."

Captain Zhukov kept his eyes from narrowing, turned at a slight noise from Captain Steele, who returned his look blankly, and finally said, "I'm inclined to agree with Mr. Pickett." He turned his attention to his German first officer. "I think that we would be best served by waiting to see what this new ship wants."

"Passive observation?" Dr. Ney asked from his comm console.

"By all means," Pickett said firmly. He gave the two captains an apologetic look and added, "If that's all right with you."

Emily and Zhukov exchanged sardonic looks. Zhukov flicked a hand in acknowledgement.

"So, we're going to leave it in the enemy's hands?" Commander Geister demanded.

"Commander," Jim Pickett said slowly in the sudden silence, "I think we would make a terrible mistake if we regarded these aliens as the enemy."

"I agree," Captain Zhukov said immediately, frowning at the German commander.

"Karl," Elodie Reynaud said, stretching out an open hand to the blond-haired man.

The German's nostrils flared and he nodded jerkily. "My apologies, Captain. It was a poor choice of words."

Captain Zhukov waved the issue aside.

"So we wait and observe," Captain Steele said, glancing around the table for any further objections. Seeing none, she rose from her seat. To Captain Zhukov she said, "If you don't mind, I'll head back to *Voyager*."

Captain Zhukov gave her an odd look but nodded. To Pickett he said, "You're free to stay here, if you wish."

Jim Pickett rose from his seat, shaking his head. "If you don't mind, I'll be in my quarters." He smiled at everyone around the table and into the comm pickup to the scientists in their detached habitats. "I've got some thinking to do."

*   *   *

Instead of going back to his quarters, Pickett stopped up in the command center to talk things over with McLaughlin.

"They're *aliens*, how can you possibly be sure?" Mac asked.

"They're aliens who went to the trouble of watching *Howdy Doody* and learning English," Pickett replied calmly. He nodded firmly. "They want something from us."

"You're going to stake all of the human race on your feeling?"

"Yeah," Pickett replied with a heavy sigh. "I think I am."

"You know, they could probably blow all of us to small particles in an instant," Mac said conversationally. "They could take anything we've got and we've got no way to stop them."

"I know," Pickett replied. Mac gave him an exasperated look. "But, that being the case, why didn't they do that already?"

Mac blinked as he considered that.

"Unless they already *have*," Jim Pickett murmured, eyes wide with sudden insight.

"Mr. Pickett, are you saying we're dealing with interstellar thieves?" Mac asked in low voice.

"It's not stealing if someone gives it to you," Jim Pickett replied with a mischievous twist of his lips.

"Damn," John McLaughlin said, turning to the displays which were now showing both alien ships in near orbit with the two human ships. "Damn! If you're right, sir, then these guys have got to be playing for high stakes!"

"Oh," Pickett said, "I always knew that."

"Damn."

"Let's think about this some more," Pickett said. "Suppose the aliens have been watching our planet and taking stuff—"

"What sort of stuff?"

"Ideas," Pickett said, "anything else and we'd probably notice."

"History is full of sightings of UFOs and strange men," Mac allowed.

"The lightest thing to lift is a thought," Pickett said. "But it's also the hardest to take away."

McLaughlin gave him a blank look.

"Consider, Mac, everyone now knows we've got a matter-antimatter drive," Pickett said by way of example. "So they've got the idea and they know it can be done." He looked to the engineer for confirmation. Mac shrugged in agreement. "But *you* know how hard it was to build the first time. And to give the idea away, you need to know all that additional technical knowledge that's required."

"Um," Mac said, his eyes unfocused as he digested Pickett's last words. "Yeah, I get what you mean."

"So, for these aliens to take our ideas, they'd have to not only learn the idea—that's the easy part—but all the little wrinkles and tricks required to make it work," Pickett said.

"Okay."

"But they want to trade with us," Pickett said now.

"They only said that they wanted to give us their faster-than-light drive so they wouldn't get in trouble," Mac countered.

"Yeah, which implies that they live in an interstellar society with a rule of law," Pickett said. "If they weren't worried about enforcement, they could just as easily run away."

"Come to think of it, when they realized their mistake, why didn't they just run away?" Mac asked.

Pickett smiled at him. "Good point, but that just makes it clearer that they were only pretending to have made a mistake."

"Huh?"

"If they made a genuine mistake, then they could have left the minute they realized it," Pickett said. "Perhaps they would have had their knuckles rapped for jumping the gun in contacting us, but if their reasons were legitimate, I'd be surprised if the penalty was all that great—if there was any at all."

"Aren't you making a lot of assumptions there?"

"I'm extrapolating from what we know," Pickett said. "They said they want to trade, they know English, they said they'd get in trouble for contacting us prematurely."

"Hmmm," Mac grunted. "So where does that leave us?"

"Hang on, I'm brainstorming," Pickett said. "What if they've already taken some ideas from us, sold them as their own, and now they're afraid that they'll get caught?"

"In that case, why not just blow up the whole planet?"

"And kill the golden goose?" Pickett asked, shaking his head. "Also, I suspect *that* sort of thing will get noticed, given their talk about interstellar law."

"Huh," Mac said. "Yeah, I suppose aliens with the reputation of blowing up any planet that gets in their way would have to be destroyed to protect any peace-loving aliens."

"Also, it's incredibly wasteful," Pickett reminded him. "If they've made a profit stealing from us in the past, then there's no reason for them to think that they might not make money from us again."

"In that case, why didn't they just disappear when they found out we didn't have an FTL drive?"

"Because some day they're gonna get caught."

"Caught by us?" Mac asked, shaking his head. "That may be years from now."

"Or sooner," Pickett replied. "They might be right in thinking that we're very close in developing a true star drive."

"Or they're just scamming us."

"In which case, they're afraid of getting caught and they want to make a deal," Pickett replied.

"Which means that they're still scamming us," Mac said. Pickett raised an eyebrow. "They sent us junk—near as we can tell—and hoped we'd fall for it. You can be certain they'll try to sell us junk again when it comes to a star drive."

Pickett gave him a lopsided smile in reply. "Your job will be to make sure they don't."

"Huh? Me? I'm no hyper-physicist!" Mac cried. He pointed in the direction the detached science modules. "Let those Eurocos guys deal with it!"

"Oh, we'll have them, too," Pickett assured him, "but, as you just pointed out, they're scientists and you're an engineer. The proof will be in the building and testing, *not* the theory."

Mac's jaw dropped. "You think we're going to build a star drive and test it?"

"That'd be the best way to know that it works," Pickett reminded him.

Mac's eyes narrowed. "What about that other ship? What's to say it's not a military vessel whistled for by our first aliens to blow us all to kingdom come?"

"If so, why are they waiting?" Pickett asked. "Of course, we've no reason to suspect that the second ship isn't crewed by the same species as the first, but it's also possible that the interstellar 'cops' have just arrived on the scene."

"Well, that'd blow our deal, then."

"That depends," Jim Pickett said.

"On what?"

"On how bribable alien cops are," Jim replied.

"Huh?"

"Well, think about it," Pickett said. "If our new aliens are the cops, they must have dealt with situations like this before. And so there are rules. Given that we now know that aliens exist as well as faster-than-light star drives and—come to think of it—the way that second ship arrived gave us *much* more information than the first ship—what's the best that can happen? Particularly if those 'cops' discover that our first aliens tried to trade with us."

"A rap on the knuckles?" Mac suggested.

"And we can now appeal to the cops for better treatment," Pickett added.

"Like a better star drive?" Mac said. He pointed in the direction of the second ship. "Like the cops' ship?"

"And wouldn't that be nice?" Pickett replied, a smile on his lips.

"Yeah," Mac said slowly, his features forming a matching smile, "that'd would be *real* nice!"

* * *

"So …" Commander Geister said as Jim Pickett finished his speech to the collected officers of *Voyager* and *Harmonie*, "assuming for the moment that you are right, Mr. Ambassador, who would get this star drive?"

"Everybody."

"You mean everyone here, or all the nations represented here?" Commander Reynaud asked.

"I mean everybody," Pickett replied. He nodded toward McLaughlin who wasn't an officer on either ship but had been included for his technical expertise. "Mac suggests that we upload the full design specifications and all the applicable techniques to the web for everyone to access."

Pandemonium broke out with words being spoken in every language available at ear-splitting volume. In the midst of it all, Jim Pickett sat silently, his hands steepled in front of him.

"*Harmonie, tais toi!*" Captain Zhukov bellowed in questionable French.

"*Voyager*, shut up!" Captain Steele added, her sturdy alto voice cutting through the noise more effectively than Zhukov's baritone.

Silence. Emily looked to Captain Zhukov and, with a quick nod, ceded the room to him.

"Thank you," Nikolai Zhukov said to her. To his officers, he said, "I will not tolerate such outbursts on my ship."

Commander Geister and Commander Reynaud hung their heads guiltily, but their eyes were smoldering.

Zhukov turned to Pickett. "Matters of distribution and dissemination are for politicians."

Pickett nodded.

"In the meantime, if your thinking is correct, I propose that the resulting starship be manned by an international crew selected from both ships."

Pickett glanced to Captain Steele for her opinion.

"That seems fair," she said. Zhukov relaxed back into his seat and then tensed as she continued, "If this does pan out, however, we're going to need a starting point."

"I see where you're going," Captain Zhukov said with a sigh. Apparently, from the way they angrily raised their heads, so did his two commanders. With a glare, Zhukov waved them silent. "*Harmonie* is the larger ship with a predetermined role that cannot safely be altered. *Voyager*, on the other hand, was built to be modular and reconfigurable."

He glanced between Geister and Reynaud. In some respects, this was a godsent opportunity—separating the two would doubtless remove whatever trouble they were experiencing. He glanced more sharply at Elodie Reynaud. Her face was more moon-shaped than normal because they were taking the meeting in one of the lower-gravity rooms but Captain Zhukov found himself wondering if she was not sick or something.

"Commander Geister," he said, glancing toward his other first officer, "I think you would make an excellent senior representative—"

"*Non!*" Karl Geister snapped in French, his hand moving toward Commander Reynaud who met it with one of her own and clasped it tightly.

Jim Pickett nodded to himself in sudden understanding. He glanced to Emily Steele, whose confusion evaporated in dawning comprehension. Her eyes danced but she twitched her head toward him, handing him the responsibility.

"Captain Zhukov," Jim Pickett said slowly, "I'm sure that either commander would be splendid but I'm afraid there seems to be a circumstance of which you're not aware?"

"Not aware?" Zhukov blinked his eyes in surprise. How could this American know more about his crew than himself? "Of what am I not aware, Mr. Pickett?"

"Ah …" Jim said, grasping for the right words. He nodded toward the French and German commanders. Then he threw up his hands and said to them, "You tell him."

Karl looked to Elodie and Elodie smiled at Karl. Then she turned to their captain and said, "We're pregnant."

"Congratulations," Emily Steele said, rising from her chair and extending a hand to the young commander. She shook Geister's hand next.

"You realize that this is against regulations," Captain Zhukov told them sternly. That done, he smiled at them and said, "When?"

"We haven't actually told anyone," Elodie said.

"So *that's* why you missed your last medical!" Captain Zhukov exclaimed. He glanced toward Commander Geister. "But you must have an idea?"

"Three, maybe four months along," Jim Pickett said, eyeing Elodie Reynaud thoughtfully. When the others turned to him, he explained, "We had a number of births on the Moon."

"You're relieved, Commander," Zhukov said, waving Elodie away. "Report to sickbay immediately."

"I don't feel all that sick, sir," Elodie replied. She burst into a smile. "In fact, I started feeling better the minute I got pregnant."

"So, morning sickness beats space sickness?" Captain Steele mused.

"Perhaps," Elodie agreed. She glanced toward Karl. Zhukov saw the wistfulness in her eyes and twitched some fingers in the direction of his other first officer. "Accompany her."

Karl jumped out of his seat and grabbed Elodie by her waist. She flicked him an agitated look then settled for a warm smile and they departed.

"She's going to need to stay in a steady gee field," Jim Pickett said as soon as they were out of earshot. "Too many changes are harmful to the fetus."

"How do you know?" Emily asked.

Jim Pickett made a face. "I know about lunar pregnancies because I was asked to oversee a study on them." Emily raised her eyebrows. "It was classified." Now everyone was staring at him. He glanced around and then returned his attention to Captain Zhukov. "The gist of it was that a constant gravity field is best for growing babies. Babies grown in a one gee field are most able to adapt to life back on Earth."

"Oh!" Emily said, eyes going wide. "And the others?"

"I'm not the only one banned from Earth by gravity," Jim Pickett told her obliquely.

"There were some studies proposed but … the funding was voted down."

"What is the chance that this baby will … run into complications?" Captain Zhukov asked.

"High."

Emily saw the way the Russian's jaw clenched and how he placed his hands on the conference table, as if making ready to rise, but then Zhukov sighed and forced himself back into his chair.

"In which case, it would make no sense to assign either of them to *Voyager*," Captain Zhukov said with a frown.

"Unless we could equip *Voyager* with artificial gravity and send her back to Earth," Mac muttered. There was a silence around the table and Mac suddenly realized that all eyes were on him. He raised his hands in a warding gesture. "Sorry! I was talking to Jenkins, who has all these crazy ideas."

"Perhaps not so crazy," Emily said glancing toward Zhukov. The Russian captain shrugged.

"I think it is something to consider," Pickett said. In response to the looks that statement drew, he expanded, "If we could convince these aliens to lend us that sort of aid, we could return *Voyager*, all our data, and our pregnant officer in the one neat, tidy package."

"Leaving us here to deal with the aliens," Zhukov grumbled.

"Exactly," Jim Pickett said, smiling.

"Better, send her for a re-supply mission," Emily said. Zhukov glanced at her. "We could do with more provisions, surely."

"All of this is supposition at best, flights of fancy at worst," Dr. Ney said over the comm console. "While I understand that it is worth thinking about, and I agree with Ambassador Pickett about the possible reasons for our aliens' behaviors, nothing is certain nor will be until they contact us once more."

"Or blow us out of space," Ensign Strasnoye added in an undertone.

"Well, if they do, our worries will be over," Peter Murray muttered. Opposite him, John McLaughlin snorted in agreement.

Zhukov pursed his lips and glared at his muttering officers. "Let us proceed upon the notion that we are going to negotiate with the aliens and that we'll get them to provide us with the plans and training to build a star drive." He waited for any objection, but the two senior scientists onboard the science habitat had been rendered speechless by his bold proposition. "In that case, we'll go with the suggestion that *Voyager* form the test bed and that its first mission should be to return to the Moon—that's where you have your base, right?" At Emily's nod, he pressed on, "So we'll need to assign crew and figure out payloads."

"Commanders Geister and Reynaud are obvious candidates—"

"If we can boost at one gee or if we get an artificial gravity," Mac interjected.

Captain Zhukov accepted the correction with a nod. "Given that, however, I suggest that Captain Steele remain in command and that we keep the alterations to her crew to a logical minimum."

"That will depend upon the sort of technological assistance we can obtain from the aliens," Emily said.

"All this depends on the aliens," Pickett said. He split his next question between Captain Zhukov and Captain Steele. "We're agreed that I'll handle that, right?" When the two nodded, Pickett smiled. "In that case, I'd like you, Lieutenant Murray, to arrange a standard transponder and set it to squawk the emergency frequency."

"Pardon?" the red-haired Englishman said.

"We have a medical emergency, one of our crewmembers needs immediate assistance, so we have every right to declare it," Pickett said.

"A transponder?" Murray repeated. When Pickett nodded, he continued, "Like on an airplane?"

"Exactly."

"And you think they'll know what it means?" Mac asked. Before Pickett could reply, he said to Lieutenant Murray, "The code is 7700, sir, and if you want some help, I'm pretty sure you'll find Sally Norman knows all about them. She started life working with aircraft."

"I'd be glad to have her," Murray said.

"How soon can you have it ready?"

"Let me see what's needed first, if you please," Murray replied tetchily.

Pickett waved an open hand in a placating gesture.

* * *

Xythir

>>What is it, Communications Officer?<< Captain Nexl rapped in response to the alert popping up on his command panel.

>>**We're picking up a new transmission from the humans,**<< Exern reported.

>>**What do they say?**<< Captain Nexl asked. He wasn't surprised. He'd expected Exern to report communications with the new ship. He was expecting them to knock any moment now.

>>**They're transmitting on a different frequency,**<< Exern replied. The captain could hear the communications officer rattling various keys and contacts on his communications panel. >>**They're broadcasting on the 1090 megahertz band.**<<

Nexl's arms twitched as some vague memory came to him about that particular frequency and its importance to humans. >>**And?**<<

>>**It is the standard frequency used by their aircraft to broadcast position and status,**<< Exern responded.

>>**And?**<< Captain Nexl repeated with increased agitation.

>>**They're broadcasting code 7700,**<< Exern replied.

>>**Which means?**<<

>>**It's their 'Emergency' code, sir,**<< Exern told him. >>**The** *Harmonie* **is signaling an emergency.**<<

>>**Because of our new arrival?**<< Captain Nexl wondered.

>>**I doubt it, sir, the transponder wasn't detected until some time after the arrival,**<< Exern replied. >>**But they're signaling an** *emergency*, **Captain! What should we do?**<<

Nexl paused. It was against interstellar law to ignore a known emergency or distress signal. But if Nexl responded, that would necessarily admit that he and *Xythir* knew about the broadcasts and their significance—which would mean revealing that they knew *much* more about Earth history than he wanted. However, if things went sour and this whole incident was reported to galactic authorities then the penalties would be—

>>**Send them a message,**<< Nexl replied. >>**Tell them that we've detected their signal and wonder if they can explain it to us.**<<

>>**But,** *Captain*,<< Exern rapped, >>**we** *know* **what it means!**<<

Nexl willed himself to silence. The young communications officer might be from another shore, but he was correct in his concern. Finally, the captain responded, >>**You're right. Tell them that we've noticed their emergency signal and by intergalactic, no, interstellar treaty, we are required to render any assistance possible and inquire as to the nature of their emergency.**<<

The Yon, Nexl thought to himself furiously, *what are they going to do? They'll be practically in knots over* this!

*   *   *

Harmonie

"Captain," Ensign Strasnoye called, "we're getting a response from the aliens."

"What is it?" Captain Zhukov said, moving toward the communication officer's console. "And tell the ambassador."

Strasnoye nodded and spoke quickly into his microphone, sending for Pickett, while at the same time gesturing at the center screen.

What is the nature of your emergency?

"Tell them that we have discovered that one of our crewmembers is pregnant and need to return her to Earth as soon as possible," Captain Zhukov said just as he spotted Ambassador Pickett race up beside him. Pickett gave him a confirming nod to which Zhukov, with a twitch of his lips, said, "They can't hear you."

"I'm getting ready for when they can," Pickett replied causing the captain's eyebrows to rise. "They just admitted to interstellar law, to covenants regarding emergencies and emergency aid, *and* they've admitted to knowing a damn sight more about our civilization than they were ever going to get from *Howdy Doody* and *Sesame Street*."

Zhukov pursed his lips. "*Sesame Street* was quite advanced, Ambassador. They might well have had an episode on transponders and emergencies."

It took Pickett a moment to recognize that the Russian was teasing him.

"Transmitted," Ensign Strasnoye reported.

"How long until—"

~One of your females is with child?~

"We've got a transmission from the second ship!" Chris Jenkins shouted across the comm link. "*Harmonie*, did you get it?"

The sound of feet alerted Zhukov and the others to the arrival of Captain Steele and John McLaughlin.

"Did you hear that, Mac?" Pickett said to the MAM engineer. "They not only know our transponder codes but they know how to select fonts on our displays."

"We're running a variant of Linux, sir," Ensign Strasnoye reported. "Our displays utilize the graphical interface."

"Shit," Emily muttered. Zhukov raised an eyebrow in her direction. "Just think about what that means for their penetration of our security."

"They're probably not much better than the average hacker," Mac assured her with a dismissive flick of his fingers. "Although," his eyes cut to Pickett, "I wonder why they know Linux so well that they can choose their display fonts."

"See?" Pickett said with a grin. "Are you beginning to see what I mean, Mac?"

"Yeah," Mac said in a dull tone. "If they've spent this much time on our software, they could easily have a full read of our technology."

"Which brings us right back to the original question," Pickett said.

Ensign Strasnoye pointed to the screen and asked his captain, "What should I tell them?"

"Tell them the truth," Pickett instructed with a glance to Zhukov and Steele for confirmation. "Tell them one of our crewmembers is, in fact, pregnant and we think that it would be best to return her to Earth or Luna as quickly as possible—"

"Why not Mars?" Emily asked. "It's closer."

"That would mean contacting the Chinese and getting them more involved," Zhukov pointed out.

"Also, this should have the desired effect," Pickett said.

"What effect?"

"Well … they've got to know that they can't just drop their ship in orbit around either the Earth or the Moon without opening an even *bigger* can of worms, so they'll work for a compromise."

"What sort?"

"Message transmitted, sir," Ensign Strasnoye reported. "Shall I append the medical details?"

"Not yet," Pickett said. The others glanced at him. "Well, don't you think the way our new aliens responded was a bit odd?"

"What, with the special typeface?" Mac said.

"They didn't respond to the emergency beacon, but they practically tripped all over themselves when they found out that we had a pregnancy aboard," Pickett explained. "Why is that?"

At his console, Ensign Strasnoye turned slightly green. "You don't suppose all those rumors about alien vivisection are true, do you, sir?"

There was a moment of horrified silence before Captain Zhukov coughed and said, "No, Ensign, I don't think so."

Chapter Eight

>>Contact those idiots!<< Captain Nexl ordered his communications officer.

>>The Yon, Captain?<< Exern asked, trying to confirm the exact identity of the "idiots."

>>Well, the Earthers aren't *that* dumb!<< Nexl responded lowly. A moment later, he added, >>Who will I be talking to, anyway?<<

>>It's hard to know, Captain,<< Exern replied. >>If nothing's changed, then I'd say that the current commander is probably Sa-li-ri-to.<<

>>Probably,<< Nexl agreed. >>And gestating, no doubt.<<

Nexl couldn't understand the intense attachment the Yon had for their gestation, but then again, Nexl wasn't a four-headed serpent. Of course, neither were the Yon but it was a useful image when determining which species should have first contact with the humans. The xeno-psychologists were all confirmed in their opinion that most Earthers would find it much harder to deal with the Yon than the Xlern; although the Xlern had to trade a great deal to ensure that certain disturbing appendices were left out of the final report. Apparently spiders and octopi were also not particularly high on the list of psychologically pleasing shapes. *Stupid two-legs!*

Of course, Nexl reminded itself, the two-legs weren't the ones who'd opened unsanctioned communications!

* * *

Ynoyon

Je-te-ji-go routed the communications to its captain.

~What?~ Sa-li-ri-to rasped.

~The round ones desire communication, Captain,~ Je-te-ji-go informed it.

~Pipe it through,~ the captain responded. Without further comment, Je-te-ji-go complied. The captain realized that it hadn't inserted the necessary noise dampeners the moment the Xlern captain rapped its opening words. *Ugh!* Sa-li-ri-to thought. *This is going to disturb the baby.*

~Yes, Captain? Is there something you wished to communicate?~ Sa-li-ri-to asked distractedly. It had only two heads directed at the display, the other two were idly teasing each other.

>>I thought, Captain, that we'd agreed that your ship would not communicate with the humans.<<

~But a pregnancy!~ Sa-li-ri-to responded, its two spare heads turning to the display, distracted by the emotions flowing through it. ~One of the humans will soon be producing offspring!~

>>I … understand how this could be of interest to you, Captain.<<

~Not just to me but to all my crew!~ Sa-li-ri-to replied. ~I understand that your species is not quite as involved in gestation as ours…~

>>Nor are the humans, really,<< Nexl rapped, interrupting.

Three of Sa-li-ri-to's heads recoiled at the implications—two of them hissing menacingly. With some effort, Sa-li-ri-to forced them out of range of the vid pickup, absently wondering if the communications officer's suggestion that they use audio only had not been a superior idea after all.

~Their biology renders them, in this instance, slightly more in concordance with ours than does yours,~ Sa-li-ri-to responded, trying not to sound tetchy. It was hard, however, as its gestation was nearing its end and it could not help but wonder what would become of it when the gestating bond was broken. It was very rare for a Yon to reform twice in a row. In fact, it was rather frowned upon. Sa-li-ri-to had two geas Yon in its thrall and, of course, there were the ship's spare Yon, but, beyond a nip or two, Sa-li-ri-to had no great experience with any of them.

Not that it mattered, the mission was supposed to complete before the birth—unless—

~What do you propose, we do, Captain Nexl?~ Sa-li-ri-to found themself asking, breaking the normal give and take of speech between the two.

It was a moment before the Xlern recovered from its shock.

>>This is falling apart, you know,<< Nexl rapped angrily. >>The only way I see is to …<<

Sa-li-ri-to lost focus for a moment as Is(sa) returned with a nice, fresh, fearful, live, fur-covered crunchy. Sa-li-ri-to was pleased with its resourcefulness as the ri- and the to- heads fought for possession, in the end, neatly tearing the scurrying thing in two and wrapping their jaws about it.

With two heads sated, Sa-li-ri-to's focus returned to the Xlern. Not wishing to admit its distraction, it said, ~Whatever you think is best, Captain.~

>>I'm pleased that you agree, Captain,<< Nexl responded. With a final salutary clatter, it broke the connection.

Oh, gods, my heads! Sa-li-ri-to thought, the notion echoing throughout its four-pronged being. *I'm going to have headaches for the rest of the day.* And, of course, analgesics were not acceptable at this point in its pregnancy. To distract itself, Sa-li-ri-to poked up a rerun of *Days of Our Lives* and tried to engulf the strange notion of arguing over how best to raise a hatchling. *Such strange things these two-sexes are!*

* * *

"Mr. Pickett to the bridge! Mr. Pickett to the bridge!" Lieutenant Ives, the communications officer called over the ship's intercom.

Pickett arrived moments later to find both captains on the bridge deck, huddled near the communications section. Emily spotted him first and said, "Our friends are calling."

We have been asked to apologize for the Yon.

"The Yon?" Pickett repeated, brows creased. "Ask them if that's the name of the other ship."

The ship is called the Ynoyon, the crew are Yon.

Pickett glanced at the communications officer, at the two captains, then gestured toward the seat saying, "Can I just type?"

Zhukov and Steele exchanged unhappy looks, but with a shrug, Captain Zhukov gestured for his officer to relinquish his post to the American.

"Can you call for Mac and Jenkins?" Pickett said, turning to Captain Steele. "We might need them." Meanwhile, he typed: **Thank you for the information. You may inform the Yon that it is true that one of our officers is pregnant. We do not have the facilities here to safely deliver the child and we are concerned about radiation and gravitic hazards.**

What can we do? was the reply.

We need to get her back to Earth or Luna as soon as possible, Pickett replied. **But we do not believe it would be beneficial to carry her in one of your ships.**

We could provide you with a suitable transportation system.

One that permitted us to accelerate at constant gravity? Jim typed back.

That's possible. We were thinking about artificial gravity. Given your urgency, we thought it best to achieve accelerations that are normally greater than your species can tolerate.

"Jesus!" Mac swore. "Artificial gravity!"

"Tell them yes!" Emily urged.

"Da!" Zhukov added, reverting to his native tongue in excitement.

We could not accept such an offer, Pickett wrote back.

"What?" Steele cried, reading over his shoulder. "Are you mad?"

"What's the idea?" Mac added, glaring suspiciously at the politician.

Pickett held up a hand, silencing them and then typed: **It would be best that any system be something we could construct and comprehend ourselves. After all, you did talk about a trade.**

We will have to consider this.

Please hurry, Pickett wrote back. **We are concerned for the safety of our crewmember and her child.**

"Signal lost," Lieutenant Ives reported, gesturing toward a secondary display.

"What did you do that for, Mr. Pickett?" Mac asked angrily. The two captains joined him with heated glares.

"Do you remember how the Indians sold Manhattan Island?" Pickett said. Captain Zhukov shook his head. Captain Steele and McLaughlin nodded, but both had pained looks in their eyes.

"That was the island on which you built New York City, *n'est-ce pas?*" Lieutenant Ives asked softly.

"Indeed," Pickett said. He sighed and glanced to Steele and McLaughlin. His gaze moved to Jenkins, who stood with his hands clenched at his side. "You all had relatives when the meteor hit?"

Their expressions were enough to answer him.

Jim Pickett blew out a long, hard sigh. "I'd been fighting for Spacewatch for three years—" he broke off, seeing their looks. He threw up his hands in surrender.

"They say it was America's worst disaster, worst defeat," Captain Zhukov said glancing from one American to the other before returning his eyes to the ambassador.

"We never quite recovered," Pickett admitted. "New York City, half of Long Island, large parts of New Jersey, Connecticut, and most of Rhode Island were obliterated in the space of seconds."

"And the third world war was nearly started," Captain Zhukov murmured, eyes dark at the memory.

"It took us hours to confirm that it was a meteor," Pickett said, his lips pursed in a sour line. "If it weren't for the International Space Station—" He stopped himself, flicking a hand open in dismissal. "Anyway, I was talking about Indians and beads."

"You were?"

Pickett shrugged. "Our alien friends have revealed that they know a lot more about our civilization than they originally admitted," he reminded them. "And now they offer us a ship—a 'transportation system'—as they called it, but they don't offer us the know-how to build our own." He glanced around for comments, found none, and continued, "So they're essentially offering us beads and trinkets."

"And you want the steam engines and the technology," Emily said.

"Should we trade for anything less?" Jim asked.

"We should contact our governments," Captain Zhukov said.

"Given what the aliens said, if we wait a bit, we might be able to talk to them directly," McLaughlin said.

"They're going to point out that we've declared an emergency and that their solution is the quickest," Pickett said.

"It is," Emily agreed. "So what do we do?"

"We tell them that without a complete understanding of their system, we can't evaluate its possible biological affects," Nikolai Zhukov replied.

Emily pursed her lips and nodded. "Well said."

"All the same, we'll want a compromise position," Jim Pickett added. "We can't wait too long."

"And we can use this as a resupply mission," Emily said. Zhukov raised an eyebrow. "We're going to need more supplies, certainly at least more fuel for *Voyager.*"

"Actually, Skipper, I think we'll probably want to cannibalize the MAM module," Mac said thoughtfully. Emily started a heated response but he cut her off. "I know that it *was* state-of-the-art, but we're going to be replacing it with a star drive."

Emily considered this with a sour expression.

"Culture shock," Jim said, nodding to her. "We're likely to see a lot of that."

"Yeah," Emily murmured. "Like the Japanese when Perry arrived."

"Exactly," Captain Zhukov agreed. The Americans looked at him in surprise. "It was your Commodore Perry who started the Japanese on the course that led to our defeat at Port Arthur less than fifty years later."

Pickett pursed his lips thoughtfully and nodded. "A good point, Captain," he said. He glanced toward the others. "We all know how quickly the Japanese caught up to the rest of the world."

"And the rest of the world regretted it for some time afterward," Emily Steele reminded him.

"There are all sorts of regret," Pickett said. "Pearl Harbor was one sort of regret, the economic miracle of Japan in the second half of the twentieth century was another."

"And now they've got the Moon," Captain Zhukov murmured.

"That's not strictly true, Captain," Pickett reminded him. "There are several international bases on the Moon."

"But it is true that the Japanese have the largest population on the Moon," Zhukov persisted.

Pickett allowed himself a small smile. "I think, Captain, that with some minor qualifications, we'll all be quite happy to cede the Moon completely."

Zhukov's brows furrowed until Pickett waved a hand around in a circle, inviting the captain to consider their current location and then Zhukov's lips twitched upwards and, with a chuckle, he said, "By which, I gather, you're suggesting that we'll shortly be awash in real estate."

"I consider it one of the many possibilities we'll want to explore," Pickett said.

"But you're an American," Lieutenant Ives objected.

"Lieutenant, I've been on the Moon for rather a long while," Pickett replied, silently inviting the young Frenchman to reconsider Pickett's history. "For years now, I've seen the Earth rise." He smiled. "In all that time, I've yet to see any lines indicating national boundaries."

"You were appointed by your president," Captain Zhukov reminded him.

"True," Pickett agreed, "and supported by the United Nations."

"I'll be happy to leave that sort of thing to the politicians, myself," Emily said. She turned to Captain Zhukov. "In the meantime, would you wish to assemble a list of supply requirements? I can't guarantee we'll be able to get them all, but it seems like it's something we should consider at this moment."

"*Harmonie's* main need is supplies to make up for those used by your crew," Captain

Zhukov said. "Beyond that, we were supplied for our full mission."

"Understood," Captain Steele replied, "but given the change in circumstances, would there not be other supplies that you might desire?"

Zhukov bent his head in acknowledgement. "I'll have Commander Geister work out a list." With a wry grin, he added, "I suppose I shall have to put replacements for my officers on that list."

"If I could make a suggestion, Captain?" Pickett asked. Zhukov frowned at the notion and relented with a quick flick of two fingers. "Would it not make more sense to promote from within? You could ask for junior replacements."

Zhukov frowned. "I'm not sure if you're aware, Mr. Ambassador, of the various political considerations that went into the formation of our original crew—"

Pickett interrupted him with a lazy smile and said in a drawl, "I suspect that you would maintain the political structure, if at all possible."

"Yes," Zhukov said slowly, "I suppose that would be possible."

"You already have a hole in your ship's roster. I don't see why you wouldn't want to fill it immediately," Captain Steele said.

"Mmm," Zhukov grunted in agreement. "I shall consider what you have said. In the meantime, I do believe that we should proceed with the assumption that we will shortly be sending *Voyager* back to Earth."

"Back to the Moon," Pickett corrected him. "Our base is on the Moon, and it makes more sense to go there than fiddle around with LEO and try to arrange supplies."

"I suppose, also, that would allow communications to be somewhat … ah, throttled," Captain Zhukov observed dryly.

Jim Pickett gave him another of his lazy smiles.

*   *   *

Xythir

Captain Nexl wanted a long relaxing immersion in warm waters, a reversion to the happier days before he had come ashore and was captured by the elders and forced into education. Instead, he had only the soothing sounds of *Black Sabbath* overlain with a loud white-noise rendition of waves crashing. That would have to do.

Time was of the essence. If nothing else, the Slitherers or the Stumblers would shortly be demanding his attention. Nexl turned, sped up, and raced up the curved walls of his quarters, carefully inverting himself, top for bottom, landing on the floor on his upper limbs. With rapid breaths, the captain performed a quick number of full body crunches, then deftly flipped right-side up, still breathing heavily.

Out of practice. A limp thing, no matter what the rank, will have a hard time attracting partners. Nexl flung his right forearm to the pile of rocks in the center of his cabin, sucked up a nice pair, passed one to his left hind-arm, and knocked them together in a quick, precise staccato.

Castanets, Nexl thought to itself. *Castanets and flamenco dancing. I don't give a* **click** *about the Slitherers, we've got to get those on the list. Maybe body paint, as well. Certainly lipstick.* Nexl recalled the excitement with which the first load of Stumbler cosmetics had on his homeworld. *That* had been an immense profit!

And now, the captain reflected to itself, *as the Stumblers say: It is time to pay the piper.*

Maybe he could get the Slitherers to agree to the pipes in exchange for the castanets. The thought pleased the captain and he dropped the two small rocks, plucked a sponge from his supply locker, washed off quickly in the dribble that was his living stream, then inserted the still-wiggling sponge into the opening of his ingestor, forcing himself to ignore the tantalizing notion of using the small thing for anything more sensual.

Refreshed, if not entirely relieved, Captain Nexl trotted out of his quarters and returned to the command deck.

>>**Has Axlu reported?**<< Nexl demanded as he stepped through the portal to the deck.

>>**Captain, he has reported back,**<< Exern replied. >>**Engineer Axlu continues in his suggestion of Plan B.**<<

>>**Axlu's been hanging around Ixxie,**<< Nexl clicked irritably. >>**And Plan B would be?**<<

>>**We provide the humans with our second-line drive, utilizing their remaining antimatter,**<< Exern replied.

>>**That won't do,**<< Nexl rapped. >>**We want them to come back, and what about their desire to learn how the system works? I thought that was why we'd agreed on Plan A.**<< Which was, naturally, to sell the Earthers on the crappiest, most energy intensive star drive in the known universe.

>>**I can get Axlu if you desire, Captain,**<< Exern offered. The communications officer was trying to slip out of his position of authority. Or perhaps, Nexl reflected honestly, Exern was tired of having the headaches the engineering officer invariably inflicted with his enthusiasm. Nexl had had to warn the engineer that such vibrations were unwelcome among the rest of the crew, but the engineer was hardened to such motions from years of working in the high vibrations of the ship's machinery. Most engineers were suitably loud and overbearing, Nexl recalled. Even over electronic communications with the aid of decibel controls, the exuberant engineer seemed to be always booming.

>>**We can't have them use up all their antimatter, they'll need it for the return journey,**<< Nexl responded indirectly. He waved his limbs in surrender as he added, >>**You'd best connect me with the engineer.**<<

>>**I'll turn the volume all way down,**<< Exern promised.

>>**Not off, however,**<< the captain warned him, keeping any tone of wistfulness out of his response.

>>**Of course,**<< Exern agreed. A moment later he said, >>**Engineer Axlu, Captain.**<<

>>**AXLU HERE!**<< the engineer rapped out sharply. Nexl waved imploringly to his communications officer, who flipped his limbs helplessly in response.

>>**Plan B won't work, Axlu,**<< the captain clicked in well-modulated tones.

>>**PARDON, CAPTAIN? COULD YOU BE LOUDER?**<<

>>**PLAN B WON'T WORK!**<<

>>**WHY?**<<

>>**The Earthers need enough antimatter for a return trip,**<< Nexl responded.

>>**THAT'S EASY. WE SIMPLY RETUNE THE CONVERTERS.**<<

>>**Won't that affect performance?**<<

>>**THE CONVERTERS HAD TO BE DETUNED TO BE SO WASTEFUL.**<< *Oh, no!* Nexl thought to himself. *Please don't pontificate! Too late.* >>**AS YOU MAY NOT KNOW, CAPTAIN, THE GRAVITY GENERATORS ARE INCREDIBLY EFFICIENT. IN ORDER TO PROVIDE OUR EXPORT MODELS, WE TYPICALLY DETUNE BY SIX ORDERS OF MAGNITUDE. IN THIS CASE, WE'VE DETUNED BY SEVEN.**<<

Oh, my body! Nexl thought, gesturing wildly for help from the communications officer.

>>**I can't modulate any lower, Captain,**<< Exern apologized.

>>**Can we retune it so that they use half their antimatter each way?**<<

>>**THAT REQUIRES ADDITIONAL MODIFICATIONS,**<< Axlu responded. >>**IT WOULD TAKE A NUMBER OF DAYS.**<<

>>**We don't have days,**<< Nexl responded. Struck by a new thought, he asked, >>**What sort of transit time would we get?**<<

>>**WE COULD TRANSIT AT 56.25 XP AND ARRIVE IN .95 OF THEIR 'DAYS,'**<< Axlu responded, >>**BUT THEY WOULD ONLY CONSUME A TENTH OF THEIR ANTIMATTER.**<<

Nexl considered that. That would enable the Earthers to make four more round-trip journeys, if they so desired. Nexl thought that the Earthers would have to be more than stupid to waste their hard-won antimatter on such jaunts but he could always hope.

>>**Very well, Engineer, we'll go with your plan,**<< Nexl responded.

>>**CAPTAIN, I AM CONCERNED ABOUT THE KNOWLEDGE TRANSFER REQUIRED.**<<

>>**Have you not prepared the necessary instructions?**<< Nexl snapped, ready to vent his growing irritation upon the engineer. Axlu had known what would be required even before they set out on this voyage.

>>**I HAVE,**<< the engineer responded succinctly. Nexl was about to congratulate him on his self-control until—>>**THESE HUMANS ARE NOT STUPID. I AM CONCERNED THAT THEY WILL NECESSARILY LEARN THAT WE HAVE DOWNGRADED THE DRIVE CAPABILITIES.**<<

>>**I don't doubt they will,**<< Nexl replied. >>**It was part of the plan, after all.**<< Before the engineer could further batter him, Captain Nexl said, >>**Your job now, Engineer,**

is to ready the equipment for transfer.<<

>>**IT SHALL BE DONE.**<<

>>**Good. Let me know when you're ready.**<<

>>**YOU MAY PROCEED IMMEDIATELY. I WILL CONFORM MY ACTIONS TO YOUR NEEDS.**<<

Trust the engineer to get the last—excruciating—word. Nexl allowed himself a slow, calming breath before waving at the communications officer.

>>**Call the Earthers, let them know our deal,**<< he clattered.

>>**As you command,**<< Exern clicked back, his response mercifully muted.

* * *

"Skipper, the real problem is you don't know how long it's going to take to get back to the Moon," Mac said, as he and Emily conferred over the crew list. "If it takes the same three weeks it took us to get here, then we have to borrow stores from *Harmonie*, but we'll be able to go with our standard crew lists."

"No, we're going to have to leave two people behind, at least," Emily replied. When Mac raised a brow, Emily explained, "We're going to have Commanders Reynaud and Geister traveling with us."

"And their doctor," Mac added. Emily shook her head. "Why not?"

"Because *Harmonie's* doctor needs to remain here."

"What if something goes wrong?" Mac demanded. "I know that O'Reilly's good at her job, but you have to admit, she's no OB/GYN."

Emily snorted a laugh. "No, she's not," she agreed, "but she's competent, and if the trip is only for three weeks, we really don't have much to worry about." Emily paused, then smiled again. "Anyway, Mac, I suspect that you're over-estimating the transit time."

Mac gave her a questioning look.

"We've made it clear that Commander Reynaud would be safest in a steady one gee environment," Emily told him. "So, how long would it take to get back at one gee?"

"Shit, Skipper, you can't believe they're gonna be *that* fast," Mac grunted. "Where are they gonna get the fuel?"

"They're talking about a gravity generator, who says they'll need fuel?"

"Huh," Mac said, raising a hand to scratch his chin. "I suppose there's something to that." He pulled out his hand calculator and tapped in some numbers. "At one gee, we'd get there in—huh, under a week, assuming we have to flip over and decelerate."

"And they were talking about going faster," Emily reminded him.

Mac snorted. "I'll believe that when I see it."

"Okay," Emily allowed. Then she grinned at him impishly. "Twenty-five bucks says it'll take less than that."

"Skipper, I hate to take your money," Mac said, reaching out to shake on the deal.

"I'll believe it when I see it," Emily repeated back to him. A moment later she said,

"Now that we've got that out of the way, who stays behind?"

"Mr. Pickett, obviously," Mac said.

"Why?"

"So he can get plausible deniability and stay in touch with the aliens," Mac said. "If he goes back, he'll be inundated with all sorts of orders, directives—you know, the usual crap."

Emily pursed her lips and nodded. "If he went back, he'd probably stay."

"No way!" Mac retorted. "He'd beat them all off with a stick and steal something to get back out here. Besides all the history he's going to make, this is his baby."

"Certainly," Emily agreed, "but there's no way they'd let him come back when they've heard the sort of stuff he'd have to say."

"Yeah," Mac said, nodding in turn. He smiled at her. "Good call, Skipper."

"I could leave Danielle," Emily said. Mac raised an eyebrow. "Zhukov's certain to promote Lieutenant Ives so they'll need another comm officer."

"Skip, what's to say that they won't have enough of their own?"

"Politics," Captain Steele told him. Mac made a face. "It'll be politic to leave one of our officers here—probably two—seeing as we're getting two of theirs."

"Only one-way!"

"True," Emily agreed. "Which brings us to the other question—who should we bring back with us?"

"Huh?"

"Someone from the Japanese base, certainly," Emily said. "They're not represented here."

"Get Admiral Tsukino," Mac said with a smile. "Wouldn't *that* throw a spanner in the works!" His grin slipped as he took in Emily's reaction. "I mean, wouldn't it?"

"Actually, Mac, it's a brilliant idea!"

"How?"

"Firstly, have you ever met the admiral?" When she saw Mac shake his head, she continued, "He was educated at CalTech, the Sorbonne, as well as being attached to the United Nations at Hong Kong."

Mac pursed his lips in appreciation of this news. He, like so many Americans, had accepted the new location of the United Nations with mixed emotions. No one argued that the mud-pile that was all that remained of Manhattan was suitable for nothing, having been scraped clean by the 600-meter-high tsunami the Manhattan Meteor had created.

The hurt to the national pride had been somewhat assuaged by the politics that the new location had engendered. The Chinese, the *de facto* sole power after the destruction that had reigned on the United States, had been gracious in their acceptance of their role as host nation.

The Chinese were very careful to accord the United States with dignity and respect, opening a new era of greater cooperation between the two nations that had resulted in the

Treaty of Mars—which had effectively ceded the Red Planet to China.

Mac was no politician, but even he could see how that treaty had redirected China's efforts, resulted in increased space travel, and permanent settlements and expansion on Mars—something that the devastated United States was neither politically nor economically capable of undertaking. That the Chinese were careful to employ JPL and other NASA subsidiaries as partners in exploration helped ease the discomfort and enrich the American West, which had emerged, after the Manhattan Meteor, as the economic powerhouse of the nation.

Somewhere in the wake of all that, Japan found itself investing heavily in lunar exploration, establishing first a base and then a set of self-sustaining colonies. As European commentators were quick to observe, the tragedy of America was the savior of mankind. The Manhattan Meteor and its heart-rending impact had affected mankind's view of its survival in a profound way; a way which forced humanity to see Earth as a fragile, easily ruined resource.

Admiral Isao Tsukino had been the first of the new wave of Japanese technocrats, pushing firmly for extraterrestrial investment. He was viewed almost reverently by the majority of the Japanese people. He was also very popular with most Americans, being a charismatic, photogenic leader very much in the mold of the century-dead President Kennedy. It didn't hurt at all that he'd married an American movie star and had two very cute children.

"What makes you think the Japanese will let him go?" Mac asked.

"Who says we'll tell them?"

"What will Mr. Pickett say?"

"I suspect he'll be overjoyed," Emily said. "They worked together for a while before—"

Mac raised an eyebrow.

"—before Pickett took ill," Emily finished.

"Well, I can't imagine Captain Zhukov and the crew of the *Harmonie* will thank you if you bring someone out here who outranks him."

"The admiral would be outside of Captain Zhukov's chain of command," Emily said with a shrug. "It would give us all a certain amount of leeway."

"Instead of getting a French admiral or American commodore," Mac observed.

Emily grinned. "Something like that." She keyed a few notes onto her display. "So … we'll see if the admiral might be interested in a little jaunt. Now, who else do we leave?"

"Well … me," Mac said. Emily gave him a startled look. He raised a hand and ticked off on his fingers, "You've got to keep your two ABs, they're vital. You need to keep Mick because he's your only life-support specialist. Lori and Harry will need to stand watch-on-watch over this 'whatever' they're going to stuff on the ship. Neither of them is a slouch when it comes to engineering, so they'll be just as quick on the uptake as I am." He paused for a breath. "Besides, they're Navy and I'm not."

"Yeah," Emily admitted reluctantly, "but I'd really like to have you riding herd on this."

"And I'd like to, Skip, but you've got to face facts. If these aliens are going to give us a star drive, then me, Jenkins, and Norman are all pretty much out of work," Mac told her. He pursed his lips. "In fact, you'd be better off leaving all three of us behind. We're civilians, after all."

"No," Emily countered, "I need at least one civilian just in case I need someone to hijack the ship."

Mac gave her a surprised look then snorted. "Yeah, so you can say that it's not your fault if you want to bug out." He tilted his head toward her. "Devious."

Emily smiled at him. "So, who should we leave, Jenkins or Norman?"

Mac shook his head, refusing to choose. "Why don't you put it to them?"

"Because, Mr. McLaughlin, if there's going to be a hijacking, I'm expecting *you* to perform it."

"Thanks, Skip," Mac muttered sourly. "I always wanted to be a traitor to my country."

"I hope it won't come to that."

"Yeah, so why did Deep Ear go offline, then?" Mac countered.

Captain Steele smiled at him. "You know, Mr. McLaughlin, your time with Ambassador Pickett seems to have worked to your advantage."

"Naw, Skipper, I was always this devious," Mac said. "How do you think I managed to get the whole MAM project going in the first place?"

*　*　*

"I don't know what it is about this guy but he seems to always talk in caps," Jenkins muttered as he inspected the latest dispatch from the aliens.

"Maybe he thinks that you have to shout at civilizations that don't know about star drives to get them to understand," Mac said as he glanced over Jenkins' shoulder. "Did you send them the specs for the drive module?"

"Yes, indeedy," Jenkins replied. "I have now, officially, violated the PATRIOT Act by providing aliens of unknown origin with classified information."

"Better you than me," Ensign Dubauer told him with a grin. She turned to McLaughlin. "So when do you think we'll be ready?"

"They're going to send us some specs for interfacing our containment chamber with their ... whatever—"

"I thought the official term was thingamabob," Lorie Dubauer interjected.

"Only for Navy types," Mac said, with a wave of his hand. "We technical people are much more comfortable with 'whatever' because it allows for a greater range of possibility."

"Anyway," Jenkins said heavily, bringing their levity to an end, "from what I get from Old Shouter over there, they should have something run up in a few minutes."

"And then?" Mac raised an eyebrow.

"Then we get to do an EVA, pick up their parts, attach them to our propulsion module, and …" Jenkins waved a hand.

"The captain says we'll be able to boost at a steady one gee," Dubauer said in a tone that mixed longing and surprise.

"Actually, you'll be boosting at over 53 gees but the eetees say that you'll only feel a steady one gee," Jenkins corrected mildly.

"And get back to the Moon in less than a day," Dubauer said, shaking her head in amazement.

"And if not, we'll be sure to do you up a proper wake," Jenkins told her gravely.

"Is that why the whole MAM team isn't being sent?" Dubauer asked, glancing to MacLaughlin.

"Now, Ensign, you heard what the captain said," Mac told her. "There's only so much room on *Voyager* and the more we save, the more room you have for supplies on the return."

Ensign Dubauer's lips twitched.

"We're going to have Harry with us," Mac reminded her, referring to Chief Harry Long, *Voyager's* non-commissioned propulsion technician, "I figure he'll sniff out any trouble before any of us notice it."

Lorie Dubauer gave him a quick grin. Chief Long's ability with propulsion systems seemed almost magic.

"In the meantime, Ensign, Sally and I will be studying up back here on *Harmonie*," Jenkins said, trying to sound soulful and put upon. "You can imagine how the two of us will slave long hours trying to fathom this technology."

"Two days," Dubauer said. "We'll be back in two days. I'd be very surprised if even *you* could make sense of it in two days."

"Yeah, but Sally …" Jenkins said with a grin.

"Miss Norman is an entirely different matter," Ensign Dubauer agreed. "She'll probably have worked out a whole new hardware interface."

"And have sold it to the aliens at a profit," Mac added.

"Actually, that'll be *my* job," Jenkins said. He frowned. "Uh-oh, more from the Shouter." He read over the new message, glanced around to see if Mac and the ensign had seen it all, then said, "So, who won the toss?"

In answer, Ensign Dubauer punched up a comm channel and said, "Captain, they're ready."

"Very well," Captain Steele responded from her position on *Harmonie's* bridge. She spoke off-screen for a moment, then said, "Tell them we're sending the EVA team now."

"That'll be Harry and Lieutenant Murray," Mac said to Jenkins.

Jenkins raised an eyebrow. "I didn't think *Harmonie* would send their chief engineer."

Mac snorted. "Apparently, Lieutenant Murray was rather insistent." He smiled as he recalled the Englishman's vehemence in dealing with his captain. "And he's got more EVA time than the next two people put together."

"Huh," Jenkins said. He flicked a couple of switches, pointed to a new screen and said, "External monitors, active."

"Systems safe," Mac said, pulling up a checklist that he'd hung at his side.

Ensign Dubauer moved into position and called back, "Systems safe."

They took two more minutes to complete their checklist. Mac nodded to the ensign when they were done and she, with a dimpled smile, contacted the captain. "All systems safe, Skipper."

"Roger," Captain Steele acknowledged crisply. A moment later, she relayed the news to *Harmonie's* watch crew.

* * *

"We're all green. Let's get going, Mr. Long," Lieutenant Peter Murray said to his American colleague.

"Aye aye, sir," Harry Long said. "Thrusting."

"Confirmed," Captain Steele called. "Prepare to activate EVA activity list one."

"EVA AL1 loaded and primed," Lieutenant Murray said. A moment later Chief Long echoed him.

"ET1 confirms your separation from *Harmonie*," Lieutenant Ives reported from communications a few seconds later.

"That's quick," Murray muttered to himself.

"'Bout what we expected, sir," Chief Long said.

"Confirm reticle sighting," Captain Steele said, continuing with the flight checklist.

"Reticle sighting … confirmed," Lieutenant Murray said a moment later as he double-checked his sight alignment with the nearer of the two alien ships.

"Confirmed," Chief Long echoed once again.

"Roger, we have you on radar," Captain Steele informed them. A moment later, she added, "Tracking confirms that you are on course. Continue with the mission."

"Aye aye, ma'am," Murray replied. A moment later, in a lower voice he said to Chief Long, "Nice sight, isn't it?"

"Yes, sir!"

* * *

"Heart-rates are nominal," Lieutenant Svoboda, *Harmonie's* chief medical officer reported. She smiled at Lieutenant Commander Reynaud as she pulled the ultrasound probe back off her belly and wiped it clean. "I'd say that everything is progressing perfectly." She glanced to the other woman in the room. "Do you have anything to add?"

Petty Officer 2nd Class Louise O'Reilly took a careful look at the various monitors before responding, "Looking good, Lieutenant." She smiled at the French commander, who was readjusting her clothing. "I'd say you're doing just fine, ma'am." As Elodie Reynaud rose from the examining table in *Harmonie's* half-gee section, PO O'Reilly added, "Although, Commander, I do have one request."

Elodie raised an eyebrow in elegant question.

Louise glanced to the medical officer before saying, "I think the lieutenant and I would both be much relieved if you'd promise to undertake in no more biological experiments until we get you back safely to the Moon."

Elodie Reynaud blushed and bobbed her head.

"We don't want any accidents," Lieutenant Svoboda added. She allowed her lips to twitch upwards. "Or should I say, any *more* accidents."

* * *

"Contact," Lieutenant Murray reported.

"Roger, we confirm contact," Captain Zhukov replied from *Harmonie's* command deck, having relieved Captain Steele, who had returned to *Voyager's* bridge in preparation for the second part of the EVA. "You are 'Go' for maneuver."

"Roger, 'Go' for thrust," Murray responded. "Thrusters engaged."

The crews had decided that Murray's suit thrusters would be sufficient and set Chief Long's as reserve. Both suits had enough thrust to complete the mission individually.

"Stand by," Zhukov said, waving over at his crewman on tracking. The crewman frowned over the display for a moment, then gave his captain a thumbs-up. "Tracking confirms your burn."

"Roger," Murray replied. "Three … two … one … cutoff."

Again Zhukov waved at tracking and waited impatiently until the crewman gave him another thumbs-up.

"Good burn," Zhukov said. "Tracking confirms you on intercept for the MAM module."

"Roger," Murray replied. "Estimate one zero minutes to intercept."

"Roger," Zhukov glanced again to Tracking. The crewman nodded. "Tracking confirms, one zero minutes to intercept." A moment later he added, "Time for a nap if you want, Peter."

Far outside in the vacuum of space, Peter Murray snorted. "With this scenery?"

"Lieutenant Murray, Chief Long, this is *Voyager*," Emily called.

"Go ahead, *Voyager*," Chief Long responded.

"Prepare EVA AL3," Emily said.

"Roger, preparing AL3," Chief Long replied. AL3 was the deceleration and docking checklist; they were currently working through the end of AL2, the capture and cruise list.

* * *

Ynoyon

Security head Su-la-ij-an contacted the captain, saying, ⸌**Our sensors indicate that the humans have rendezvoused with their MAM propulsion unit.**⸍

⸌**Very good,**⸍ Sa-li-ri-to replied. Su-la-ij-an was convinced that parasites inhabited every shadow and was more willing to bite than to chew; Sa-li-ri-to had ordered them to report mostly to assure themself that the security officer hadn't engaged its weaponry without authorization.

~I do not understand why the spiders simply didn't use their tractor beam, Captain,~ Su-la-ij-an noted in a tone full of suspicion.

~We agreed that it was better to not startle the Earthers too much,~ Sa-la-ri-to assured them calmly. ~Remember, we want them as partners, not subatomic particles.~

~Partners?~ Su-la-ij-an replied. ~I thought we were going to make profit on them.~

~There is short-term profit and long-term profit, Security,~ Sa-li-ri-to reminded them. ~It is one thing to make a large profit once and quite another to make a decent profit for our offspring.~

~Oh,~ Su-la-ij-an said. ~Our offspring will trade with these humans?~

~Hopefully at greater profit than our ancestors,~ the captain said.

There was a pause as the security chief digested this. ~That would be good.~

~I'm so glad you agree,~ Sa-li-ri-to replied with ill-disguised acerbity.

~We shall continue to monitor events,~ Su-la-ij-an said stiffly.

~And keep us informed,~ Sa-li-ri-to reminded.

~As you say,~ the security chief confirmed, closing the connection.

* * *

"Okay, Lorie, it's up to you," Captain Steele called over her comm link.

"Roger, Captain, preparing for EVA AL9," Ensign Dubauer replied through her suit comm. She and Commander Geister had rendezvoused with the MAM module slightly before Lieutenant Murray and Chief Long came to a stop, with the alien payload just one meter away from the top of the MAM module.

"Now the fun starts," Mac said from his perch behind Captain Steele.

"Status check," Captain Zhukov called from *Harmonie*.

"*Voyager*, all systems go," Emily told him quickly.

"EVA team two, set," Commander Geister replied quickly. There had been some argument against having the commander on the EVA, but he'd pointed out that he was one of the most experienced officers in extra-vehicular activity, adding that as he would be a watch officer on the return trip, it behooved him to ensure that everything was in the best possible order.

"EVA one, set," Lieutenant Murray reported.

"This is *Harmonie*," Captain Zhukov now said, "activate AL9."

"Initiating AL9," Commander Geister said. "Removing access ports 23, 24, 25."

"Roger," Emily said. She glanced over to Mac, who hung upside down behind her, his eyes glued to a different set of monitors.

"Green light on 23 and 24," Mac reported. A moment later he added, "Green on 25."

"Confirming, access ports 23, 24, 25 open," Commander Geister said.

"We show that here," Emily confirmed.

"Now we get to the really tricky part," Mac muttered.

"Ensign Dubauer, are you in place?" Emily said, ignoring him.

"In place, Skipper."

"This is Chief Long, I'm in place too, Captain," Chief Long said.

Emily nodded to herself but said nothing. In a monitor, Captain Zhukov's face showed concern. He said, "Captain Steele?"

"For what we are about to receive," Emily murmured. Louder, she said, "Commence AL10."

"Activity List one zero," Commander Geister repeated. "Ensign Dubauer, close the valve on your ambient helium feed."

"AH Feed 3 closed," Ensign Dubauer reported a moment later.

"Chief Long," Geister prompted.

A moment later, Chief Long reported, "Connecting valve MAM-4 closed."

"Visual confirmation," Emily ordered.

"I'm on it," Lieutenant Murray said. It took him some moments before he confirmed, "I have visually inspected and confirm that line 4 is isolated."

"Roger," Emily said. "You may proceed."

"And with this, we say goodbye to our MAM drive," Mac said mournfully.

"I know," Emily agreed in a soft voice.

"If the aliens have sold us a bill of goods, we've got a long walk home, Captain," Mac added.

"We're starting to turn," Chief Long reported. There was a long silence and then he said, "Okay, ambient helium disconnected."

"Confirmed," Emily said in a flat, professional voice.

"Removing the feed line," Ensign Dubauer said. Minutes later, she said, "Line cleared."

"Ready for AL11," Commander Geister reported.

"Roger. Commence AL11," Emily said. She glanced at the master timer and saw that nearly three hours had elapsed. "Med check."

A moment later, Lieutenant Svoboda replied, "All suits nominal."

"That's a relief," Mac said.

"I thought you wanted to add more hours to your log book," Emily teased. Mac snorted and shook his head. He was slated as the second backup; Lieutenant Cohen was already suited and waiting at the egress module just in case.

"Okay, so all they have to do is run the plumbing between the helium tank and the antimatter containment unit, and then slide this mating collar over our interface module, and we're set, right?" Mac said.

"That's what the aliens say," Emily replied. "Then our guys reverse the flow on the AM valve—"

"And hope everything goes right or there's going to be a bright flash," Mac muttered.

"And hope everything goes right," Emily said. "Then we dock *Voyager* back to the propulsion unit, test the interface couplings, and … we're off."

"Sort of like hooking up a nuclear reactor to a horse and buggy," Mac said sourly.

"Who was it that said, 'Any sufficiently advanced technology is indistinguishable from magic'?" Jim Pickett called from his link on *Harmonie*.

"Arthur C. Clarke," Captain Zhukov replied immediately.

"Well, this is clearly not magic," Pickett said.

"Yeah, that makes it engineering, which means it can go wrong," Mac muttered.

"It also means we can possibly understand it," Pickett reminded him. Mac accepted this with a grunt.

"Bypass inserted," Commander Geister reported.

"Confirmed," Lieutenant Murray said. "We're ready to mate the alien artifact."

"Roger, commence AL12," Emily responded.

"You worked hard to keep us from having a thirteenth activity list, didn't you, Skipper?" Mac asked *sotto voce*.

"Anything that takes that long requires switching crews," Emily declared.

"Da," Captain Zhukov agreed from his ship.

"Lieutenant Cohen, get ready," Emily called.

"Righto, Skipper," Alan Cohen called back cheerfully.

"I'll go check his suit," Mac said, moving away quickly.

"He's been out before, you know," Emily called after him. Mac sketched an agreeing wave but said nothing. Alan Cohen was more than competent as *Voyager's* navigation officer, and had been eager to add to his EVA log book—although this maneuver would nearly double his hours in a spacesuit. After a moment, she called on her comm, "Lieutenant McElroy to the bridge."

Danielle McElroy arrived moments later and seated herself.

"Bring up the separation checklist, Danni."

"On it, Skip," Danielle McElroy assured her with an easy grace. While Alan Cohen was competent, Lieutenant McElroy was probably the shining light in Captain Steele's command. Emily had earmarked her for early command and always found the younger woman's enthusiasm and professionalism a joy to treasure.

"*Harmonie*, this is *Voyager*, preparatory to separation," Danielle called over the comm link.

"This is *Harmonie*, Acknowledged," Lieutenant Ives replied. Just as Danielle had been seconded to handling the separation on *Voyager's* side, so had Lieutenant Ives over on *Harmonie*.

"I've got a green light," Emily called to the EVA team. "I confirm solid contact with the AA."

"Roger, we confirm that the alien artifact is mated with the propulsion module."

"Okay, everyone, time to come back," Emily called.

* * *

"Why the long face, Ambassador?" Captain Zhukov said, as the jubilant crews gathered for a celebratory dinner. "We have made history today."

"Certainly," Pickett said, carefully schooling his expression into something more cheerful. "I was just thinking …"

"Eh?" Emily Steele had noticed the exchange and now glanced between the Eurocos captain and the American ambassador.

"It isn't that we've cannibalized our most advanced propulsion system, nor that we've accepted an alien technology with hardly a quibble …" Both captains were now frankly staring at him. He shrugged. "It's that I've got to wonder what they learned from it all."

"How do you mean?" Captain Steele said.

"Well, we've told them that we have an emergency and yet we're taking a sleep cycle before we detach *Voyager's* crew and command module from *Harmonie* and start her back to the—to Luna," Pickett finished, hastily amending himself to use the more internationally recognized name. Officially, it was called the Confederated Colonies of Luna, but as the majority of the colonies were under control of the Japanese, there was a lot of grumbling at the notion of allowing Luna a separate seat on the United Nations—and some notion that *that* organization should be named the United Interplanetary Nations.

"Well, they have to know that we sleep," Emily said.

"True," Pickett agreed, "but what they've learned is how quickly we can react in an emergency situation."

"Which is pretty damned quick," Emily said, glancing to Captain Zhukov for support.

"Indeed. I am amazed at how quickly we managed to produce procedures for something this radical," Zhukov allowed. Privately, he planned to write a rather lengthy and detailed report to various parties back on Earth suggesting that, as an example of coordination and improvisation, this was unique in history—with special attention to be paid to the lessons learned.

"That's what I mean," Pickett said, his features twitching toward a frown and back again when he caught himself. "What I'm saying is that the aliens now know how quickly we can cobble something together under the direst circumstances."

Zhukov's brows furrowed in consternation.

"I see what you mean," Emily said. "Well, we did *have* an emergency and we did show how quickly we could hack something together, so I don't think it's all bad."

"If we're quicker than the aliens, it may be cause for alarm," Pickett said. "And if we're slower than the aliens, it may be cause for complacency."

Captain Zhukov smiled knowingly to Captain Steele. "We discussed this earlier."

Now Pickett looked surprised.

"I'm pleased to say that we are at least ahead of you on this one, Mr. Ambassador," Emily said, smiling back at the Russian captain.

"I suspect it's a result of our years of learned military paranoia," Zhukov murmured.

"What?" Pickett demanded.

"Well, that sleep cycle?" Emily responded. Pickett nodded slowly. "Do you think we really needed it?"

"So you're putting one over on the aliens?"

"Officially, we're just ensuring that our crews are safely rested for our final evolutions," Emily replied. "Besides, it gives time for Commander Geister to familiarize himself with my ship."

"I'm actually sorry to lose him," Zhukov confided. "I'm sorry to lose *both* of them, although I'm glad that I finally discovered the reason for their ... disquieting behaviors."

"Well, I'm glad to hear that you injected some disinformation into the flow to the aliens," Pickett said, raising his glass to the captains. They nodded in return. "Am I to presume that the sleep cycle won't be the same for all our crews?"

The two captains smiled and nodded again. "We've got the science team working on everything we can pass them and we've upped the size of our night watch to allow us to process what we've got from the aliens on their gravity drive."

"Won't the increased computer use give that away?" Pickett asked.

"It could," Emily agreed. "If they've been monitoring us that closely and know how to interpret the data."

"In which case we'll be learning more about their capabilities," Captain Zhukov observed.

"But we can always say that the extra computing power was being used to work out the course to Luna and other parts of the emergency mission," Emily added.

"So they might guess but they won't know," Pickett murmured approvingly. The two captains exchanged pleased looks. Pickett raised his glass and swallowed the last of his drink. Rising from his chair, he said, "I've got some dispatches of my own to write."

"Do you need a crewman to guide you to your quarters?" Captain Zhukov asked, rising out of courtesy from his chair.

"No," Pickett said, waving him back down, "I can manage, thank you."

Shortly after the ambassador left, the dinner broke up. Captain Zhukov invited Captain Steele back to his cabin for a final consultation.

"Without betraying national security, how long do you think you will be on your mission?" Captain Zhukov asked as they entered his spacious cabin—"spacious" being a relative term. Zhukov's cabin included enough room to have a partition between his sleeping area and his working area, including a number of comfortable folding chairs, allowing him a somewhat secluded area in which to conduct private meetings such as this.

"A day each way, a day for everyone to recover from the shock ..." Emily's voice faded as her eyes grew unfocused while she concentrated on the problem.

Zhukov suddenly found himself staring at a much younger face—more open, less guarded. A face that was quite attractive, he realized. He coughed to distract himself from that line of thinking. The noise distracted Captain Steele and her eyes focused back on the present.

"Sorry," Zhukov murmured.

"Five days at least, maybe seven," Emily said crisply. "That is, if everything works as planned."

"Of course," Nikolai Zhukov agreed.

"It could be that they're taking advantage of our situation to cripple your command and eliminate mine," Emily said.

"That is a possibility," Captain Zhukov agreed. "Perhaps even one that your—our—ambassador may not have considered."

"It's a long shot, really," Emily said. "Pickett's right. If they wanted to hurt us, they would have gone straight to Earth and launched an attack."

"What sort of an attack?"

"Easiest thing to do would be an epoch-changing meteor," Emily replied with a quick shrug.

"Twenty years ago they might have succeeded," Zhukov said. "But now? With your Six Sigma?" He shook his head. "I think not."

Six Sigma was the name generally applied to the U.S. Spacewatch; a collection of earthbound and orbiting telescopes, courier ships, interceptors, and other spacecraft designed to guarantee within six standard deviations, 99.99966%, that no object was on an intercept course with Earth—and to intercept and deflect any that was.

"Maybe that's why they waited," Emily said. "Until we had Six Sigma, we couldn't guarantee that they *wouldn't* consider such an option."

"Possibly," Zhukov allowed with a wave of one hand, "or they might have waited until the Manhattan Meteor created such a change in the balance of power."

"You mean they were unwilling to deal with a lone superpower?" Emily asked with a snort. "Wouldn't that have been easier?"

"Perhaps," Zhukov replied. "We can't know for certain as we have never had dealings with aliens before."

"That we know of," Emily corrected. Nikolai raised an eyebrow. "There were all those UFO sightings through history."

Nikolai shrugged, his face impassive.

"Well, that's neither here nor there," Emily said with a shrug of her own, "and I propose that we do something very unmilitary and discard all the worst scenarios in favor of the better and best scenarios."

"Normally, it's wise to plan for the worst," Captain Zhukov said.

"The worst is that the aliens are leading us down the garden path and will destroy *Voyager* and *Harmonie* on their own schedule, for their own very alien reasons."

"Or for very human reasons," Captain Zhukov countered. "Perhaps to keep this encounter a secret?"

"As I said, I think there's no profit to be had in planning for annihilation," Emily replied. "I think that we need to consider what happens when *Voyager* returns and what we'll do next."

"In which case we should get the ambassador to join us," Captain Zhukov said.

Emily pursed her lips. Then she shook her head. "I think, for the moment, we should consider the military implications."

Nikolai regarded her in silence before slowly nodding his head.

CHAPTER NINE

Moonbesu Nihongo, Near Side, Luna

"ADMIRAL, WE ARE GETTING A STRANGE COMMUNICATION RELAYED FROM THE Americans," Ensign Sato alerted Admiral Isao Tsukino, ranking officer of Moonbesu Nihongo, Japan's premiere moon base.

"Yes?"

"They claim to be onboard the *Voyager* and requesting contact with you," Ensign Sato continued.

"Put them through," Admiral Tsukino said, suppressing a sigh. The Americans were always "viewing with alarm" and "suggesting" or acting out in their various ways. *Voyager* was a Navy ship so Admiral Tsukino expected—

"Admiral Tsukino, you are connected," Ensign Sato said, clearly making the announcement to both parties.

"Admiral Tsukino?" a female voice inquired. There was something odd with the signal. "This is Captain Emily Steele of the spaceship *Voyager*."

"Captain Steele, how may I help you?"

"I'm inbound from Jupiter on the *Voyager*," Captain Steele replied. "I have Commanders Reynaud and Geister from *Harmonie* along with me. Commander Reynaud is pregnant and in need of prolonged medical care."

"I see," Admiral Tsukino said slowly while thinking rapidly. "And Commander Geister?"

"Commander Geister is the father-to-be," Emily explained tersely. "Captain Zhukov has detached the pair for the duration. My understanding is that your medical facilities are the most advanced on Luna. I request their use in this humanitarian case."

That would give the Moonbesu a great deal of clout, particularly when any similar "incidents" occurred. It was a strange, if plum, offering.

"We are also requesting that you aid us in resupply," Captain Steele continued, "and I've another request that Captain Zhukov and I would like you to receive in private."

"Is your ship capable of landing?"

"We would prefer an orbital transfer," Captain Steele replied.

Admiral Tsukino schooled his face firmly, even though the conversation was without visuals; he didn't want anyone on his staff to guess at his mood.

"You say you came from Jupiter?" Admiral Tsukino asked, bringing up a separate window on his display and tapping in course vectors.

"Indeed, Admiral, in a rather precipitous manner," Captain Steele agreed. "I would be happy to say more in private."

"Very well, I'll have a shuttle sent to rendezvous with your ship; you may come down with it," the admiral replied, keeping a predatory gleam out of his eyes. It was a rare American captain who disobeyed orders; perhaps the admiral would be able to negotiate this situation to Japan's great advantage.

"I'd prefer it if you met me aboard, Admiral," Captain Steele replied. "Time is of the essence, sir."

"Very well," Admiral Tsukino said. "Let my comm tech know your resupply requirements, and I'll scramble up to you on a shuttle when you're in orbit." He paused. "And when might that be, Captain?"

"Twenty minutes, sir," Emily Steele replied with a touch of humor in her voice.

"Then we shall dock with you in thirty minutes, Captain," Admiral Tsukino replied, rising from his comfortable chair and gesturing peremptorily for his staff.

* * *

Voyager had the standardized docking collar at the front of the ship, and the Moonbesu shuttle had no problem making the rendezvous. There was a quiet flutter while pressure seals were checked, and then the pilot announced that they were opening the hatch.

Admiral Tsukino was the first one through, and found himself entering into a crowded but functional command deck. A trim woman moved forward easily in the microgravity, sketched a quick salute, and then extended her hand to him.

"Captain Emily Steele, United States Navy, commander of the XSS *Voyager*," she said.

"Admiral Tsukino," the admiral said, grasping her hand firmly but releasing it quickly. Two commanders in the garb of Eurocos moved to introduce themselves. The Frenchwoman was not quite noticeably pregnant, but the admiral had no trouble accepting the fact.

"We thank you for your hospitality on such short notice, Admiral," Commander Geister said a bit stiffly.

"Admiral, if you don't mind, we're going to need to get those two dirtside; our medicos want Commander Reynaud back in a gravity well as soon as possible," Emily said demurely.

"I understand," the admiral said, gesturing for the two commanders to head toward the shuttle. As they moved by, he nodded to Captain Steele. "You said you wished to speak with me?"

Emily smiled and nodded. "Would you join me in the galley, sir?"

The admiral motioned for her to lead the way.

* * *

The galley was cozy, as was to be expected. What was not expected was the other man already seated. He rose when the admiral entered.

"Admiral Tsukino, this is John McLaughlin, the project leader for our MAM system," Captain Steele said.

"I thought we were having a private conversation, Captain," the admiral said with the beginnings of a frown.

"I thought you'd prefer to hear some of this from Mac directly, sir," Emily said.

Admiral Tsukino glanced at the grizzled man for a moment, and then allowed himself to settle in his seat.

"You may have noticed that we made good time getting here from Jupiter," Captain Steele said.

"Indeed."

"In fact, Admiral, we boosted at a steady 53-plus gees while internally we experienced lunar normal," Captain Steele explained. "You may have noticed the strange attachment at the end of our command module."

"And we used less than a tenth of a kilogram of antimatter," Mr. McLaughlin added.

"This is alien technology?" Admiral Tsukino said, turning to Captain Steele for confirmation.

"They donated it to aid us in our emergency," Captain Steele said.

"I suspect it's only the tip of the iceberg," Mr. McLaughlin added.

"And why would that be, Mr. McLaughlin?" Admiral Tsukino asked.

"Please, sir, call me 'Mac.'"

"Only if you call me 'Admiral,'" Tsukino said with a straight face.

Mac gave him a look and muttered, "Not my first choice but …" and louder said, "Well, Admiral, these aliens seem to want to trade with us."

"Really?"

"They say that they were confused by the signatures from *Harmonie's* fusion drive and our MAM drive into thinking that we'd developed FTL travel."

"'Confused'?"

Mac gave him a wry grin. "Exactly my thought, Admiral. Particularly when you consider that for our normal parallax, they'd have to have detected our signatures over twelve thousand light-years away."

"I see," Admiral Tsukino said, glancing toward the US Navy captain.

"I spoke with Captain Zhukov, sir, and we feel that—well, militarily, we feel—we are well over our heads," Captain Steele told him.

"So you'd like me to come out there with you and make this an even bigger international disgrace?" Tsukino guessed.

"Success is what we're hoping for," Emily replied, "but we feel that having an admiral with your known abilities available in real time would be a great advantage, sir."

"Why me?"

"You're the nearest," Mac told him bluntly. "Also, while Eurocos and the U.S. are well represented, there, so far, is no representation from Japan."

"We'd like to present a consensus if possible," Emily said.

"And if it all goes into the crapper, you can blame it on the little Jap," Tsukino said dryly.

"Admiral, if it 'goes into the crapper,' we'll all be dead," Emily told him.

"I note, Captain, that you and Captain Zhukov have not tried to get some superior in your chain of command," Admiral Tsukino said.

"Sir, you *know* the sort of superiors we have," Emily told him frankly. "They've made their reputations saying 'no' and 'not possible.'" She looked at him and shook her head. "That's not the reputation you have, sir."

"Which is why I've been banished to the Moon."

"Bullshit!" Mac burst out. The two officers glanced at him, surprised. "Sir, you don't expect anyone except the lamest of your superiors to buy that bullshit. You certainly can't expect any spacer to!"

Admiral Tsukino raised an eyebrow.

"You're here, sir, because you're too good at what you do to stand by and let some jackass screw it up," Mac said. "Which is why we need you at Jupiter, sir. Because this is the most important thing that's ever happened to us and we need the best."

Admiral Tsukino turned his head to Captain Steele.

"He's right, sir," Emily said. "You know that everyone in the different services keeps an eye on the other services." She waited for him to respond and, when he didn't, continued, "Captain Zhukov and I have both watched your career with a mixture of panic and elation—"

"Panic, Captain?" Tsukino said mildly.

"Sir, the number of times we were sure you'd be called home …" Emily told him, shaking her head in amazement.

"Anyway, Admiral, you have to come with us," Mac said.

"I do?"

"We took two people off the ship, we need to bring two back, plus the mass difference," Mac said glibly. "Because none of us knows this alien antigravity system well enough to figure out how to account for the mass difference."

"And how, Mr. McLaughlin, do you explain all the extra mass of supplies we're loading?" Admiral Tsukino asked.

"Well, we'd already accounted for that with the eetees," Mac said. "We told them we'd be bringing about three tons of supplies back and they told us which buttons to push when we were ready."

"Really?" Admiral Tsukino said, looking toward Captain Steele.

"Actually, Admiral, it really is that way," Emily said. "We're like old wooden ship sailors suddenly launched into the age of steam."

"And so you figured that we survived your Commodore Perry once, we should be able to handle a whole new batch of aliens?" Admiral Tsukino asked with a straight face.

"Well, Japan's had a great deal of experience in that area," Mac admitted.

"And you Americans are more used to being on the giving than the receiving end of things," Admiral Tsukino said.

"Really, sir, we just think that having the best minds—open minds—available is to all our advantage," Emily said.

Admiral Tsukino glanced from her to the engineer and back before sighing. He lifted his wrist communicator to his lips.

"Ensign Sato," he said.

"Communications, Ensign Sato, Admiral," a young woman's voice came back promptly.

"Execute Rainbow," Admiral Tsukino said.

"Very well, Admiral," Ensign Sato replied. "Operation Rainbow has been activated. Shall I join you?"

In response to the surprised looks of the Americans, Admiral Tsukino said, "She's my plus one."

"And you've singled her out as an up-and-comer for early promotion, partly because of her excellent political contacts but mostly because she's been consistently rated excellent in all her duties," Emily Steele said, taking in his growing surprise with a satisfied look. "She's also cute as a button."

"And likes girls," Admiral Tsukino admitted with a sigh. "Something which is a huge selling point with my wife."

"Well, I know—"

"Mac, you're not to play matchmaker," Emily warned him.

"Yes, ma'am," Mac agreed, adding under his breath, "I'll leave that to you."

Captain Steele glowered at him before returning her attention to the admiral. "Sir, you are now the ranking officer of the Jupiter Mission."

"And, conveniently, have absolutely no standing in your chain of command," Admiral Tsukino replied with a wry grin. "It is something that both you and Captain Zhukov are both noted for." He paused a moment then said, "How soon can we leave?"

"As soon as our supplies are loaded, Admiral," Captain Steele reported, "and when your ensign arrives."

"That will only take her as long as is necessary to bring her gear and mine across from the shuttle," Admiral Tsukino said, taking quiet delight in the expressions of the two Americans. "Do you wish to communicate with your superiors at Far Side Base?"

"Um ... no, if you don't mind, Admiral," Emily said, her cheeks going pink.

"It's okay, Skipper, I sent them a time-delayed whip squeal with the latest," Mac said. "I can append it to say that we've invited Admiral Tsukino along as liaison for Japan."

"That won't be necessary, Mr. McLaughlin," Admiral Tsukino told him. "My second-in-command will shortly have instructions on that matter."

"We should break orbit as soon as we can, Admiral," Emily said.

"Yes, I'd like to see these new additions to our solar neighborhood," the Admiral said. He turned his head to the ship, adding, "And I'm sure you want to show off your latest capabilities."

"I'd be happier if I could explain them to you, Admiral," Emily admitted, "I surely would!"

*   *   *

The White House, Washington, DC

"Mr. President, you should see this," Ron Grimminger said as he burst into the Oval Office. He grabbed a remote and flicked on the TV.

"Ron, we're in the middle of planning what we're going to do with the veep—" Secretary of State Ellington said before the sound of the TV cut him off.

"—reporting from Goldstone, this is Jennifer Smith," a young news reporter was saying. "We've just received confirmation that a spaceship approached lunar orbit at an unheard-of acceleration and then departed on a course for Jupiter." Jennifer pulled someone into view. "With me is Christopher Rogers of the Deep Space Network. Tell me, Mr. Rogers, what does this mean?"

"We've identified the ship as an experimental U.S. Navy ship," Rogers said. "Beyond that, I cannot speculate."

"Oh, geez, turn it off!" President Merritt shouted, waving wildly. Grimminger complied. "What's it mean, and why didn't we know sooner?"

"I don't know what it means, sir," Grimminger replied. "Except that we're pretty much at the end of our cover up and we're going to have to go live before we find ourselves buried under a flood of questions."

"If that was *Voyager*, why didn't we hear from them?" George Morgan demanded of Elijah Wood, the Navy secretary.

Wood shrugged. "Perhaps we'll hear something through the network."

"Then Rogers should have told us," Grimminger said. His phone rang and he flipped it open. He held up a hand to the group and listened closely in the ensuing silence. "Oh, my god!"

"What?" The president demanded.

"I don't believe it," Grimminger said, hanging up and pocketing his phone. "We just got confirmation from Deep Ear," he said to the others. "*Voyager* rendezvoused with a shuttle from the Japanese moon base, debarked Commanders Reynaud and Geister of the *Harmonie*, and took Admiral Isao Tsukino and his comm officer with them."

"Kidnapped?" Morgan grunted in surprise. "They kidnapped a Jap?"

"No, apparently they went willingly," Grimminger said.

"What's it mean, then?" the president demanded.

Grimminger shook his head. "I don't know, sir. But Deep Ear verifies that *Voyager* was accelerating at fifty-three gees."

"Fifty-three gees?" the president repeated.

"Fifty-three times the force of gravity," Grimminger expanded.

"A human body can only take about twelve gravities before it gets crushed," Admiral

Roberts, Admiral Kinnock's replacement, said.

"*Voyager* could never generate that sort of power," Grimminger said.

"So there's a mistake," the president decided.

"No, sir," Grimminger said, shaking his head. "No mistake. Deep Ear and the Deep Space Network both confirm the acceleration. At that rate, *Voyager* will be back at Jupiter in less than a day."

"But it took three weeks to get there in the first place!" Brian McPhee exclaimed.

"Yes, sir," Grimminger agreed. "Our best technology can get to Jupiter in three weeks. They got to the Moon from there in a day. And they'll get back in a day."

"And at a speed that kills humans," Admiral Roberts noted sourly.

"So what does that mean?" the president asked.

"Aliens have got the ship," Roberts said. Grimminger spluttered but the admiral steamrollered over him. "What else can it mean?"

"They were communicating with the Japanese," Grimminger pointed out.

"So the aliens know our languages," Roberts replied.

Grimminger's phone rang again and he answered it. This time, he didn't have to wave for silence.

"I see," he said after a moment. "Keep us informed." He pocketed the phone again. "We have a decode from the DSN. Captain Steele reports that she returned with *Voyager* to debark Commanders Reynaud and Geister at the Japanese moon base because Commander Reynaud is pregnant and they needed the best possible medical facilities in the shortest time.

"The aliens responded to the emergency by providing us with a specially rigged antigravity drive," Grimminger concluded. "The crew of the *Voyager* and *Harmonie* are in good condition. *Voyager* has acquired more supplies for both ships and is returning to continue with the mission."

"So *not* aliens," the president said, turning to Admiral Roberts.

The admiral's eyes were glazed with amazement. "They've got an antigravity drive!"

"What's that mean?" the president asked.

"It means, sir," Grimminger said, before the admiral could respond with something acidic, "that the aliens have given us, free of charge, a way to colonize the entire solar system."

"So, they're *good* aliens?" the president said, turning from advisor to advisor for confirmation.

"Maybe," Grimminger said finally.

* * *

Harmonie, Jupiter Orbit

"So, what have you got?" Jim Pickett said to the two bleary-eyed technicians the next morning.

"A splitting headache," Chris Jenkins said. Sally Norman grunted in agreement.

"Anything from the scientists?" Sally asked hopefully.

Pickett shook his head.

"I would have been surprised," Chris said. "I'll bet they're like us—they've got plenty of theories but no way to test them."

"Well, tell me what we do know," Pickett said.

"We know that *Voyager* pulled away at a steady 53 gees while maintaining only one-sixth gee internally," Sally said. "So that means that the alien tech can support a gravity differential of nearly 54 gees—"

"And do it for nearly a day on just a hundred grams of antimatter," Chris finished. "Sally, Dr. Ney, and all the others did a search through the theoretical abstracts that are available and came up with a good three hundred solid leads."

"Three hundred?" Pickett was surprised.

"The thing is, that means that probably two hundred and ninety-nine are wrong," Sally told him.

"They could all be wrong," Chris said. "The aliens could have discovered something we just don't know."

"Really, we don't have enough data to begin to come up with an answer," Sally said.

"Well, I know that Mr. McLaughlin on *Voyager* will be getting as much telemetry as he can," Pickett assured them.

"I'm sure he will," Sally agreed. "It's just …"

"Just?" Pickett prompted.

"'Any sufficiently advanced technology is indistinguishable from magic,'" Chris said, quoting Arthur C. Clarke's famous observation.

"Which means that we're in luck," Pickett said.

The two technicians gave him questioning looks.

"It's obviously not that sufficiently advanced because we *can* distinguish it from magic," Pickett told them.

Jenkin's expression slowly changed to one of enlightenment.

"Keep at it, you two," Pickett said, rising from his seat and giving them a reassuring grin.

"Aye, sir." Sally Norman replied.

As Jim Pickett turned to leave, the overhead speaker called out, "Will the ambassador report to the bridge, please?"

The two technicians exchanged looks with Pickett who shrugged and moved off with a wave, "Duty calls."

The bridge of *Harmonie* was a short distance from where Jenkins and Norman were working, so Jim Pickett arrived in less than a minute. Captain Zhukov, Lieutenant Milano, and Ensign Strasnoye were huddled near the communications section; Pickett met them there.

"*Voyager* is returning," Captain Zhukov told him.

"And?" Pickett prompted, realizing that the captain would not have called for him simply with that news.

"The aliens have sent another communication," Captain Zhukov said, pursing his lips tightly. Pickett raised an eyebrow. "They want to know what we'd like to trade."

"For what?" Pickett replied immediately. The others looked startled and he realized that they weren't used to politicians or trades.

"They didn't say," Captain Zhukov admitted.

"Ask them 'for what'?" Pickett said to Strasnoye. The young ensign gave his captain a quick look but Zhukov merely nodded in confirmation, so the ensign tapped out the question.

The response came back after several seconds: **We are willing to offer you access to a faster-than-light drive.**

The three officers gasped at the response but Pickett grunted. He raised an eyebrow to Zhukov and gestured to the ensign's seat at the keyboard. "May I?"

Zhukov's frown lasted for only a second before he said, "Ensign, give the ambassador your seat, please."

With a nod of thanks, Pickett took the seat from the ensign, adjusted it and pulled the keyboard into a more comfortable location.

Given the circumstances as you've described them to us, we believe that we would require not only the drive itself but a complete technical understanding of the underlying workings and associated physics, Pickett typed back slowly. Behind him Captain Zhukov and Lieutenant Milano gasped in surprise. Aloud, he said, "They claim that they thought we'd developed an interstellar drive. If we're asked, we should be able to explain how it works."

"Mmm," Zhukov murmured in agreement.

Is there a better drive than the one we would have developed with the signatures you detected? Pickett typed now. **Would you like to trade us that knowledge as well?**

"Mr. Ambassador?" Zhukov said in a disbelieving tone.

Pickett chuckled. "Captain, these guys claim to have come here because they picked up our 'faster-than-light' drive's signature. But we've got good reason to believe that that's a crock. The whole issue of the minimal distance the parallax would place them at for detection calls that whole thing into question."

"I'm sorry, Ambassador, but could you explain that more?" Lieutenant Milano asked politely. To his captain, he added, "From a navigational perspective, I understand the whole issue of parallax and distance, but I'm not sure about the rest, sir."

"Mr. Ambassador?" Zhukov said, now asking Pickett to explain.

"Lieutenant, if their claim was honest, then they would have been able to pick up a signature from over twelve thousand light-years *and* it would have to have been transmitted faster-than-light itself," Pickett said. "In fact, it would have had to have moved as several thousand times the speed of light, given that *Voyager* hasn't been operating her MAM engines that frequently and the only time the *two* signatures would have been generated was when both engines were thrusting."

"Which either would have been at the exact moment we braked into Jupiter orbit, or … when did *Voyager* first fire her MAM engines?" Lieutenant Milano said.

Pickett frowned, then gestured to Ensign Strasnoye. "Would you put that question to my two techs, Norman and Jenkins?"

Ensign Strasnoye nodded and keyed open a comm channel to the two techs. Pickett repeated the question to them.

"We only tested *Voyager* two times, Mr. Ambassador," Chris Jenkins said, a tone of reticence in his voice. Pickett guessed that he was afraid to reveal too much information.

"The aliens said they picked up signals from the MAM and the fusion drive and confused the two for an FTL signal," Pickett told him. "We need to know when that could have happened."

"I see," Jenkins replied thoughtfully. A moment later he added, "From what Sally and I remember, sir, that could only have happened when *Harmonie* fired her big engines for the orbit."

"And that was two hours before our friends appeared," Captain Zhukov said, stroking his chin thoughtfully.

"Which means that for their story to be true, the signal would have had to have traveled … how fast?" Pickett said, spreading his question between the three officers.

"Roughly three point six light-years per second," Ensign Strasnoye replied immediately, glancing to his superiors to see if they agreed. "That is, if they spent an hour between receipt of signal and arrival here."

"Which would mean that they could travel at the same speed," Lieutenant Milano noted.

"Which means that's the baseline for a decent FTL drive," Pickett said with a small smile. "Unless our friends are lying, of course."

"And if they're lying?" Captain Zhukov prompted.

"Well, then we know that they didn't detect any fake FTL signal," Pickett replied, "which means we have to wonder why they bothered appearing here when they knew that we didn't have an FTL drive."

"Doesn't it also mean that they've known about us longer?" Lieutenant Milano said.

Jim Pickett smiled at him.

"Certainly, that would explain their choice of communication," Ensign Strasnoye murmured.

"Even that is intriguing," Pickett said.

"How so, sir?"

"Well, Ensign, if they know much about us, they must know that the United States of America, after the Manhattan Meteor, is not the greatest power in these parts," Pickett said. He ignored the sharp breaths of the three men behind him as they acknowledged his statement of the obvious but unspoken political reality.

"In fact, the Chinese are arguably the most powerful nation on Earth and the greatest space-faring nation off Earth," Pickett continued. "So, by all rights, they should have contacted them first."

"More so given that theirs is one of the oldest civilizations,," Lieutenant Milano added in agreement.

"Perhaps they found learning Chinese more difficult," Ensign Strasnoye ventured.

"Chinese is no more difficult than English," Captain Zhukov said waving a hand in negation.

"True," Pickett agreed. "Which once again brings us back to the question: Why speak English?"

"Maybe they thought *Harmonie* would understand?" Strasnoye suggested.

"Then why wait until *Voyager* arrived?" Lieutenant Milano countered.

"Hmm," Captain Zhukov murmured in agreement.

"Again, gentlemen, we come back to the riddle of our alien friends," Jim Pickett said. He stared at the keyboard. "I wonder what they're thinking, right now."

A signal lit on one of the panels and Ensign Strasnoye leaned forward to examine it. He moved to a spare seat and began rapping in inquiries before turning first to Pickett and then to his captain. "Sir, we've incoming traffic from Earth."

Captain Zhukov raised an eyebrow.

"It's encrypted, sir, and directed to Mr. Pickett," the ensign explained.

"Here, let me see," Pickett said, moving to take the seat from the ensign. He looked at the challenge code, grunted and quickly tapped in a response. When the message decrypted, Strasnoye said, "It's an audio signal, sir."

"Put it on the speakers, if you please," Jim Pickett told him kindly. Lieutenant Milano and Captain Zhukov glanced at him in surprise and he just shrugged. "Either it's important and you need to know or it's stupid and we'll all get a laugh."

At the captain's nod, Strasnoye started the playback.

"Mr. Pickett, this is President Merritt," the familiar voice began. "I have not had an update from you in a while and just now I've learned that *Voyager* returned to lunar orbit, off-loaded some unauthorized crew, and took Admiral Tsukino and his aide back with him."

In the background, another voice yelled, "Are you crazy, Pickett?"

"That would be Elijah Wood, the secretary of the Navy," Jim Pickett explained blandly to the others.

"I'm told that *Voyager* moved at impossible speeds and that the media has found out," the president continued, ignoring the outburst. "We're running out of time here, Pickett. We need results. We need something we can tell the people without setting off a panic. And we need it fast."

"And who gave permission to put a Jap on my ship?" Wood shouted from the background.

"Shh, Elijah!" the president said. "I'm sure there was a good reason." His voice grew louder as it neared the microphone once more. "As I said, Pickett, we need results. We need 'em quick and we need 'em to be good. Respond immediately to this message."

There was a slight hiss of static and then Ensign Strasnoye reported, "Message ends, sir."

* * *

Ynoyon, Jupiter Orbit

A hiss of noise alerted the commander just a moment before the primary voice of Je-te-ji-go spoke on the communicator.

~**Sir, the grubbers have received communication from their homeworld,**~ it reported.

~**And?**~ Sa-li-ri-to demanded.

~**It was encrypted but we broke it—**~

~**What about the stumpers?**~ Sa-li-ri-to asked, referring to their Xlern "partners."

~**It was not difficult, I imagine they broke it, too,**~ the communications officer responded. ~**It was from the U.S. president to the ambassador.**~

~**And?**~ Sa-li-ri-to repeated with more venom in its tone.

~**The president reports that they cannot contain the news much longer and demand that the ambassador produce results.**~

~**Ah!**~ Sa-li-ri-to hissed with pleasure. ~**Now we can up the stakes. Contact the stumpers.**~

~**Sir, they've already initiated the next phase of the plan,**~ Je-te-ji-go reminded him.

~**Tell them to speed things up,**~ Sa-li-ri-to replied. ~**Tell the grubbers that we cannot linger long without a profitable trade.**~

* * *

Harmonie

"We picked up something that seemed to come from the second alien just a few minutes before we were contacted by the first," Dr. Ney reported from the detached science modules orbiting Jupiter.

"Could you pass us a copy?" Jim Pickett asked, glancing to Captain Zhukov to see if he was in agreement. The captain nodded.

"I suspect it was a side effect of the main transmission," Dr. Ney reported. "It was very intermittent."

"We'll take anything we can get," Captain Zhukov said, stepping toward the mike. "This may be the first break we've had."

"Indeed," Dr. Ney agreed. "We'll pass it along, then."

Captain Zhukov glanced to the ambassador. "And how do we respond to our friends' request?"

"I think we should tell them that we have to wait until we have rendezvoused with *Voyager*," Pickett said.

"They seemed rather hasty."

"They seemed more pushy than hasty to me, sir," Pickett said, "and given that they had some sort of communications from the other alien ship, I suspect they were feeling the pressure from their friends."

"If they're traders, they're probably right in saying that they can't linger long," Captain Zhukov said.

"Sir, if they're traders, they'll stay as long as it takes to complete their trade," Pickett told him, flashing a smile. "I think they decoded the president's message and are using it to pressure us."

Zhukov was silent for a moment. "Why?"

Pickett opened one hand in a throwaway gesture. "I think something fishy is going on."

"Something fishy," Captain Zhukov repeated without assurance.

"Well, we have to admit that there are some inconsistencies in their story."

"True but we can't forget also that they're aliens and unlikely to think the same ways we do," Zhukov countered.

"Which is why I'll be happy to see how Admiral Tsukino views all this."

"So you counsel that we wait until we can hear the admiral's views?"

"I think we shouldn't mention anything about the admiral at all, sir," Pickett said. "If the aliens know about him, let them tip their hand. If they don't know about him, he may be our ace in the hole."

Zhukov nodded slowly. "Very well, Mr. Ambassador, we'll do it your way." He gestured to the communications officer. "Tell them that we're awaiting our rendezvous with *Voyager*."

* * *

Ynoyon

~**Those insolent two-legs!**~ Sa-li-ri-to hissed when the message was relayed to it. ~**They feel sure of their fangs to take on so!**~

~**We could implement Plan Z, Captain,**~ Su-la-ij-an of security offered eagerly. Sa-li-ri-to shuddered. They had no idea what Plan Z was but could easily guess that destruction and mayhem were involved—security officers throughout the known galaxy were irresistibly drawn to acts of destruction. Perhaps it was because they spent so much of their time in utter boredom.

~**No,**~ the captain said quickly. ~**We shall confer with our 'allies.'**~

~**The grubbers would be better,**~ Su-la-ij-an rasped softly. For a moment, a whisper of fear coursed through the sinews of the captain, but then they realized that the security officer had only been grumbling about the Xlern and not with any grand strategy in mind.

~**Perhaps,**~ Captain Sa-li-ri-to responded, ~**but that is not a possibility. Stick to your orders.**~

~**As you say,**~ Su-la-ij-an replied sullenly. The captain cut the connection and contacted the communications officer.

~**Get me the Xlern skipper,**~ Sa-li-ri-to said, using the most offensive Yon term for a ship's commander, having connotations of one who hauled refuse at a loss.

The comm officer was struck voiceless, but a moment later, the channel opened.

>>**Xlern** *Xythir*, **Exern, communications,**<< a Xlern clicked at him.

~**Your commander, I will speak with him,**~ Sa-li-ri-to hissed.

>>**Connecting,**<< the Xlern clicked back. There was a long pause until finally, the tone changed.

>>**Captain of the** *Ynoyon*, **this is the captain of the** *Xythir*,<< the stumbler captain clicked.

~**Why aren't the grubbers falling all over themselves?**~ Sa-li-ri-to demanded without preamble. ~**We are at risk here and must minimize it immediately.**~ That last was an understatement of the first magnitude.

>>**I confess myself also surprised by their behavior,**<< the *Xythir's* captain responded. >>**I would have thought that our kindness and willingness to negotiate would have achieved concrete results by this time, if not sooner.**<<

Sa-li-ri-to's primary heads snapped at this. The stumbler was right: something was wrong. Wrong was not a good thing to occur in such delicate times.

>>**They demand that they wait until their other ship returns,**<< *Xythir's* captain added.

~**Perhaps they do not quite trust us,**~ Sa-li-ri-to mused.

>>**I told you that story about mixing up their fusion and antimatter drives was too stupid,**<< the Xlern clicked back.

Sa-li-ri-to's second and third jaws snapped on empty air in fury. A stumbler to talk *this* way? Sa-li-ri-to was tempted for a moment to order the security geek to implement whichever plan blew up the stumblers and put the blame on the grubbers. But their better brains held sway and the lesser two slowly lost their anger.

~**What do you suggest?**~ Sa-li-ri-to said finally.

>>**I suggest we wait until their ship returns,**<< the Xlern captain replied. *Nexl—that was its name*—Sa-li-ri-to suddenly recalled. >>**We know that their 'Ambassador' is under pressure to produce results, we cannot hope to increase it much more ourselves.**<<

~**Yes,**~ Sa-li-ri-to hissed. ~**You are correct, Captain. Much though it irks me, we shall have to conduct an exercise in patience.**~

>>**Profit will ensue,**<< Nexl clicked in agreement.

~We must do something to keep them off balance, however,~ Sa-li-ri-to responded. ~We cannot allow them time to consider all the options.~

>>I think we will find them ready to go to our 'home' in a short while,<< Nexl replied.

~And then *we* will have the sharper fang, yes!~

* * *

Harmonie

"Welcome aboard, Admiral," Captain Zhukov said as the smaller man, in the full dress of a Japanese Space Services admiral stepped through from *Voyager* to *Harmonie*.

"Thank you, Captain," Admiral Tsukino said, taking the outstretched hand and shaking it quickly. "Permission to board?"

"Granted, sir," Captain Zhukov said. He nodded to the man behind him. "This is my executive officer, Lieutenant Milano." He nodded to another man behind him. "And Lieutenant Murray, my chief engineer."

"Gentlemen," the admiral said with a nod, moving onto *Harmonie* to make room for those behind him. "May I introduce my aide, Ensign Sato?"

"Delighted," Captain Zhukov said, taking the young ensign's hand in his quickly before letting her move forward to shake hands with the others.

"Permission to board, sir?" Captain Steele's voice rang out warmly.

Captain Zhukov turned and bestowed a huge smile upon her. "Of course, Captain Steele." He waved her grandly aboard. "Consider my ship your ship."

Emily smiled back at him and stepped aboard.

"You made good time," he added in a lower voice.

"Historic," Emily agreed with a smile lighting her eyes. "We burned all of two hundred grams of antimatter roundtrip." She glanced around to see who else was on hand to greet them then said, "Any luck with our friends?"

Zhukov shook his head. "Admiral, we would probably all be more comfortable in a higher gravity location."

"If we could pry the secret of antigravity from our alien friends, we could adjust wherever we desired," Admiral Tsukino said in oblique agreement.

"Oh, sir, that has been much on our minds!" John McLaughlin said as he brought up the rear of *Voyager's* party.

"Ambassador Pickett is restricted to lunar gravity, so we have made arrangements to communicate with him via comm link, if that's acceptable, Admiral," Captain Zhukov said, waving the way forward and indicating the distant Ensign Strasnoye as courier to their final location.

"I would prefer meeting the ambassador in person," Admiral Tsukino said. "Perhaps I could join him?"

The two captains exchanged quick glances and, by some unspoken accord, Emily elected Nikolai as spokesperson. Zhukov said, "Of course, Admiral." To the distant ensign he said, "Please bring the admiral and his aide to the ambassador."

Ensign Strasnoye accepted this change in plans with a sharp nod and gestured the admiral off to his right. Zhukov and Steele waited until he'd departed before they permitted their eyes to meet.

"I see that the admiral is all that we'd expected," Zhukov murmured to her.

"More," Emily assured him, gesturing for him to lead on. With a snort, he moved off.

"I'm glad to see that your mission was a success," he told her.

"We've got three tons of supplies; we'll need help bringing them aboard," Captain Steele told him by way of reply.

"Lieutenant Milano?" Captain Zhukov said.

"I've parties designated and ready, sir," Lieutenant Milano reported crisply. He paused a moment, adding, "I've detailed Lieutenant Immelman to lead the effort."

"Good choice," the captain said. "Coordinate with …" he turned to Captain Steele.

"Ensign Dubauer has the watch," Emily responded.

"Coordinate with Ensign Dubauer, then," Captain Zhukov said.

"Aye, sir," Lieutenant Milano replied, speaking quickly into his communicator as they all continued onto the wardroom. "He's on it, Skipper."

"Thank you," Zhukov replied, even as he caught Emily's sidelong glance to gage his reaction to receiving the unofficial honorific as the ship's commanding officer. Nikolai allowed the corner of one lip to twist upward in recognition of the title and its meaning—it was quite something to gain the confidence of a foreign officer under such circumstances. Well, he'd *tried* hard enough, he knew.

They filed into the chairs of the wardroom and Lieutenant Milano arranged the communications console so that all could see, and programmed it for the space where the ambassador was hastily receiving the admiral and his aide.

"Admiral Tsukino, I cannot tell you what a pleasure it is to greet you on this historic event," Jim Pickett said over the console.

"Mr. Pickett," the admiral replied, "I followed your career with great interest until …"

"Until I fell into a bottle," Pickett finished as the admiral groped for words.

"Until your tragic accident," the admiral corrected him. "In your own way, sir, you were an inspiration to the rest of us."

"And how are things on your Moonbesu Nihongo, Admiral?"

"I suspect they will shortly grow more exciting," the admiral predicted.

"Indeed, I rather expected that you had been planning for a future where your moon base was somewhat more than a watering hole," Pickett said.

"I understand that perhaps your Far Side base might want to challenge that assumption," Admiral Tsukino returned neutrally.

Pickett guffawed. "If it weren't for your base, sir, I would not have been able to convince others to construct ours."

The admiral managed a bow, even though sitting. "If so, I am glad to have had a hand in such a worthy endeavor."

"Our world and our solar system will never be the same," Pickett said, waving his hand to gesture toward the alien starships outside of *Harmonie*.

"For good or for ill," Admiral Tsukino agreed. His eyes creased just slightly as he continued, "And why is it, Mr. Ambassador, that I imagine you to be somewhat relieved that your two captains chose to kidnap me here?"

Pickett smiled. "I imagine, Admiral, that from the moment you were contacted by *Voyager*, you had guessed the nature of its mission and made your plans accordingly."

"You flatter me, sir," Admiral Tsukino said.

"Crap," Pickett replied. "I just don't underestimate you, sir."

Admiral Tsukino raised his hands above his waist to spread them expressively in front of himself. "I suppose that I did draw certain conclusions and made contingency plans accordingly."

"While all the admirals in all the other fleets would have been wetting their pants and trying to figure out ways to distance themselves from this nightmare," Pickett said.

"I don't think you're being fair, sir," Admiral Tsukino said, allowing his lips to purse into a thin line. "I believe that there are several ranking officers in many nations who would have been thrilled to be offered the chance."

"And none of them were conveniently on the Moon where they could be masters of their own thoughts," Pickett replied with a snort. "No, the moment you were mentioned, you became the obvious and *only* choice for reasons which, judging by your actions, were as immediately apparent to you as they are to me." He took a breath. "So, Admiral, shall we stop pussyfooting around and get down to business?"

"And what business is that, Mr. Ambassador?"

"Captain Steele briefed you on what we know—"

"She was busy with her command and we had less than a day—"

"And your aide, the commendable Ensign Sato, needed no prompting to cozy up to Lieutenant McElroy and Ensign Dubauer—"

"Mostly with Ensign Dubauer, sir," Ensign Sato corrected him demurely.

"I hope you two didn't spend all your time gossiping about aliens and officers," Pickett said with a look so frank that the young ensign dimpled in response. He chuckled. "Good! That means I don't have to worry about playing matchmaker for you two."

"Sir!" Ensign Sato said, turning horrified eyes toward her admiral.

Admiral Tsukino cut her off with a hand raised palm outward. "Sato, I trust your judgement implicitly. Your actions can only reflect highly on you, your family, your service, and your humanity." She drew a breath, but he cut her off before she could speak. "I will hear no more of this, if you please. Have I not always made it clear that I allow my officers to follow their hearts as long as they remember their duty?"

Ensign Sato nodded curtly.

"Good!" Admiral Tsukino said. "And if not, I believe I gave you express permission to do so, in your capacity as my aide."

"Sir."

"Then enough," the admiral said, turning back to Mr. Pickett. "You were saying?"

"I was saying, Admiral, that if there's anything more I can add to bring you up to speed, you have only to ask."

"You are most kind," Admiral Tsukino replied, "but I suspect that, like the rest of us, I have far too many questions for which we as yet do not have answers."

"As my old drill sergeant used to say, sir, 'There's no stupid questions, only a question unasked,'" Pickett replied. "I encourage you to ask any questions that may not have occurred to us."

"Sir," Ensign Sato spoke up, "I have a question which I share with Ensign Dubauer." Pickett motioned for her to continue. "How come we haven't met these aliens yet?"

"A good question," Pickett said. He turned toward the pickup on the communications console. "Any guesses?"

In the wardroom, the two captains exchanged looks and shook their heads.

"They're saving it," Mac ventured.

"For what?" Admiral Tsukino asked.

"I don't know," Mac confessed. "Either they're saving it because they're afraid their appearance might alarm us or … because they're afraid of us."

"They could also be worried about contagions," Emily Steele said.

"Yes, that's a very good point, Captain," Admiral Tsukino replied.

"Theory says that if they're more advanced than we are that their bacteria might kill us," Lieutenant Milano added diffidently. "But they must know decontamination protocols …"

"Why not have us meet in suits?" Mac asked.

"Indeed," Admiral Tsukino agreed. "Although the construction of a suit will give away much information about their body shape."

"Yeah," Mac said. "Which is probably why they've not done any EVAs where we can see them."

"Have they left their vessels?" Admiral Tsukino said. "I'd heard nothing about this."

"We don't know if they have," Captain Zhukov assured him. "We know that we haven't detected anything like that."

"But we're not watching them actively," Mac reminded him.

"We didn't want to appear aggressive," Jim Pickett explained in response to the look on Ensign Sato's face.

"And they are asking what we want to trade for an FTL drive," Admiral Tsukino said. He turned to the pickup. "What do you propose?"

"Honestly, Admiral, we decided that the question belonged firmly with Ambassador

Pickett," Captain Steele said after exchanging glances with Captain Zhukov.

"They felt it was beyond their pay grade," Jim Pickett observed dryly.

"I don't doubt I'd do the same in their circumstances," Admiral Tsukino agreed. His grin slipped and he turned his full attention on the ambassador. "And you want me to be the sacrificial officer?"

"No, sir," Pickett replied, shaking his head fervently. "I've been making my own cock-ups … er, mistakes all my life. I don't really need anyone to take the fall for me." He paused and allowed a wolfish grin to cross his face. "In fact, Admiral, I plan to put all the blame squarely on my shoulders."

Admiral Tsukino absorbed this for a moment and then leaned back and roared with laughter. It was some time before he could control himself enough to look back at the ambassador and splutter, "Nothing ventured, nothing gained."

"Indeed," Pickett said, allowing himself a smile in return.

"And any spoils you acquire will redound firstly to your home nation," Admiral Tsukino said with a hint of admiration in his voice.

"Not quite, sir," Pickett replied. The admiral gave him a silent look. "This is an international mission, sir. I intend to treat it as such. If this doesn't work out to the benefit of all mankind, it will ultimately work out to our loss."

"I'm glad that you see it that way, Mr. Ambassador."

"It's the only way, sir," Pickett replied. "Our nations may not understand it, but anyone who's seen the Earth from the Moon knows that there are no lines on it, no borders, no boundaries."

"Very well, Mr. Ambassador," the admiral said after a sharp glance into the American's eyes, "I accept your credentials." He paused for a moment. "So, what do we do now?"

"First thing, sir, I'm going to need a letter of *carte blanche* from the United Nations," Pickett replied. "All trade items, and I suspect they will mostly be in the form of knowledge and know-how, will be traded equally, and all goods received from the aliens will be the joint property of every human being alive within the solar system."

"Why do you say the solar system, Mr. Ambassador?" Ensign Sato asked in her soft voice.

Jim Pickett smiled at her. "Just in case our alien friends have some humans tucked away where we don't know about them."

"You're afraid they might stuff the ballot box?" Mac asked from his seat in the wardroom.

"Something like that, Mr. McLaughlin," Pickett replied.

"Very well, anyone within the solar system," the admiral agreed. "And why do you want me to coordinate this? Surely this is more your purview, Mr. Ambassador?"

"Because I won't be here, sir," Pickett said.

"What?" Captain Steele roared, half-jumping out of her seat in the wardroom.

"In fact, Admiral, with your permission, I'd like us to detail an ambassadorial team."

"And the composition of that team, Mr. Ambassador?" Admiral Tsukino inquired, his eyes going quickly to his aide and then back.

"Both captains and Mr. McLaughlin to start," Pickett said without pause.

"Pardon?" Captain Zhukov said.

"Why both?"

"Well, unless I miss my guess, they're not going to take us on their ship—and we don't want them to—and we'll need someone to captain whatever ship they give us in trade."

"That's one captain," Admiral Tsukino said.

"The other will be for *Voyager*," Jim replied. "Before we accept a 'pig in a poke' from the aliens, we'll want them to prove that they've really given us the technology and know-how."

"You want to turn *Voyager* into a lab?" Captain Zhukov demanded incredulously.

"With respect sir," Mac replied, "she already is."

"And while all this is going on, Mr. Ambassador, what am I going to be doing?" Admiral Tsukino asked in a low voice. Out of the corner of his eye, Jim saw Ensign Sato cringe and guessed that the admiral was verging on full-on pissed.

"Admiral, while we're gone, sir, we're going to need you to keep the mission here going, to keep our physicists and technologists trying to figure out the FTL drive, to keep in contact with Earth—hell, sir, we're going to need you to be the admiral of Jupiter."

Admiral Tsukino was so flabbergasted by the notion that he didn't see Captain Steele in the monitor mouthing "admiral of Jupiter" to Captain Zhukov.

"I have a different proposition, Mr. Ambassador," Admiral Tsukino said. Pickett motioned for him to continue. "Captain Zhukov has trained for the Jupiter mission and knows the *Harmonie's* systems far better than anyone. I propose that he remain here with his crew and scientific mission while I accompany you and Captain Steele."

"But what if there's another ship?" Mac asked.

"I think you'll find, Mr. McLaughlin, that I have commanded a spaceship a time or two in my career," Admiral Tsukino replied.

"I was rather hoping to keep you here, sir, to deflect any flak," Pickett said. "With Captain Zhukov detached, your argument about your inexperience can be used against any demands that *Harmonie* return to Earth."

"I rather suspect that Captain Zhukov has had some experience in high stakes diplomacy, Mr. Pickett," Admiral Tsukino replied drolly, glancing at the captain to gage his reaction.

"Enough to prefer to avoid it," Mac judged in a low voice.

"Actually," Pickett said now, giving Captain Zhukov a regretful look, "I'm afraid the admiral has made some good points."

"Against them, Admiral, you might want to consider that Captain Zhukov and I have achieved a certain degree of harmony and concert in our actions together," Captain Steele said.

"Mmph," Admiral Tsukino grunted in acknowledgement. "There is that. Conversely, as we have said, I have acquired a fair amount of experience dealing with politicians from differing nations and have had a greater depth of command experience."

Captain Zhukov sighed and leaned back in his chair. "Much as I would like to disagree, I have to confess that Admiral Tsukino's abilities would be better placed at the disposal of the exploration team."

"That would mean a supernumerary of three," Captain Steele said, meaning that, along with Pickett, the crew of the *Voyager* would have two additional passengers.

"With respect, Captain, I believe I could be rated watch-ready with your communications equipment," Ensign Sato spoke up.

"I've already done watch duty, Skipper," Jim Pickett reminded her with a smile. "I imagine I could handle it again."

"And I, too, have some knowledge of spaceships," Admiral Tsukino reminded her with a wry grin.

"Even with a regular crew of thirty, if we have to split for another ship, we're likely to be short-handed," Steele told the others. Her lips twisted into a grimace and she looked toward Pickett. "I suppose the decision is really yours, Mr. Ambassador."

"Thank you," Jim said, relieving the sting in his words with a smile. "Of course, all this depends upon the aliens making us such an offer but ..." and he continued to outline his decision.

* * *

Xythir

The two leggers' message was concise and to the point: **While naturally we are desirous of establishing trade with you and wish to help you avoid any consequences from your early contact with us, we feel it imperative to know what we are trading for. We must also ensure that we can reproduce the underlying technology necessary so that we can show that we invented it ourselves.**

With that in mind, and in order to speed up our negotiations, we suggest that perhaps one of our ships docks with one of yours and that you show us some of your faster-than-light capabilities.

Please contact us at your earliest convenience.

>>**Yes!**<< Nexl clattered triumphantly. >>**Yes! They're buying it!**<<

* * *

Harmonie

"Captain, you should see this!" Commander Murray called urgently.

"What is it, Mr. Murray?" Captain Zhukov replied as he approached the navigation console.

"C'est encroyable!" Lieutenant Ives exclaimed in a hushed voice.

"We're getting readings over in telemetry," Ensign Strasnoye reported. "Strong and varied gravity fields focused on *Voyager.*"

"A tractor beam," Commander Murray surmised. "But, Skipper, look at the Xlern ship! She's split along her central axis, opening nearly half her width."

"We're getting some radar bounces off the interior," Ensign Strasnoye reported. "Strong signals."

"Good, stick with it, Gregor," Captain Zhukov said quietly. He followed Murray's finger as it outlined the opening in the alien's hull. Compared to it, *Voyager* was invisible.

"Most of that ship must be cargo space," Lieutenant Milano surmised.

"How much space?" Captain Zhukov asked. "And, Ensign? Be sure to see if you can spot any cargo containers or other cargo."

"Yes, sir," Ensign Strasnoye replied promptly.

"*Voyager* has entered the shadow of the cargo door," Commander Murray reported.

"Telemetry clean," Ensign Strasnoye reported, referring to the telemetry from *Voyager.*

"Communications a bit warbly, but stable," Lieutenant Milano added a moment later.

"Sir! Cargo door is closing!" Ensign Strasnoye reported.

Captain Zhukov keyed his mike. "*Voyager*, Godspeed."

"*Voyager* acknowledges," Ensign Sato's voice came back through a growing hiss of static and noise. "See you soon!"

The static grew louder and nothing more was heard.

"The cargo door is closed, Captain," Ensign Strasnoye reported.

"Keep recording, expand sensor sweep," Captain Zhukov replied. He turned to Lieutenant Ives. "How are the science modules doing?"

"They report good telemetry, sir," Lieutenant Ives responded immediately, adding by way of explanation, "I've been keeping an eye on them."

A moment later, the whole ship shivered, and Commander Murray yelled, "Bloody hell!"

"Sir," Ensign Strasnoye reported, "the alien ship has disappeared."

CHAPTER TEN

Voyager

"CAPTAIN, WE'RE READING AN INCREASE IN LUMINESCENCE ON OUR EXTERIOR sensors," Chief Petty Officer Harry Long reported.

"We're picking up conducted noise, too," Lieutenant McElroy added a moment later.

Emily Steele exchanged a look with Jim Pickett and then thumbed her comm link. "I'm on the way. Pass the word to the admiral, too, please."

"Aye, Skip," Danni McElroy told her.

Pickett yielded right of way to the captain with a wave of his hand and then followed hard on her heels.

"How are you feeling, Mr. Pickett?" Emily called over her shoulder.

"Just fine, Captain, just fine," Pickett replied jauntily. The aliens had managed to produce a steady one-sixth gee on the "down" side of *Voyager's* living quarters, much to the relief of everyone aboard—and the consternation of McLaughlin, CPO Long, and Ensign Dubauer in particular as they tried to imagine how it was achieved.

"They play with gravity like it was a toy or something," Mac had muttered sourly when the field was first activated.

"It probably *is* for them," CPO Long had replied just as crossly.

Ship's time had indicated that they'd been aboard the alien ship for a little more than an hour.

"Cargo door is opening, Skipper," Danni McElroy reported before they were halfway to the bridge. "I've got Alan on his way up here, and I've engaged the spectral matching computers to see if we know where we are."

Emily reached the bridge, took one look at the external monitors, and shook her head. "No need," she said. She pointed at a set of bright shiny stars in the distance. "I'd say we are smack dab in the middle of the Pillars of Creation."

Lieutenant McElroy shook her head in immediate negation then took a breath and narrowed her eyes at the view in front of her.

"Cargo door completely open," CPO Long reported.

"Harry, come up here and look at the stars," Captain Steele told him. She heard a hiss of surprise from the CPO and then the sounds of his movement before he cut off his comm.

"We'll have to take it in turns," Pickett said, glancing around the crowded bridge. It wasn't so crowded when they were in zero-gee because they could stack people up and around in different orientations but with only one "down" that became impossible. "I'll wait until the admiral and his aide have had a look."

"Very well," Emily acknowledged absently, waving him away. She barely heard his

"Well, firstly, Ensign, we can't be quite certain that this ship is actually crewed by just one species," Danni pointed out. "But, as far as all previous communications, this seems to be the only alien who communicates in all caps. That's why Chris Jenkins called him 'the Shouter.'"

"Perhaps he is a different species and unaware of such distinctions."

"I dunno," Danni replied. "He's been their go-to guy for engineering stuff, and if he runs true to form, he might be a little deaf."

"What's that, Lieutenant?" Mac piped up as he moved to take his position in front of the viewport. "I couldn't hear you."

"I imagine that in your case, Mr. McLaughlin, your deafness is for a different reason," Lieutenant McElroy teased.

"I'm generally unable to hear bureaucrats when they speak," Mac said, glancing to Ensign Sato to see if she caught the joke.

"And you seem to be particularly incapable of hearing the word 'No,'" Danni added.

The comm screen flickered back to life. **YOUR REQUEST IS GRANTED.**

Thank you, Danni typed back even as she called out loud, "We're moving!"

"Admiral, Ensign, if you'd return to your stations, please," Lieutenant McElroy said to them as she activated a number of screens and called down to engineering to say, "Harry, get ready!"

"Roger, Lieutenant!" Harry Long's voice called back over the comm link.

In a moment, *Voyager* was bathed in the light of many stars. Moments later she was completely outside the alien ship.

HOW LONG DO YOU REQUIRE YOUR OBSERVATIONS?

Thirty minutes, Danni typed back immediately. "We've got thirty minutes! Everyone look lively!"

Back in the wardroom, Pickett smiled to Captain Steele, "Lieutenant McElroy seems to have everything well in hand."

"Yup," Emily replied, with a pleased smirk. She clicked on a comm stud and said, "Danni, relay anything interesting down here."

"Sure thing, Skipper!" Danielle McElroy replied. "So far there's nothing much except confirmation of your initial hunch."

"'Assessment,' Danni, that was an assessment, not a hunch," Emily corrected.

Danni snorted. "As you say, Skipper, an 'assessment.'"

Thirty minutes later, they were back inside the alien ship, the cargo door closed and they were once more in darkness.

"Where to next, I wonder?" Jim Pickett said aloud.

"If they've studied us, I imagine we'll get another two surprises," Emily said.

A little less than twelve minutes later, Lieutenant McElroy reported, "Cargo door opening again, Captain!"

"I wish we had a probe," Emily muttered.

feet and his muffled, "Hi, Chief!"

"Lord in heaven!" Harry Long declared as he took his place near the external viewport. "Would you look at that!"

"We've got positive spectrums on five stars, Skip," Danni reported. "You were right: we're in the Pillars of Creation."

"What's the mission clock say, Danni?" Emily snapped, not taking her eyes from the view that spread out in front of her.

"Huh?" Lieutenant McElroy grunted, taken by surprise. She recovered quickly. "Thirty-nine minutes since door-close, Skip."

"Seven thousand light years in less than thirty-nine minutes," CPO Long breathed as he looked down at the screen where the mission clock was displayed.

Captain Steele motioned him aside and tapped in some numbers. "That's over ten thousand light-years in an hour."

"If the gravity and the engines are coupled, Skip, I'd say we should buy," Harry Long said.

"Probably," Emily agreed. She heard a noise behind her and spotted Admiral Tsukino. "Harry, why don't you let the admiral up here?"

"Of course, ma'am," Harry Long reported, dipping his head in a half-salute and moving off, nodding to the admiral as he passed back down to his duty station.

"Why all the excitement—" Admiral Tsukino began only to cut himself off abruptly. "Oh!"

"We've confirmed spectral signatures on five stars, sir," Emily reported. "We're in the Pillars of Creation, seven thousand light-years from Earth."

"And our speed?"

"We seem to have moved at something in excess of ten thousand light-years in an hour, sir," Emily told him.

"Impressive," Admiral Tsukino said, gesturing to be allowed a closer view of the outside. Captain Steele moved backward, smiled awkwardly at Ensign Sato, and then motioned her forward to join her admiral. After examining the view for several minutes, Admiral Tsukino said, "Would you mind, Captain, asking the aliens if they could place us in free space for better observations?"

"Certainly, Admiral," Emily Steele replied, not quite hiding the surprise in her voice. "Danni …?"

"On it, Skip," Danni replied, moving to click open the right channels. "I just hope we don't get the Shouter again."

They got the Shouter. **I SHALL RELAY YOUR REQUEST TO MY CAPTAIN.**

"Imagine if this guy actually talks that way," Danni muttered to no one in particular.

"It should not be difficult to represent lower case letters," Ensign Sato said.

"We can, Ensign. This guy just doesn't seem to use them," Danni replied.

"This is not something consistent throughout the species?"

"Wouldn't you need a probe with the alien technology?" Pickett asked.

Captain Steele dimpled as she corrected herself, "I wish we had an alien probe."

"What do you think we'll find?"

"What's about two thousand light-years from the Eagle Nebula and the Pillars of Creation?" Emily replied.

Pickett shrugged.

"Cygnus X-1!" Lieutenant McElroy's voice boomed over the intercom. "People, we got ourselves a black hole fine on the starboard bow!"

"*This* I've got to see!" Captain Steele said, surprised to find her words echoed by Ambassador Pickett. They smiled awkwardly at each other and then explained in another disconcerting unison, "I've wanted to see this since I was a kid!"

Pickett smiled at her and motioned for her to precede him once more. "Rank hath its privileges."

"Indeed it does," Admiral Tsukino spoke up from behind them. "And, Captain, if you don't mind, I'm going to pull it."

Emily bowed her head to him with a smile and waved him ahead, but raised a hand to stop his ensign from following. "Rank hath its privileges, Ensign."

"As you say, Captain," Ensign Sato replied with a dip of her head.

"Don't worry, you'll get a chance to see, too!"

On the bridge, Lieutenant McElroy had squeezed herself as far to one side as she could and still perform her duties.

"We've got a good confirmation on six stars," Danni reported as the admiral took his place in front of the viewport. "There's not much to see on normal wavelengths, I'm displaying X-ray frequencies."

"Is there a health hazard?" Admiral Tsukino asked immediately.

"No, sir, we're too far," Danni replied. "I reckon we're a good eighty light-years away but we can still see it."

"Please keep an eye on our radiation levels," the admiral instructed. Danni nodded in response. He continued, "And, if I may, I suggest that as soon as we've got confirmation, we let the aliens know that we're ready to depart."

Emily, who had crowded in behind him, nodded in agreement. "I'm quite ready to continue the grand tour, sir."

"I'd like five minutes more," Lieutenant Cohen called up from his room. "I've got telemetry recording, Skipper."

"Okay. In five minutes, we'll let our friends know that we're ready to go," Steele replied, glancing to the admiral who nodded in agreement.

* * *

Xythir

>>**The stumblers don't seemed much impressed, Captain,**<< Ixxie rapped softly.

>>**They may be too busy dealing with unwanted excretions,**<< security officer Noxor clicked snidely.

>>**Whichever, our next destination is certain to appeal to them,**<< Captain Nexl responded. He rapped to Exern, >>**Inform engineering that we are ready to depart.**<<

>>**Yes, Captain,**<< Exern replied without enthusiasm. He transmitted a pre-recorded message to the engineer and shunted its reply to a Boolean screen so that all he had to contend with was a burst of bright white light—the conversion of the engineer's loud affirmative into a less frenetic signal.

A moment later, the starship *Xythir* was no longer in the vicinity of the black hole.

* * *

Voyager

"Cargo doors opening," Ensign Sato reported, having relieved Lieutenant McElroy on communications.

"Engaging sensors," Lieutenant Cohen added. "We've got a star in plain view, good spectral reading."

"I'm picking up some noise on a number of frequencies," Ensign Sato reported.

"This is the captain, I'm on my way," Captain Steele said. She'd taken the time during the jump to catch some rest.

"Captain, you're not going to believe this!" Lieutenant Cohen called.

"I believe the radio noise is intelligent," Ensign Sato said.

"What is it? Talk to me," Captain Steele said as she charged up the stairs to the bridge.

Lieutenant Cohen turned to her with a huge grin. "Positive spectral identification: Gliese 581."

"Radio noise coming from multiple locations," Ensign Sato reported. A moment later she added, "Lieutenant McElroy to the bridge, please."

"What is it, Sato?" Captain Steele said, turning to the diminutive officer.

"Captain … I'm not sure if I am interpreting the readings correctly," Ensign Sato replied, ducking her head to avoid meeting Emily's eyes.

Captain Steele moved over to the displays and gave them a quick look over. "Route that traffic to the software routine that Jenkins set up. You'll find it in the miscellaneous folder."

Ensign Sato nodded briskly. A moment later, a new window popped up on the console with three different displays: one showing the frequencies observed, another showing strength, and a third one blank.

"If there's intelligence in the signals—" Emily began, only to halt when the third screen displayed in large red letters: *Jackpot!* "—well, there's intelligence in the signals."

"Didn't someone send a radio signal to Gliese back in 2008?" Lieutenant Cohen asked.

"Yes," Emily said. She gestured to the communications console, adding with a smile, "I imagine that they might be getting a reply in the next decade or two."

"I'm here!" Danni McElroy announced cheerily as she stepped up on the bridge. "What've you got?"

"Take a look for yourself," Captain Steele said, gesturing to the display while Ensign Sato did her best to make herself invisible. Emily pressed a comm stud and called over the intercom, "We've just positively identified our current location as the star Gliese 581. We've also just determined that there are numerous intelligent signals originating from the planets of this solar system."

"I wonder what they're saying to our buddies, Skip?" Danni said, brows suddenly furrowing. "Are they saying hello or get lost?"

Emily thought about it for a moment, then switched her comm link. "Ambassador Pickett, should we ask our aliens if they're in contact with the locals?"

"Interesting …" Pickett said. "Yes, let's see what they say."

"Very well, sir," Emily said, keying the connections closed. She turned to Ensign Sato. "Sato, would you do the honors?"

Ensign Sato turned to Lieutenant McElroy, who smiled at her, waving her to the controls. "It's your watch, Ensign."

Ensign Sato moved to stand in front of the communications panel, put her fingers on the keyboard and began typing, **This is** *Voyager*, **we have a question: Are you in contact with the local life-forms in this system?**

NEGATIVE. THE LIFE-FORMS HAVE NOT ACHIEVED STARFLIGHT. THEY ARE PROTECTED BY THE SILURIAN CONCORDANCE.

"Admiral, Mr. Ambassador, you need to hear this," Captain Steele said repeating the response word for word.

"Hah!" Pickett cried so loudly that his voice carried in a slow echo from his quarters back up to the bridge. "Ask them about the Silurian Concordance."

Ensign Sato nodded that she'd heard and quickly typed in the question.

THE SILURIAN CONCORDANCE IS UPHELD BY ALL SPACE-FARING RACES. SECTION 8 SPECIFICALLY PROHIBITS CONTACT WITH—

* * *

Xythir

>>**AXLU, WHAT ARE YOU TAPPING?**<< Captain Nexl demanded at almost the same volume as his insufferably noisy engineer. >>**Exern, why did you let him respond?**<<

>>**He's been our primary contact with the stumblers, sir,**<< Communications Officer Exern replied. >>**Your orders were to keep communication to a minimum.**<<

>>**JUST FOR THIS PURPOSE!**<< the captain rapped back fiercely.

>>**I have cut the engineer's link to the stumblers,**<< Exern replied quietly.

>>**Great, now they'll wonder what's happening,**<< Nexl responded. He tapped several extremities together angrily, then continued, >>**Better put me through.**<<

>>**Very well, Captain, you are in contact with the stumblers,**<< Exern told him redundantly as the red "live" light had illuminated on the captain's controls.

* * *

Voyager

"Get them back!" Captain Steele shouted. Ensign Sato flinched and nodded at the same time.

"It's nothing on our end, Skip. It's them," Lieutenant McElroy said, turning to both glare at her captain and put a reassuring hand on the young ensign's shoulder. She gave Sato a quick pat and turned her full attention to her commanding officer.

"Ensign Sato, please try to raise them," Captain Steele said in a more controlled voice.

"My guess, Captain, is that they're now experiencing 'technical difficulties,'" Pickett said over the comm link.

"Sir?" Emily said, not noticing that she'd used the honorific.

"I think our shouting friend may have given away some information that he was not supposed to release," Pickett replied.

"He's a tech," Lieutenant McElroy agreed. Captain Steele motioned for her to continue. "I think he's their engineer. That would explain why he spoke to us first, to get the technical stuff right."

"And once they started with him, they continued," Pickett surmised.

"So, what is the Silurian Concordance?" Emily said to herself.

"I suspect, Captain," Jim Pickett replied, "that that's the three hundred trillion-dollar question."

"I'm getting a signal," Ensign Sato replied. "Here it comes."

We apologize for that. We regret that our communications were cut short. We are ready to make our return to your departure point. When we arrive, we will be ready to receive your embassies.

"The doors are closing," Danni reported.

"Signal's gone, Captain," Ensign Sato said, turning her dark eyes to the tall American.

"Are you recording all the other traffic?"

"That's gone, too," Ensign Sato said after a quick glance at her console. She re-ran the trace and said, "It cut off at the same time as their engineer was cut off."

"Did it come back when the other alien contacted us?" Emily asked.

"No, Skip, they kept the outside lines dead," Danni McElroy reported.

"Okay," Emily said with a sigh. "Ensign Sato, if you can set up a program to analyze what data we captured, that would be most useful." She turned to Danni and said, "We should get some rest." To Lieutenant Cohen, she said, "The bridge is yours."

"I have the conn," Lieutenant Cohen said in the age-old acknowledgement. "The doors are closed, Captain."

"Call me again if anything unusual occurs," she said, then, seeing the lieutenant's expression, amended herself with, "I mean *more* unusual than what we've seen already."

"Aye, Skip," Lieutenant Cohen agreed laconically. Emily turned and followed Lieutenant McElroy back to their quarters hearing Cohen say, "You did well, Sato."

"Thank you, Lieutenant," Ensign Sato replied. "If I am to be permitted to concentrate on the captain's request then I shall have to ask you to monitor our frequencies."

"Send 'em over," Cohen replied readily.

After that, their voices fell out of Steele's earshot.

* * *

"They're going to up the stakes," Pickett said as he and the admiral mulled over the last communication from the aliens.

"How could they do that?"

"A number of ways," Pickett replied, lifting one hand to tick off items with the other. "They're certain to put some sort of time limit on us and I wouldn't be surprised if they try to raise the ante."

"How so?"

"Their new guy used the word 'embassies,'" Pickett replied. "That's inviting us to present multiple ambassadors."

"Which makes sense, because we have multiple nations to represent," Admiral Tsukino replied mildly.

"Divide and conquer, Admiral," Pickett told him. "They're in a superior position and they're trying to get as much as they can."

"But aren't they in an inferior position?" Admiral Tsukino countered. Pickett gestured for him to continue. "They have violated their own rules; they admitted that. They need to come up with some plausible way to give us knowledge to explain their mistake to the rest of the aliens."

"Except that their 'mistake' stinks from all angles," Pickett replied. "We're pretty sure that they couldn't have confused the two different signals and so they're trying to run some sort of scam on us."

"A scam which will give us interstellar travel seems more like 'a gift horse,' some would say," the admiral said.

"Except, sir, that we have not just one alien ship, but two," Pickett said. "And they're pretty obviously of different design and quite possibly belonging to different species."

"And?"

"The second batch of aliens arrived ostensibly to up the ante," Pickett replied. "Why?"

"Do you mean: Why, if it was an honest error?" Admiral Tsukino asked. Pickett nodded. "Perhaps both aliens were involved."

"Then why didn't they arrive together?"

"Any number of reasons: they could have been further away; they could have been off-loading cargo, or—"

"And that's another thing," Pickett said, raising a hand in apology for his interruption. "If they're traders, they can't linger here too long unless they know they're going to make a suitable profit."

"I agree," Admiral Tsukino replied. "And so the question is what they would perceive of as profitable?"

Pickett nodded. Then he stiffened. Admiral Tsukino raised an eyebrow in a silent implication for the ambassador to speak. "What if they already have a list?" Pickett said.

"That would make things easier," the admiral replied. "In fact, I suspect they have *two* lists, one for each alien."

"Two?"

"Well, they're going to have to teach us enough to let us 'manufacture' a star drive and then they're going to have to trade us a better star drive to show to the rest of the stars that they were dealing legitimately."

"Two lists, two star drives," Pickett repeated, trying the sound out on his lips. He bobbed his head up and down for a moment as he digested the implications. With a twinkle in his eyes, "So what if we only offer to trade for *one* drive?"

Admiral Tsukino looked at him for a long moment and then laughed.

* * *

Harmonie

"We're picking up gravitational shifts," Chris Jenkins reported.

"Setting tracking rate to high," Sally Norman replied.

"Bridge, this is Jenkins, we're getting something on the gravitics," Jenkins reported.

"We copy and concur," Dr. Ney reported from the detached science modules. "Please send your data to us."

"Sending," Norman said.

"This is Captain Zhukov," Jenkins' console sounded. "How does this compare with—never mind, the alien ship has returned."

"Right on schedule!" Sally cried. She turned to Jenkins and shouted, "Did you see that spike, Chris? That's right when you thought it would be!"

"There is strong evidence for the fifth force," Dr. Ney added. "Captain, I believe we may have a theory regarding their current mode of transportation."

"Current mode, Dr. Ney?" Captain Zhukov replied. "Do you expect more?"

"I can't be certain, Captain," Dr. Ney said. "The readings seem to confirm one of our leading theories, and with that we can make several guesses about faster-than-light transportation."

"*Harmonie*, this is *Voyager*," Captain Steele's voice came over the comm link. "We're back. And, *boy*, did we see the sights!"

Chapter Eleven

Harmonie

"Welcome back, Captain, Admiral," Captain Zhukov said as he stepped aside to permit them entry through the hatchway.

"Thank you," Admiral Tsukino replied. Emily merely smiled and waved. "It's been quite a trip."

"We had some good luck on our end, too, sir," Captain Zhukov said.

"Really?" Emily said, moving close up beside the admiral. "Did you get good readings?"

"Not only that, but Dr. Ney and your Mr. Jenkins have formulated some novel inferences," Captain Zhukov replied. He gestured for them to precede them. "They're ready in the inner wardroom." He glanced beyond them to the empty hatchway. "Will Mr. Pickett be joining us?"

Admiral Tsukino shook his head. "He's staying on *Voyager*. We're expecting communications momentarily from the aliens."

"Really?"

"Indeed, I'm surprised they let us dock with you," Emily said. She shook her head as she added, "Although perhaps they are hoping that we'll use up all our fuel."

"We should have our engineers consult on the possibility of refueling your reaction tanks from ours," Captain Zhukov said with a worried frown.

"Right now, Captain, I think I'd really like to get that briefing done," Admiral Tsukino replied. "We're expecting the aliens to up the pace at any moment."

"Really, why?"

"Ambassador Pickett believes—and we agree with him—that our main alien contact may have 'leaked' some information that we weren't supposed to get," the admiral replied.

"We're arranging a download of all our data," Emily said.

* * *

"So what you're saying is that we have a good chance of working out the principles of their star drive ourselves?" Admiral Tsukino asked as Dr. Ney and the others finished their presentation.

"Quite possibly," Dr. Ney replied. "But … how long this will take, I cannot say."

"A crash program would take how long?" Admiral Tsukino asked, glancing around the table for an answer.

"Twenty years?" Chris Jenkins suggested.

"If we had a massive investment for the project," Captain Steele said. "This would have to be an international effort, certainly."

"And won't those inhabitants out at Gliese 581 have responded to our message by then?" Admiral Tsukino asked.

"You know," Emily Steele said thoughtfully, "that could get us into trouble."

"Pardon?" Dr. Ney blurted in surprise. "How?"

"We might be then seen as guilty of contacting a non-star-faring race when we had faster-than-light travel," Emily answered.

"Like these aliens are in trouble by contacting us," Captain Zhukov said in agreement, leaning back in his chair, his lips pursed. He turned to Captain Steele and said, "Do you think they planned this?"

Emily started to shake her head vigorously then stopped. "Ambassador Pickett said that the aliens might want to set a deadline …"

"Twenty years seems rather a long time," Dr. Ney said.

"But it *will* present us with a quandary," Captain Steele insisted.

"Should we arrange to get our star drive *after* we receive a reply from Gliese 581?" Captain Zhukov wondered.

"I don't think we're going to be allowed that much time, Captain," Chris Jenkins said. The others looked at him and he shrugged. "I think that we've got enough pressure right now to come to a deal with the aliens, regardless of the Gliese 581 issue."

"Also, our knowing about intelligent life on Gliese 581 was a direct result of their intervention," Captain Steele said in agreement.

"We break no protocols if we fail to reply," Admiral Tsukino observed.

Captain Zhukov snorted. "I wonder how many contacts were never made for similar reasons?"

"I begin to see something of the reason for this Silurian Concordance," Admiral Tsukino said.

A hail from the bridge interrupted them. "Captain Zhukov, we're picking up a transmission from the alien ship."

"Let Pickett handle it," Captain Steele said urgently. Captain Zhukov's eyes widened and he turned to Admiral Tsukino.

"The captain is correct," the admiral told him. "Mr. Pickett and I have discussed the options at length. He can handle this while we concentrate on the matters before us."

Zhukov pursed his lips for a thoughtful moment then nodded. "Very well," he said, keying the comm link to the bridge. "Bridge, this is the captain. Ambassador Pickett will handle it from *Voyager*."

"Aye, sir."

* * *

Xythir

>>**We're being hailed on subspace by the Yon ship, Captain,**<< Communications Officer Exern tapped quietly. >>**They want a full copy of our log.**<<

>>**Tell them that we've just opened phase two of communications and are too busy to respond at this moment,**<< Captain Nexl rapped in reply, pleased with the ease at which the answer came to him.

>>**Aye, Captain,**<< the communications officer responded with a slight tremble in his tapping.

>>**It's time to show these stumblers what a few hard raps can really do,**<< Captain Nexl said to himself. He keyed open his outside comm link to the transmission already in progress. **At this time, we would like to meet directly with your emissaries.**

The response which came back did not please him at all: **We would be happy to have our ambassador meet with yours.**

We insist upon having representatives from all your parties, he wrote back.

We would be happy to do so, if you will provide representatives from both your ships.

We see no reason to overextend our contacts at this time, Captain Nexl replied.

Then we shall not encumber you with more than one representative.

Impasse. Nexl twitched in muted anger. The whole reason to use American as the contact language was because they were most likely to produce a "cowboy" in response. Someone big on swagger but small on sensibility. This stumbler was not a cowboy. Where was *Howdy Doody* when one needed it?

We cannot conceive of a trade not involving all parties, Nexl responded.

Our representative is empowered to negotiate for all parties.

Is your representative able to handle all the technical and scientific information?

For that, others will be consulted, the stumbler replied. **Is it not the same with your crew? Were we not talking originally with the chief engineer of your ship?**

The prior communicator is indisposed, Nexl rapped back. *Indisposed! Confined to quarters with rocks to hold it down! That idiot Axlu had endangered everything!*

Nexl could only hope that Axlu's subordinates were not so knotted in their thinking. **His position is unimportant.**

Then who am I communicating with? Are you empowered to make decisions?

Nexl's limbs quivered with fury at the temerity of the question. How dare some puny two-legger from a useless ball of rock question his authority?

Are you still there? The stumbler prompted.

Nexl shivered to calm itself. **Whom am I communicating with?**

I am Ambassador Plenipotentiary James Earl Pickett. I am empowered by our United Nations, the stumbler responded. **With whom am I communicating?**

Ambassador! United Nations! Oh, no! Nexl thought in panic.

>>**Exern, I need you to break contact immediately!**<< Nexl rapped over the internal link.

>>**Captain?**<<

>>**Just DO IT!**<< Nexl rapped so loud that one of his rocks cracked against the other. He wondered if perhaps the engineer Axlu had always been so loud or if somehow it had gone so noisy in anticipation of its encounters with the stumblers.

>>**Connection broken,**<< Exern reported a moment later with quiet raps.

>>**Get me the slitherers!**<<

>>**Captain?**<<

>>**JUST DO IT!**<<

Meekly, a moment later, the communications officer tapped, >>**I have Je-te-ji-go, of communications, sir.**<<

>>**I need to talk with your captain at once,**<< Nexl rapped as soon as the new link went live.

* * *

Voyager

"Try again, Danni," Pickett said as the communications officer gave her latest report. He glanced at the clock. It had been ten minutes since the link with the alien ship had been broken.

"Nothing, sir, not even carrier," Danni replied. "It's like they've become a hole in space."

"*Voyager*, this is Jenkins, we think we've picked up signs of communications between the two alien ships."

"What sort of communications?" Pickett snapped.

"It might be some sort of dedicated gravitic wave," Jenkins said. "It's not clear and we're only picking up enough on the various arrays to give us a hint, but we're pretty sure that it's being frequency modulated."

"Frequency modulated gravity waves?" Danni said to herself. "Can they do that?"

"Chris, is Mac monitoring this?" Pickett asked.

"I don't know, sir," Jenkins admitted. "We're just out of our meeting with the admiral."

"Please send the data to Mac when you get the chance," Pickett said.

"Will do!"

A noise from the forward hatchway alerted him to new arrivals and he looked up just in time to see Captain Steele float down onto the bridge, zero-gee having returned slowly after *Voyager's* separation from the alien ship.

Captain Steele raised an eyebrow questioningly to which Pickett responded with a shake of his head.

"Mr. Ambassador, what happened?" Emily asked as she made room for Admiral Tsukino.

"They broke off," Pickett said with a frown.

"And you can't get them back?" Emily shot at Lieutenant McElroy. Danni shook her head and Emily returned her attention to Pickett. "Any idea what happened?"

"Jenkins tells me that they may have opened a link to the other ship, using a gravity wave," Danni said while Pickett nodded in mute agreement.

"They were upset that we were only going to send one person," Pickett added with a frown. "They were hoping"—he glanced to see Admiral Tsukino's reaction—"that we would send emissaries."

"Did you not tell them that you were ambassador for the United Nations?" Admiral Tsukino asked.

"I did."

"And then they cut off," Danni said. "And now, if Chris is right, they're talking to their buddies."

"They're scared," Emily guessed. "Things aren't going according to plan."

"I believe you are correct, Captain," Admiral Tsukino agreed. He turned to Pickett. "Now what, Mr. Ambassador?"

Pickett shrugged and shook his head.

"Danni, get everything we've got to date zipped into a high-compression signal and send it back to Earth. Ask *Harmonie* to repeat," Emily ordered.

"Aye, Captain," Danni replied crisply, tapping in a quick set of commands. A moment later she said, "On the way."

"That was quick," Pickett said.

"I sorta figured we might need something like this," Lieutenant McElroy told him, adding in a softer voice, "just in case."

"Of course, if they blow us up, Earth will find out just at about the same time the aliens arrive in low earth orbit," Jim Pickett said in a voice without inflection.

* * *

Ynoyon

~**The Xlern captain is rattling for you, Captain,**~ Je-te-ji-go reported to its commander.

Sa-li-ri-to's two minor heads snapped before its main head replied, ~**I shall hear him.**~

~**As you wish,**~ Je-te-ji-go said, switching the link through.

~**What is it?**~ Sa-li-ri-to asked without preamble.

>>**The stumblers have an ambassador,**<< the Xlern's tedious rapping responded.

And tongues, Sa-li-ri-to thought to themselves venomously. *At least they can form sounds, even if they cannot properly roll their* esses.

~**Was this not expected?**~ Sa-li-ri-to responded. ~**Why is this of concern?**~

>>**The ambassador claims he represents their United Nations,**<< the Xlern replied, its rapping overlain with the trembles of fear.

If only we could nip these spiders where it hurts most and get them to see sense! Sa-li-ri-to hissed to itself. Of course, their collective heads did not say anything; the Xlern captain would probably shake itself into individual limbs if it knew of the Yon breeding plans. The Xlern were inferior in so many ways, but until control was achieved, they had to be treated as if they actually had the same four brains of a proper Hydra.

~**In the meantime, while you are slipping in your fear, our sensors have detected that the Earthers are increasingly monitoring the very wavelengths we are using to communicate,**~ Sa-li-ri-to hissed. ~**We still have to receive your report on the excursion.**~

>>**It went as planned,**<< the Xlern captain tapped in reply. >>**Although we had some trouble at Gliese 581.**<<

~**Trouble?**~ Sa-li-ri-to interrupted. ~**Was not that planned?**~

>>**We should talk of it later. Right now the question is what to do with the Earthers?**<<

~**That would be simple: take their emissary aboard and start the trade,**~ Sa-li-ri-to said, allowing their lesser tongues to sound in chorus.

>>**If they are monitoring our transmissions, they might work out how the Amuksli Drive works,**<< the Xlern captain protested.

~**And is that not what we want?**~ Sa-li-ri-to replied. ~**I grow tired. You know what to do.**~ Without waiting, they cut the connection.

* * *

The White House, Washington, DC

"Mr. President, Goldstone has an update from *Voyager*, sir!" Navy Admiral Roberts exclaimed as he burst into the Oval Office, waving actual paper as if in proof.

"Paper, Joel?" the president drawled, eyeing the secretary with disapproval. Part of the president's campaign had centered on "eliminating waste."

Roberts eyed the offensive papers as if he had just noticed them and hastily dropped his hand by his side. "Sir, we've heard from *Voyager*."

"Yes, you said," President Merritt replied mildly. He waited a beat before adding, "And?"

The side door opened and Ron Grimminger, the White House science advisor stepped in, a tablet in his hands.

"They've been to Gliese 581!" Grimminger exclaimed, face split wide in a grin. "They found signs of life!"

Roberts spared him a killing glare before saying to the president, "*Voyager* visited three different locations shuttled inside the first alien ship."

With a wave of his hand, President Merritt ordered him to continue, while with his other hand gestured for Grimminger to show him his tablet.

"They were in the Eagle Nebula, the place where the old Hubble telescope shot that superb photo of the birthplace of stars," Roberts continued, "and then they were taken to view the black hole, Cygnus X-1."

"It says here," the president said, waving toward the tablet that Grimminger had slipped him, "that the aliens broke off communication."

"It also says that our scientists have some ideas of how the aliens' star drive might work," Ron Grimminger added in an undertone.

The president tilted his head up from the tablet to give Grimminger a wolf's head grin. "Catching up on 'em already?"

"Well, sir," Grimminger temporized, "we've got ideas. It takes time and money to make them into working prototypes."

"Yeah," Merritt grunted, a wince on his face. He gave the issue a dismissive wave and looked over to his press secretary. "Does this give us something for the press?"

"I'll need to see what we've got, sir," Anne Byrne replied, "but I think we can do something with it."

"I've got us a free slot in the United Nations feed, sir," Secretary of State Ellington told him. "I had to twist some arms but I think, all things considered, it's our best venue."

"Fly all the way to Hong Kong?" the president asked in dismay.

"No, sir, we'll record it here in the Oval Office and drop a feed through to Hong Kong," Ellington replied. "It's been done before."

It was one of those painful reminders of the impact the loss of the United Nations in New York City meant to the country.

President Merritt frowned then grunted. "It'll do."

Ellington rose to leave, saying, "I'll alert the Chinese."

Merritt gave that a sour look but nodded; there were some things that playing second fiddle to the rest of the world required. To the others, he said, "Okay, that's out of the way. Where does that leave us?"

"Well, sir, the reason for this latest transmission—and it was repeated through *Harmonie* so the Euros have it by now—is that the *Voyager* and Ambassador Pickett were worried about the abrupt way in which the aliens cut off communications."

"What?"

"It seems that the aliens wanted our people to send multiple ambassadors, not just the one," Grimminger said.

"Pickett refused, saying that he was Ambassador Plenipotentiary for the United Nations," Roberts added with a glower.

"What? I thought he was our man!" the president swore.

"Well, he does have credentials from the United Nations," Grimminger said. "John ran that through as soon as he could, sir."

"I shouldn't have let him leave," the president grumbled, eyeing the door through which the secretary of state had so recently departed with disfavor.

"No matter, sir," Brian McPhee, the president's chief of staff piped up, "it puts us in a superior position."

"Only if we don't fuck it up," the president snapped. "If we screw *this* pooch, the whole world will *never* forgive us."

There was a silence as everyone digested this unassailable display of logic.

"Well ... not for long," Grimminger said softly to himself. He wasn't quiet enough and found all eyes on him. With a shrug, he added, "I mean, once the aliens come raining bombs down on us."

A slow groan ran around the room. Roberts, the Navy admiral, rose from his seat. "Should I put us on alert, sir?"

Greg Merritt eyed the eager man through half-lidded eyes. With a sigh, he answered, "No, Joel, I don't think that'll do much good, will it?"

"It might piss off the aliens more," McPhee added.

"Sir, I've got a sketch of your speech ready," Anne Byrne said. "I've included a plea for compassion from the aliens toward the end."

"Send it to Grimminger's tablet," the president said, pointing to the tablet in front of him.

"It's already there, sir," Anne told him with a smile. "That flashing icon, if you press it."

President Merritt looked down at the tablet, saw the flashing icon, grunted, and pressed it. He scanned it quickly. "It'll do."

"I'll get the crew in here," Anne said, rising from her chair.

"Bring some press, too," the president called after her. Anne raised a hand in a wave of acknowledgement as she went through the side door.

*   *   *

Eurocos Headquarters,
Noordwijk aan Zee, The Netherlands

"Well, Werner, what is it?" Anne-Marie Foquet said as she gestured for the others in her office to be seated for this hastily-called meeting.

"The Americans have screwed up," the Eurocos' chief science adviser told Eurocos' chief executive. "We've just decoded the transmission from *Harmonie*. The aliens have broken off their negotiations."

"Why?" Antonio Scarli, the executive secretary, asked. He was Italy's highest-ranked member of Eurocos and he'd earned his position both through political pull and sheer hard work. "I thought they took *Voyager* on a tour, along with the Japanese base commander."

"Admiral Tsukino," Anne-Marie said to him, supplying the missing name. She turned her attention back to Werner Ulke. "And?"

Werner's lips twitched but he had no immediate response.

"I'd like a copy of the full report, Werner," Anne-Marie said into the silence. "I think we should take a good, hard look at it before we draw any conclusions."

"It might be too late if the Yanks have blown it," Ulke replied unhappily.

"I think we must hope that they will recover from the situation," Anne-Marie said.

"And if they don't?"

"Well, then, our problems will be over," Antonio Scarli said to the German with a grin.

* * *

Moscow, Russia

"The American president will address the United Nations," President Vatutin said as he entered the meeting room, throwing his briefcase on the table. He speared Boris Kalinsky, the minister of science and technology, with a glare. "Why?"

Kalinsky was prepared for the assault. "We have a new dispatch from *Harmonie*."

Vatutin's aide rushed in with a message in his hand, calling, "Sir, the American president just sent this!"

Vatutin grabbed the message, scanned it quickly and pursed his lips sourly. "*This* tells us why—he plans to announce the aliens to the world."

"What?" Vladimir Novitsky cried. The Space Exploration Bureau's chief had known that the time would come, but he wasn't prepared for it to be just then.

Vatutin simmered for a moment then sighed. "I doubt we could have kept the news from our own people much longer."

"Does it say why he's going to address the UN?" Sergei Korolev, the spacecraft design chief, asked.

"Apparently, the American's man has fucked up," Vatutin said with a sour smile. He waited until he had their complete attention. "The aliens have broken off negotiations."

"Oh, shit!"

* * *

The White House, Washington, DC

The light over the camera went red and Anne Byrne waved a hand to the president of the United States. The teleprompters rolled and Greg Merritt, seated behind his desk at the Oval Office looked into the cameras and smiled.

"Greetings," he began. "I am Greg Merritt, President of the United States. I am here today—and I must apologize for not being able to address this august body in person but the demands of the moment require me to remain here in the capital.

"I am here today to tell you that an international team in orbit around Jupiter has made the most momentous discovery in the history of our kind."

He paused for a moment, then continued, "Somewhat less than three weeks ago, the Eurocos fusion ship *Harmonie* arrived in orbit around Jupiter after a three-year journey to begin an historic mission of scientific discovery.

"It had barely settled into its explorations when it discovered that it was not alone." Again, he paused.

"A ship, not of Earth, joined it in orbit," the president continued. "When we learned of this here in America, we immediately dispatched our fastest spaceship, the *Voyager*, to render whatever aid it could.

"When *Voyager* arrived, the alien ship, with which all previous attempts to communicate had failed, opened communications with our ship. We later discovered that the aliens had scanned our old television shows and had learned English through *Sesame Street*." Here the president allowed himself a quick grin.

"Accompanying *Voyager* was our special representative, James Earl Pickett, a man with a distinguished career who volunteered his services with commendable alacrity." Here, the president looked directly into the cameras although, in the Oval Office, his eyes were actually on Anne Byrne, registering his opinion of her choice of words used to describe Pickett. He continued. "While we were engaged in communications with the alien ship, *another* ship appeared and joined in the dialog.

"At this time, an emergency arose onboard *Harmonie*, and the aliens gallantly offered to transform *Voyager's* propulsion system so that she was able to return to the Moon in less than a day instead of the three weeks that had been required for her outbound voyage.

"Under our guidance," the president lied stoically, "*Voyager* arrived at the Japanese moon base and took aboard much-needed supplies, as well as the distinguished Admiral Isao Tsukino, who offered his services unstintingly.

"Upon return to Jupiter—again, in less than a day thanks to the alien technology— Admiral Tsukino, Ambassador Pickett, and Captain Emily Steele, as well as a handpicked international crew on *Voyager*, were conveyed by the aliens on a whirlwind tour of the local galaxy, including the Eagle Nebula which, as you know, is the home of the 'Pillars of Creation'; the black hole of Cygnus X-1; and, finally, the solar system Gliese 581, where our astronauts were able to detect intelligent radio signals from among that sun's planets."

The president paused for a long moment.

"Upon their return, Ambassador Pickett was appointed to continue negotiations," the president continued, "negotiations which would hopefully lead to acquiring interstellar drive technology and allow our world access to all the glories and possibilities of interstellar, faster-than-light flight."

He allowed a small frown to cross his face.

"However, we have just been informed that, for reasons unknown, the aliens have chosen to break off negotiations."

He took a slow, steady breath and looked down for a moment before raising his face once more to the cameras.

"We hope that this is just a momentary hiccup in what has proven, up to now, to be an amazing journey of peaceful discovery and an enlightening explosion in the horizons of possibility available to all mankind." He paused again. "When Americans landed on the Moon, we left a placard which stated: 'We came in peace for all mankind.'"

Pause.

"Again, we come in peace for all mankind," the president continued. "We hope and we are confident that we will overcome our current situation and see the opening of a new and brilliant chapter in the history of our race. We are committed—as are our friends in Europe, Japan, China, and the rest of the world—to provide equal access to all our gains in technology to every government. We are hopeful that, shortly, we will be able to make the great announcement that we have continued—even, completed—negotiations with these aliens, and will embark on that new, brighter day."

Again, he paused.

"Until then, we will all remain hopeful and confident that, having sent our very best people to the stars, they will return with the very best results."

He smiled into the camera.

"I thank you for your patience in listening," he said now in conclusion, "and I wish every one of you the very best, from my nation to yours."

Off script, he added, knowing that his constituents would demand it, "And may God save us all."

Chapter Twelve

Xythir

>>Exern, connect me to the stumblers, request their 'Ambassador Pickett,'<< Captain Nexl said. He'd spent several minutes after his heated conversation with the damned slitherer in the quiet of his quarters, listening to the soothing tones of Mike Oldfield's *Hergest Ridge*. Copying it was a violation of interstellar copyright laws but—shatter it!—so many of the stumblers had already stolen it that he figured he'd never be prosecuted himself.

It was a bad attitude for a captain of a starship that thrived on selling intellectual properties, Nexl knew, but really he couldn't care less. The music was soothing. It reminded him of why he wanted to trade with the stumblers—the Earthers he corrected himself diplomatically.

His tracking console had lit with the information that Exern had detected transmissions from both Earthers ships back to their homeworld. Doubtless they were both saying something along the lines of "whip your limbs together one last time, folks, the aliens are pissed!" If he could have, he would have let them stew longer, but time and space waited for no one.

This is Ambassador Pickett. To whom am I speaking?

I am Captain Nexl of the Xlern ship Xythir, Nexl responded. **I regret the previous breakdown in communications.**

We had not had the chance to thank you for your amazing tour of the nearby galaxy, the two-legger typed back.

In our mutual interests, we thought it useful to provide you with an indication of the value of the technology we wish to trade.

Indeed. It was quite an enjoyable journey, the two-legger replied.

As you know, we are under some pressure to repair our error and continue with our normal mission, Nexl tapped back, glad that their method of communication did not allow for the transmission of emotions, even as he thought: *If we don't fix this, we're gonna be pulled limb from limb!*

Our engineers have made great strides in grasping your technology, Pickett now typed. **We are convinced that we could quickly develop a star drive that would equal yours.**

Nexl's upper limbs shot straight out in shock. Were they serious? *Calmly,* he told himself.

Doubtless so, Nexl typed back, **but if any aliens were to arrive while you were still in the process of developing this technology, it would be bad.**

How is that?

The penalties for early contact would be … unfavorable to our concerns, Nexl tapped in response. **And there are some within the league of star nations who consider it best to eradicate any illegal activities.**

Why might that concern us? Pickett asked.

I was not clear, Nexl typed back, **if it were determined that you were not qualified to trade, there are those who would consider it wisest to eliminate you.**

Your allies would destroy a sentient race?

Sentience is defined by star travel. Under the circumstances, some of the sentient races might classify your planet as a source of potential infection and cleanse it.

What do you propose? the ambassador asked.

We believe that we could coordinate with your scientists and engineers, Nexl typed in reply, still amazed that the Earthers would bother to differentiate between the two specialties, **and quickly give them the knowledge and tools to build your own star drive. We believe that your small ship would be well-suited as a test bed.**

On that we agree, Pickett replied. **And in return for this, would you require anything in exchange?**

We believe that you understand the concept of trade, Nexl replied. **We are traders and not used to giving things without return, except in rare circumstances.**

Is this not one of those rare circumstances?

Nexl reached for a small rock with his forelimbs and passed it back to the bigger hindlimbs before launching it against the nearest non-functional surface. The resounding *crack!* was a most satisfying distraction. He really wanted to get his tentacles on the Earther and tie it into the sort of shape that the Earthers called a pretzel. *Of course,* Nexl realized, *such a drastic re-arrangement of Earther limbs would be fatal. But that,* he reflected, *was precisely the* point.

That would not explain our contact with you, Nexl responded after it recovered itself. **What we propose is to exchange with you both the technology of a simple primitive star drive and that of our most complex technology. Then, when asked, we would all mutually maintain that we had traded just that technology with a fellow star-traveling racc.**

We would want to establish treaties of trade and exchange ambassadors with both your nations, Pickett replied.

Nexl was ready for that. **We are mere traders. We are quite willing to provide introductions to our governing bodies, but whether they are willing to exchange representatives is outside our grasp.**

What about navigational aids? Pickett responded. **We would certainly be interested in trading information with you regarding routes, species, and their trade preferences.**

Never! Nexl thought angrily. **All things are open for trade,** Nexl replied, **provided suitable exchange can be arranged.**

Have you any idea what you'd like to learn from us in exchange for your star drive technologies? Pickett now typed.

Nexl's limbs shivered with pleasure. *Oh, yes! We've got a little list!*

We have not had a chance to obtain a decent account of the technologies you possess from which we might create trade, Nexl typed back, lying with all four top limbs.

It is difficult to provide such a list without some understanding of your needs, Pickett responded.

Liar! Nexl thought happily to itself. It had hoped to negotiate with one of the two-legs' engineers or scientists. Failing that, with a gaggle of emissaries all bent on offering their best deal. This Pickett was neither and, Nexl admitted, seemed to have a great understanding of the basics of trade.

Would you consider trading a brief history of your species in exchange for the basic star drive technology? Nexl typed back. **While you are building your prototype drive, we can examine it and see if there is any potential for trade.** He didn't wait for the human to reply before adding, **Naturally, we expect that as your population grew, the amount of your inventions grew accordingly, so if you were to omit, say, the last two hundred years of your history, you would doubtless be saving revelation of your most important innovations.**

Let's see if they'll swallow that! Nexl thought happily. In truth, because of the variations of mineral deposits and civilization growth, the most useful inventions were among the first discovered. Later discoveries tended to be things that were duplicated among multiple races and so of much lesser value.

That was not to say that there weren't some technological jewels in the later years—the Mykorran were quite eager to get the rights to integrated circuits for their burgeoning sexual pleasure trade while the TyrrinAlgols were just as eager to replace their chain abaci studios with four-math electronic calculators.

All that, however, was for the future. Now …

On behalf of the people of Earth, the Moon, Mars, and solar system Sol— Pickett's response broke off. **Permit me to amend: on behalf of the human race, I accept your suggestion.**

Yes! Nexl couldn't wait to slap the slitherers with *this* news!

Your trade is accepted, Nexl responded in the English version of the interstellar common contract. **I will instruct our engineer—the dratted Axlu, twist it!—to open an entry port to our training facilities.**

I shall trust the details of the technological exchange to our engineers and scientists while my crew will provide you with a copy of our history. Pickett typed back.

Excellent!

A moment later, Pickett responded, **We know that you have had some experience with our form from your viewings of our television. In this historic meeting, is there anything we should consider in selecting our personnel?**

Nexl wiggled its limbs in appreciation of the question. It paused for a moment and then typed, **Personnel who might be alarmed by multiple limbs should be left behind.**

How many limbs?

We have four mobility limbs and four manipulator limbs, Nexl typed back happily. **Our contact engineers have suggested that those who are afraid of octopi or spiders might not be good candidates for contact with our species.**

Hee, hee! Nexl thought to itself. *I hope Pickett is squealing with fright! Giant spiders!*

* * *

Harmonie

"Giant spiders?" Peter Murray said. "They're like giant spiders?"

"I can't tell you that for certain," Pickett replied. "Their captain merely told me that those who might be squeamish with spiders or octopi would probably be best left behind."

"Is there anyone here who has that problem?" Captain Zhukov said, scanning the wardroom's occupants.

"I was bitten by a poisonous spider once," Chris Jenkins spoke up in the silence.

"Will this cause you problems in working with these aliens?" Captain Steele asked.

Jenkins grimaced. "I can't say for sure."

"Then you're out for the moment," Pickett declared. When Captain Zhukov looked ready to object, he quelled him, stating, "This is first and foremost a diplomatic mission. *My* mission."

"As you say, Mr. Ambassador," Admiral Tsukino rumbled in agreement.

"Chris, you're good with data," Captain Steele said, "could we put you in charge of giving the aliens the history dump?"

Jenkins bit his lip. "Look, Skip, I'm sure—"

"I'm sorry, Mr. Jenkins, but we can't risk it at the moment," Pickett cut across him. "When our people have had a chance to get to know these aliens, if you decide you might be comfortable in your dealings with them, then we'll re-open the issue."

"Okay," Chris said glumly.

"I'd like Ensign Sato to participate," Admiral Tsukino said.

"She's got a degree in engineering, with honors," Jenkins said approvingly.

"You've had a chance to talk with her?" Admiral Tsukino asked in surprise.

"Well, not as much as Ensign Dubauer," Jenkins replied with a twitch of his lips, "but some."

"Lori Dubauer would be a good choice," Captain Steele said.

"I'd like to send Ensign Strasnoye," Captain Zhukov spoke up. "He, too, has a broad grasp of technology and science."

"Who should lead this endeavor?" Admiral Tsukino asked, glancing around the room.

"That's easy," Pickett replied, glancing toward Emily Steele. "It's your ship, Captain."

Admiral Tsukino nodded slowly. "Very well, Mr. Ambassador, as soon as you can arrange it, we will transfer our team to the alien ship."

"I think that we can leave that with the normal communications officers," Pickett said. "I'm pretty sure that the people back home would like to know that they don't need to worry about Armageddon just yet."

"I wonder if we could weasel an FTL comm system out of them," John McLaughlin muttered.

"That's an excellent idea, Mr. McLaughlin," Admiral Tsukino said, pouncing on the notion. "Captain Steele, would you object to letting Mr. McLaughlin, here, lead a team to investigate that possibility?"

When Steele seemed to hesitate, Pickett spoke up, "I agree with the admiral. If we can demonstrate our technical prowess on our own, it will help with our negotiations with aliens."

"And while that's being done, Captain Zhukov, I'd like to get with you, your chief engineer and" Admiral Tsukino turned inquiringly to Captain Steele, "perhaps your Lieutenant McElroy, to discuss our future."

"Future?" Pickett repeated with a raised eyebrow.

"Long-term," the admiral explained, adding, with a smile, "We are very shortly going to be a group of nations with interstellar travel. How best to exploit that?"

Pickett's eyes widened in enlightenment. "I think that's an excellent idea, Admiral."

"Thank you," the admiral replied. He rose from the table. "Now, I think we'd best put our plans into action."

*   *   *

"The aliens have opened a hatchway for us and they've illuminated it with a standard red light as well as a radio beacon at 121.5 megahertz," Captain Steele said as she and her detachment assembled at *Voyager*'s airlock. They were all wearing their suits. Admiral Tsukino and Ambassador Pickett stood at the hatchway to see them off.

"This is all voluntary," Pickett now said. He glanced to each in turn. "If you've got cold feet about this, let us know now."

"Mr. Ambassador, I'll admit to butterflies in my stomach but I will not admit to cold feet," Lori Dubauer told him with a grin.

"Very well," Admiral Tsukino said. He glanced fondly at his young ensign, wearing the smallest spacesuit among the group, and the only one sporting the flag of the red sun on a white background. "We will be monitoring you and be ready to support you in any way."

He motioned for Pickett to follow him and they stood back, allowing Chris Jenkins to close the hatch and check the security of the seal.

"You're good, Skip," Jenkins said over the intercom.

"Good seal on this side," Emily agreed. "Gregor, would you please open the outer hatch?"

"As you wish, Captain," the ensign responded.

"When the hatch is open we'll proceed in file and make for the sled," Captain Steele reminded them.

The "sled" was nothing more than a long steel tube with two cross-tubes and the simplest of wiring to allow them to connect their suit intercoms together. It had lights at the front and four strategically placed clusters of cold-jets that used liquid nitrogen for thrust in the age-old standard of low-thrust systems everywhere. As backup, the four each had their suit thrusters—each quite capable of getting them to their destination.

When they were hooked up, Emily said, "Transit time will be about ten minutes. Be sure to take as many pictures and readings as you can. This is our first real chance to get good readings on this ship."

"Aye, Skipper," Lori Dubauer replied.

* * *

They were about halfway across when Lieutenant Ives called from *Harmonie*, "Captain Steele, I'm picking up some strange vibrations on the sled's telemetry."

"Yes, I've noticed it, too," Emily said. "Some sort of rhythmic vibration."

"Oh, sorry!" Ensign Dubauer said in distressed tones. "It was just me, Skipper, I was tapping on the frame."

"*Harmonie*," Emily called, "do you copy?"

"Roger, Captain," Lieutenant Ives said.

"'In space, *everyone* can hear you tap,' Lori," Captain Steele reminded her.

"Yeah, I forgot," Lori Dubauer said demurely.

"You were tapping Morse code, weren't you?" Ensign Sato spoke up suddenly.

"'*The secret is to ...* '" Ensign Strasnoye translated, pausing uncertainly.

"'*...bang the rocks together, guys,*'" Lori finished. "I was thinking of some old English radio show from the turn of the century."

"*The Hitchhiker's Guide to the Galaxy*, by Douglas Adams," Lieutenant Murray piped up on the frequency, to the surprise of everyone.

There was a moment's silence, then *Harmonie's* chief engineer explained, "When Lieutenant Ives saw the signal, he sent it to me for an opinion." His tone changed as he continued, "I had only just thought of trying Morse."

"What's the secret, then, Lori?" Emily said.

"Oh!" Lori replied, surprised at all the excitement her simple twitching had generated. "The story was a comedy about aliens coming to Earth to destroy it."

Lieutenant Murray snorted in pique.

"Sorry, Lieutenant, I know that's selling it short," Lori apologized.

"I wasn't surprised at you, Lieutenant," Murry replied quickly.

"Then who?"

There was a moment's silence. "I'm afraid that I was surprised, actually, that your captain was not more aware of science fiction references."

"Is there a reason why this is important?" Emily asked.

"Actually, Skip, it's more of a joke," Lori said. "The quote is supposed to come from this alien galactic radio broadcast where the announcer says hello—"

"And we'll be saying a big hello to all intelligent life-forms everywhere,'" Lieutenant Murray interrupted. *"And to everyone else out there, the secret is to bang the rocks together, guys.'"*

"Ah, Douglas Adams," Lori said wistfully, "one of England's greater comic geniuses."

"And so we're the intelligent life-forms?" Captain Steele ventured.

"In Morse?" Lieutenant Murray snorted.

"Uh, no, Skip," Lori added in a small voice, "I was thinking that we're about to bang some rocks together, actually."

"Hmm," Captain Steele replied thoughtfully, "I suppose we are." A moment later, she called over the ship frequency, "Lieutenant Ives, would you be so kind as to play us some background music in honor of our upcoming endeavor?"

"I can do that, Captain," Lieutenant Ives replied quickly, clearly feeling that *Harmonie* could do with some restoration of pride in light of Lieutenant Murray's undiplomatic snort.

"Do you happen to have the twentieth century English song, 'Tubthumping' by the group Chumbawamba?" Emily said, adding, "It was rather the unofficial theme song for our ship when we started working on the propulsion system."

"Here it is, Captain," Lieutenant Ives responded. "I'm sending it on your sub-channel B for those who wish to filter it out."

"Thank you," Emily said, even as the opening words began: *"'We'll be singing, when we're winning ...'"*

* * *

"Contact lights, everyone," Captain Steele told the sled riders nearly four minutes later.

Lights flicked out from their suit helmets.

"Telemetry has you on profile, Captain," Lieutenant Ives reported.

"Lori, let's have a ping," Emily said.

"Aye, Skipper, radar ping to active," Ensign Dubauer replied, turning on the sled's limited radar set.

Ping! The noise rang in their headsets echoed almost immediately by an echoed return.

"Range is 7.2 meters," Dubauer reported. Another ping and she added, "Range 7.0 meters, closing at .2 meters per second."

"Very well," Captain Steele replied. *"Harmonie,* contact in fourteen seconds."

A moment later, Lieutenant Ives said, "Roger, we put you now at ten seconds to contact."

"Roger," Emily replied. "Ensign Sato, prepare to launch the magnetic grapple."

"Ready," the ensign said immediately.

"Launch."

They were less than a meter from contact. The grapple accelerated as its magnetic field pulled it to the alien hull.

"Solid contact, ma'am," Ensign Sato said. "Launching second grapple." They'd agreed that they'd anchor the sled fore and aft on the side of the alien's hull just beside the airlock mechanism.

"Brace for impact," Emily warned. They had rotated the sled so that their feet were facing the alien ship. A moment later, Emily's feet felt a gentle push.

"*Harmonie*, we're down," Emily said. With a quirk of her lips, she added for history, "We're ready to make the next leap for mankind."

"Roger, Captain," Admiral Tsukino responded, having come to the bridge in anticipation of the history they were making. "Godspeed and good luck!"

* * *

Xythir

>>I EXPECT EVERYONE TO COMPORT THEMSELVES AS BEFITS THEIR DUTIES,<< Axlu rapped out loudly with its hind uppers while waving one of its forelimbs pointedly in the direction of Engineer Apprentice 4th Class Xover, of which Axlu had noticed an alarming tendency toward poor practical jokes, and another toward Security Apprentice 3rd Class Doxal, who seemed to embody the worst of Security Officer Noxor's paranoid beliefs. Either was likely to precipitate the sort of untoward event that might bring the full weight of the Traders' Guild down upon them all. And *that* would be the worst possible thing for all concerned, particularly the Earthers, who might find themselves on the wrong end of a political cover-up.

>>THE EARTHERS ARE NOT SOPHISTICATED, WE ALL KNOW, BUT NEITHER ARE THEY TO BE CONSIDERED INFERIOR,<< Axlu said. He waited until he was certain that the others had responded with appropriate levels of quivering and shaking then consulted the monitors. >>DO YOUR DUTY, FOR YOUR SHIP, FOR YOUR SHORE, FOR THE GUILD.<<

Axlu consulted the monitors and then tapped the stud that opened communications to the airlock and training area.

IF YOU FOLLOW THE ILLUMINATED MARKERS ON THE FLOOR, THEY WILL LEAD YOU THROUGH OUR AIRLOCK SYSTEM, INTO THE SHIP, AND THEN TO OUR TRAINING FACILITY, Axlu typed to the alien two-leggers.

>>Sir,<< Xover rapped lightly, >>what if they can't do that?<<

Axlu flicked a quelling limb toward the apprentice.

Roger, *Xythir*, came the typed response over the agreed communications frequency.

Jenkins had managed to convince the aliens to change the way they communicated to include using lowercase letters, to the relief of almost everyone. **We are following the illumination.** A moment later, the message came, **How will we activate your airlock mechanism?**

    WE WILL DO THAT FOR YOU, Axlu replied.

    We would like to learn how in case there's an emergency.

    THAT WILL COVERED IN OUR MEETING.

    Excellent.

Axlu twitched at the alien's response but made no reply. As soon as he was certain that all aliens were in the outer airlock, he typed, **CLOSING OUTER DOORS.**

    Waiting.

Axlu was surprised at the reply until he realized that Xover hadn't closed the outer door.

    >>**XOVER, THE OUTER DOOR, IF YOU WOULD.**<<

    >>**Engineer?**<< Xover rapped back.

    >>**CLOSE IT!**<<

Xover trotted to the appropriate panel at full speed and quickly ran a limb over the appropriate protrusion.

    Outer door closed, the alien typed. Axlu wondered briefly if the two-legs might make more proficient engineer apprentices than his current trainees.

    FOLLOW THE LIGHTS, THE INNER DOORS WILL CLOSE BEHIND YOU. DO NOT BE CONCERNED.

    Wilco, came the response.

    >>**Officer Axlu?**<< Trade Apprentice Nevan rapped softly.

    >>**YES?**<<

    >>**What is '*wilco*'?**<<

    >>**It is a compression of two of their English words: will comply,**<< Security Apprentice Doxal clicked. Adding, >>**It is commonly used in their more warlike work divisions.**<<

    WHEN YOU HAVE COMPLETELY ENTERED THIS ROOM, THE OUTER DOOR WILL CLOSE AND WE WILL INSERT AN ATMOSPHERE SUITABLE FOR BREATHING. Axlu now typed. **AT THAT POINT, YOU MAY REMOVE YOUR VACUUM SUITS.**

    Very well, came the reply.

Axlu rapped its forelimbs together in a staccato motion that said nothing, rather indicating impatient waiting.

    >>**They do not seem to be moving very slow,**<< Xover noted.

    >>**NO, THEY DO NOT,**<< Axlu agreed. He was not surprised to be handed this task. Typically, it was something assigned to the trade officer or, at most, an engineer apprentice. Axlu knew that he had received this less pleasant task as a result of his unwanted revelation to the two-legs. Captain Nexl had made it clear that this was Axlu's chance to clear the dark

ink with which that incident had stained his honor. For himself, Axlu was somewhat relieved to be given a list of approved topics which he could communicate to the two-legs.

The two-legs entered the fore room and Axlu waved to Xover to close the outer door.

>>**Door closed,**<< Xover reported a moment later. In a softer tone he said, >>**Engineer?**<<

>>**YES?**<<

>>**Why are we piping more air into the room?**<< Xover asked. >>**The pressure is already acceptable.**<<

Doxal rattled his upper limbs in a staccato that indicated derision before rapping out, >>**We are confusing the aliens. We do not want them to know that they can breathe our air.**<<

>>**TRUE,**<< Axlu agreed, although secretly he wondered if this particular deception was well-advised. Security Officer Noxor had insisted upon it, however, and Axlu was in no position to argue. From an environmental standpoint, however, it represented a danger if any emergency arose. Axlu only hoped that the captain had considered that there might be emergencies. >>**YOU MAY STOP THE AIR, NOW, APPRENTICE.**<<

>>**Stopped.**<< Xover reported.

YOU MAY NOW REMOVE YOUR VACUUM SUITS, Axlu typed to the aliens.

>>**They are—they are quite tall,**<< Trade Apprentice Nevan rapped cautiously.

>>**On average their height is four times that of our own standing height,**<< Doxal rapped in agreement. >>**However, it should be noted that our forelimbs are easily able to reach the upper protuberance known as the 'head.'**<<

>>**Some of our hind uppers might not reach,**<< Nevan noted.

>>**For offensive purposes, the proper response is to press hard upon the small spheres in their heads. They are called 'eyes' and are used for sight. A sufficient application of force on the eyes will render any two-legs incapacitated,**<< Doxal replied with a great amount of enthusiasm.

>>**WE SHALL NOT ENGAGE IN SUCH EXTRANEOUS ACTIVITIES, APPRENTICE,**<< Axlu rapped forcefully. >>**OUR MISSION IS PEACEFUL.**<<

>>**It is important to be prepared, Engineer,**<< Doxal replied.

>>**INDEED,**<< Axlu agreed. >>**IN THIS INSTANCE, IT IS REQUIRED THAT YOU BE PREPARED TO FOLLOW MY INSTRUCTIONS.**<<

>>**Just so.**<<

>>**They are quite awkward in appearance,**<< Nevan observed.

>>**They must think so as well,**<< Doxal said, >>**for most of their visual art deals with the destruction of one another through various forms of violence.**<<

>>**I prefer their attempts at humor,**<< Xover responded.

>>**ENOUGH DISTRACTIONS! ATTEND YOUR DUTY!**<<

>>**As you wish,**<< Doxal responded with overtones of disgruntlement.

We have removed our suits and are ready to proceed, the alien leader typed.

THE DOORS TO THE TRAINING ROOM WILL NOW OPEN, Axlu typed in response, signaling to Xover to open the door.

>>**Here they come!**<< Nevan rapped. >>**Just like newlings flopping onto the shore.**<<

>>**Ugly newlings,**<< Doxal observed.

>>**XOVER, PREPARE TO ENTER THE TRAINING ROOM,**<< Axlu rapped.

>>**I thought I was entering,**<< Doxal responded indignantly.

>>**YOUR ATTITUDE IS INSUFFICIENTLY CONDUCIVE TO A POSITIVE OUTCOME,**<< Axlu rapped back.

Doxal shifted back and forth on his lower limbs in an involuntary display of pique and shame.

>>**I am ready, Engineer,**<< Xover reported.

PLEASE PREPARE YOURSELF, ONE OF OUR ENGINEERS WILL NOW INTRODUCE OUR SPECIES TO YOU, Axlu typed to the aliens.

Is there a screen we should watch? the alien typed back.

Axlu's hind upper limbs twisted with amusement while his forelimbs waved Xover out of their observation room.

Xover moved steadily, if not with great speed, through the door that connected to the hallway, and then paused to hit the exterior alarm for the training room.

Axlu noted that the aliens all turned toward the sound, much like any Xlern would.

>>**PROCEED,**<< Axlu ordered his apprentice.

>>**With all the pride of elders receiving a new batch of flounderings, I now welcome these aliens onto our shores,**<< Xover clicked humbly, aware of his position as the first representative of his species to a whole new school of aliens.

*   *   *

"Captain, there's something at the door!" Ensign Dubauer cried as they all jumped at the strange rapid tapping.

"Steady everyone," Emily warned as the door opened.

When the door finished opening, they all stood frozen in place.

The alien's body was shaped like a slightly squashed ball, being just a bit wider than it was tall. The body was about sixty centimeters—two feet—from side to side and the same from top to bottom. The skin was a mottled mix of blues and greens. Dark spots in the front marked eyes but, surprisingly, another pair of dark spots were also on each side of the body.

The alien stood on impossible limbs, four of them. The limbs were darker in color than the body. Above the body, nearly in line with the lower limbs, were four thinner, whip-like, tentacular limbs which were, if anything, slightly darker.

The alien trotted forward.

"Skipper! Look at its hands!" Lori shouted, pointing to the upper manipulators. Each of them were curled around what looked like brightly colored marble stones.

"Maybe they're gifts," Ensign Strasnoye suggested.

"Stand still," Emily ordered. She slowly raised her hands, palms out in the universal gesture of peace.

The alien paused and, in a motion that was almost a blur, rapped the two rearmost, larger rocks together to produce a quick burst of percussive sound.

"It's not Morse," Ensign Strasnoye said.

"Skipper, look at the screens," Lori said. Emily turned her eyes to the nearest screen and saw that it now read: **Welcome on board our ship.**

"They use the rocks to communicate?" Ensign Strasnoye cried in surprise. He gestured to the alien and then to the screen.

The alien rapped the rear rocks and added the fore rocks to produce a second, higher-pitched sound.

We sense the compressions on our bodies and translate them, the screen now read, That is interpreted into your words.

"Oh, Dear Lord!" Lori Dubauer said with a groan. "They really *do* bang the rocks together!"

We were hoping you'd notice, the translation of the alien's rapping scrolled upon the screen.

"I owe Mr. Jenkins fifty dollars," Ensign Sato said quietly. Emily turned her eyes upon the diminutive Japanese officer, who explained, "I bet him that the aliens had no sense of humor."

The alien rapped both sets of rocks again. **In our experience, all sentient species have a sense of humor. We believe that it is a requirement for the sort of thinking required to produce interstellar flight.**

"If you can't take a joke, you shouldn't try?" Lori ventured.

Ensign Sato moved in one quick fluid set of motions and, before Captain Steele could react, was directly in front of the alien. She was on her knees, one hand raised in a broad gesture.

"Are those your eyes?" Ensign Sato said as she indicated the two dark spots in the alien's front.

We call them opticals, the alien replied. **Our analyses indicate that, while we share your range on the colors you call blue and green, we see somewhat more into the range of what you would call infrared.**

"My name is Kasumi Sato, how do you call yourself, honorable sir?"

I answer to the sound X-o-v-e-r, came the typed response.

"Xover? Is that correct?" Ensign Sato replied.

Your accent is strange but it will do, came the translation of Xover's rapping.

"You know, Skipper, I wish the eetees had told us about the whole rapping thing earlier," Lori Dubauer commented in an aside to Captain Steele. "I can feel a major migraine coming on."

We felt that it would be difficult to explain, Xover responded, having obviously "heard" the remark in spite of Ensign Dubauer's intentions.

"I'll trade a migraine for a star drive any day," Lori declared, taking a step toward the alien. Xover skittered back and Lori halted. "I'm sorry, I didn't mean to scare you."

"You are much taller," Ensign Sato observed from the floor.

I apologize, Xover typed. **I am afraid that I reacted in fear.**

"No need to apologize," Emily said, waving the objection away. "I am sure that we will all have to learn to overcome instinctive reactions while we get to know each other."

Xover's upper limbs twitched but he clicked no rocks together so Emily took the motion as alien body language.

"My name is Emily Steele and I am the captain of *Voyager*, the smaller of our two ships," Emily said. "Are you in command of this ship?"

Xover's upper limbs, particularly the front ones, jerked spastically and it wobbled up and down on its lower limbs.

I? Captain? You honor me! Xover typed. **I have no pretensions ever to captaining a ship. I am a mere engineer apprentice and quite expendable.**

"Well, we'll try not to expend you, Xover," Emily said in a dry tone. "However, in that case, I ask if you are equipped to train us all on this drive technology?"

Ah, very good, Captain! came the typed translation of Xover's rapid rapping with both sets of upper limbs although mostly with the higher-pitched rocks of the fore limbs. **No, I am merely the *hors d'ouevres* as it were, the introduction, sacrificial, if needed.**

"Shouldn't you be over that worry by now, Engineer?" Lori Dubauer asked, earning a scowl from her captain. She responded with a shrug, adding aloud to Xover, "I mean, you must have known coming in here that we were unarmed."

Whether or not you carry projectile weapons or implements of destruction does not mean that your limbs have been removed, came Xover's response.

"By 'unarmed,' Ensign Dubauer is saying that we have not brought weapons with us, not that we have removed any limbs," Emily explained.

Our databases were ambiguous on this, Xover said by way of apology. **They will be updated. As for the issue of weapons, your species evolved with limbs capable of destruction.**

"Ah!" Emily cried. "I see your point."

"We were worried about your rocks," Ensign Strasnoye spoke up. "On our world, they were used as one of our earliest ranged weapons."

Also on ours, Xover responded. **Of course, any such action also rendered us speechless.**

"Which must have put your species at a certain disadvantage," Emily guessed. "Although I imagine your rear upper limbs were used for long ranges and the near limbs used for communication."

Correct, Xover typed back. **We refer to our upper limbs as pikki.**

"And your lower limbs, what do you call them?"

Tek, Xover replied. A moment later it rapped some more and the screen showed, **One might consider them our low-tek form of motion.**

"Xover, did you draw straws to see who could get the record for the first alien pun?" Lori Dubauer demanded with a groan.

Draw straws?

"It is a very basic method of selecting randomly from a group of people," Emily answered.

I volunteered and the engineer selected me, Xover replied.

"For your puns?"

I was selected by the engineer because my attitude was conducive toward a positive outcome, Xover replied with lengthy rapping of both fore and rear pikki.

"Your engineer must have a great sense of humor," Lori Dubauer guessed.

Without meaning any disrespect, I am not sure that I have ever seen the engineer show any signs of humor, Xover rapped in response.

"I am sorry, Xover, but we seem to be getting distracted from our purpose," Emily said, casting half-hooded eyes censoriously in the direction of her ensign. Lori Dubauer accepted the partial rebuke with a guilty nod and a shrug of her shoulders. "Given that we do not intend you as our *hors d'ouevres* nor any other meal, perhaps you can explain to us the steps we will take to learning about this star drive?"

Firstly, Captain, I believe that the rest of the team will enter and make acquaintances, Xover typed back.

"If you're all typing, how will we know which of you is which?" Ensign Strasnoye now asked.

In multiple conversations we will tag each line with the speakers' name, Xover replied. **Much like your close-caption television systems.**

"You know—" Lori began in surprise, only to cut off when Captain Steele kicked her foot. Ensign Dubauer turned her eyes questioningly, but Emily quickly jerked her head in the negative, her lips set in a thin line.

"This is not the time," Captain Steele said out loud. "Would your fellow crew members feel more secure if we were to step further away from the door?"

I imagine they would, Xover replied, not moving from his position.

With hands at her sides, Emily gestured for the others to move further back into the room. When they were near at the far wall, Xover took a few quick steps further into the room, although still only a quarter of the way from the door.

A new line of text appeared on the display screen although Xover had clicked no rocks.

Axlu: WE WILL ENTER NOW.

"Axlu?" Lori said, turning her head toward the captain, then back toward Xover. "Is

Axlu your chief engineer?"

Xover: Engineer officer, yes.

"We have met him," Emily said, allowing her lips to quirk upwards briefly.

"Did he not always communicate in upper case?" Ensign Sato asked, her question directed mostly toward Ensign Strasnoye, the communications officer.

"It appeared so," Gregor replied neutrally.

"Is there a particular reason that his communication was always in upper case letters?" Emily asked.

Xover: You"ll see.

The door opened. Behind Xover, Emily saw three more Xlern move into the room.

They were all colored in greens and blue but they had variations in their mottling, including some brilliant combinations that gave the impression of streaks of gold or flame yellow.

The aliens stood for a moment and then one moved up to stand beside Xover. He rapped a sequence of booming bangs as his thick upper limbs hurled the large rocks he gripped together and apart in rapid succession, the sound filling the room and echoing painfully.

Axlu: I AM AXLU, ENGINEER OFFICER, I WELCOME YOU TO OUR SHIP.

"Oh," said Lori in small voice, "now I see."

CHAPTER THIRTEEN

"PLEASE BE QUIET," EMILY STEELE URGED AS SHE RUBBED HER FOREHEAD soothingly. "I need some aspirin."

"Earplugs," Lori Dubauer added.

"Perhaps some noise-cancelling headsets," Ensign Sato suggested.

Ensign Strasnoye was not with them in the briefing room; he'd gone directly to *Harmonie's* sick bay as soon as he was out of his suit.

"They use rocks to communicate," Lori said to a quizzical Chris Jenkins. She reached into her pants pocket and pulled out her wallet, peeling out a crisp bill and passed it to him. "And they tell puns."

"Told ya," Chris said, pocketing the bill with a grin. "Murray Leinster wrote about it in *First Contact*, way back in the last century."

"They have humor?" Admiral Tsukino asked, eyes going toward his ensign.

Ensign Sato nodded and then winced at the pain of the motion.

"Except the Shouter," Lori said. "Xover says that he's got no sense of humor."

"I suspect he's right," Ensign Strasnoye concurred. He smiled at Chris Jenkins. "On the other hand, Engineer Apprentice Xover has a very well-developed wit."

"Even made the first human-Xlern pun," Lori said with a quick smile.

"Apparently a sense of humor is a trait common to all star-faring species," Emily added, turning to be sure that Ambassador Pickett didn't miss her words.

"Humor is associated with deceit," Admiral Tsukino said.

"It's a form of deception," Pickett agreed, "but we suspected as much of these aliens. In fact, there's some argument to support the notion that trade of any sort embodies a willingness to deceive."

Admiral Tsukino waved the issue aside, turning to Captain Steele. "Headaches aside, how was it?"

"It was amazing," Emily said. "Admittedly we didn't do more than make basic introductions and assignments but …" words failed her and she could only shrug apologetically.

"What we don't know, Admiral, is how long it will take us to absorb what they have to teach," Ensign Sato said demurely into the silence that fell.

"Sato is right, Admiral," Lori agreed. "One of the limiting factors is the time taken to rap out a message and then get it translated."

"How fast are they communicating, then?" Pickett asked.

"Because they use two sets of limbs they are pretty much able to keep up with our speech rates," Emily said. "But given the amount of information they have to impart …" she flicked her hand open in an indeterminate motion.

"I did some guesswork with Mac," Pickett told them, "and we figure that under normal circumstances, it would take at least ten people eight years each to absorb and convert this sort of scientific and technological leap into something usable. And that's the lowest number. The upper limit is about two people-centuries."

"But they're saying they don't have much time," Lori said.

Pickett's face twisted in a sour expression.

"Mr. Ambassador?" Admiral Tsukino said.

Pickett sighed and shook his head. "It's not that we don't know that they're scamming us—that's a given. It's that we don't know how *much* of this is a scam."

"Sir?" Emily said, inviting him to explain.

"You know that we've got a long list of questions regarding their reasoning for this contact with us in the first place," Pickett said. "There are questions as to how they could have made their 'mistake' and then there are questions as to how much of mistake it actually was."

"Meaning what, Mr. Ambassador?" Captain Zhukov, who had been sitting silently at the end of the group, now asked.

"They claim that their contact with us is in violation of interstellar agreements," Pickett replied. "That this violation is so serious that the interstellar community might consider annihilating us as part of their reaction."

"That does seem a bit far-fetched," Captain Steele agreed.

"No," Pickett said, "*that* part I can see. It depends upon how strictly controlled the interstellar community actually is." Only Captain Zhukov nodded in understanding, so he continued for the sake of the others, "If the community were a loose integration or a confederation, then I suspect our alien friends wouldn't have bothered contacting us at all unless they were certain of making a profit. They *certainly* wouldn't have worried about giving us a star drive—that probably would happen all the time in such a loose union. If, on the other the hand, there was strict and absolute control, then the aliens would never have tried to pull this scam on us at all. They would have stayed away and pretended that they never even noticed us.

"So that leaves us with a community that's somewhere in between," Pickett said, raising his hands extended and bringing them closer together to illustrate the constraints. "In which case, the question is: how closely will the aliens' actions be scrutinized?"

"I still don't get it, sir," Jenkins said, glancing around to see if he was the only one.

"If they really are expected to follow the law—or *mostly* follow the law—then what they're trying won't work," Pickett said. "Because no matter how quickly we learn this new technology that we're going to pretend was home grown, a cursory examination of our literature and industry will prove that that's not so."

"You're saying that we couldn't possibly leap from fusion and antimatter drives to star drives?" Emily asked.

"Not without new evidence to send us down that track," Pickett said. "Until we got some indication that the aliens were using gravity, we didn't even know where to look to see how our current model of the universe was wrong."

"And we haven't proved that it is wrong," Emily said. "At least, if you discount the evidence of our recent trip to the stars."

"Exactly," Pickett said. "And so the aliens must be operating in a society where they aren't under excessive scrutiny for this sort of operation, but they *are* under enough scrutiny that they have to at least *pretend* that we invented our star drive."

"Sounds almost mobster," Jenkins said. "Semi-legal at best."

"Well, they're making sure that we're going to do everything in our power to protect them," Emily remarked.

Pickett raised a finger in her direction while nodding emphatically. "And those are the best sort of scams."

"How?" Admiral Tsukino asked.

"They're the sort of scams where your victim is loudly protesting your innocence," Pickett replied. He shook his head wonderingly. "Which is why I really want to know what's going on."

"Won't it be enough that we get a star drive?" Captain Steele asked.

"That's certainly what they want us to think," Chris Jenkins observed.

Pickett nodded slowly in agreement. "Which leads me to this question: if this is the bippy prize, what did we *really* earn?"

"But, aside from a simplified history, they've got nothing from us!" Jenkins protested.

"Nothing that we've given them," Captain Zhukov replied, turning searching eyes on Ambassador Pickett. Pickett met his look and smiled grimly.

"So the question becomes, what of ours do they already have that they value so highly?" Admiral Tsukino asked.

"And so highly that they're willing to risk getting caught," Pickett added.

"Well," Jenkins said, "they've got television."

"Which, according to Xover, doesn't do them much good," Emily said.

"Why not?" Pickett asked in surprise.

"We did some simple communicating," Emily told him. "And we found that their eyes process images at the rate of seventy per second. Our transmission rate of thirty images per second is less than half their normal vision—they see only a series of slowly changing images, not motion."

"Okay, Skipper, why did they send us *Howdy Doody* when they first contacted us, if they couldn't get a sense of motion out of the images?" Chris Jenkins now demanded.

Emily looked at him blankly for a long moment then shrugged.

"Could they not have recognized the transmission as coherent, decoded it, and run some simple interpolation on it to produce images suitable for their vision?" Lieutenant Ives suggested. "After all, it seems that traders would have to be adaptable."

Emily turned to Chris Jenkins. "At a guess, how long would it take you to do something like that?"

"We pretty much did it when they sent their first transmission to us," Chris replied with a shrug. He nodded toward the French lieutenant. "That backs your suggestion up pretty strongly, sir."

Jacques Ives blinked owlishly and looked rather pleased with himself.

"Which means that your friend Xover might have been pulling the wool over your eyes," Pickett said.

"Possibly," Admiral Tsukino agreed. "But, Mr. Ambassador, what are our alternatives?"

Pickett frowned and shook his head. "There's no way we can back out now," he said, "and that's what bothers me."

Admiral Tsukino turned to Captain Steele. "Did the aliens say how long they thought it would take us to learn this technology?"

Emily shook her head. "They said that tomorrow we'll start training and that will give them a chance to gauge our speed."

"Do we need to do something about the noise levels?" Lieutenant Ives asked.

Emily smiled and shook her head. "We're each going to try a different approach and see how it works."

"And the recorders?" Captain Zhukov asked.

Emily glanced toward Lieutenant Ives, who beamed and said, "My people tell me they worked perfectly."

"Do we have anyone who can analyze them, maybe try to figure out a way to translate directly from their clicks to speech?" Pickett asked.

Captain Zhukov nodded approvingly at the idea but Emily shook her head. "I got the impression that their clicking was their native language and what we saw on the screen was a translation," she said.

"That would make things more difficult," Lieutenant Ives observed.

"I think it's worth doing, however," Pickett said. "I'd be happier if we had a fundamental understanding of their speech."

Admiral Tsukino gave him a probing look.

"I think there could be many applications, including a direct Xlern to human speech system," Pickett explained. Admiral Tsukino waited and Pickett added wryly, "*And* we'd be able to learn what they're *not* saying."

"It could be very useful," Lieutenant Ives agreed. "However, I don't know if we have the available resources."

"There's also the issue of time," Emily added. Pickett gave her a questioning look. "To get a good correlation—it wouldn't be a proper direct translation—would require a lot of observations before their 'speech' patterns could be determined accurately."

"So give it to the NSA," Pickett said. "They'd probably enjoy the challenge." He glanced toward Captain Zhukov as he added, "And send it to your people in the FSS. Let 'em both know and they can race each other."

Captain Zhukov chuckled evilly at the notion. The FSS was the Russian successor to the infamous KGB and was no more loved by the average Russian than its predecessor. The National Security Agency in the United States ran a close second as the world's most loathed spies.

"I wonder if either would be willing to admit to having deciphered the communications, however," Captain Zhukov said.

"Heck, give it to all the world and make it a priority," Pickett said. "That'll mean that it'll be a matter of national pride to announce the breakthrough."

"I wonder how the aliens will feel about that," Admiral Tsukino mused.

Pickett smiled, turning to Lieutenant Ives. "Would there be a way you could embed the data in something that our alien friends might not notice?"

"Sir?" Lieutenant Ives asked, confused.

"Well, I think it'd be nice to pull one over on them for a change," Pickett said. "And if we could present them with a direct translation system without their knowing that we'd been working on it …"

"I like it!" Chris Jenkins said.

"It could be a trade item," Captain Zhukov suggested.

"Actually, I think we would do better to offer it to them *gratis*," Pickett said with a twinkle in his eyes.

"Free?" Admiral Tsukino said.

"What's the catch?" Emily asked.

Pickett winked at her. "Wouldn't it be possible to insert a recording circuit in the unit? Something the aliens might not notice?"

"I'm not sure they would be very happy if they found out," Emily objected.

"It's also possible that they might be impressed by our duplicity," Captain Zhukov said. "After all, they do not seem to be operating with complete honesty."

"They're traders. They'll want to be sure that they got the best of the trade," Pickett said.

"Very well," Admiral Tsukino said. "Lieutenant Ives, if you could get your people to consider the ambassador's suggestion, I'd be delighted to hear your results."

"I'm sure we can think of something, sir," Jacques Ives replied.

"Excellent," Admiral Tsukino said. "In which case, we'll revisit this issue." He turned to Captain Steele. "In the meantime, I suggest that you and your people rest, recover, and prepare for the next session."

"Aye, sir."

* * *

Axlu: VERY WELL, CAPTAIN, WE WILL ACCEPT YOUR DIVISIONS FOR THE MOMENT, the monitors displayed the next day after the chief engineer had announced that they would separate into two training groups: one theoretical and one practical.

IF I DISCOVER THAT THERE IS GREATER EFFICIENCY IN A DIFFERENT GROUPING, I SHALL REQUIRE THAT YOU CONFORM.

"Barring any political considerations, we will be happy to comply," Emily said. The simple earplugs that Louise O'Reilly had recommended did a marvelous job of reducing the jarring clack of the rocks that the engineer used for his communications to something much less painful, but the subsonic noise still rumbled her chest in an uncomfortable fashion.

Axlu: POLITICAL?

"Two of our group come from the same nationality," Emily said. "It would be best if myself and Ensign Dubauer worked on different tasks." A quick glance toward the other three in her group made it clear that they were not unaware of the issue, nor did they find her suggestion unpalatable.

Axlu: I DO NOT LIKE POLITICS. IT IS INELEGANT AND INEFFICIENT.

"I agree, sir," Emily said with a quick grin. "However, you said that we would be splitting up, where will we go and with whom?"

Axlu: THE THEORETICAL GROUP WILL REMAIN HERE WITH ME AND TRADER NEVAN. THE ENGINEERING TEAM WILL FOLLOW ENGINEER APPRENTICE XOVER AND SECURITY APPRENTICE DOXAL TO THE FABRICATION ROOM.

"Fabrication room?" Emily repeated, eyes going wide. "I thought we would be responsible for our own fabrication, sir."

Axlu: OF COURSE, BUT FIRST YOU MUST KNOW THE MATERIALS AND PROCESSES REQUIRED. I WOULD ALSO BE SURPRISED IF YOU HAVE THE NECESSARY RAW MATERIALS ON YOUR SHIPS. WE WILL LOAN YOU THE RAW MATERIALS; FABRICATION WILL BE THROUGH YOUR MACHINES.

"How do you know if our fabricators will be capable?" Emily asked mildly, her heart racing in ill-concealed excitement.

Axlu: PERHAPS THEY ARE NOT. HOWEVER, IT HAS BEEN OUR EXPERIENCE THAT THE FABRICATION PROCESSES ARE NOT THAT MORE COMPLEX THAN THOSE REQUIRED FOR FUSION REACTORS OR ANTIMATTER ENGINES. The burly engineer—burly, that is, compared to the thinner Xover and the lithe Nevan, although dwarfed by the obvious physical prowess of Security Apprentice Doxal, whose very motions indicated a high degree of suspicion—now gestured irritably toward the door. **ENGINEERS, FOLLOW MY APPRENTICE.**

"Yay, we get the punster, Sato!" Lori Dubauer squeaked with false glee.

"Perhaps it is our pun-ishment for being so good with engines," Ensign Sato said, nodding obsequiously to the more flamboyant of the two aliens leading them.

"We'll see you two later," Emily said, tapping her comm unit meaningfully. Ensign Dubauer caught the motion and nodded: If needed, they would call.

The door slid shut noiselessly and Emily turned to Engineer Officer Axlu.

"We're ready."

Axlu: VERY WELL. DOXAL, REDUCE THE ILLUMINATION WHILE I BRING UP THE HOLOGRAPHIC DISPLAY. The engineer lowered its fore mannies toward Emily and Gregor in a motion that Emily interpreted as a nod of recognition before moving all four upper mannies side-to-side in a motion that drew Emily's eyes to the edge of the room.

The room went dim. A blue dot of light appeared in the center of the room, hovering slightly above them.

Axlu: GATHER AROUND.

Emily nodded to Gregor and they moved to either side of the dot. At some mannie motion from Axlu's right forelimb, Doxal waved its manipulators in a way that seemed to be interfacing with some sort of remote tracking device—or gesture sensor. In response, a small red dot appeared at a distance.

Doxal made another gesture and the two dots shrank almost to invisible while the red dot grew in intensity, so that it was still visible. It started to orbit around the blue dot. Then it speeded up and then—it was a blur of motion, a cloud nearly, surrounding the blue dot.

Axlu: NEXT.

Doxal waved again and the blue dot brightened, split and became a blue dot and a green dot, joined so tightly together that it was difficult to see where one began and the other ended. "Hydrogen," Ensign Strasnoye said, waving at the hovering image. "And now the isotope deuterium."

"With exaggerated sizes for the particles and not to scale," Emily added. She turned to Axlu, "The electrons should be orbiting at a far greater distance—larger than this room."

Axlu: MUCH LARGER, came the alien's typed agreement. **NEXT.**

"Tritium. One proton, two neutrons," Emily said when she spotted another green dot. A third green dot appeared and then there was a flash of light and the green dot was a blue dot with a much smaller red dot flying from it.

"Helium produced by neutron bombardment," Gregor guessed.

"Two protons, two electrons, two neutrons," Emily added. "That is the most stable isotope of helium."

Axlu: AND WHAT DETERMINES THAT IT IS HELIUM?

"The number of electrons," Gregor Strasnoye said immediately.

"The number of protons," Emily said. She darted a quick glance toward the ensign and said in a low voice, "Remember ionization."

"It is very difficult with noble gases," Gregor replied.

Axlu: SO YOU SIGNIFY BY PROTON QUANTITY.

"Yes," Emily said, "although we also make a distinction between electron energy levels, separating them into various shells." She pursed her lips and said, "Could you display carbon, the sixth element?"

Axlu: MAKE IT SO.

Doxal seemed to move reluctantly, certainly with less alacrity than before, but the image suddenly brightened to display six blue dots enmeshed with six green dots and six red dots moving in a complex dance that gave the red cloud a mottled, bulging look.

Emily frowned at the image. "Is this a display of ground state or some elevated energy states?"

Axlu: NEXT.

Doxal seemed as surprised by the response as the humans but in short order they witnessed a torrent of images as the number of protons, electrons, and neutrons grew until it stopped at the largest display.

"Is that element 126?" Emily asked.

Axlu: NO. IT IS ELEMENT 184.

"We have only produced artificially up to element 126," Emily said.

Axlu: ELEMENT 184 REQUIRES SPECIAL PRODUCTION TECHNIQUES.

"Do we need it for the star drive?"

Axlu: NO. THIS IS THEORY. Then to the apprentice, **DOXAL.**

The image shifted, zooming in until only one large proton was in view. It seemed to pulse or alter.

"In our understanding, these larger particles are themselves composed of more fundamental particles," Ensign Strasnoye observed.

Axlu: NEXT.

And so it went, working through elements, particle and sub-atomic particle physics, and then into field theory, through to electromagnetic fields.

Axlu: WE WILL BREAK NOW.

"We could continue," Emily offered.

Axlu: IT IS NECESSARY TO EXCRETE AND TAKE ON SUSTENANCE.

"Bathroom break," Emily muttered to herself. She glanced to the Russian ensign.

"We could use our suits," he suggested.

Emily grimaced. Certainly, their spacesuits were equipped to handle bodily waste, but there was a limit, she preferred to have something in reserve.

Axlu: DO YOU WISH TO USE OUR FACILITIES?

"I'm not sure our physiology is capable—" Emily began.

Axlu: WE EXCRETE THROUGH OUR CENTRAL VENT. OUR EXCRETORY RECEPTACLE IS A LARGE HOLE WHICH WE STRADDLE. WOULD THAT MEET YOUR REQUIREMENTS?

Emily took a moment to process the words: the aliens used a hole in the ground.

"Would there not be an issue of possible contamination?" Ensign Strasnoye asked. Emily raised an eyebrow at the mournful tone in his voice. Apparently the ensign was more desperate than she'd imagined.

Axlu: NO. I AM AN ENGINEER. SUCH THINGS ARE CONSIDERED. WASTE IS PROPERLY RECYCLED.

Emily wondered if the alien's way of waving its limbs right now indicated that it was laughing at them.

"Go on, Ensign, if you have the need," Emily said with a wave of her hand.

Axlu: FOLLOW ME, ENSIGN.

"We can switch off," Ensign Strasnoye suggested, trailing behind the smaller alien in case Captain Steele decided to pull rank.

"I'll wait for your report," Emily said, taking some delight in the ensign's widened eyes. Clearly he hadn't considered that she had decided to see if it was safe before risking her higher rank—and dignity.

Ten minutes later, the ensign and the engineer returned. Ensign Strasnoye smiled at the captain and gave her two thumbs up. "It's better than any zero-gee facility."

Emily, led by Doxal, discovered that this was indeed so. The aliens had provided gripping bars over their excretory hole and also had provided some rudimentary wipes which, when Emily thought about it, might be more likely a normal fitting on the alien starship than a sop to the human trainees.

Much relieved, she returned to the training area, for the next session.

Three hours later, she was quite ready to return to *Harmonie* and *Voyager*. The lessons had progressed from exploring the limits of human understanding to the fundamentals of new math and physics. Emily hadn't felt so intellectually stimulated and physically exhausted since she'd finished her second doctoral dissertation.

She was extra careful to ensure that all her people double- and triple-checked their suit integrity before allowing them to enter the airlock, hook up to their sled, and let *Harmonie's* bridge crew guide them autonomously back "home."

* * *

"The earplugs worked," Emily said.

"I didn't need anything once we'd left you with the Shouter," Lori Dubauer told her.

"I thought my noise-cancelling system was sufficient," Ensign Strasnoye added.

"I'm afraid that I concur with Ensign Dubauer," Ensign Sato said. "It was only in the presence of their engineer that my ears hurt."

"You call him 'the Shouter'?" Emily said to Ensign Dubauer.

"It is not very respectful," Ensign Sato said in a soft voice, glancing sideways toward Lori.

"Heck, it's not my name," Lori said. "That's what I got from Xover when you were on the john."

Ensign Sato looked momentarily confused while she deciphered "the john" and then nodded.

"How did it go?" Emily asked the two "practical" engineers.

"Skipper, we built a gravity-wave detector," Lori chirped. She turned to Captain Zhukov, "I think, sir, that your scientists could produce a more accurate unit within the week."

"And why would we want that, Ensign?" Admiral Tsukino asked mildly.

"Sir, I'm thinking that we could use it to properly track any communications between the two alien ships for starters," Lori responded immediately, "and, once your people can do it, we can send the plans back home and have our guys build bigger ones." She smiled mischievously, glancing toward her captain. "Ones that'll let us talk to home."

"Actually, Admiral, I believe that the gravity arrays would be more beneficial for an early warning system," Ensign Sato said demurely. She caught Ensign Dubauer's look and added, "Lori, they could be used to detect meteor interactions in the Oort clouds."

"That far?" Emily said.

"With a sufficiently large separation, Skip, you could probably pick up the orbits of the planets ten thousand light-years out," Lori said with a shucks-that's-easy shrug.

"Really?" Emily was impressed.

Captain Zhukov turned to Admiral Tsukino. "I would say that that is an excellent investment, sir."

"I suspect there'll be the usual moaning and whining from the crackpots," Pickett said, "but it'll get funded in the States the minute you say 'meteor.'"

No one laughed at that. The horrible destruction of Manhattan and most of the United States' East Coast was still too deeply seared into their culture.

"Did the aliens seem to realize what they were giving us?" Emily asked Lori, before adding in an aside to the group, "When we finished, we'd only just started on the new theories of gravity and five-force interactions."

"Skip, I think that Doxal guy was pretty sore about it, but he sees everything as a threat," Lori said.

"He is one of their security and safety officers," Ensign Sato said as though trying to soothe her training partner.

Lori smiled in reply and shook her head. "He's a paranoid dork." To her captain, she added, "Xover is definitely the best of the best, however. If he were human, I'd recommend him for promotion or whatever."

"Well, *Ensign*, I'm sure the eetees will be quite happy to know that," Captain Steele said with a grin. She added an open-handed wave of her hand to remove any sting from her gibe.

Lori laughed and then yawned, setting off all the rest of the training crew.

"You should get some rest," Pickett said, glancing toward Admiral Tsukino.

"I'd like Lori to spend a moment with our scientists before she heads off," Admiral Tsukino said.

"I will join her," Ensign Sato said in a rare display of decisiveness.

Admiral Tsukino made no reply and Lori rose quickly, reaching a hand toward the Japanese ensign and dragging her out of the room.

Pickett followed them with his eyes and then cut his gaze back to Captain Steele who met his look with quirked lips.

"It is one of the more pleasant duties of a commander," Admiral Tsukino said to the ambassador, "to ensure that the needs of his personnel are met in all matters."

Captain Zhukov stifled a chuckle.

Emily yawned, gesturing toward Ensign Strasnoye. "I think, Captain Zhukov, that your ensign will want to get his rest as soon as possible." More directly to Gregor, she said, "We're going to have another brain-burning day ahead of us."

"I think I can jot some notes before I collapse," Ensign Strasnoye assured her.

"Well, if you can't, don't worry because I'm going to do the same," Emily said. She rose and with a nod, said, "Admiral?"

Admiral Tsukino waved her away. "Sleep as soon as you can, Captain."

In a moment, the only ones left in the room were the admiral, Captain Zhukov, and the ambassador. Admiral Tsukino glanced at the other two. Captain Zhukov met his gaze but dropped his eyes, saying, "If you don't mind, I should be getting my people ready for tomorrow."

"Certainly, Captain," Admiral Tsukino said with a nod and a wave of his hand. "Please keep me informed."

"Yes, sir."

Pickett remained quiet until the sound of the Russian captain's feet had disappeared. Then he smiled at the Japanese admiral. Admiral Tsukino raised an eyebrow.

"I just love seeing a master at work," Pickett told him with a grin, obliquely acknowledging the way in which the admiral had effortlessly inserted himself into the chain of command.

Admiral Tsukino snorted and gave Ambassador Pickett a slow nod. "As do I, Mr. Ambassador."

Together they sat silent for a long moment, reflecting on what they'd learned that day and considering the implications.

"I suspect we'll see the other shoe drop in a couple of days," Pickett said finally.

"I wonder how our alien friends will react when we get our gravity detectors online," Admiral Tsukino replied.

"I think they won't know until the first transmission from Earth," Pickett said.

Admiral Tsukino thought on that. "Yes, I rather imagine you are correct, Mr. Ambassador." After a moment, he gave the American a conspiratorial smile. "I'm sure you'll be more than pleased to see how they react when we 'put one over on them' as it were."

"Let's say that I'm always happier to be giving than receiving," Jim Pickett said.

* * *

"I'm not decent!" Captain Steele called from her cabin when she heard the soft knock on the door.

"That's what I was hoping," John McLaughlin replied with a chuckle.

"Mac?"

"I thought you'd like a chair massage, after all you've been through," Mac replied.

"Oh!" Emily said. She thought about the offer for a moment longer and then brightened. "Oh, in that case come right in!"

Ensuring that her pajamas weren't likely to go floating away from her, she unstuck her chair from the Velcro floor and repositioned it further away from the small outcropping that counted as a desk in the "luxurious" captain's quarters of the small courier. Idly she wondered if, with all that mass, the captains of the alien ships had more spacious quarters, or if they were just as tightly crammed.

"Assume the position," Mac teased lightly.

"Ready," Emily said, having gone through the slow zero-gee motions of pulling the Velcro-footed chair up, turning it around, and pushing it firmly back onto the carpet before gingerly moving herself to sit in it with the chair back to her chest.

"Shoulders and neck, right?" Mac asked as he slid aside the thick fireproof fabric curtain that was vainly pretending to be a door. He slid the door closed again so that he would have enough room to kneel and then positioned himself behind Captain Steele's well-muscled—and quite tense—back.

"Ooohh!" Emily groaned as Mac's fingers found the first knot on the side of her shoulder and teased it out.

Mac worked on her shoulders, neck, arms, and lower back for a good twenty minutes. "Well, I'm done," he said, moving away from the chair.

"You pamper me," Emily said.

"Nah, as I told you the first time, this is enlightened self-interest in action," Mac replied. "Tense captains make bad decisions."

"And it's always easier to get them to change their minds when you're the one giving the massage," Emily said.

Mac's eyebrows twitched upwards in acknowledgement. "That, too." He held open the fabric door, saying, "Sleep well, Skipper."

"Thanks, Mac," Emily replied. She brought a hand to the back of her neck, rubbing it. "At least the damned headache is gone."

"If you're in a lot of pain, Harry brought his needles, you know," Mac reminded her. Harry Long, *Voyager's* engine-room watch stander had acquired a skill in acupuncture somewhere in his long career.

"If I do that, you know I'll get those puppy-eyed looks from Louise," Emily replied. "She hates it when she's not consulted on matters medical."

Mac smiled at her. "You'd be surprised, Skipper, she's Harry's best customer."

"Customer?" Steele repeated with a twinkle in her eyes.

Mac smiled. He was always amazed at how well she knew the crew.

Emily tapped her forehead knowingly. "I see all."

"Explains the headaches, then," Mac said.

Emily laughed and waved him away.

"Goodnight, Skip," Mac said closing the door and carefully arranging it so that it was lightproof before moving off toward his own bunk.

He was halfway there when he noticed Captain Zhukov coming from the opposite direction. The Russian captain paused for a moment then nodded to Mac, who nodded in return. As they shuffled past each other, Mac said softly, "Don't keep her up too late, sir."

"I—I—I was only planning on—" Nikolai Zhukov stuttered in response.

"Ain't my business, sir," Mac told him with wry grin. "If it was, I'd say that the two of you needed it." His expression changed, growing stern. "But if you break her heart, sir, then you'll answer to me."

"To you?" Zhukov repeated, all attempts at pretense evaporating.

Mac grinned again. "I'm not in the chain of command, sir. Civilian. Don't forget that."

Captain Zhukov drew himself up to his full height and pronounced stodgily, "Mr. McLaughlin, I assure that I am only on ship's business—"

Mac cut him off with a raised hand, palm out. "Sir," he said, grinning again, "you might as well save your breath. Neither you nor the captain can lie worth shit."

Zhukov drew in another breath and let it out, defeated.

"It's okay, sir," Mac assured him, patting the Russian captain on the shoulder, "I was betting on you."

Zhukov twitched, speechless.

"As soon as she met you, we started betting," Mac lied. They had actually started betting long before that when *Voyager* had broken lunar orbit and shaped course in a straight-line intercept for Jupiter. Mac nodded to him. "I made fifty bucks, so I can't complain."

"Your whole crew knows about this?" Zhukov said, jaws agape.

"Sir, *everyone* knows about this," Mac told him.

"The Admiral?"

"Sir," Mac began patiently, "no matter what navy or service, do you think a person gets to become an admiral without being able to know what's going on?"

Zhukov slumped. Mac patted him reassuringly and moved beyond him in the crowded float way. "Be sure to pull the damned door tight, sir."

"Pardon me?"

"That way you won't be disturbed, sir," Mac called back over his shoulder. He didn't have the heart to tell the young captain that there was a bet going on when the two captains would get *caught*.

* * *

Xythir

>>**What did you** *do*?<< Captain Nexl demanded of Axlu when the other arrived on the bridge. It had been eight days since the two-legs had first come aboard.

>>**I DO NOT UNDERSTAND.**<<

Nexl waved its rear mannies at the communications officer who clicked in explanation, >>**We're getting gravity waves emanating *from* Earth.**<<

>>**REALLY?**<< Axlu rapped back, its body moving in all directions in agitated excitement. >>**WHY THE LITTLE TWO-LEGS... !**<<

>>**Is that all you have to say?**<<

>>**DO WE KNOW WHAT THEY'RE SAYING? DO WE KNOW WHERE THE SIGNALS ORIGINATE? WHAT'S THEIR TRANSMISSION SPEED? HAVE OUR SENSORS PICKED UP ANYTHING ON THE FIFTH WAVE?**<< Axlu asked rapid-fire.

>>**That's not the point!**<< Nexl rapped loudly, its lower limbs all a-quiver with irritation. >>**They're not supposed to do this!**<<

>>**I WARNED YOU, CAPTAIN, THAT THE TWO-LEGS ARE VERY INVENTIVE.**<<

>>**Wasn't that why we decided to contact them, Captain?**<< Exern added in the engineer officer's defense.

>>**Well ... yes but they're supposed to be too awed and tired to consider something like this for at least another of their months,**<< Nexl replied. >>**And, sure as water is wet, the slitherers will -** <<

An alert rocked out of the communication officer's panels.

>>**Captain, the captain of the *Ynoyon* is hailing us.**<< Exern declared.

>>**Yes,**<< Nexl rapped feebly, >>**I was expecting this.**<<

>>**Shall I put it on?**<<

>>**Certainly,**<< Nexl said, its fore mannies jerking outwards in a sign of exasperation. >>**After all, this day-cycle can get no worse.**<<

>>**I MUST RETURN TO THE TWO-LEGS BEFORE MY APPRENTICE...** <<

>>**Yes, yes! Go!**<< Nexl rapped.

Axlu decided, as it trotted off, that reporting that the two-legs had mentioned some sort of surprise gift would probably not improve the captain's mood. Or digestion. Or cognition.

Perhaps they were going to mention their development of the gravity-wave pulse generator. Yes, that would be nice, Axlu thought to itself as it clambered into the drop-level and punched in his destination.

With more courage than it felt, Captain Nexl tapped out, >>**Put the slitherer on.**<< Exern clicked a short acknowledgement.

>>**Captain,**<< Nexl tapped when the line went live. With all that was going on, Nexl

couldn't remember if the commanding Hydra was Sa-li-ri-to or Sa-ri-to-li and didn't really care. *Bunch of slithering biters!*

~Captain, how do you explain this?~

>>Explain what?<<

~Did your ship not notice the gravity waves emanating from the Earther homeworld?~

>>Oh, that.<< Nexl replied. >>I had words with my engineer. It was always a possibility that they would prove resilient and adaptable.<<

~Yes, it was expected,~ Sa-li-ri-to replied. ~Their alacrity is the surprise.~

As that was obvious, Nexl made no response.

~Do you have any suggestions?~ Sa-li-ri-to prompted.

>>Obviously, we must keep them occupied,<< Nexl tapped back.

~More occupied,~ Sa-li-ri-to agreed. ~We shall start the second phase.~

>>My crew are not able,<< Nexl complained.

~I was not clear. *We* shall start the second phase,~ Sa-li-ri-to replied.

>>Don't we then run the risk of giving away for free what we need to survive?<< Nexl worried.

~No.~

>>Why?<<

~Because we shall also start the trading demands.~

>>We have not learned enough of their history,<< Nexl complained. >>We will reveal ourselves!<<

~No matter.~

>>They may demand legal representation!<<

~Not until they have acquired a star drive technology,~ Sa-li-ri-to corrected.

>>Are you so certain?<<

~If not, we have our arrangements in hand.~

>>We do,<< Nexl concurred. He did not feel relieved, however. The two-legs were behaving too unpredictably. >>I fear we could lose on this deal.<<

~Against backwards two-legs?~ Sa-li-ri-to said derisively. ~They only have one brain each, I do not see them competing against us.~

Nexl clenched down on an angry retort. What the Yon was saying sounded too much like their initial pitch: "With your limbs and our brains, what can go wrong?"

Nexl *hated* "what can go wrong?" It was practically an invitation for a detailed—and exceedingly painful—demonstration of precisely that.

* * *

ESA Eurocos Headquarters,
Noordwijk aan Zee, The Netherlands

"The Americans seem to have stolen a march on us," Konstantin Alexandrov, the Russian liaison officer, noted with a gimlet eye spearing Science Adviser Ulke accusingly.

"They put out a contract and set a prize for the highest bidder," Anne-Marie Foquet said mildly, "for the first team to develop a working gravity-wave antenna and generator."

"It should be remembered that our EU team was the third to complete the requirements," Antonio Scarli said to the Russian. "I don't consider that a poor result."

Konstantin kept his face impassive in spite of the unspoken criticism of the Russian efforts.

"Actually," Werner Ulke said, "I was surprised—and somewhat pleased—to see that MIT beat both Stanford and CalTech in getting a working version first."

That pride, the Russian reflected sourly, would be because so many Europeans had flocked to the prestigious college when its tuition had become so competitive in the aftermath of the economic collapse brought upon the United States by the impact and devastation of the Manhattan Meteor. German was spoken more often on the campus than English.

"I wonder if it isn't because there are two Americans on that team and only one European," Alexandrov said.

"I understand that your Ensign Strasnoye had shown a remarkable grasp of the newer math and physics required," Werner Ulke said, "and we know from your captain that all information is being shared directly."

Alexandrov eyed him glumly, well aware that the German had made it clear that the two Russians were foremost in the Eurocos effort with the unspoken implication that any failing was *their* fault. "I wonder," Alexandrov said, "if the Americans will be as willing to share their gravity-wave communications as they have been with everything else."

"It won't matter, Konstantin," Anne-Marie Foquet said, "as I've been told—confidentially—that the English have just got their system working over in Cambridge."

"That's good news," Alexandrov said in a voice without feeling.

Antonio Scarli exchanged an amused look with Werner Ulke. The entire world had been shocked and sympathetic over the massive losses the United States had suffered in the catastrophe of the Manhattan Meteor. As the waters receded, there had been a quiet re-evaluation of the world order, which had left the rest of the world somewhat relieved that "the world's policeman" was having to deal with being a second-rate power. The Russians, already a second-rate power, seemed to have enjoyed the turnabout surprisingly less than the rest of the world. Perhaps, the Americans' loss of super-power status had merely underscored to the Russians how far Russia herself had fallen.

It was not so strange, Scarli, thought. Typically, tragedies made Russia happy. The notion of a happy Russian was practically an oxymoron.

"Well, so they have 'stolen a march,'" Anne-Marie said with a wave of her hand. "Werner, how do we make sure that it doesn't happen again?"

Werner Ulke pursed his lips. "Our reports from *Harmonie* indicate that our fabrication systems can produce eighty percent of the required materials needed for the first star drive."

"What would happen if we were to withhold them?" Alexandrov asked, glancing around the room with a predatory gleam in his eye. "Would that not require our American friends to prove that they are dealing with us in good faith?"

Werner's lip twitched even as he shook his head. "I'm afraid that's not an option. If it were, it would be up to your captain to implement it."

"Indeed?" Alexandrov returned blandly. He flicked the fingers of one hand dismissively. "Well, if it's not an option, I suppose we'll just have to continue to hope that our American friends do not attempt to—how do they say it?—'steal the limelight'?"

* * *

Xythir

Xover: **I am not sure this is a good idea.** The typed response lit the displays around the walls of the circular room.

"We're only talking a few hundred grams of various metals," Lori told him cajolingly. "Surely your ship loses that much in wastage."

Xover: Which is why I am uncomfortable, Xover typed back.

"You aliens are centuries more advanced than us," Lori replied. "There's probably nothing that you haven't thought of. We were hoping that perhaps we might surprise and please you—and besides, it'll give us a chance to learn more about your extruders."

Beside her, Ensign Sato nodded vigorously. "We are hoping that you will find it pleasing. If you do, we thought you would like to provide a set to your engineer officer."

Xover: A set? Xover's response, even typed, seemed dubious.

"In fact, you might even find them profitable," Lori persisted.

Nevan: Profitable? Nevan moved closer to Xover and waved its limbs rapidly.

">>**Profitable trade is good,**<<" came the sound through Lori's earbud. She glanced over at Ensign Sato and saw the other nod; she had heard something, too. Whether it was the same or translated the same way would be something they would talk about later, but for now, it seemed that the translators that Jenkins, Norman, and Lieutenant Ives had sweated over were finally beginning to work out.

Lori suppressed a grimace as she considered the strange partnership of the French communications officer and the jack-of-all-trades Jenkins. Somehow the two had made some profound connection, further abetted by the ever-inventive Sally Norman, and they had quickly cobbled together something that Lori herself—and from what she'd heard elsewhere, both captains and the admiral—would have sworn to be impossible.

Lieutenant Murray and Dr. Ney had been involved, too, and Lori suspected that the admiral—who turned out to be a secret Sudoku fanatic—had added his skills to the project, which was code-named Babelfish in honor of the *Hitchhiker's Guide to the Galaxy*. The book, the video, and the audio—all three—had gone around both ships and the science habitats like oxygen. *Don't Panic!* had become the unofficial slogan of the self-styled International Interplanetary Interstellar Communication Enterprise which the Americans had converted into "ICE-cubed"—the "cubed" for the three 'I's in the acronym. The Europeans had become attached to the word "Enterprise" and were now alternately suggesting that *Voyager* be so renamed when the first star drive was ready to test or that the entire mission be called Enterprise.

Doubtless the aliens knew nothing about all this inter-ship scuttlebutt and would have been hopelessly confused even if they did. That, of course, bothered Lori not in the least, partly because she was certain it didn't matter but also because, with the possible exception of Xover, she had found the eight-limbed aliens deceitful—and not very good at it. She wasn't certain which bothered her most.

She and Sato had spoken of this together several times in the past week and had slowly come up with the concept of their "gift" to the aliens. They were reasonably hopeful that the aliens would take it at face value, even though Chris Jenkins disclosed that the history he'd sent over had included references to ancient Troy.

"How long will it take?" Lori said now, pressuring Xover without acknowledging what Nevan had clicked.

">>**Let me see your data,**<<" came the translation of Xover's clicking some moments before the screens around the room displayed: *Xover: Submit data.*

Hmmm. Lori was desperate to compare notes with Ensign Sato on what she'd heard but this translation seemed to confirm the hypothesis that the aliens' translators were not accurate.

"Transmitting," Lori said, pressing the button on her communicator.

Communicators, of course, were not much more than radiation-hardened, tough, advanced smartphones. *Well,* Lori thought with a hidden smile, *perhaps a bit more.*

The communicators, by virtue of their function, had built-in frequency scanners and decoders. It was never certain on what frequency another communicator might transmit, particularly in emergencies or when dealing with different military services or nations, so the communicators were marvels at picking up the merest scraps of radio—really, all electromagnetic radiation. Lori had twitted Jenkins about that when he'd proudly relayed his part in developing the gravity-wave communications systems. Now she was afraid that the smug civilian might actually be working on a way to put *that* into a communicator, too.

In this instance, however, the aliens had agreed to allow the communicators Wi-Fi access to their onboard systems, so it was only a matter of conforming to the alien specifications for transmitting three-dimensional data. Not an easy task, but really, it was only a matter of asking the right questions and submitting a few test patterns.

Just after Lori sent the file to the aliens, there came a series of rapping noises that her hidden communicator couldn't translate. The noises seemed to come from the ship's walls and Lori guessed that it was the aliens' computer systems informing Xover that it had received Lori's transmission.

">>**This will not take long,**<<" Lori's earbud translated. A moment later, the wall displays showed, *Xover: Not long.*

Xover waved an upper limb—pikki—in what had become the inter-species "follow me" gesture and moved over to one particular wall. Lori, Ensign Sato, and Nevan trotted behind.

">>**Observe.**<<"
Xover: Watch.

The section of the wall moved, revealing a larger room beyond theirs, and Lori and Sato pressed themselves against the transparent plastic to view the proceedings.

In a matter of moments, four small bronze objects were sintered into existence. Robotic tentacles scooped them up, deposited them in a place behind one of the opaque walls, and, a moment later, a slot opened between the two rooms and the finished products slid into view.

Lori gestured to Ensign Sato. The smaller woman lowered her head in an abbreviated bow—somewhat more than a nod, at least—and moved forward. She and Lori had agreed on this already, as Lori had admitted that her fingers were not as thin as the Japanese woman's.

"Sato will demonstrate," Lori said.

Ensign Sato picked up one of the bronze … disks. There was a loop at the back of the disc, through which she put her index finger. Quickly, she put the other disc on the opposing finger.

"Watch! Listen!" Lori said with a huge grin before nodding to Sato.

Sato brought the two discs together in a quick motion and then apart as they rang softly in the air. *Ching.*

The tone was perfect, pure, resonant.

Ching! Sato made the noise louder. Before the echoes had faded completely, she clapped the discs together in rapid succession. *Ching-Ching-Ching-Ching!* And then she tapped them together softly and kept them together. *Chong.*

"Now, Sato, say hello," Lori told her with a grin. Sato turned to face Xover directly and rapidly brought her fingers together in the complex raps that the aliens used for their greeting.

">>**Hello.**<<" Lori's earbud said into her ear.

??: Hello, the walls displayed.

"These two pair are designed specifically for you, Xover," Ensign Sato said, removing the tuned castanets from her fingers. She bowed toward the alien, adding, "If you would, I would be honored if I could place them on you."

">> **…** <<" Lori's earbud clittered.

Xover: Shock. Pleasure. Awe.

The greener alien, its skin churning with shades of color, stepped forward and lowered itself.

Delicately, Ensign Sato placed each of the four castanets on the alien's upper limb "pikkis." When she was done, she stepped back and bowed again.

"Say something, Xover!" Lori implored excitedly.

Tentatively at first, Xover clanged the little castanets together. *Ching.*

Then it tried them again, tried the larger, deeper back ones separately, then the smaller lighter front castanets. *Ching. Chung. Ching-Ching.*

And suddenly it was dancing around the room, twirling and prancing, bucking and leaping in the air, all while clattering the four castanets in a symphony of sounds.

Lori found herself shouting with joy and saw that Sato had tears streaming down her face.

"Nevan, we have a file for you, too!" Lori called out loud.

Xover raced back over to them and halted, all upper limbs outstretched. And then, unmistakably, it bowed, prostrating itself and lowering its upper limbs to its sides.

When it stood again, Xover chimed out, ">>**Blessings of the Xlern upon you.**<<" It pranced back again and twirled, chiming out, ">>**I must show my captain!**<<"

In a flicker it was gone, leaving Nevan behind. The trader apprentice moved slowly toward Lori.

">>**Please?**<<"

Nevan: ?? The walls displayed.

"I'm sending the file now," Lori said warmly. "We also have files for Security Apprentice Doxal and Engineer Officer Axlu."

Nevan appeared not to hear, rushing toward the extrusion machines with what almost appeared to be a half-fearful, half-hopeful motion.

"Poor thing's in shock," Lori said to Ensign Sato.

"The chimes are very beautiful," Sato replied, unabashedly wiping the last of the tears from her eyes. "I did not imagine that they would be quite so moving."

"Yeah," Lori agreed, moving to wrap an arm around the smaller woman, "I think we done good."

"And tomorrow we will do better," Ensign Sato said with a quick smile.

CHAPTER FOURTEEN

"DOES EVERYONE UNDERSTAND?" EMILY STEELE ASKED ON THE CLOSED communication link of their sled as they closed toward the *Xythir*.

"I believe so," Ensign Strasnoye said. "We are to give the engineer officer and the security apprentice their chimes when we arrive."

"And, after lunch, Lori and I will suggest to Xover that we have thought of some improvements," Ensign Sato continued on cue.

"Exactly," Emily said with warmth. "We want to build the excitement."

"And test to see if our bugs work," Lori added, her smirk audible over the link.

"Also to see if our friends might have questions on the composition of our materials," Emily reminded her.

"'Cause we don't want 'em to know they're bugged," Lori said in agreement.

"It would not be amenable to good relations," Captain Steele agreed, her lips curving upwards.

"Sure, we got it, Skip," Lori told her. "So we wait until you've got a 'go' on the data dump, then lay this new idea out after lunch."

"I am more concerned with the other proposed arrangements," Ensign Strasnoye added.

"You mean bunking on the alien ship, Greg?" Lori asked.

"More, I am concerned about adding a second shift," Ensign Strasnoye said. "Stretching our original team to split shifts will reduce our efficiency, at least in the short run."

"True," Emily agreed. More true than she wanted to admit. The idea had been the admiral's and it made sense: by doubling the training team, they could cut in half the time to produce a working star drive. If the aliens accepted the proposal, it would help all considered; if they rejected it, however, that would indicate either a reluctance on their part or provide a glimpse into the aliens' sleep cycles—valuable information when trying to understand the alien society.

The proposal was to double the number of trainees, pairing the newer trainees with one of the original team. Switching the sleep schedules of half the team would be awkward, as would integrating the new people into the groups and the training … but the payoff could be huge.

Not only would it remove any tension over the composition of the team, but it would also allow Emily to inject Charlie Vincent into the mix. Ensign Charles Vincent was a good solid software engineer without the flash and speed of Chris Jenkins, but still reliable and quick-witted. Emily trusted that he'd be able to implement Jenkin's plan without being detected … if the admiral gave the go-ahead.

The others were all unknowns to her, but judging by the reaction of Ensign Strasnoye, they were all well-qualified: Ernst Schuyler and James Saxon were both ensigns with distinguished records while Carol Mason was an outstanding crewman who reminded Emily very much of Chris Jenkins, with her intense focus and her brilliant creativity. The only problem with the plan that Emily could see was that it would separate Sato and Dubauer— the two had forged tight bonds and were more than just friends. Still, they knew their duty.

"Contact in three … two … one!" Lori Dubauer called out, waking Emily out of her reverie.

"Secure lines," Ensign Strasnoye said.

"Bowline secure," Emily reported. She'd decided to rotate command and duties on the sled so as to keep everyone alert—and also to increase the cohesion of the team.

"Stern secure," Sato added.

"Dismount," Lori called.

"Moving off," Greg Strasnoye announced. He led the way to the airlock, followed by Dubauer, Sato, and then Emily herself.

They cycled through the airlock and into the receiving room where they shucked off their suits.

">>**Greetings!**<<" Xover chimed, skittering forward and halting abruptly as if he suddenly recalled that the team was not composed of eight-limbed Xlern.

Xover: Hello, came the translation on one of the wall displays.

"Hello," Emily said before the others could react. She didn't want anyone to make the mistake of using the translations of their earbuds instead of the alien computers. She noted that only Nevan stood with the other alien. "Are we early?"

Xover: We were told to greet you and start our lessons. Axlu and Doxal are waiting in their room.

Hmmm, Emily thought to herself.

"Lead the way, Xover," Lori said with an impish grin. "And did you get a chance to play with your castanets?"

">>**Bliss!**<<" Emily heard through her earbud. She wondered for a moment just how the translating computer had come to select a word which she was certain hadn't been uttered before but she knew that the adaptive artificial intelligence software used was written by Jenkins and Norman, so she was willing to accept the word at face value.

">>**Trade!**<<" Nevan exclaimed. Given his specialty, Emily could readily imagine the joy of the bluer alien.

"Well, I wish you all success in today's endeavors," Emily said, waving with one hand before gesturing for Gregor to follow her.

">>**And you in yours,**<<" Nevan responded.

Nevan: Likewise, the walls displayed.

Emily wondered how much longer she could hold off before announcing the "invention" of translation software. The admiral and the ambassador were divided over whether to present the technology for free or offer to license it. Emily tended to side with Pickett's belief that the aliens were "in it for the money" and would accept a trade or license agreement more readily than a straight-out gift. Still, there were the conflicting notions of "don't look a gift horse in the mouth" and "don't accept a Trojan horse."

The door to the learning room opened and Emily was not surprised to see that Axlu and Doxal were already present.

It looks pissed, Emily thought as she assessed the alien engineer's stance. She chided herself on thinking that she had learned to read alien body language in just a week, but she still couldn't shake the feeling.

"Before we begin, Engineer Officer Axlu, I wanted to ask if you had had a chance to experience the gifts my two ensigns had presented your other two apprentices?"

Oh, yeah, pissed, Emily thought to herself as she watched the way the alien suddenly shifted on its lower limbs—tek—and the way the hind upper limbs—hind pikki—tensed on his body. Beside her, she could feel Gregor move closer, clearly reflecting her opinion.

">>**OF COURSE,<<**" was the instant translation of the alien's rock banging.

Axlu: I HAVE, came the lagged words on the walls.

"If you would, we were hoping to make you a similar present," Emily told it.

">>**I AM ABOVE SUCH THINGS!<<**" The engineer boomed.

Axlu: IT IS NOT NECESSARY. The wall display translated.

"Please wait until you have had a chance to examine them before deciding," Emily said. "Is that not the sign of a good scientist?"

Axlu's limbs twittered in agitation as it mulled over her statement. Then it moved toward her.

"Gregor?" Emily said, prompting the ensign to open his messenger bag and place a small wrapped bundle in her hands.

"We thought, perhaps, that you would appreciate a set made especially for you," Emily said, unwrapping the package to reveal eight specially crafted chimes. Emily didn't feel it necessary to mention that each chime was specially crafted to produce a more muted sound.

">>**EIGHT IS TOO MANY.<<**" Axlu rapped.

Axlu: TOO MANY, the walls displayed.

"We thought that, as befits your rank and position"—*not to mention also volume*—"that you might find it convenient to have greater capabilities. So we designed two specifically for each of your upper limbs.

"If I might be honored by accoutering you?" Emily finished, moving to place the package back in Gregor's outstretched arms while selecting the first, larger chime. "I shall begin by placing the two lower chimes on your fore pikki and then the two higher chimes, if you are willing." *Tweeter and woofer, as it were,* Emily thought, reflecting Lori's original suggestion. Emily was still not certain that equipping the booming engineer with *stereo* was the best of ideas.

"**>>VERY WELL.<<**"

Axlu: ACCEPTED.

The bulky engineer approached Emily. She deftly slid one chime down the left forelimb, then another down the right one.

"If you would try them to see if they are located suitably, I can make adjustments if necessary," Emily said. Their studies of the alien physiology had indicated there was a suitable inflection point on the upper limbs.

Axlu obliged. *Bong.*

"Now the uppers," Emily said. This time she thought that the alien seemed eager to present its pikkis for adornment. "This will produce a higher, lighter note. Combine the two for greater volume."

"**>>TAKE THE WHOLE PLUNGE.<<**"

Axlu: PLACE THEM ALL.

Emily hid a smile and moved, with Gregor trailing her, so that she could place the rear chimes. Axlu obliged by lowering itself to make the task easier.

When all eight chime-castanets were placed, Emily stepped back.

"Can you try them all in order from rear bottoms to front?" Emily asked.

Boommm. Bink. Bong. Chime.

"We could sell them whole choirs, tuned specifically to each alien," Lori had chortled when she started expounding on the full set of possibilities. "Each of them has to be handmade, as it were, because of the differences in each alien's limbs."

Rather like a fingerprint, the thickness and form of each alien's limbs were different from any other. To keep the chime-castanets firmly in place meant that a "one size fits all" approach was inefficient. Also, as Lori had pointed out, "Everyone loves tailor-made!"

Booommm. Booommm-boomm (chime, chime-chime, chink). Bink. Bink-boommm, bong-bink, bong-bink, chime-chime, bong.

And suddenly, just as Lori had reported with Xover, Axlu was prancing around the room, like a one-Xlern bell orchestra.

"Oh, my lord," Emily breathed out softly, closing her eyes.

"⬒⬒⬒⬒⬒⬒⬒ ⬒⬒⬒⬒!" Gregor said softly.

"Oh, yeah," Emily agreed fervently, "*such* a heavenly sound." She opened her eyes and without saying a word, gestured toward Doxal.

The alien trotted forward and knelt even as Gregor opened a second bundle.

"Wait until the engineer officer has finished before you try yours," Emily suggested as she fitted the four chimes. If the security apprentice seemed offended by the lesser offering, she could not detect it in his body language nor in the way he quivered with anticipation as he waited for Axlu's beautiful song-dance to complete.

The engineer officer stopped abruptly, mid-chime, as though he suddenly remembered his location and his dignity.

"**>>DOXAL? FOUR?<<**" There was a pause as if Axlu were considering this. "**>>I**

SHALL SEE YOU GET MORE WHEN YOU PASS TO OFFICER.<<"

">>**It would be my honor,**<<" Doxal chimed back in response. He moved awkwardly toward the engineer officer, as if uncertain.

">>**TAKE A MOMENT TO FAMILIARIZE YOURSELF,**<<" Axlu ordered.

">>**Oh, may I?**<<" And there was no mistaking the wistfulness in the other's response.

">>**I ORDER IT,**<<" Axlu responded. Emily realized that she no longer even bothered to check the translations on the wall displays.

Not waiting for its senior to change its mind, Doxal raced toward Emily, chiming all the while and stopping with a huge crescendo of its deeper rear chimes before kneeling, now just barely touching the fore chimes and then rising again with another clash to repeat the gesture in front of Gregor before he raised himself again and raced in a whirl around the edge of the circular room, leaping and bucking with all the abandon of a young colt horse, chiming and booming to punctuate its impromptu dance-gallop.

Emily, caught up in the excitement, hastily dumped the wrappers onto Gregor's arms and then caught herself, glancing at him and smiling.

"Ensign, did you ever take dance?" Emily asked. Gregor flushed in surprise and jerked his head in a nod, pushing the wrappers back into his messenger bag and pulling the strap off his head.

"As a child, I took ballet," he announced.

"Well, warm up," Emily warned him, moving away and starting a series of stretches even as she was overwhelmed with an urge to join the cavorting Xlern in its musical odyssey. *Great choice of words, there, Em.*

She ignored herself as she completed a quick set of stretches, took her mark, and began a series of moves that led to a *grand jeté* which she took straight into a *pirouette*.

Gregor spun around in front of her and, with a quick set of movements, matched her *pirouette* with his face locked on hers.

Emily was suddenly aware of the silence in the room and brought herself to a stop. Gregor stopped a turn later.

">>**WHAT WAS THAT?**<<" Axlu said.

">>**You two were spinning in the same place.**<<" Doxal added, his chimes pitching high in what Emily decided was a tone of awe.

"I'm sorry," Emily apologized, "but Doxal, you made such a beautiful song and such a great dance that we felt we just had to join you in your expression of joy."

">>**AND YOU SPIN ON ONE LIMB?**<<"

"It is a form of dance developed many centuries ago," Emily explained. She gestured to Gregor. "In Ensign Strasnoye's home country, it has been developed to high art."

Ensign Strasnoye bestowed her with a wry grin and gave her a deep bow. "I should enjoy dancing with you again sometime, Captain, if it were possible."

Emily dimpled and nodded in response.

">>**WE**—<<" Axlu began only to cut short as the door opened suddenly.

">>**CAPTAIN?**<<"

Emily and Gregor spun around to face the new alien.

">>**TO WHAT DO WE OWE THE HONOR?**<<" Axlu said. Emily thought that his chiming seemed a bit off, as though the engineer officer were not on good terms with his captain. *Prancing about is frowned upon, I imagine.*

Emily stepped forward, hand outstretched in greeting. "Captain, I am Captain Emily Steele of the United States Experimental Starship *Voyager*."

">>**Those things, the stumblers made them?**<<" a different voice, belonging to the captain rapped out. The sound of his rocks were jarring compared to the more mellow—and purposefully muted—tones of the chime-castanets.

Emily glanced at the wall displays to see what the alien computers made of *that*. The wall displayed: **Nexl: Did the humans make those?**

Nexl. Now they knew the alien captain's name. Emily decided to ignore that revelation for the moment.

"We would be happy to make more, Captain," Emily said pleasantly. She glanced back toward Axlu and Doxal who, being four-legged, had no difficulty looking sheepish, particularly with their upper limbs dangling listlessly at their sides.

">>**How much?**<<"

Nexl: In exchange for what?

Emily was quite ready to tell it they were free but stopped herself just before she spoke. Instead she said, "We would be happy to offer them to you free for use within the limits of our solar system."

">>**But the money is *outside* your little system?**<<"

On the display: **Nexl: And outside?**

Emily hid a smile. "Our intent was merely to ease communication," she replied. "However, we now realize that there are greater possibilities and would like to license them to you in exchange for cooperation in combined artistic endeavors."

">>**What?**<<"

The wall showed: **Nexl: Explain, please.**

"You may have noticed that myself and Ensign Strasnoye were happy to join in participating in the sound and movements of Security Apprentice Doxal. Are you familiar with the notions of dance and music?"

Nexl considered for a moment the awesome possibility of engaging the Bolshoi Ballet to perform on his home-world. The credits would roll in; he'd become a fleet admiral or even a master trader.

">>**We are familiar with this concept, although it is foreign to us,**<<" Nexl lied quickly.

The display read: **Nexl: Yes.**

Emily glanced toward Gregor with a raised brow. The ensign returned her questioning look without expression, but she was certain that he, too, had noticed the discrepancy in the length of Nexl's tapped response and the alien computer's terse translation. How long would it be before they could honestly state that they suspected the alien computer of deliberating filtering the alien's raps?

"I thought that it would give our people back home much pleasure and relief if we could work together, in our spare time, to produce some choreography that would express the joy of your people and ours combined," Emily said. She wasn't at all sure how the admiral would respond when she told him of her impromptu plans to stage a *ballet* with the aliens but she was certain that, once he'd heard the recordings of this session, she'd have no problem getting Nikolai Zhukov on her side. Of course, she admitted privately, she had a special *in* with the Russian captain now. "We could split the profits from such a production."

">>**Anything that would relieve suspicion would be beneficial,**<<" Security Apprentice Doxal allowed. Emily was surprised at its words, for in her experience, security personnel were more apt to be suspicious and paranoid than worry about culture. *Perhaps,* she thought to herself, *the little goat has got the music bug.*

">>**I would volunteer myself to this task,**<<" Axlu said.

">>**Pardon?**<<" Captain Nexl responded.

">>**I would volunteer myself to this task,**<<" Axlu repeated.

">>**Are you all right?**<<" Nexl asked. ">>**You are not as forceful as usual.**<<"

">>**I'M PERFECTLY FINE, CAPTAIN,**<<" Axlu boomed back, causing everyone to take an involuntary step back.

Emily was as surprised as the alien captain as she realized that for the first time she hadn't heard the engineer speak in all caps.

">>**Captain,**<<" Doxal now chimed, ">>**the aliens gave two sets of round-rocks to the engineer officer in accordance with its rank.**<<"

Ah, clever prancer! Emily thought, watching Ensign Strasnoye to see if he was thinking along similar lines. The ensign gave her an imperceptible dip of his head: he had.

">>**How many would I get?**<<" Nexl asked, moving toward Axlu.

Emily glanced at the wall for the typed translation but there was nothing.

"I imagine that your captain would be entitled to three sets of chime-castanets," Emily said, trying to sound as if she'd thought of this on her own, "in deference to his higher rank."

">>**Three?**<<" Nexl said. It took a step back, then sideways in the alien version of a pace. ">>**Three would be good.**<<"

The display read: **Nexl: That would be acceptable.**

"Our people can have them prepared for you by our next training cycle," Emily said.

">>**Next cycle? That long?**<<" Nexl said.

">>**Perhaps we could use our replicators,**<<" Axlu suggested, once again using an uncharacteristically normal volume.

">>**Captain, if I may,**<<" Doxal chimed inquiringly. ">>**The aliens have utilized special tuning algorithms with the engineer officer's sets of round-rocks. I suspect we** would find it difficult to reproduce. Also, I consider that, from a trade perspective, this is an attempt on their part to acquire greater standing with us.<<"

Nexl's upper limbs twitched in what Emily had come to brand a "thinking" expression.

">>**Very well. I shall get Ixxie to work on this,**<<" Nexl rapped back. ">>**Please extend courtesy responses to the stumblers.**<<"

">>**As you command,**<<" Axlu responded. Then, seeming to catch itself, added, ">>**I SHALL DO SO.**<<"

Nexl hesitated a moment, gave Emily a sketchy bow from its fore body, then turned and left.

There was a moment's awkward pause and then Doxal said, ">>**I must report to my superior.**<<"

">>**AND DOUBTLESS VOID YOURSELF,**<<" Axlu boomed back, then waved his limbs toward the door. ">>**Go, take a break.**<<"

Doxal dipped its fore body in salute, waved limbs toward Emily and Gregor, and trotted out the door.

"I take it that Security Apprentice Doxal is taking a break," Emily said. She turned to Gregor, "Now's your chance."

"I—" Gregor began only to stiffen when he saw Emily jerk her head commandingly toward the door. "I think that's a good idea, Captain."

Emily waited until he'd left before moving slowly toward Axlu.

"Engineer Officer Axlu, may I ask you a question?"

">>**Naturally.**<<"

"Our translators showed your words in upper case letters only when we first contacted you," Emily began. "In our parlance, speaking in all capital letters is akin to shouting." She paused, to see if the engineer were going to reply, then continued, "When we met you, we discovered that you do, in fact, make all your communication at a very high volume. Is there a particular reason for this?"

">>**Captain,**<<" Axlu chimed back softly, ">>**can you keep a secret?**<<"

Emily was surprised at the question.

">>**One officer to another?**<<" Axlu added.

"One officer to another," Emily allowed.

">>**I do it to keep command,**<<" Axlu admitted.

Emily frowned as she thought on that.

">>**Do you not find that those who are loudest are those who are most readily obeyed?**<<"

Oh! "You mean you shout to cow your subordinates?" Emily squeaked in surprise. "But what about your commanders?"

">>**I shall never admit this if you repeat it,**<<" Axlu warned, ">>**but I have discovered that even superiors find it best to deal with me in the quickest manner possible.**<<"

Emily snorted. Axlu shouted at its captain to keep Nexl from harassing it.

">>**Does not your engineer employ similar tactics?**<<" Axlu wondered.

"My engineer—" Emily stopped herself. Lorie Dubauer was listed on the roster as *Voyager's* engineer but everyone knew that the real engineer was Mac. A flash of one of her moments with Mac came to her memory: puppy-dog eyes were just as good as shouting, weren't they? "My engineer indeed employs similar tactics."

">>**I had rather thought as much,**<<" Axlu admitted. ">>**In my contact with other engineer officers, I have noted that we must sometimes employ drastic methods to ensure that our superiors do not … engage in over-enthusiastic actions.**<<"

"Don't you feel worried by telling me this?"

">>**You said you would keep this secret,**<<" Axlu replied. ">>**Besides, I would be surprised if you were to engage in similar conversations with any engineer officer any time in the near future.**<<"

The door whooshed open and Ensign Strasnoye and Security Apprentice Doxal returned.

"Well," Emily said in a voice pitched low, "we've resorted to using noise suppressors in your presence."

">>**AH, THAT IS A GOOD PRECAUTION,**<<" Axlu boomed back in response. Then, softly, ">>**However, I can safely assert that these marvelous round rocks of yours inspire me to treat them with the courtesy due any delicately shaped material. I would not wish to damage them.**<<"

Good excuse, Emily thought to herself. She wondered if Axlu got sore from straining itself by rapping so loudly all the time. *No, probably it's inured to it by now.*

">>**If everyone is ready, we shall begin without further interruption,**<<" Axlu now said.

Emily purposefully turned toward one of the displays, waiting until she could read the translation before saying, "We're ready."

">>**Good. As you recall, we were working on an introduction to the effects of what you wish to call the 'fifth' force.**<<" Axlu said. The light dimmed and the 3D display filled the room, surrounding Emily and Gregor as they began the next lesson.

* * *

"An interstellar ballet? Really, Captain Steele, I was quite surprised by the suggestion," Admiral Tsukino said when she reported back that evening.

Emily's lips twitched. "To be honest, sir, I sorta surprised myself."

"It's a good idea," Pickett declared firmly. "It will cement our relations with the Xlern and ease public opinion back home."

"Well, nothing's going to happen on that front for a while," Emily replied with a slightly wistful tone. "As it is, though, it seems to have aided in getting the aliens to accept our new wrinkles to their plan."

"So they've agreed?"

"Not only that but they suggested that we allow a separate crew to run the sled back and forth every day with any supplies or dispatches we might want to send," Emily said.

"If we weren't stretched so thin, I'd recommend posting a separate group to liaison with the training groups," Captain Zhukov said.

"That's not a bad idea," Pickett said.

"How many would you send?" Admiral Tsukino asked.

"Four: an officer in charge and three enlisted watch standers," Captain Zhukov said, glancing toward Emily for her reaction. She merely nodded in agreement.

"I could let you have Danni—Lieutenant McElroy," Emily said. "That would give us a good communications person on-site."

"If you do that, I could release to her three of my yeomen," Zhukov replied, glancing toward Admiral Tsukino and the ambassador.

"How many of them know ballet?" Pickett asked to the surprise of the others. He explained, "We could have them double as our ballet team if we worked it right."

"Why would we want that, Mr. Ambassador?" Admiral Tsukino now asked.

"Because it would disarm any alien worries that we were staging or attempting to stage an armed takeover," Pickett replied, "and it would let us accelerate our cultural contact. It would also send a calming message back home."

"I don't understand," Captain Zhukov said.

"Even just the early images would be useful," Pickett said. "People at home would see the aliens playing with our guys, doing pratfalls, making that beautiful music …"

"Very well," Admiral Tsukino said, "you've made your point." He turned to Emily. "Captain Steele, can you put this to the aliens tomorrow?"

"I'll want you to be careful how you put it, Emily," Pickett said to her. "We don't want to get the wind up their sails."

"I'll run it by Axlu," Emily promised. She rubbed the back of her neck wearily.

"Too much dancing," Captain Zhukov teased her.

"Too much higher math," Emily corrected tartly. She shook her head. "If this is what we're supposed to have figured out ourselves, I hate to imagine what the *better* drive is going to be like."

"Mac said to tell you that you're doing great, Captain," Pickett assured her.

"Is Mac getting all this?" Emily asked.

"Mac, Dr. Ney, and Commander Geister," Pickett replied.

"Commander Geister?" Emily said in surprise, glancing toward Captain Zhukov.

Nikolai smiled. "It appears that our impetuous commander has become somewhat of a force of nature since his arrival at the Japanese moon base."

"I was both surprised and amazed," Admiral Tsukino admitted. "Once he was certain that Commander Reynaud was comfortable, he threw himself into the administrative tasks that I had to leave behind." He glanced at Zhukov as he said, "Did you know he was fluent in Japanese?"

"Chinese, Russian, French, and Thai, if I recall," Zhukov responded, earning a look of admiration from Emily Steele. She always struggled to remember the details of her personnel records.

"Yes," Admiral Tsukino said with a quick tightening of his lips, "he apparently was quite forceful in demanding that we share what we knew with our Chinese associates."

"Good for him!" Pickett said. The others gave him surprised looks. "This isn't going to work if we try to hush it up."

"Be that as it may," Admiral Tsukino said with a wave of his hand, "it remains that Commander Geister extended his communications to the U.S. Naval base on Far Side—I believe you are associated with it, Captain—and has received an *ex tempore* commission to act as liaison between my moon base and yours."

Emily couldn't tell how the admiral felt when making that admission.

"Karl was always a superior officer," Captain Zhukov said. "What surprises me is that you've said nothing about Elodie."

"Ah, I was getting to her," Admiral Tsukino said with a grin. "While your Commander Geister took over my moon base, your Commander Reynaud seems to have absconded with the combined research teams of all the Moon and Mars combined."

"She was fluent in Chinese as well," Pickett guessed with a glance toward Zhukov who nodded, his lips twitching.

"Between the two of them, we now have top scientists daily assessing every scrap of information we can send their way," Admiral Tsukino finished. He glanced at Captain Zhukov. "And I've put in commendations through Eurocos for the both of them."

"I'll see what I can do on my end," Jim Pickett said. The others were confused. "Aside from the obvious American honors, I can probably get a word in with the Japanese and Chinese embassies, maybe arrange some rather public recognition of their efforts."

"And improve your relations at the same time," Captain Zhukov said approvingly.

"While you've been ably running your ship, Captain, and Captain Steele has been our highest ranked officer in our contact team," Pickett said, sitting a little straighter, "Admiral Tsukino and I have had several high-level conversations on the nature of the post-contact society."

Captain Zhukov pursed his lips thoughtfully. "Good."

"No doubt you'll share it with the rest of us when you deem us ready," Emily said, carefully using a teasing tone of voice.

"The first thing the admiral and I agreed upon," Pickett told her, "was that it was more important to complete the current mission than to engage in any wild speculation."

"And the second thing, sir?" Captain Zhukov asked, half-hiding a grin.

"We agreed was that it was both too early and too late to consider planning for a post-contact society," Admiral Tsukino said, "but we felt ourselves in the best position to make such an undertaking without rancor or excessive politics."

Captain Zhukov exchanged glances with Captain Steele and both smiled. "So what you're saying, sir," Emily said, "is that you'll set the agenda and thereby control the outcome?"

"Welcome to interstellar politics, Captain," Pickett told her with a smile of his own.

"Of course, all this is speculative," Admiral Tsukino conceded. He frowned at Pickett. "The ambassador and I are likely to find ourselves out-voted."

"And possibly relieved," Pickett reminded him.

"Even from the Moon, I could not see any lines drawn on the surface of the Earth," Admiral Tsukino replied obliquely. His meaning was clear enough to Captain Zhukov and Captain Steele, they nodded in agreement. "My oath is to my country; my duty is to my species."

"Of course, all this may be thrown out the airlock when the aliens drop the other shoe," Pickett warned.

"If it was easy, anyone could play," Emily said, earning a chorus of laughter.

* * *

"You know, Skip, I never did sign on for singing and dancing," Danni McElroy said as she helped the sled crew finish storing the latest set of supplies.

"Is that a complaint, Lieutenant?" Emily asked in a deceptively mild tone.

Danni snorted. "Nope, not me, no way, Cap'n!"

"Good, because I'd trade in a hot second if I thought I could get away with it," Emily told her warmly.

"That, Captain, is because you've got a dancer's body," Danni said. She ran a hand down her own body in counterpoint. "Whereas what I've got is this ungainly mass of muscles and misaligned nerves."

"You'll do fine, Danni," Emily assured her. "I saw your personnel records, remember? I *know* you took ballet."

"Captain, my records indicate that I took ballet for four years. What they *don't* say is that my dance teacher begged me to quit," Danni told her. Danni carefully kept from adding that her dance teacher was also her martial arts teacher and that Danni went on to get her black belt in *aikido* shortly thereafter.

"Lieutenant, I don't think it will matter that much, if you don't mind me saying," Yeoman Kees van der Bilt said.

"And why's that?" Danni challenged. "Is it because Alexei spent a year with the Bolshoi? Or that Georges studied at the Paris Opéra?"

"No, ma'am," Kees said. "It's because they'll all be watching the aliens dance, Lieutenant."

Danni pursed her lips and said to Emily, "I suppose he's got a point, Skip."

"Well, then," said Emily, "I guess that's settled. If you'll excuse me, I've got to get my brains pumped full of *n*-space manifold theory."

Danni paused for a moment before saying cautiously, "Do you know if that's really necessary, Captain?"

Emily turned back to face her full on. She pursed her lips then said, "Well, one way or another we'll know soon enough."

* * *

Ynoyon

~It is time,~ Sa-li-ri-to said to communications, ~contact the two-legs.~

~What frequency, Captain?~ Je-te-ji-go asked.

Sa-li-ri-to's two lesser heads hissed menacingly, and communications correctly deduced that commanding had no preference.

A moment later, communications reported, ~We are connected to their Captain Zhukov, commanding of the *Harmonie*.~

Sa-li-ri-to bobbed their primary head in understanding and waited for their sound to go live.

~Translate to text,~ Sa-li-ri-to ordered, its two lesser heads moving toward the input consoles. Its rearward head was hunting a small edible, leaving the combination with a feeling of anticipation and elation.

Alien ship, this is Captain Nikolai Zhukov of the Eurocos fusion ship *Harmonie,* **with whom do I have the pleasure of communicating?** The screens displayed the human words in the twisty letters of the Yon script.

The two lesser heads moved closer to the input modules, opening their mouths to let their four-pronged tongues jab swiftly on the control surfaces, composing the message, **We Sa-li-ri-to Commanding. We wish discuss teaching theory construction of Yunuffili Drive. You give eight most talented. We start teach in two hours. Sa-li-ri-to done.**

~Commanding?~ Je-te-ji-go asked, two of its heads twining in bemusement. ~Did you mean to send such a message?~

~Yes,~ Sa-li-ri-to calmly replied. Sensing the others' confusion, they explained, ~Always best to confuse your enemies. Let them think you have fewer heads.~

~Ahhh, strategy!~ Communications hissed in comprehension, three of its heads bobbing appreciatively.

~The humans say that two heads are better than one,~ Sa-li-ri-to added, two of its heads bobbing with glee.

Je-te-ji-go communications gave a three-headed snort of amusement. ~How will they react when they meet us!~

Sa-li-ri-to hoped that their horror and confusion would cost the humans several days' worth of frustration. After how easily they'd overcome the obstacles set by the Xlern, they—all four heads—did not wish to underestimate them.

* * *

The White House, Washington, DC

"Sir, we've just received word that the second set of aliens have contacted *Harmonie*," Ron Grimminger announced as he stepped into the briefing room. He looked around and saw that he'd interrupted Charles—Charlie—Sumner mid-word.

"Charlie was just telling us the details," the president said, gesturing for Grimminger to take his seat. "Charlie?"

"Yes, Mr. President," the national security advisor continued with a gimlet glance—really, a gloat—toward Grimminger. "We detected communication over the gravity-wave network. Apparently the second set of aliens, the Yon, have indicated that they are ready to train personnel on the working of the 'Yunuffili' drive."

"Yunuff illi?" the president repeated.

"We think it's the name of another alien species or just the inventor's name, sir," Grimminger interposed smoothly, casting a warm—and triumphant—glance at the nation's head spy. "And it's pronounced as one word—Yunuffili—my people tell me."

"Was this some sort of deliberate ploy?" George Morgan, the secretary of defense, wondered aloud. "All our people are engaged with those walking spiders."

"They're more like octopuses, George," the president corrected with the supercilious air of an ill-informed dilettante. He frowned for a moment then added with a glance toward Grimminger, "But it's a good question."

Grimminger shrugged. "It's possible. Certainly *we* see it as divisive, and that may be enough."

"The Euros could learn about this super-drive and leave us in the dust," Morgan complained. "We should demand that we be equally represented."

"That might not be too easy, Charlie," Navy Secretary Wood said. Morgan glared at him. Wood turned his attention to the president. "It's just that we're a little over-represented with the Xlern. Demanding more representation with these new aliens might be seen as being greedy."

"We can't play the Manhattan Meteor card too many times, Mr. President," Brian McPhee, the chief of staff, said in a bid to forestall the president's standard reaction.

"There's also this," Grimminger added. "The aliens have made no bones about the fact that this 'better' drive will also be harder to master." The president's brow furrowed. Grimminger raised a hand. "We might actually get a head start by having the easier drive while the Euros are still fumbling with the other."

"The Euros outnumber our crew nearly six to one," Admiral Roberts reminded them. "No matter what we want, our people are only human and there are too few of them."

"What about *Odyssey*, Mr. President?" Charlie Sumner asked, happily ignoring the horrified gasps coming from the military types.

"Charlie!" George Morgan cried, shaking his head, eyes wide and desperate. In a more controlled voice, he continued, "Now's not the time to bring that up—"

"What's *Odyssey*?" President Merritt cut across him, glancing around the room angrily. "And how come I didn't know about it?"

"It was in the original specifications, sir," Elijah Wood said defensively.

"It was only intended as a follow-on," Admiral Roberts added quickly. "You know, just in case."

"In case what, Joel?" Merritt demanded. "And what's this got to do with the aliens?"

The eyes of all the military types fell accusingly on Sumner—promising painful retribution to be delivered at a later date—then turned demandingly to Ron Grimminger.

Nervously, Ron licked his lips before beginning, "Well, sir, you know that in our experimental projects we always like to build in some redundancy if possible." He paused to see if the president was following or—better yet—leaping ahead.

"Redundancy?"

"We weren't sure that *Voyager* would work," Admiral Roberts admitted. "A matter-antimatter engine was something totally new. It could have failed or blown up or something."

"*You* told me that it was perfectly safe," the president said angrily to Grimminger. "We could not handle a major reverse. The public would crucify us."

"Yes, sir," Grimminger agreed demurely, "although, if you'll recall, I believe that what I said was that the military felt it was reasonably safe."

"Regardless, Mr. President," Elijah Wood said quickly, before the president could vent his ire on him, "*Voyager* worked flawlessly and has performed better than desired."

"Once," Charlie Sumner muttered under his breath.

The Navy secretary speared him with a glare before continuing, "Of course the Navy had hoped that would be the case but we wanted to be prepared for all contingencies."

"*Someone* tell me what this *Odyssey* is right *now*," the president growled, eyes flashing. He knew bullshit when he heard it and he only liked the sound of it when it came from his lips.

"*Odyssey* is *Voyager*'s sister ship," Ron Grimminger said.

"Her twin, actually," Admiral Roberts corrected. "She's flight ready, with a handpicked crew. All she needs is the fuel."

"Where's Ned?" the president demanded. The others exchanged startled looks at this sudden change of topic. "The veep was in charge of space exploration, right?"

Heads nodded slowly.

"Did he know about *Odyssey*?" Greg Merritt demanded, his voice growing louder. "And isn't he on the Moon?"

"He's been detained, sir," Elijah Wood said soothingly. "We were planning on bringing him back to the capital as soon as—"

President Merritt popped out of his seat, glaring down at the assembled luminaries, finger pointing at each in turn. "Please don't tell me that you were planning on sending him home on this *Odyssey* when she was ready."

"No, sir," Admiral Roberts said quickly. "We were planning on getting him back on the next available shuttle."

"When?" The others looked at him in confusion. "Before or *after* this ship was ready?"

"Well … after," Roberts admitted slowly.

"But, sir, I don't see why that matters," Charlie Sumner said. "Everyone knows that the vice president is crazy."

"Everyone but the people who agree with him, Charlie," the president replied. He turned to Admiral Roberts. "And can you swear that none of them are in the Navy? That none of them might be able and willing to release the vice president and bring him to this damned ship?"

"I'll get right on it," Roberts said, springing from his chair and racing out of the room.

"Charlie, your people need to handle this," Merritt said to his Security Chief. "You need to be *certain* that Ned doesn't get together with another crazy friend."

Sumner nodded, turning to Navy Secretary Wood, "Who got command of this ship?"

"I don't know," Wood admitted, "that's more of a Navy affair. I'm sure that Harry Kinnock picked someone who was reliable, particularly given that Emily Steele was given command of *Voyager* and you know what sort of loose cannon she is."

"The sort that gets results," Grimminger said approvingly. "Wasn't she in overall command of the project?"

"Yeah," Wood said, pursing his lips tightly, and making a pained face, as if he'd bit into something very sour.

"What?" Sumner prompted.

"Well, if I know Harry, he'll have picked her exact opposite for the number two command," Wood said in a voice that slowly drained white with worry.

"Someone all spit and polish," Grimminger guessed.

"Exactly the sort of person to follow Ned Alquay zealously," Wood finished. He popped out of his chair, muttering, "I'd better go see how the admiral is doing."

"Mr. President, I think we should send orders to Far Side, demanding that in all circumstances *Odyssey* should remain grounded," Grimminger proposed.

"Ron's right, sir," Morgan chimed in, rising from his chair. "If you don't mind, I'll see to it personally."

"Yes," Greg Merritt replied in a tight voice, "you *do* that. The last thing we need is an interplanetary incident."

"If anything involved the aliens, sir, it would be an interstellar incident," Secretary of State Ellington corrected mildly.

"It would be *bad*," the president said. "That's all that matters."

* * *

Harmonie

"Eight," Admiral Tsukino repeated. "That's the same size as our basic team with the Xlern."

"And how many do we have supporting them here on *Harmonie* and *Voyager?*" Jim Pickett asked.

"That will leave us practically bare," Zhukov said, frowning at the admiral and the ambassador. "Even counting the scientists, particularly given their specialties, we are going to be short-handed."

"That is probably their intention," Pickett said, frowning. The others looked at him. "Oh, perhaps not their prime reason, but I don't doubt that they want to keep us off guard and too busy to think."

"And that, perhaps, is why they chose to contact us here at Jupiter instead of on Earth," Zhukov agreed sourly.

"You said short-handed," Pickett prompted.

Zhukov shrugged. "Not in watch-keeping. We can run with just fourteen personnel in four watches. But we only have another forty-four personnel—forty-two with Karl and Elodie on Luna—and most of those are working three shifts to analyze what we're getting now."

"So we reduce our capacity by fifty per cent," Admiral Tsukino said.

"Or do we shift more people to dealing with the newer drive?" Pickett wondered.

"There's also the question of computing power and simulations," Zhukov added.

"Not to mention the additional drain on stores for prototype parts," Pickett reminded him.

"We've got two 3D fabricators working flat out," Zhukov said in agreement. "Either we divert one to the new drive or ..." he waved a hand in surrender.

"Emily—" Captain Zhukov caught himself, deftly ignoring the droll looks that passed between the ambassador and the admiral "—Captain Steele, rather, was of the opinion that Axlu is close to wrapping up the theory side of things."

"Then we could assign her to lead the new team," Pickett said absently. The sudden chill that fell cued him to his error. He flicked open the fingers of both hands in apology. "I didn't mean—"

"We're short of command staff," Admiral Tsukino admitted.

"And I have too many duties here on *Harmonie*," Zhukov said in agreement.

"However, it would not appear politic to put our American captain at the head of successive operations," Pickett agreed. He cocked an eye toward the Russian captain. "Perhaps your Lieutenant Murray?"

Zhukov frowned. "I had thought of that, but at this moment, *Harmonie* is our only ship with a functioning drive. I'd hate to deprive us of our most experienced fusion engineer at this juncture."

"But they'll howl back home if we put Emily in command a second time," Pickett observed.

"There's also the issue of command for the first starship," Admiral Tsukino said. "Given her theoretical knowledge, your captain would be ideal."

"Perhaps we're viewing this too militaristically," Pickett said with apologetic looks for the two naval officers. "The ability to lead a scientific team does not reside solely with our officers. Perhaps we should consider some civilians instead." He turned to Captain Zhukov. "Perhaps Dr. Ney would—"

"No!" Nikolai swore.

"I would no more desire to lose Dr. Ney than I would to lose your 'Mac,' Mr. Ambassador," Admiral Tsukino added smoothly, "and for almost the exact same reasons."

"You want to keep them working on the broader scientific principles," Pickett said after mulling on their surprising declarations for a moment. He sighed. "Then we're back to square one. It seems that our available pool of officers is limited to those already employed with the Xlern or those still on *Voyager*."

"As our thinking is that *Voyager* will serve as life support and command for at least one of the star drives," Admiral Tsukino said, "that would seem to be the only logical solution."

"Couldn't we cross-train some of *Harmonie*'s people on *Voyager*'s systems?" Pickett said, glancing to Zhukov. "I mean, I'd really like to be able to say that our first starships are composed of international crews."

"How would your president react to that, Mr. Ambassador?" Captain Zhukov asked mildly.

"He'd be pissed but my credentials come from the UN," Pickett said with a dismissive wave, reminding them of the extraordinary powers he'd been granted by the world's assembled governments. "Besides, the bastard threw a party when he learned that I was marooned on the Moon."

"The difficulty with cross-training is that my personnel are all being utilized in some other capacity at the moment," Zhukov said thoughtfully.

"Yeah," Pickett agreed sourly. "We don't have enough warm bodies of the right type up here."

"If we had either Commander Reynaud or Commander Geister, I would have gladly recommended one for the position," Zhukov said glumly.

"It's a pity we couldn't just pop back to the Moon and steal—" Pickett muttered to himself only break off with wide eyes.

Admiral Tsukino and Captain Zhukov exchanged amazed looks.

"Mr. Pickett, perhaps your skills were wasted in political office," Admiral Tsukino said after they recovered. "You would have made an exemplary officer."

Jim Pickett was only able to give him a stunned, hurt look.

* * *

Voyager

"*Voyager*, you are cleared for departure," Lieutenant Ives said in response to the hail. "Good luck, Captain Milano."

Acting-Commander Giovanni Milano replied, "Thank you, Jacques." He flipped open a channel to engineering, "We are cleared, Mr. Long, you may engage the drive when ready."

"For what we are about to receive …" CPO Harry Long intoned as he flipped the switch that fired the alien engines for the third time ever. A moment later, Commander Milano reported, "Telemetry confirms departure at five-three gravities."

"Course locked in," Acting-Lieutenant and Executive Officer John McLaughlin added.

"You may stand down the second watch, Mac," Giovanni Milano said. "We'll call you if we need you."

"Aye, sir," Mac said, feeling uncomfortable in the strange uniform that Admiral Tsukino had forced him to wear.

"Mr. McLaughlin, given all that I have heard about you, I can think of no one else to whom I would give this opportunity," Admiral Tsukino had said when Mac had reluctantly reported to his quarters. Mac had been quick to note that Mr. Pickett was conspicuously absent, as was Captain Steele. Captain Zhukov and a very nervous-looking Lieutenant Giovanni Milano, *Harmonie*'s Italian navigation officer, were the only others present.

"It was only a matter of time, I assure you," Captain Zhukov said to the admiral. Admiral Tsukino accepted this Delphic prophecy without reaction which, if anything, made Mac feel even more insecure.

"I'll bite," Mac said finally, "what opportunity are you proposing, Admiral?"

Slowly and carefully Admiral Tsukino and Captain Zhukov laid out the situation and their need.

"Oh, no!" Mac said as soon as he caught on, shaking his head vigorously. "I got out of uniform thirty years ago, sirs, and I vowed never to go back."

Admiral Tsukino nodded. "Captain Steele said that this was how you'd react."

"She knows me pretty well," Mac admitted.

"She told me to say, 'We need you, Mac,'" Admiral Tsukino added.

"That's very nice, sir, but I don't see why that means that I should wear this brand-new uniform of a naval force that doesn't exist and is not recognized by any nation on Earth," Mac protested.

"She said, 'Somebody's got to be first,'" Captain Zhukov told him.

Mac's lips thinned. "A civilian navy?"

"Perhaps," Admiral Tsukino replied. "Certainly a trading navy. A search and contact navy."

"*Voyager's* still a Navy ship," Mac protested.

"Absolutely," Captain Zhukov agreed, "but in the interests of interplanetary need, Ambassador Pickett and Captain Steele have agreed to place her at the disposal of this new exploratory navy."

"Captain Zhukov will loan you Lieutenant Milano, who will be acting commander," Admiral Tsukino added, "but we need you to be executive officer."

Mac had spluttered, but even as he tried to raise further arguments, he knew that he was only a lamb bleating on its way to the slaughter.

And so, somehow, under the aegis of Ambassador James Pickett, John McLaughlin became the first lieutenant in the United Nations Free Trading Navy and *Voyager* was now operating under call-sign UNS *Voyager*. Which meant, if things didn't work out, that Mac would be the first—and hopefully the only one—to be put up against the wall and shot as a traitor.

Probably what bothers me most, Mac admitted to himself, *is how much* fun *this is.* He'd always felt like a pirate at heart and now, unless things went just right, he was going to be one. His attempts to get *Voyager* to broadcast the pirate flag were politely quashed by both the admiral and the ambassador.

Well, John, you did a good job. Here's your reward: a harder job. You get to go watch-on-watch on an alien technology that no one really understands in a ship that was just commissioned only a few months ago. And where are you going? Right into the thick of things to raid Far Side and Moonbesu Nihongo for officers. Should be fun.

"Mr. McLaughlin, you should really get some rest," Acting-Commander Ives said with more urgency.

"I'll try, Captain, I'll try," Mac promised before sketching an abbreviated salute and moving off.

*   *   *

"United Nations Ship?" Captain Steele demanded the moment she stepped into Pickett's quarters. "What's this crap, Mr. Pickett?"

"Captain," Pickett said, gesturing for her to take a seat. He was now firmly ensconced in one of the low-gee quarters aboard *Harmonie*.

Emily frowned at him but sat out of years of military training and common courtesy.

"I presume you're referring to our dispatch of UNS *Voyager* back to lunar orbit?" Pickett said when she'd sat and leaned forward on her elbows to glare at him.

"That ship belongs to the United States Navy and you know it," Emily said hotly. "You didn't say a thing about changing *that.*"

"And it still does," Pickett said soothingly. Emily raised an eyebrow and opened her mouth to speak but he cut her off with raised hands. "However, as ambassador of the United States, I have seconded it to the United Nations for the duration."

"Why?"

"The first reason is that it will confuse just about everyone," Pickett said with a small smile. "Operating under commission to the United Nations means that she is technically not subject to U.S. laws or commands—"

"Is that why you sent Mac in that ridiculous uniform?" Emily snapped. Then, because she couldn't resist, "And how *did* you convince him to take a commission in a navy that doesn't exist?"

"Actually, it *does* exist," Mr. Pickett corrected her mildly. "While it currently only has one commissioned officer and one ship under a slightly shady charter, its existence is, if anything, overdue."

"What are the aliens going to say?"

"*That* is why I created the navy in the first place," Pickett told her with a smile.

"Pardon?"

"The fact that the nations of our system have so quickly banded together to declare one unified naval force to police our actions both here and among the stars will, I predict, prove to be of unimaginable value in dealing with our alien friends," Pickett told her.

"Huh?" Emily said. "But *you* invented it."

Pickett spread his hands palm down in front of him. "As in accordance with my acknowledged position as ambassador for the United Nations."

"What does the admiral say about all this?" Emily demanded. Then she shook her head. "Never mind. The two of you are in it up to your necks." She frowned. "What I don't get, though, Mr. Ambassador, is why you picked Mac?"

"Aside from him we have a very limited number of civilians," Pickett explained. "While I imagine I could convince Chris or Sally to join the UNS, that sort of concentration of one nationality might appear suspicious."

"Why not some of the EU scientists?"

"Because we needed ship personnel, not scientists," Pickett replied. He shook his head. "Mac was really the only choice."

"You know he's a pirate at heart," Emily warned him.

"I think he's a free independent spirit," Pickett admitted, "but I'm not sure that he isn't more committed to freedom and fair trade."

"Okay, I suppose I can see that," Emily admitted. "But why not just make him captain, instead of XO?"

"Partly because he really isn't up for the task," Pickett said.

"And Lieutenant Milano *is*?"

"Acting-Commander Milano has many years of service," Pickett corrected her mildly. "He's used to command." He smiled. "Admiral Tsukino and I both formed a high opinion of him. We think he'll do well."

"If not, your navy's first ship will be its last," Emily told him frankly. A moment later she added, "How will the aliens take this?"

"I'm hoping it will cause them as much consternation as their latest moves caused us,"

Pickett told her with a grin.

"And if we get more people?"

"That's the real reason. We need more officers, particularly those suited for command, and we need crewmen, too," Pickett said.

"Just as long as they get back quick," Emily pronounced.

"Why's that?"

Emily grinned at him. "Because, aside from getting this system's worst migraine, I think I've finally cracked the alien gravity drive."

"When can we build it?"

"Not too long from now," Emily told him with a wave her hand. "Say tomorrow?"

Chapter Fifteen

Moonbesu Nihongo

"YOU *WILL* COME BACK TO ME," ELODIE REYNAUD SWORE AS SHE GAVE KARL Geister one last, tight hug.

"I shall do my best to ensure that he remains unharmed," Lieutenant Fukui added consolingly.

Elodie moved from hugging Karl to hugging Ryo Fukui.

"I'll hold you to that, Ryo," Elodie told him.

"And we shall do our best to ensure that all are thriving when you return," Commander Raiden Tanaka, Moonbesu Nihongo's executive officer, now acting commander, added in a surprisingly deep bass voice. "I only wish we could spare more personnel."

"It's a question of capabilities and availability," Karl Geister replied. "You could only let Ryo go because we were able to trade you Commander Reynaud," he added, gently touching the nose of his lover with one outstretched finger.

"It's not a fair trade," Elodie protested, "I'm going to be quite useless in another four or five months."

"You'll be one of the first mothers on the Moon," Karl corrected her.

"And an honor to all," Commander Tanaka agreed with a slight bow in her direction. He lifted his communicator so that the others could see as he asked Base Operations, "Any word from *Voyager?*"

* * *

Voyager

"This would work better if we could land," Acting-Commander Milano muttered bitterly.

"I agree, sir, but we don't have the reaction mass required," John McLaughlin, the *very*-acting-lieutenant, replied. "And with the base on lockdown, we're lucky to have got this far."

"But is it really necessary?" Giovanni Milano wondered.

"The extra fuel is important, sir," Mac assured him. "They've accumulated another whole kilogram and, what with *Odyssey* being grounded, they've no use for it. With antimatter, it's always a question of 'use it or lose it.'"

"And the containment field? Will it hold when we more than double the amount of antimatter?"

"It held more than that originally, sir," Mac told him with a shrug. He didn't mention that that was before the aliens had added their gravity drive. Nor did he bother mentioning that *Voyager* was an experimental ship.

"What about this Gallegos?" Milano now said. "Can we trust him?"

"Jorge?" Mac replied with another shrug. "He's a good man."

"Docking lights," Harry Long announced from the conn. "Radar contact solid, Foxtrot Sierra Two, you are 'Go' for docking."

"Roger, *Voyager*," a woman's voice replied.

"Lieutenant Longton?" Harry Long squeaked in surprise.

"Is that you, Harry?" Lieutenant Commander Sarah Longton asked. "Docking in five … four … three…two … one."

A series of bumps, rattles, and booms vibrated through the ship and then settled.

"I hate docking," Harry Long muttered. Then he recovered, checking his panels and called, "Good lock. Prepare to open the airlock."

A few moments later, Commander Milano opened the lock and grinned "up" at the people on the other side.

"Welcome to the *UNS Voyager*," he said, beckoning them forward. "I'm Commander Milano."

"Commander?" a deep southern male voice drawled. "Last I heard you were a lieutenant."

"Captain Lee, is that you, sir?" Mac called past his commander.

"John McLaughlin, I should have expected you here," Captain John Lee replied. "I always had you for a pirate."

"Too right," Mac replied. "Now if you and your crew will just step inside so we can talk things over …"

"Mr. McLaughlin, I don't know what you think you're doing but I've got orders from the White House," Captain Lee told him sternly. "*Odyssey* has been ordered to remain on the Moon, and I can't help but think that what applies to one of our ships should apply to both."

"Ah, well, sir, I'm sorry to hear that you feel that way," Mac replied. "But I've got my orders, too."

"From Captain Steele?" Lee guessed. "She isn't here, is she? As she and I have the same rank, I think that under the circumstances, you'll have to let my orders supplant hers."

"My orders come from Ambassador Pickett, Ambassador Plenipotentiary for the United Nations," Mac replied. Behind his back, Mac moved a hand in a circular "crank it up" gesture to Harry Long. In a smaller voice, he said, "Skipper, you'd better get back to the deck."

Commander Milano hesitated, then, with a slight smile for the boarding Americans, started back down the ladder, sliding past Mac with little difficulty.

"What in hell's that?" Captain Lee cried when he caught sight of McLaughlin's uniform.

"The uniform of the United Nations Navy," Mac returned quickly, not bothering to add all the various caveats that he normally supplied when answering that question. "I was commissioned lieutenant."

"Which makes you a traitor," Captain Lee declared angrily.

"No, sir, I was a civilian and free to give my oath," Mac said. "We need to present the aliens with a solid front moving forward."

"Why?" Sarah Longton's question was honest.

"Well, Lieutenant, there are a lot of reasons but I'm not prepared to discuss them at the head of an airlock," Mac replied. He turned his attention to Jorge Gallegos. "All I can say is that all our futures depend upon making the right choices."

"I couldn't agree more," Captain Lee replied, "which is why I'm calling on you, Mr. McLaughlin, to return this ship to its rightful sovereignty and yield to the authority of the President of the United States of America."

"I can't do that, sir," Mac told him quietly.

"Why not?"

"I'm not the captain," Mac said with a grin. "Besides, *Voyager* had been loaned out to the United Nations for the duration." He smiled at the stodgy Navy Captain. "I imagine the paperwork will catch up, eventually."

"Lieutenant," Harry Long called, "we're ready."

"Captain," Mac said, moving slowly down the ladder, "we're about ready to head over to Moonbesu Nihongo, and we can't alter our plans." Mac didn't add that he wasn't sure if they *could* change plans, it had taken some serious thought to determine how to use *Voyager's* gravity drive for a simple orbital change—it seemed too much, like using a sledgehammer to crack eggs. "We'd surely like it if you came along—we could use more command personnel."

"What for?" Sarah Longton asked.

"Commander, we're about ready to commission our first two interstellar ships," Mac told her with a grin. "We've already got two ships to command and we're going to need a *lot* more officers."

"That's all very well," Captain Lee said, "but you're not going anywhere with this shuttle still docked. You don't have the reaction mass for it."

"We're not using reaction mass, sir," Mac told him. "Now, if you'll just undock, we'll be on our way."

"And what if we don't, *Mister* McLaughlin?" Captain Lee demanded. "We're not closing our hatch so if you blow the clamps, you'll be killing us." Lee smiled. "You're stuck here until we decide to let you go."

"Skipper, they're being obstinate," Mac called over his shoulder.

Commander Milano made a rude noise and clambered back up the ladder. "Captain Lee, I beg you, please do not force our hand."

"What are you going to do?" Lee demanded.

"I'm sorry, sir," Mac said to Commander Milano, "I hadn't expected it to work out this way."

"Well, we all make mistakes, Lieutenant," Commander Milano replied, glancing toward the American Navy captain with an unreadable expression.

"So!" Captain Lee cried exultantly. "Here's what we'll do: you'll follow us onto our shuttle and we'll return to Far Side One."

"I don't think so, Captain," Commander Milano told him. Over his shoulder, he called, "Chief, carry out your orders!"

"Aye, sir, thrusting in three … two … one!" A force suddenly pushed everyone 'down' toward the rear of *Voyager*, causing Captain Lee to pile on top of Commander Longton who piled on top of Lieutenant Gallegos, who found himself falling toward the floor of *Voyager's* bridge. Mac and Commander Milano had sensibly pressed themselves to the side of the hatchway.

While they were still in a groaning heap, Mac closed and dogged both airlock doors. Clambering back down the ladder, he moved to help the surprised Navy officers back to their feet.

"Welcome aboard *Voyager*, Captain," Mac said as he lifted Captain Lee to his feet. "Next stop, Moonbesu Nihongo. We can drop you off there."

"Rendezvous in five minutes, sir," Harry Long called to Commander Milano.

"*Five minutes?*" Captain Lee repeated in amazement. At Mac's gesture, Captain Lee went to peer at Harry Long's instrument panels and then glanced over to Mac. "So it's really true? It's not some sort of stunt?"

Mac shook his head. "No, sir. There are aliens out there. *Voyager* was equipped with a gravity drive to get Lieutenant Commander Reynaud back to the Moon. We took less than a day to get here."

"Mac—Lieutenant—" Lieutenant Gallegos said with an awkward smile, "I brought up all the antimatter."

"We figured you'd know if we didn't," Sarah Longton explained.

Mac smiled and nodded. "We should move it to our containment unit."

"Soon," Gallegos agreed fervently.

"Jorge, you should *see* what they did to the drive," Mac said, suddenly aware that he had a fresh, kindred spirit to regale. "We're pulling fifty-three gees—"

"I only feel about one-sixth gee," Captain Lee complained.

"That's on the inside, sir," Mac told him. "On the outside, externally, we're running fifty-three."

"How is that possible?" Sarah Longton asked.

"Captain Steele says that she can almost explain it," Mac replied. "She says that she hopes to know by the time we get back."

"So what are you here for, Mr. McLaughlin? More antimatter?"

"No, sir," Mac said. "As I said, we're really recruiting."

"I'll volunteer," Jorge Gallegos said immediately. Mac saw Sarah Longton look at him hopefully, and felt that the Commander was wavering.

"Well, there'll be promotions all around when the navy gets going," Mac said, using the one line that Captain Steele had provided him with and aiming it directly at Captain Lee.

A light on the communications panel lit just as a chime sounded. "We're being hailed," Mac said, glancing around the room. "We're going to be docking with the moon base's shuttle shortly." He glanced toward Jorge Gallegos, "We'll need to undock your shuttle."

"How are you going to get the antimatter?" Captain Lee demanded.

"I've got Mick ready in the airlock," Mac replied. He glanced toward Lieutenant Gallegos. "Although I'm sure he could use help. You have it in a TCM, right?"

"That's the only way to move it," Captain Lee said. The transportable containment module was a self-powered unit that included not just the antimatter but the super-conducting magnets and other gear needed to contain it.

"That's what we figured," Mac said. With a smile, he added, "And we would have aborted the docking if we didn't see it."

"It could have been empty," Captain Lee said.

Mac shook his head. "Not with the magnets under load. If you turned them on with nothing in the chamber the thing would tear itself apart."

Lee nodded in agreement. "You were really after the antimatter, then."

"No, sir," Commander Milano replied. "Mac thinks that it would be nice to have it as an 'ace-in-the-hole' but we really are looking for more personnel."

"Is that all the antimatter?" Mac said now to Captain Lee.

"It had to be," Captain Lee admitted. "Anything less and the containment unit would have torn itself to bits."

"So *Odyssey* can't move," Mac observed. He glanced pityingly at Captain Lee. "You're a captain without a ship, sir."

Captain Lee glowered at him.

"We're coming up on the docking point," Harry Long called out. "We'll need to get that shuttle off our docking port."

"You could take the shuttle back down to the moon base, Captain," Commander Milano said politely to the American captain.

"Or we could arrange for the moon base shuttle to ferry up an additional pilot," Mac added quietly, glancing to Lee's reaction.

"Can you get me a channel back home?" Captain Lee asked suddenly.

"We've got a line standing by through Moonbesu Nihongo," Commander Milano reported, passing a headset to the American captain.

"You knew what I was going to do?" Captain Lee demanded, his eyes narrowing.

"Well, sir," Sarah Longton spoke up, "if anyone asked me to bet on whether you'd want to sit dirtside or take a ship command …"

"*Voyager*, you are online with U.S. Navy Headquarters, Admiral Roberts is standing by," a voice said quietly through Captain Lee's headset.

"If you don't mind, sir," Lieutenant Gallegos said quietly as he moved on down the ladder toward the side airlock, "I'm going to help Mick with that TCM."

"This is Captain John Lee. May I speak with Admiral Roberts?" Lee began.

* * *

ESA "Eurocos" Headquarters,
Noordwijk aan Zee, The Netherlands

"Well this is all very unusual!" Werner Ulke protested. "First this American Pickett decides to create a brand new navy without asking anyone, and now we've got half our officers submitting their resignations!"

"Captain Zhukov, I note, did not submit his resignation," Alexandrov, the Russian liaison, noted.

"Oh, come on, Konstantin! That's probably just because he sent it directly to the Kremlin!" Antonio Scarli snarled. "As for Commander Milano, we've approved his request." The other looked at him and he shrugged. "It was decided that there was a lot of good sense in the idea. We need to present a common front to these aliens—and any who come after them—particularly with regards to policing and customs enforcement."

"I note that the ambassador said that the United Nations Navy was solely peaceful in nature."

"And they snagged Tsukino as its first admiral!" Anne-Marie Foquet said in awe.

"It is truly an international force," Alexandrov said. "It's a pity there are no Chinese representatives among the officers."

"Something that Admiral Tsukino has vowed to correct as soon as possible," Foquet told him frostily. "I understand that he's invited them to propose a commodore, captain, and a slew of junior officers. He's also offered, as soon as available, a gravity-courier ship—"

"That'd have to be *Voyager*," Alexandrov muttered to the knowing nods of the others.

"—for their transportation," Foquet finished with an acknowledging nod for the Russian's interjection.

"He's also said the same things to India, Australia, South America, South Africa, the Turks … pretty much everyone," Werner Ulke noted.

"And Ambassador Pickett has proposed establishing a United Nations fund for their Navy," Antonio Scarli added. The others snorted derisively; the United Nations was famous for its inability to fund anything.

"What I like is his proposal that the UN receives royalties on the patents for the starships and ancillary discoveries," Anne-Marie noted. "That should provide them with a steady income."

"He's also asked that they be able to charge duties on cargoes, inspection fees, and a surtax to provide for emergency services," Alexandrov added.

"None of which is necessarily new," Anne-Marie countered. "Most nations and conglomerates"—she spread her hands to indicate the European nature of their organization—"do much the same."

"And what is the government reaction to this?" Werner Ulke asked.

"Still forming," Antonio Scarli told them. With his connections to the Italian government, he was the most directly connected to the political side of things. "I expect that we'll see a lot of action. Pickett and Tsukino will be able to get what they want simply by pushing hard enough."

"What about this latest, though?" Alexandrov asked. "This proposal to put an American in command of *Harmonie?*"

"It was either that or let him have one of the new ships," Scarli replied. "And given that *Harmonie* is just about to become obsolete, I know which one I'd choose."

Anne-Marie Foquet failed to mention the secret communications she'd had just recently from Captain Zhukov. *Harmonie* was not necessarily obsolete, just waiting the appropriate time for an upgrade.

"As would I," Ulke said in agreement. He turned to the Russian liaison. "But surely this is as much of a decision for the Kremlin as it is for us here?"

"I wouldn't know," Alexandrov said with a shrug. The Euros were so gullible; he was convinced they'd swallow this lie without question.

"It seems a shame that your government doesn't see fit to provide you with more intelligence, Konstantin," Anne-Marie Foquet observed dryly. "One might almost wonder if they question where your loyalties lie."

Alexandrov flushed and glared at her but said nothing.

"Anyway, with regard to this latest set of developments, how do we stand?" Anne-Marie said to the others.

"I would say that once again we should accept what is truly a *fait accompli*," Scarli said, glancing around for disagreement and finding none.

Into the accepting silence, Konstantin Alexandrov said, "Has anyone given thought to where this will lead?"

"Aside from Ambassador Pickett and Admiral Tsukino?" Anne-Marie Foquet said.

Alexandrov accepted that with a pained smile.

"Offhand," Ms. Foquet continued, "I'd say no. Why, do you have some suggestions?"

* * *

Xythir

>>**You said we'd crowd them,**<< Nexl chimed sourly to the *Ynoyon's* captain. >>**Instead even your people are exhausted by their enthusiasm.**<<

⁓Patience, rock-basher,⁓ Sa-li-ri-to rasped back. ⁓**It was not expected that they'd use their little ship to get more personnel. But, that is no matter.**⁓

>>**They're about ready to commission their first ship,**<< Nexl chimed discordantly. Drat the stumblers, but their chime-castanets were inspired. Nexl was eager to bring the

inventions back home and wanted nothing more than to move to the next phase of the plan as quickly as possible.

    ~**And they will have their second in another eight days or so,**~ Sa-li-ri-to responded.
    >>**??!!**<< Nexl chimed back.
    ~**Say that again, most esteemed ally,**~ Sa-li-ri-to returned with a tone of confusion.
    >>**That quickly?**<<
    ~**Indeed, that quickly,**~ Sa-li-ri-to replied. ~**Their brains seem well-integrated.**~ This was an admission which irked the four-brained Hydra to no end.
    >>**Then it is time to begin the serious negotiations,**<< Nexl said. >>**When they balk, we'll spring our trap.**<<
    ~**Yes,**~ Sa-li-ri-to hissed happily. ~**They will never know until it is too late.**~ Nexl chimed happily to himself.
    >>**Let me know when you are ready,**<< he said to the Yon captain.
    ~**With pleasure.**~

* * *

Harmonie

"Emily reports that they'll have their first prototype ready for tests tomorrow," Captain Lee reported to the group assembled in the wardroom.

"Lorie Dubauer and Sato worked miracles," Captain Zhukov said in agreement.

"And all this has been transmitted back to Earth?" Captain Lee said, turning to Commander Milano. The ex-Italian officer nodded. "Aye, sir."

It had only been two days since Captain Lee had accepted command of *Harmonie*, allowing Captain Zhukov to head up the team onboard the *Ynoyon* challenged with mastering the more advanced star drive technology. In that time, Commander Milano had discovered that working with Captain Lee was easier than he'd imagined. Captain Lee had been blunt and honest in his self-assessment as "a steady plodder who works by the book, nothing more."

Lee insinuated himself into the stressed crew easily enough and made certain that he'd met and worked with all four watch crews before engaging himself with the "freebooters" of the ship.

"My job is to make sure that we all have a functioning base," Lee had told his crew. In this, so far, he'd succeeded.

"It's obvious," he now said, "that *Voyager* will be the test craft for that." He frowned at the others. "But what about the next ship?"

"Yeah, we have a distinct lack of hulls," Jim Pickett agreed.

"We won't risk *Harmonie*," Admiral Tsukino and Captain Lee said in unison.

"Of course not," Captain Zhukov agreed.

"The aliens have been pressing us to talk turkey," Pickett added. "I suspect we can hold them off until we get *Voyager* successfully launched but not much longer."

"It's a pity we can't think of some nifty thing to give the Yon," Lee muttered.

"I'll give Sally Norman two more days," Pickett said with a smile. "I'm pretty sure she's feeling the heat already."

"It was Ensign Dubauer who came up with the chimes," Captain Lee reminded them. "I've put her in for a commendation, by the way."

"As have we," Admiral Tsukino told him. "It was in the packet *Voyager* brought back to Luna."

"Well, I've added to it, if that will help," Lee persisted.

"It will, if she stays with the Navy," Pickett agreed. He held up a hand to forestall Captain Lee's next words. "You can't blame her if she decides to bolt for the UN Navy."

"Either way, she's a good officer."

"I'm surprised to hear you say that, Captain," Admiral Tsukino remarked. "I would have thought her … unusual methods would have been somewhat … irksome to your command style."

"I didn't say that I wanted to command her," Lee replied with a grin, "just that she's a good officer."

"You know, from what Ensigns Sato and Dubauer have said about the aliens' construction capabilities, I wonder if we couldn't get them to provide us with a hull," Captain Zhukov suggested.

There was a moment's silence as the others absorbed this notion. Then, Jim Pickett said, "I think they hope we'll ask."

"I wonder how much they'll want for it?" Admiral Tsukino said.

"You know, trading hulls will be a limiting factor for a while," Captain Lee remarked. "If we don't have enough of them, we may find ourselves overwhelmed."

"Spoken like a true economist," Jim Pickett said approvingly.

"It was my minor in college," Lee admitted.

"I'll add it to my list of things to explore," Pickett said.

"Be sure to include life support and telemetry," Captain Zhukov said.

"In fact, if you want, I'll start putting together a complete list," Captain Lee offered, glancing to the admiral and Zhukov for agreement.

"That would be excellent," Admiral Tsukino agreed. "And now, where should we send *Voyager* on her maiden interstellar mission?"

The others looked at him in silence until Lee said mildly, "Should I add navigational charts to our list?"

*   *   *

Xythir

"Greetings to everyone on Earth. This is Lieutenant Danielle McElroy and I'd like to introduce our dancers," Danni said to the recorder. She nodded to Georges who turned on his recorder.

"I am Georges Darlan of Orleans, France."

"I am Kees van der Bilt of the Netherlands."

"I am Alexei Andryovich Semovich of the Russian Federation."

"And these are Engineer Apprentice Xover," Danni panned the camera to Xover who, prompted, waved one fore-pikki in greeting, "Security Apprentice Doxal, and Trade Apprentice Nevan." The recorder panned to the other two, who also waved although Nevan added a half-bow as a flourish of its own.

"Finally, we have the great honor to present Engineer Officer Axlu," Danni said. "We have agreed to set the gravity here to lunar normal, which is one sixth of Earth's standard gravity."

Axlu waved his fore-pikki and then chimed a deep bass riff with his two rear sets of chimes.

"And now," Danni said, returning the recorder to her face, "we are pleased to perform for you the first interplanetary ballet production: excerpts from the Nutcracker Suite by Piotr Ilyovich Tchaikovsky."

Then, she placed the recorder on its stand and moved back to show herself dressed in a leotard.

The music began and the lights dimmed.

As Captain Steele had predicted, no one commented on the human performers. It was Nevan, Doxal, Xover and, above all, Axlu who stole the show.

Try as they might, the aliens could not perfect a pirouette, having four lower limbs, but they'd managed to pull off some amazing arabesques and their *grand jetés* were awesome. Danni's choreography had been tweaked by suggestions from Ensign Strasnoye, Yeoman Semovich, Captain Zhukov, and, surprisingly, Captain Steele.

They performed the Dance of Mother Ginger's Children, with Danni on stilts as Mother Ginger and the rest as the children, and then they moved on to the Dance of the Flowers, with Doxal floating on high—using a special low-gee field—as Dewdrop.

Danni had arranged for some of the *Harmonie's* crew to be the audience and their enthusiasm gave the performance just the right sense of excitement.

"I should like to thank everyone on *Xythir*, *Harmonie*, and *Voyager* for their help in creating this event," Danni said at the end of the performance after they'd taken their final bows. "One thing which might have escaped your attention is the fact that all the percussion sounds in this performance were produced by the Xlern themselves."

In demonstration, Xover, Doxal, and Nevan came out with a quick musical dance which culminated in the introduction of Axlu performing with his double set of chime-castanets. Danni could see that the personnel in the audience were awestruck and could only hope the music would have the same affect for audiences on Earth.

When they'd finally signed off, Danni rushed to Axlu and bowed from her waist. "Engineer Officer Axlu, it was an honor to perform with you."

">>**We should do it again sometime.**<<" Axlu agreed.

">>**With sharp edges,**<<" Doxal added. Danni and the others knew that the security apprentice was devoted to all things warlike. She and Captain Steele had discussed the possibility of teaching the aliens fencing, but Ambassador Pickett had come down firmly on the side of less life-threatening arts, so in their spare time, they were busy trying to convert the principles of aikido to eight limbs.

"You were amazing," Alexei Semovich said to Axlu then waved to include Doxal and the others.

">>**Thank you,**<<" Doxal said. ">>**I found it very refreshing.**<<"

"As do we," Danni said in agreement.

">>**Well, enough of this, pleasant though it was,**<<" Axlu said, waving to his subordinates. He bobbed down in a bow to Danni. ">>**Lieutenant McElroy, we must take our leave and resume our training.**<<"

After he left, Lori Dubauer approached Lieutenant McElroy. "We're ready to build the first counter-gravity generators," Lori Dubauer told her excitedly. "Xover has accepted our challenge."

"Challenge?"

"We bet that we could get our unit built before he could," Ensign Sato explained with a nod toward her partner.

"What did you bet?" Danni asked, brows furrowed in curiosity.

Lori smiled at her. "I had a talk with Chris and we came up with something suitable."

Danni observed this with widening eyes then shrugged. "Just don't embarrass the skipper or your ass'll be grass."

"Understood!" Lori told her, sketching a quick salute and racing off toward the alien ship's machine room. Ensign Sato followed, hot on her heels with a speed and enthusiasm that was extraordinary for one so normally given to circumspection and caution.

Danni was surprised when she saw that Axlu and Captain Steele weren't heading toward their training room but rather followed Lori at a more leisurely rate.

">>**It is time to consider practical aspects,**<<" Axlu said to Captain Steele as they passed by. ">>**After which we should discuss hull requirements, life support, and power.**<<"

"Understood," Emily agreed. She nodded toward Danni, giving her a quick grin as she added, "Again, Lieutenant, great work."

"Just all part of communications, Skipper," Danni told her with an answering smile.

Captain Steele nodded abstractedly but Danni could see that her attention was directed toward the upcoming introduction to the aliens' fabrication facilities.

*   *   *

Ynoyon

The aliens were pink. Well, mostly pink. Parts of them were a bright yellow and their bodies were blends of shades of pink and yellow.

"Don't let them bite you," Lieutenant Murray said to Captain Zhukov as he greeted them at the *Ynoyon's* airlock. "They apologize but they seem rather desperate to get a good fang into one of us."

Lieutenant Murray pointed to one alien which was trying with no success to slither up on them unnoticed. "Individuals are called 'Yon' and seem not very intelligent."

"Is it true that they're controlled by the larger conglomerates?" Captain Zhukov said.

Murray nodded. "Sometimes. Apparently, the big Hydras will bite one of the singletons and put it under some sort of compulsion." Murray shrugged. "Trouble is, there's no way of distinguishing from one acting under compulsion or on its own."

"Leading to a very great deal of deniability," Lieutenant Alan Cohen said with a grin, his American accent a harsh contrast to Murray's crisp English accent. "They don't have fangs, *per se*, but teeth—lots of 'em—and some very interesting manipulative … tongues, I suppose we'd call 'em."

"The tongues do the delicate work while the teeth do the slicing and dicing, as it were," Murray said in agreement. "So far we've identified a number of ruling Hydra."

"As near as we can tell, they take their names from their member Yon," Cohen said. "Their captain is a Hydra called Sa-li-ri-to."

"So four heads are better than one?" Sally Norman asked, moving apart from the other waiting officers.

"Hey, Sally!" Cohen said. He looked her up and down. "Nice uniform."

"Mac says if I work hard enough, he'll promote me," Sally Norman said, glancing at the single ring that marked her as an ensign. She grinned at the U.S. Navy lieutenant. "Be careful, I might outrank you soon."

Lieutenant Cohen chuckled. "I'd serve under you any time."

"Lieutenant," Zhukov said warningly. Lieutenant Cohen's remarks had concealed a not-too-subtle double entendre.

"Sorry, sir," Cohen said then to Norman, "Sally."

"Well, I'm glad you're all here," Peter Murray said, breaking the awkward silence. He nodded to the captain. "Particularly you, sir."

"I can imagine," Zhukov agreed. "So where do we stand?"

"We've split into two groups, one theory and one practical," Peter Murray told him, "much like they did on *Xythir*. I'm in the practical group. Lieutenant Cohen is heading the theoretical."

"I'll keep you in charge of the practical group, and I'll take over the theoretical," Captain Zhukov said. He glanced about his group. "Lieutenant Fukui, I'd like you to join me." Lieutenant Fukui accepted that decision with a nod. "That'll leave you Lieutenant Gallegos and Ensign Norman to add to your practical team," Zhukov concluded.

"Excellent," Murray agreed. He glanced around the room, ignoring the one Yon slithering quietly on the floor. "I expect we'll be met in a moment." He made a slight face. "These chaps seem to like showing us who's boss."

Nikolai accepted that with a nod. "While we're waiting, why don't we get ourselves introduced and then start bringing us newcomers up to date with what you've learned."

"First thing is: a lot of the theory builds on what was learned from the Xlern," Peter Murray began without preamble. "They seem to be concentrating more on the maths in the theory section."

"They're working with materials in the practical area," Ana Szymzyck added. "Lieutenant Murray and I have been talking about what we've seen so far and we think—"

"Yeoman," Peter cut her off with a shake of her head. "'Loose lips sink ships,' you know. That can wait for later."

Ana Szymzyck blushed, her lips pressed firmly together.

"Ana and I have some insights we think you and the admiral might want to hear at a later time," Murray explained, managing to spare the young yeoman an apologetic look.

The outer hatch opened and the room was suddenly full of single Yon and Hydra. Actually, there were only two Hydra but the sudden increase in motion and heads made them seem greater in number. One detached itself and moved toward the wall by the airlock, and two of its heads moved to manipulate a series of controls.

I am Ja-ki-ro-ni, scrolled across a wall display. *I greet you.*

"And the free Yon?" Lieutenant Murray asked.

They are no matter, Ja-ki-ro-ni responded.

"If we are not going to be interacting with them, why are they here?" Nikolai Zhukov asked.

You are new, came the oblique response.

"I am Captain Nikolai Zhukov," Nikolai said. He gestured to the others and introduced them.

Captain is greater than lieutenant?

"It is," Zhukov said. "I have replaced Lieutenant Murray as this group's commander."

Strange, came the response.

"We understand that time is of the essence," Nikolai said, "so we assigned as many qualified personnel as we could to speed things up."

Commendable.

"We have assigned the new personnel to the appropriate learning groups and would like to start training," Zhukov said.

I shall make my superiors aware.

Zhukov moved warily as several of the single Yons moved toward the group.

"I would appreciate it if you could have your Yon remain out of reach," Zhukov said. "We are not completely comfortable with them."

They are harmless.

"Nevertheless," Zhukov persisted.

As you say, Ja-ki-ro-ni replied. One of its heads made a hissing sound and another darted out, biting one of the free Yon. The Yon instantly moved closer to the Hydra, curling itself in close to the main body.

"As near as we can tell, the Yon merge into Hydra for survival and maybe for reproduction," Lieutenant Cohen said, pointing toward the large bulge at the ends of the four individual Yon which formed the Ja-ki-ro-ni Hydra.

"How do they get food, then?" Sally Norman asked, gesturing to Ja-ki-ro-ni. "They seem less mobile when … conjoined like that."

"I think they do something with the free Yon to get them to work for them," Midshipman James Saxon said. The others looked at him. "It makes sense. Sort of like worker bees and queen bees."

"That's as good a theory as any," Zhukov agreed.

Ja-ki-ro-ni moved one head from the control panel.

This division is acceptable, the walls displayed. *The theory group will follow the Yon Ka(se), the others will follow me to the fabrication area.*

"You know, skipper," Peter Murray said affably, "if you'd told me two years ago that I'd be following a pink snake to learn how to build interstellar drives …"

"I like to keep my officers on their toes," Nikolai replied with a grin. "You wouldn't like to get bored, would you?"

"I haven't been bored in years, Captain," Murray said. He took on a bemused look. "It might be pleasant, come to think of it."

Zhukov smiled and waved goodbye as he led the theory group a few paces behind the quickly moving single Yon.

* * *

Harmonie

"I don't like it," Captain Lee said without preamble as he entered the wardroom for the usual daily meeting with Admiral Tsukino, Ambassador Pickett, and the other senior officers.

"It's a risk we're going to have to take at some point, John," Emily Steele told him, "and *Voyager* is ready." She'd spent all her time in the past week arranging the disassembly of the old propulsion module, its cannibalization, and the assembly of the new star drive. "In fact, if we wait much longer, we'll start to lose our antimatter reserves."

"We haven't seen any sign of antimatter from either of their ships," Lee said with a grimace. "I think that's because they don't use it."

"Or it could be that their shielding is better than ours," Emily said with a shrug. "Also, we can't be certain that they don't have it, we've got too much background radiation affecting our instruments to know."

"But Pete Murray says he's ninety percent confident they don't have antimatter," Lee persisted, "and I got the distinct impression that your Engineer Axlu was rather disturbed at the whole notion."

"I don't know if I'd called him 'disturbed,' sir," Emily said. "He seemed more like he was amused. Almost as if antimatter were quaint."

"Which adds to my point," Lee said. He turned to Admiral Tsukino. "Sir, I am concerned that we could be needlessly endangering our personnel."

"I'm glad to hear that, Captain," Jim Pickett now spoke up. He gave the captain a sympathetic look as he added, "Unfortunately, I don't see what choice we have." He held up a hand to forestall any protests. "The aliens have made it quite clear that they expect us to negotiate with them once we've determined that the star drive performs as expected."

"I understand, sir," Lee said with years of engrained respect for civilian authority. "I just wonder if we aren't dancing too much to their tune."

Pickett smiled at him. "Welcome to the club, Captain."

"Also, if we let *Voyager* go, we're completely at their mercy," Lee said.

"We've still got *Harmonie*," Captain Zhukov reminded him.

"But that's it," Lee said. "We've got no backup and without a gravity drive or something similar, we're a long way from any aid."

"Yes, I agree," Captain Zhukov said with a sour look of his own. "I rather think our alien friends planned it that way."

"We all do," Emily said now. She glanced to the new captain of *Harmonie*. "But John, short of installing a gravity drive on *Harmonie*, what choice do we have?"

Lee frowned and shook his head. "None."

"So we're at an impasse," Nikolai said. "Our group on *Ynoyon* are stymied." He bit his lip and shook his head. "No matter how we come at it, we just can't seem to wrap our heads around this new math they're pushing on us."

"And it's nothing like what the Xlcrn taught us," Emily said in agreement. "If I didn't know better, I'd swear they were deliberately throwing us off."

"It all started when we showed them that construction of the gee-coils," Pickett recalled.

"They were quite surprised by that," Admiral Tsukino agreed.

"I think they were pissed," Emily said. She waved a hand. "Oh, Axlu was thrilled, and praised Lori and Sato highly for their inventiveness. But after that …"

"After that, the Yon went on a slowdown," Captain Zhukov recalled.

"And the Xlern started pressing us to move faster," Emily added.

"None of which really matters at this moment," Pickett said. "They've invited us to have *Voyager* make her maiden jump and then they've requested that we start serious negotiations."

"And we can't really deny them," Admiral Tsukino said. "They've been dealing in good faith."

"Right up until they found out about our 3D technology," Pickett reminded him.

"It wasn't that we had 3D technology," Emily said, frowning in thought. "Ensign Sato was the one who pointed out that they have decent extrusion facilities of their own."

"Then what was it?" Captain Zhukov asked.

"It was when we showed them how we could go from software to hardware," Emily said, her lips pursed as if she were trying out the feel of that answer. She shook her head, unsatisfied. "No, it was more than that."

"I don't understand," Lee said.

"It was around the same time," Emily said, "but I'm not sure it was just that ability that ticked them off."

"What else did we do?"

"Well, we sintered some small parts for that super-conducting magnet …" Emily said with a shrug. "It wasn't a big deal, but the way Xover reacted, you'd think we'd invented the LED or something."

"Anything else?" Pickett said.

"*Weellll*, after that Axlu and I got into a discussion about meta-materials and how we'd done some stuff with refractive indexes and then—" Emily broke off and snapped her head up, with a triumphant look on her face. "That's it! They don't know about meta-materials." She pursed her lips again. "And I'll bet they can't sinter multiple elements the way we can."

"Why would that cause them to be mad?" Captain Lee asked. "Surely they just take that as something else they'd want to trade?"

"I see two possibilities," Pickett said after a moment's silence. "One is that they already have a full list and if they add something else, they'll have to sweeten the pot some more. The other is that perhaps we're demonstrating abilities that will put us more quickly in a competitive position with them."

"There's no reason both can't be true," Admiral Tsukino observed.

"And either could be bad," Pickett said. He saw the confusion on some faces and explained, "As long as they feel that they're getting better or equal in trade with us, they have an incentive to come to a deal."

"Yes …?" Admiral Tsukino said invitingly.

"Well, if they suddenly feel that they're on the losing end of the deal …"

"All they have to do is call in their goons," Lee finished sourly.

"Which means that it's imperative we get *Voyager* to make her jump and for us to get an agreement," Pickett said.

"I see," Lee said. "You're saying that we're better off cutting a bad deal than we are in letting them call in the cops."

"Yes."

"So, who is going to command *Voyager*?" Admiral Tsukino asked, eyeing the three captains with a grin.

"I would say that the choice is obvious," Captain Zhukov said, grinning at Emily Steele.

"I'm not so sure," Jim Pickett said, giving Emily a sad look. "I think we have to be aware of public opinion back home as well as the image we'll be projecting to outsiders."

"Are you saying that you want me to join the United Nations Navy?" Emily said sharply. "Because I won't do it. I swore an oath."

"I understand," Pickett said with a sigh. "Well, then, I suppose Captain Milano—"

"Excuse me, Mr. Ambassador," Admiral Tsukino cut across him, hand raised in interruption. He turned to Captain Steele. "I believe I understand your feelings, but I'm afraid that I cannot disagree with Mr. Pickett. I think it imperative that the captain of our first starship be someone who operates beyond regular politics."

Emily nodded jerkily and drew a breath. "I'm sure that Giovanni will do a great job—"

"In the past it has not been inconsistent with oaths for officers to take secondary service as part of a United Nations peacekeeping effort," Admiral Tsukino pressed on over her.

"I don't believe we're at war with anyone," Captain Zhukov said in Emily's defense.

"We could be," Pickett said.

"In the interests of world peace, world trade, and our interstellar presence, Captain Steele, would you be willing to second your services to the United Nations Navy?" Admiral Tsukino asked formally.

"Take it," Captain Lee told her urgently. Emily gave him a surprised look. "You need to look at it two ways: is it good for our country and is it consonant with your oath?"

Emily froze as she considered his words. Finally, she ducked her head. "Okay."

Chapter Sixteen

"*Voyager*, you are clear for thrust," Commander Milano radioed from *Harmonie's* command deck.

"Are *we* ready?" Emily said, glancing around at her command crew. It was a strange mix. Ensign Sato was at the conn, Lieutenant McLaughlin stood close behind, and Ernst Schuyler finished out the officer team.

Chief Long had insisted in staying in the engine room despite "not knowing a damn thing about them" as Mac had half-growled when first presented with the idea. He was not alone: Mick Hsu, Bill Pusser, and Louise O'Reilly had all insisted on keeping their billets. Emily wasn't quite sure whether they chose out of loyalty to her, to Mac, or sheer terror at the thought of leaving the one ship they'd called home for so long now.

She'd done her best to ensure that they understood the risks, but it seemed that nothing, not even the possibility of being hopelessly marooned at some unknown point in space, could separate them.

It was a terribly small team but Mac assured her that they'd manage to make the jump and back again—if it were possible.

The last question had been: where?

Part of the answer to that lay in the physics of this star drive. The aliens, particularly the Yon, seemed to have just arrived in Jupiter orbit, but the Xlern were adamant that *Voyager* could only activate the star drive's jump capability when far enough out of the solar system—at forty times the distance from the Earth to the Sun. Jupiter was at just over five times that distance which meant that *Voyager* had to journey another 35 AU to get to the heliopause.

Fortunately, the Amuksli drive was able to produce a more efficient gravity field than the one *Voyager* had employed on its emergency return to Earth, so the time to get to the heliopause was a little over two days.

However, while operating in normal space, the Amuksli demanded a greater amount of energy, so the journey would consume over two hundred milligrams of antimatter. The Xlern had been apologetic about that, saying that the total voyage would consume all of *Voyager's* antimatter supplies. Emily decided not to mention that *Voyager* had an extra 1.5 kilos of antimatter that it had brought back from Far Side.

Voyager's size, construction, and fuel supply precluded her from using gravity-wave communications, but she managed to remain in radio contact with Earth and, thence, back to *Harmonie* in Jupiter orbit. Because of the need to bounce signals back to Earth, the total transit distance was nearly 45 AU which meant that there was one-way lag of six hours, so any round-trip communications would require twelve hours.

With such a great delay, it was decided to let *Voyager* operate independently, merely sending updates.

The jump itself would consume a mere fifty milligrams of antimatter, for a total consumption of three hundred milligrams, which, as far as the aliens knew, would allow *Voyager* only two round trips to the heliopause and follow-up star jumps.

With the Amuksli drive, there was a slight additional penalty for each extra thousand light-years in distance, but the biggest energy requirement was just to get into the jump itself. Even so, there was no question on the first destination. Gleise-581 would have been a natural choice, but now that it was known to be inhabited, it was ruled out unanimously.

Instead, the jump would be much closer to home: Alpha Centauri at a mere 4.37 light-years. Alpha Centauri wasn't a single star but a binary star system with a third star, Proxima Centauri, somewhat closer to Earth at 4.22 light-years.

Voyager wasn't equipped with all the exploration gear that everyone would have liked, but Ensigns Dubauer and Sato had managed to put together a couple of decent probes to augment the radio and visible light capabilities of the ship herself.

"Roger, *Voyager* is thrusting for the heliopause," Emily radioed back.

"*Voyager*, this is Admiral Tsukino," a new voice called. "On behalf of the United Nations and all the crews working out here, I wish you good luck and safe journey."

"Thank you, Admiral," Emily replied. "We'll see you soon."

"At least we *hope*," Mac added darkly. Emily turned and smiled at him. Mac's lips twitched, but he turned his head to the displays, reporting, "We're pulling a solid three hundred and fifty gees."

"So at least that part is working as designed," Emily teased.

"I'm sure it will all work, Skip," Mac said. "It's just that … well, I wish I understood it a bit better."

"And how well did you understand the MAM engines?"

"A bit better," Mac told her with a twist of his lips. He pushed a comm link and said, "Engineering, this the XO. How's it looking down there?"

"Just fine, sir, just fine," Harry Long replied. "All the lights are green where they're supposed to be and all the doohickeys are hickey-ing right along."

"Well," Mac said, "just as long as they're hickey-ing, we're fine." He turned to Captain Steele. "Did you hear, Skip?"

"I heard," Emily said. "In which case, I think we can stand down the second watch." She smiled at Mac. "Get some rest."

"Aye, ma'am," Mac replied, stifling a yawn. He pushed the "all hail" and said, "Second watch, stand down." His voice boomed throughout the small ship.

* * *

Xythir

>>**Security Officer Noxor has an emergency message for you, Captain,**<< Exern reported.

>>**Put it through,**<< Nexl said in a soft, bored chime. Noxor was wont to have an emergency every few days. The last one had to do with an issue about the paint the stumblers were going to use on their old ship. Apparently Noxor was convinced that their choice of "patriot red" was some attempt to produce a secret blinding light weapon.

>>**Captain Nexl, Security here,**<< Noxor rapped. The Security Officer had declined the offer of personal chime-castanets on the grounds that they were a security breach. Of course, such behavior was normal in security officers, so Nexl placed no emphasis on it. Nexl was still recovering from his encounters with the kinder, gentler, *quieter* Axlu and the revelation that the engineer officer had known all along that he was painfully loud.

Nexl had gotten his own back—serving a special meal of slightly fermented edibles which, for the unprepared, produced a nasty ethanol poisoning, causing headaches and minor pains until flushed out of the system. Nexl was not at all surprised when Trade Officer Ixxie reported that the humans had developed similar intoxicants. Apparently, contrariness was not only a universal norm, it was also a terrestrial norm as well. That revelation had eased the last of Nexl's concerns about dealing with the stumblers—their dealing on the chime-castanets promised profits all around. Nexl had notions of buying himself a trading fleet.

Xythir was a fine enough ship but too large for most trading missions, a bit of a fuel-fiend, if truth be told. Nexl wondered idly if it might be traded with the stumblers at a profit. It had, after all, been part of the overall strategy to use outsized ships to make first contact—adding to the whole shock and awe effect.

>>**Captain!**<< Noxor prompted.

>>**Captain, here,**<< Nexl returned, realizing that he had been thought-profiting or "wool-gathering" as some of the two-legs called it. >>**What is the issue? Is the ship in danger? Will the two-legs overwhelm us?**<<

>>**No,**<< Noxor responded. >>**But you asked me to keep touch on developments around this system.**<<

>>**And?**<<

>>**We have an emergency.**<< Noxor repeated.

* * *

This was his first ride in the rocket sled and Jim Pickett wished it would be his last. Unfortunately, that would mean he would be stranded on the alien ship and, as he and Admiral Tsukino had decided long ago, having either the ambassador or the admiral aboard an alien ship would qualify as "a bad thing."

Unfortunately, the aliens had been adamant and persuasive.

"**>>We helped you in your emergency. We are now requiring that you repay us,<<**" Captain Nexl had said when he had been forced into a corner by Pickett's maneuvering.

"If my presence is absolutely required, then I shall be glad to oblige," Pickett had said. "Please understand, however, that my medical condition requires that I undergo no more than a one-sixth gravity acceleration at any time."

"**>>That will be done,<<**" Nexl had replied. "**>>Time is of the essence or lives will be lost.<<**"

"I'm on the way," Pickett had replied. Between the two of them, he and Admiral Tsukino wondered if the aliens hadn't simply panicked and were trying the worst of hardball tactics. Pickett had a plan for dealing with that.

"Prepare for contact," Danielle McElroy warned. She'd insisted on ferrying Pickett over herself.

"Ready," Pickett replied.

"Three … two …" Pickett felt his feet touch something and bent his knees to help absorb the gentle impact.

"Latch on," Danni said to her crew.

"Latched fore."

"Latched aft."

"Okay, Mr. Ambassador, you can start toward the hatch, sir," Danni told him.

"On the way," Pickett replied, undogging the line that tied him to the sled and moving toward the airlock.

Entrance, pressurization, and movement into the main room were all anticlimactic. Pickett just had time to undog his helmet before he found himself surrounded by eager space-hands who skinned him out of his suit and set him gently on the ground.

"Want to make sure you look your best, sir," Danni assured him.

"Thank you," Pickett replied. He was wearing a simple shirtsleeve outfit, differentiated from all the others only by the UN flag sewn above his pocket.

A blue-green blur whisked toward him, and it took Pickett a moment to realize he was—face-to-body?—with his first alien. He sent a silent blessing to Lori Dubauer for her inspired notion of the chime-castanets because he could immediately tell by the fact that this alien wore two pairs on each of his four upper limbs that he was dealing with Axlu, the engineer officer.

"Engineer Officer Axlu, I greet you," Pickett said, giving the smaller alien a quick bow.

"**>>I greet you, Ambassador to the Stars,<<**" Axlu replied. "**>>I hope that your surname does not indicate a preference for stolen goods.<<**"

Huh? Jim thought to himself.

"Oh, Lord!" Danni McElroy swore as realization struck her. "Engineer Officer, I'm afraid that you have used two de-references in your humor."

"**>>And this is improper?<<**" Axlu chimed back softly.

"It takes a certain type of mind to follow," Danni said delicately. She turned to Pickett and explained, "I've been trying to teach them puns. Sometimes they're very good at them, sometimes they go a bit overboard."

"**>>Pickett to picket fence. Fence to receiver of stolen goods.<<**" Axlu said. "**>>This does not work?<<**"

"It would perhaps have been more obvious if you'd gone directly from the name itself," Pickett replied. "As in, perhaps, 'I hope you will not go on strike.'"

"**>>Strike as in physical blow?<<**" Axlu was perplexed.

"Strike as in ceasing to work," Pickett replied. "As when workers go on strike for better conditions."

"**>>I shall think on that,<<**" Axlu promised. "**>>Captain Nexl will be here shortly.<<**"

"He said it was an emergency," Jim said, hoping to garner further information from the engineer officer. Axlu was clearly an outlier of his species, much as Danni McElroy and Lori Dubauer were exceptional in their own rights. He suspected that that was perhaps why the three got along so well, although he knew Captain Steele had also struck up a good relationship—at least, a good working relationship—with the Xlern formerly known as Shouter. For himself, Pickett was thrilled to learn that Axlu was willing to use volume as a method of coercing action out of subordinates and superiors alike.

"**>>I believe my captain is correct in his evaluation,<<**" Axlu replied, "**>>although it could just as easily be considered poor workmanship, if you will pardon my saying so.<<**"

Pickett raised an eyebrow and turned to Lieutenant McElroy who shrugged in a first-I-heard-of-it look.

There was motion at the outer door and suddenly Axlu was moving to one side. "**>>Ambassador Pickett, Captain Nexl,<<**" Axlu said.

"Captain Nexl, it is a pleasure meeting you," Pickett said, nodding his head in a half bow.

Aside from his three sets of chime-castanets, Nexl looked not much different from the engineer officer or any of the other Xlern that Pickett had seen. If anything, Nexl was wirier than the sturdy Axlu, but its coloring was not so different, perhaps with slightly larger swirls of blue in places. As far as he had been able to determine, coloration was not an indication of rank or status but might have something to do with origin at birth. The Xlern spoke of "different shores" in the same semantic style that people spoke of different cities.

"**>>I wish it were under better circumstances,<<**" Nexl replied. He swiveled around. "**>>What I have to say is best said alone. Will you accompany me to my bridge?<<**"

"As I've said earlier, I cannot tolerate more than a one-sixth of standard gravity," Pickett replied carefully. "Beyond that, Captain, I am at your service."

"**>>You will need to communicate with your people,<<**" Nexl said. "**>>We shall go** to the command deck. Axlu, see to the ambassador's gravity.<<"

">>**As you order.**<<" Axlu said. He moved to a wall, tapped in a number of instructions and turned back. ">>**Completed.**<<"

"I'd like—" Pickett said, turning toward Lieutenant McElroy.

">>**Come, time is of the essence and our proposed solution is drastic,**<<" Nexl cut him off.

"Lead away," Pickett replied, stomping firmly on his temper.

">>**He shall not be harmed,**<<" Axlu assured the remaining humans.

Pickett found himself scrambling to keep up with the captain. As soon as they were out of earshot, Nexl said, ">>**At some point, Ambassador, I shall require an explanation of how you can understand me.**<<"

"It's simple, really," Pickett explained. "Our people have been working on an experimental device to translate your clicks into our speech."

">>**And it's faster than our computers,**<<" Nexl noted. ">>**Will you trade?**<<"

"It's mostly of benefit to us," Pickett replied, careful to remain neutral on the topic.

">>**This is a transporter,**<<" Nexl said as a door irised open. ">>**It operates similarly to your 'elevators.'**<<"

Pickett followed the eight-limbed alien inside without faltering.

">>**While it may not be useful to others,**<<" Nexl continued, ">>**we need to trade.**<<"

"Now?"

">>**Now.**<<" Nexl responded. The transporter slowed and stopped, the door irised open. Pickett had time to notice that it was a double-door combination like most elevators—one on the elevator car itself and one in the wall to which it emptied. ">>**What I propose will require trade.**<<"

"Perhaps you'd care to explain," Pickett said, as his eyes adjusted to the dim light.

">>**Communications Officer, replay the recordings,**<<" Nexl ordered. Pickett was startled to see movement near a collection of panels set at a wall and realized that the command deck was occupied. Nexl waved an upper limb in a different direction. ">>**This is Security Officer Noxor. He reported this to me.**<<"

"Security Officer," Pickett said with a noncommittal nod toward the third alien in the room. "Would I be correct in assuming that security involves intelligence gathering and threat analysis?"

">>**The human is dangerous,**<<" Noxor said.

">>**The human has a translating device and can hear anything you say,**<<" Nexl responded. ">>**You might consider that a security lapse.**<<"

"It was not intended to shame," Pickett put in immediately. "We were simply eager to better understand you."

">>**Spy,**<<" Noxor rapped tersely.

"Understanding requires gathering intelligence," Pickett returned as smoothly as he could. He was aware that the atmosphere was less than friendly. "Captain, you said that this was urgent?"

">>**Look at the screen,**<<" Captain Nexl said. ">>**Exern, adjust for human vision.**<<"

"What am I seeing?" Pickett asked after a moment.

">>**The moon orbiting Mars,**<<" Nexl replied. ">>**The moon you call Phobos.**<<" It turned to the communications officer. ">>**Magnify.**<<"

The image blurred and then steadied again showing much greater detail.

">>**See that increase in luminance, there?**<<" Captain Nexl said, moving forward and bracketing a section of the display with two fore mannies.

"Yes," Pickett said slowly. "Some sort of construction."

">>**It is a ship,**<<" Noxor rapped.

"I could well imagine it might be," Pickett replied. "Of course it could also be a habitat or a metallic asteroid being rendered—"

">>**It is a ship,**<<" Noxor repeated.

">>**Show the human,**<<" Nexl ordered with what Pickett took to be an air of resignation.

This time the image bloomed without any shudder and focused sharply on the shape of a near-completed ship. Judging by the spacesuits surrounding it, Pickett decided that it was about the size of a courier ship. In fact, it looked *very* much like a replica of *Voyager* except—

"Is that your gravity drive?" Pickett said, moving forward to point to the after section of the ship.

">>**Not quite,**<<" Noxor rapped back. ">>**It's an accident about to happen.**<<"

"What?" Pickett said. "This ship is doubtless being built by our Chinese friends. They have established a set of thriving colonies on Mars and its moons and certainly are capable of—"

">>**They will kill everyone within six hundred thousand** *xlernen*,<<" Noxor rapped incessantly.

"How could that be so?"

">>**Inferior materials,**<<" Captain Nexl said, its upper limbs quivering with what Pickett took to be anger.

"If they do that, then …" Pickett began. The repercussions would be ghastly. "How do you know the materials are inferior?"

">>**Your** *Voyager* **was built on a keel of lunar titanium with aluminum and high-strength steel,**<<" Captain Nexl said. ">>**This has none of those components. It will not withstand the stresses of the gravity drive.**<<"

"How can you be certain?" Pickett asked without thinking.

Before he could withdraw the question, Noxor answered, ">>**We have been monitoring the supplies delivered. There was no titanium and the metals provided were**

low-grade ore from the lesser moon.<<"

If the aliens were correct, then when the Chinese fired off their drive, their ship would be destroyed along with everyone within a—how big was a "xlernen" compared with a meter?—certainly within a large radius.

The Chinese would not accept that the explosion was the result of inferior materials or poor construction. Admitting such things would entail a loss of prestige—and probably a fatal admission of error for at least one or more officials. Instead, they would point the finger either at the UN team responsible for disseminating the information or—worse—at the aliens themselves.

"We must warn them," Pickett said. "I shall return to *Harmonie* and—"

"**>>That will be too late,<<**" Noxor rapped harshly.

"What do you suggest?" Pickett said, turning to Captain Nexl.

"**>>We need to go to them now,<<**" Nexl said. "**>>But to do that, we must trade.<<**"

Pickett's mind whirled. He thumbed his comm link. "Lieutenant McElroy, can you get either Ensign Dubauer or Ensign Sato?"

"They're in the fab with Xover, sir," Danni replied easily. "Is this urgent?"

"Yes," Pickett replied. "Tell them that I require plans for our communicators—the ones the Xlern just learned about—immediately."

"Sir?" Danni sounded alarmed.

"We're conducting a trade," Pickett said. He turned to Nexl. "Will that suffice?"

"**>>Engineer Officer Axlu, execute emergency translation,<<**" Nexl said by way of reply. He turned to Pickett. "**>>You should warn your personnel.<<**"

"Warn them?"

"**>>Engineer Officer Axlu offered this witticism,<<**" Nexl replied. "**>>It said, 'You are going to get the jump on** *Voyager*.'<<"

"Get the jump?" Pickett repeated, his eyes widening as the meaning became clear to him. "I've got to warn *Harmonie*!"

"**>>Channel open,<<**" Communications Officer Exern said.

Pickett didn't stop to think. "*Harmonie, Harmonie*! This is Pickett, we're jumping to Mars orbit—now!"

* * *

Harmonie

"Sir!" Lieutenant Jacques Ives of Communications cried just as Captain John Lee saw the *Xythir* disappear. "Ambassador Pickett!"

"Put it on screen," Lee said calmly. "I'm sure he has an explanation." As an afterthought, he added, "And send a sitrep to Admiral Tsukino."

"On it," a different voice returned. Lee recognized it as belonging to Commander Milano.

Pickett's voice came over the speakers, "*Harmonie, Harmonie*! This is Pickett, we're jumping to Mars orbit—now!"

"Just like that," Lee muttered to himself. He turned in his seat. "Navigation, when will you get a good view of Mars?"

"We'd have to adjust the antennae, sir," Commander Geister said. "And then with the light lag, it'll be thirty-four minutes or so before we get first sight."

"Make it so," Lee said.

"Aye, sir," Commander Geister replied.

"Admiral for you, sir," Lieutenant Ives reported.

"Admiral Tsukino, Captain Lee, sir," Lee said. "*Xythir* just jumped away from us. We received a transmission from Ambassador Pickett at the same time—" he glanced to Ives for confirmation and the French communications officer gave him a nod "—that's confirmed."

"Warn Earth," Admiral Tsukino said. "Copy the message to Moonbesu Nihongo and your Far Side base, if you'd please."

"Earth, sir?" Lee said, asking for more details.

"Eurocos, NASA, the Chinese Space Agency, and the Japanese Space Service Headquarters in Kyoto, as well as the United Nations General Assembly and Security Council," Admiral Tsukino said.

"But not the press," Lee said.

"No, Captain, I think we can leave that to the individual organizations," the admiral replied, much to Captain Lee's relief. "Ambassador Pickett has been summoned for an emergency."

"Aye, sir," Lee replied. "As near as I can guess, the emergency involves Mars."

"And probably the Chinese," Admiral Tsukino said, half to himself. "I'm not surprised."

"Sir?"

"I couldn't imagine them standing idly by," Tsukino said. "I rather think they've done something that's upset or worried the Xlern."

"What about the Yon?"

"I don't know," the admiral replied. "Why don't you contact them and see if they have any suggestions?"

"Will do, Admiral," Lee said, nodding toward Commander Geister who'd been listening in. The German nodded and moved over to his station, opening a hail to the remaining alien ship.

"Let me know if you find out anything more," Admiral Tsukino said, signing off.

"Will do," Lee repeated to the dead connection. He took a moment to sit back in his chair, glad to be in the artificial gravity of *Harmonie*'s bridge, and spent a moment exuding the same calm that the admiral had displayed. Lee had been in the service—and in space— long enough to have learned the hard lesson that panic kills. His crews followed his example and reacted calmly to what could only be described as an extraordinary event. Although, after so many weeks in contact with two alien races, perhaps they were just numb to any new shock.

* * *

People's Liberation Army Shipyard, Phobos

"With the commissioning of this ship, we will leap to the forefront of interstellar exploration," Admiral Wang Anbai pronounced, "and take our rightful place among the stars."

"Indeed, sir," Commander Ren Wenwu agreed. "I merely present my engineer's concerns that we have not tested any of the components of the systems nor have we certified the pressure vessel for habitation."

Commander Ren normally viewed Lieutenant Ma's concerns with disdain. In this instance, however, the lieutenant had the backing of his senior non-coms and *they*, at least, were people Commander Ren trusted.

"We know that *Voyager* was built with lunar materials," Ren had said. "What we're using is the lightest stuff they can ship up from the surface. It's not the same at all."

"Captain," Admiral Wang now said, "we know that the American ship, *Voyager*, has already departed for the edge of our system and will shortly make a star jump to Alpha Centauri. Our orders are clear: We are to meet with *Voyager* and demand representation on her as part of the historic United Nations voyage."

Captain Ren noticed how the attributions changed before and after the introduction of Chinese personnel to the international effort.

"Sir, I understand," Ren said deferentially, "and heartily concur with our goals. I am merely expressing the concerns of my chief engineer."

"He is not the captain," Admiral Wang said.

"He is responsible for the power systems of the ship," Captain Ren replied. "I would be remiss in not apprising you of his concerns, Admiral."

"Very well," Admiral Wang replied, glancing out the viewport to where the gleaming new ship—proudly wearing the People's Republic of China's brave flag with its five golden stars on its red background—floated close by the orbital space station. "You have conveyed those concerns and now I'll convey you—What in the name of the Republic is that?"

The admiral's finger pointed to the right of *China* where the light was suddenly blocked by a large, dark shape.

"Phobos shipyard, this is Ambassador James Pickett, requesting immediate response," a voice gabbled out of the speakers around them. "This is an emergency."

"Do you speak English?" Captain Ren asked the admiral, glancing at the speakers and then back to the huge darkness. "I think that might be one of the alien ships."

"Here?" Admiral Wang said. He turned to his yeoman. "Get someone here who speaks round-eye."

* * *

Xythir

"Welcome aboard, Admiral, Captain," a cheerful tall woman in U.S. Navy garb greeted them as they undogged their suit helmets. "I'm Lieutenant Danielle McElroy detached from *USS*—now *UNS*—*Voyager*."

Captain Ren gave her a curt nod while Admiral Wang made no response. Their accompanying translator kept his eyes on his admiral.

"You might want to put these on your ears, sirs," Danni said, extending two small earbuds toward them. "We had to work fast but we think we've got them to work for you."

"What are they?" Admiral Wang said to his translator, a burly sergeant who stood close by. Sergeant Yin Shushei was a small arms specialist first and an English speaker second.

"Admiral Wang asks what are these devices?" Sergeant Yin asked.

"Translation devices," Danni told him with a smile. "We jiggered them so that they should be able to translate from Xlern to Mandarin." She made a face. "There might be a few bugs, so if you hear something that seems off, you might want to run it by me."

"Do they translate to English as well?"

"No," Danni said, shaking her head. She didn't bother to mention that she and Ensign Sato were both fluent in Chinese and had often used it for private conversations. If the Chinese didn't know, she wasn't going to tell them—particularly given the vibes she was picking up from Captain Ren and, especially, Admiral Wang.

She'd met her share of big-wigs too big to be wrong and the admiral had that swagger in spades.

She noticed that the admiral handed his earbud to the sergeant and that the captain was less than thrilled to insert *his* earbud. He jumped, startled, when he heard, ">>**Are they ready?**<<"

"That's Xover, engineer apprentice," Danni said to the translator.

">>**The captain and the ambassador are coming,**<<" Xover continued. ">>**They request we wait in the display room.**<<"

"Xover, why don't you come show yourself so that our new friends can get used to you?" Danni said, waving toward the Chinese spacers.

Captain Ren saw Admiral Wang take an involuntary step backward as a four-legged creature trotted over to them and stopped.

">>**Which one is the admiral?**<<" Xover asked in a tone which Captain Ren was willing to bet was one of a worried subordinate keen to impress.

"This is Admiral Wang Anbai, Xover," Danni said, waving both her hands in the direction of the admiral.

">>**Ah, he is brighter than your Admiral Tsukino!**<<" Xover exclaimed. ">>**You were not correct when you called them 'brass,' Lieutenant. They seem to prefer gold.**<<"

"It's an old saying," Danni assured the alien with a wave. "Sirs, if you'd accompany us, we're going to head to a display room. The captain and the ambassador will join us shortly."

"Do you know if the displays will show Chinese characters?" Sergeant Yin asked.

">>**Of course,**<<" Xover replied in a tone which Danni had no problem reading as annoyance. Xover and Axlu, engineers both, prided themselves on their abilities. ">>**We can handle any squiggles you stumblers need.**<<"

"Yeah but it's not *Howdy Doody*, is it?" Danni quipped.

Admiral Wang turned to look briefly at Sergeant Yin, then Captain Ren.

"*Howdy Doody* was the first television images used to communicate with the Xlern, sir," Captain Ren reminded him. Admiral Wang grunted in response.

As they entered the training room, Danni said, "This is the room where Captain Steele and Ensign Strasnoye spent their time learning the theory behind the Amuksli drive."

"Theory which we have yet to learn," Captain Ren said sourly. Danni waited until Sergeant Yin had translated before reacting, something that she found harder than she had imagined.

"The admiral decided that until we were certain we had the theory correct, we should not disseminate it," Danni said. "We don't want someone to suffer an accident."

Captain Ren made no response but his stiff movements made his feelings plain.

"That seems very … thoughtful of the admiral," Admiral Wang remarked. Danni took the pause as a veil for sarcasm. She was finding it harder to like these stuffed shirts.

"I'm glad the admiral thinks so," Danni replied when Sergeant Yin finished translating, feeling that she was giving as good as she got. "Xover, can you run a test of the displays for Chinese?"

">>**The Chinese displays are rimmed with red,**<<" Xover replied. ">>**Initiating tests now.**<<"

"Admiral, Captain, if you would look at the displays, Xover is running some language tests. Please let him know if there are any problems."

The three Chinese spacemen quickly picked out the Chinese characters on some of the displays. *The quick brown fox jumped over the lazy dog.*

"Is that what the displays were programmed for?" Sergeant Yin asked as he provided a translation.

"Look again," Danni said.

China is one of the countries with the longest histories in the world.

"That is from our Constitution," Sergeant Yin said. He glanced at Danni. "Did you provide this material?"

">>**Was it correct?**<<" Xover asked.

"Eminently so," Captain Ren replied in Chinese. "Are you aware of our history?"

">>**We have been provided with a précis from** *Harmonie.*<<"

Captain Ren sniffed but said nothing more.

The door opened and another Xlern entered, followed swiftly by Ambassador Pickett.

"Admiral Wang, Captain Ren, thank you for meeting with us," Ambassador Pickett said, nodding politely to the two officers.

"**>>I am Nexl, captain,<<**" the Xlern said. "**>>I greet you.<<**"

Sergeant Yin translated smoothly and waited for the admiral to respond.

Admiral Wang spoke quickly in a low voice to his translator.

"Admiral Wang asks by what right do you invade the territorial space of the People's Republic of China?" Sergeant Yin said.

"**>>We apologize for intruding without prior communication,<<**" Nexl replied. "**>>We are trying to avert a catastrophe.<<**"

"How so?"

"**>>We were aware of your construction efforts,<<**" Nexl replied. "**>>You are to be commended for your alacrity. However, your choice of materials is unsuitable for their purpose.<<**"

"Huh?" Danni said. "Is the captain saying that the Chinese ship is defective?"

"*Voyager* was built with titanium and aluminum, as well as high-strength steel," Pickett said to her.

"Of course," Danni said with no surprise. "She's an experimental ship, we didn't know what sort of stresses she'd get." Her eyes widened as she leaped ahead. "Do you mean they didn't use titanium for the keel?"

"The Xlern say that they used locally produced materials," Pickett told her, his eyes straying to the Chinese officers. "Axlu is convinced that—"

"Geez, it'll blow up for sure!" Danni interrupted him. "So the Xlern came here to beg them not to use their death trap?"

"Yeah," Pickett agreed, frowning at the lieutenant. "Our Chinese friends might not be too happy with your choice of words."

"I'd rather that than have them smeared across the system," Danni said. "The captain said that the g-drive could rip a regular ship to pieces. She wasn't too sure how long it'd be before we have to retire *Voyager*, for that matter." Her expression grew pensive and she moved closer to Pickett, lowering her voice as she added, "I think the skipper had the idea that was another thing our friends wanted to trade with us."

"I'd already guessed that," Pickett told her. He turned to Captain Nexl. "Captain, can you have the stress diagrams displayed for our friends?"

"**>>Gladly,<<**" Nexl said, "**>>anything to avert a catastrophe.<<**"

The displays shifted and showed a model of the Chinese ship. The ship took on colors ranging from a gray through to a flaming red.

"**>>We have adjusted to your ocular abilities,<<**" Captain Nexl said. "**>>The red is where failure will occur.<<**"

"And when will this failure occur?" Captain Ren asked.

"**>>This simulation shows the stresses within the ship as it engages the gravity drive,<<**" Captain Nexl replied. "**>>Your antimatter containment unit will fail first, creating a chain reaction gravity wave which will fatally warp any organic life-forms**

within roughly three hundred of your kilometers.<<" Captain turned to Xover. **">>Show that display.<<"**

"**>>As you order, Captain.<<"**

Admiral Wang grunted as the imagery showed the space station ship being shredded and its contents shooting out into open space. Further away, parts of the surface of Phobos glowed with sudden intense heat, the result of gravity interactions with its material.

"This is not what happened to the American ship," Captain Ren objected.

"We used different materials, sir," Lieutenant McElroy reminded him, "and we've only fired that particular drive a few times."

"**>>Indeed, we were going to trade the technology to produce Amuksli drive-compatible components at an early date,<<"** Nexl confirmed.

"Ask him what did the Americans trade for this visit," Admiral Wang ordered his translator.

"**>>The admiral is correct in understanding that we owe our existence to continued trade,<<"** Captain Nexl replied. "**>>However the admiral should understand that in order to have trade, there must be trading partners.<<"**

Admiral Wang grunted. Captain Ren said, "What do you mean?"

"**>>A disaster of the magnitude we envision could easily curtail all trade,<<"** Captain Nexl replied. "**>>We were motivated to prevent that.<<"**

"How do we know that you were not bribed by the Americans?" Admiral Wang said. Danni turned away so that the Chinese spacers could not see her flushed cheeks.

"I am here under the auspices of the United Nations, Admiral," Jim Pickett replied stiffly. "Such actions are outside my charter." He took a deep breath and continued more calmly, "I had regretted that the demands of our situation had not allowed us a way to incorporate your nation more closely in our contact with the aliens." He paused, trying to think of the best way to solve that problem, one that had clearly grated more on the Chinese government than it had made public.

"You said we could use more hulls, sir," Danni reminded him. "Perhaps we could interest the Xlern in helping us set up a shipyard here."

Sergeant Yin gave her a look of undisguised amazement.

"Trade allows all to prosper," she said directly to him. Then, to Captain Nexl, she said, "Sir, it would seem that perhaps this incident could be turned to all our advantages."

"**>>It would require some trade,<<"** Captain Nexl told her. Danni grinned at him and wagged her arms over her head in what she'd come to view as the human equivalent of the Xlern laugh. Captain Nexl wagged his fore-pikkis back at her. "**>>Lieutenant, am I correct in observing that you seem to embrace the irreverent?<<"**

"You are quite correct," Pickett said, grinning at the communications officer. "It is a trait that seems to be associated with the best of traders." He turned back to Admiral Wang. "Admiral, I understand that the People's Republic of China has a great interest in showing its people how well it can master new technologies and that there is, perhaps, a feeling among its people that the Republic has not been properly recognized in our dealings with the aliens.

"Could we perhaps not use this now as an opportunity to correct the situation?"

Admiral Wang thought for a long moment. "It would require approval of the Party."

"The Xlern and Yon are traders, Admiral," Pickett observed. "They feel that we are currently in their debt for the technology transfers they have bestowed upon us. I know, through the United Nations Security Council, that the People's Republic of China has agreed in principle to exchanges in return for that technology.

"If the Xlern were to license your fabrications techniques to you, would you honor the UN resolution?" Jim asked carefully.

Sergeant Yin provided a halting translation and was interrupted several times by the admiral and once by Captain Ren.

During this exchange, Danni sidled over to the ambassador and nudged him lightly, shaking her head. She could tell that Sergeant Yin had mistranslated several of Pickett's words.

"Excuse me," Pickett said, raising his voice above the Sergeant's and earning a dark look from the admiral. "It occurs to me that my words might not be interpreted as well as I'd like."

Sergeant Yin glowered at him, saying in Chinese to the officers, "He says that you cannot trust his words."

"Xover," Danni said moving over to the small blue-green alien, "could you put a translation into Chinese of what Ambassador Pickett said?"

">>**It will not be accurate,**<<" Xover protested, ">>**but it is done. Even-numbered screens.**<<"

"Admiral," Danni spoke up, "I've asked the Xlern to provide translations."

Pickett nodded and moved toward Admiral Wang. The admiral glanced warily at him and then at the screens as he followed Pickett's open-handed gesture.

"Is this accurate?" Admiral Wang demanded of his translator, pointing to the screens. "Is this what the round-eye said?"

"No, Admiral," Sergeant Yin protested. "It is garbled, probably in translation from the alien tongue."

"Actually, Admiral," Danni said in fluent Mandarin, "I believe that the aliens are doing a much superior job than your sergeant."

"You speak Mandarin?" Sergeant Yin said, unable to keep his eyes from betraying his panic.

"Better than you speak English," Danni said frostily. She turned to Admiral Wang and bowed from the waist. "My parents were teachers in Beijing for a number of years."

"How many languages do you speak, Lieutenant?" Admiral Wang asked her directly. Sergeant Yin moved to one side. The admiral spared him one dismissive glance.

"I'm fluent in about five, Admiral," Danni admitted with a shrug. Impishly she added, "I'm working on Xlern."

"Parlez-vous français?" the admiral asked.

"Je parle français, Amiral," Pickett replied unexpectedly. The two conversed for several minutes in French before they broke apart, the ambassador offering his hand and the admiral solemnly taking it. Then he turned to Captain Nexl.

"Captain, I have a request of you and your ship," Pickett said. "It concerns our present dilemma."

">>**What can we do?**<<" Nexl responded.

Pickett smiled at him. "We'd like to take the admiral on a quick jaunt. We'll leave Lieutenant McElroy and the others here." Danni gave him a sharp look but he ignored it. "Between Ensigns Sato and Dubauer, I believe we can quickly identify any problems that might adversely affect the starship *China*."

">>**Where do you wish to go?**<<"

"I think we can just about catch *Voyager* before she makes her first jump," Pickett replied. "I'm sure that Captain Steele would be overjoyed to have Admiral Wang onboard."

"Shit!" Danni whispered in awe.

">>**But—**<<"

"You have already demonstrated that your ship can make jumps within our heliosphere, and have been willing to do so in an emergency," Pickett said brusquely. "The emergency will not end until we can correct the impropriety of not involving the personnel of the People's Republic of China in the first star jump." Pickett smiled. "Admiral Wang has kindly consented to represent his people in this matter."

">>**But—**<<"

"If it's a matter of trade," Pickett interrupted again, "I remind you that you've already been paid."

">>**Engineer Apprentice Xover, make it so,**<<" Nexl clanged out. Pickett noted that the alien captain had not rapped his chime-castanets loudly nor very brittlely which he took as a sign of the alien's resignation and lack of irritation.

Pickett bowed lowly to the alien. "I thank you for your kindness in this matter."

">>**It is still a good trade,**<<" Nexl admitted reluctantly.

* * *

People's Liberation Army Shipyard, Phobos

"It just disappeared!" Lieutenant Ma said, jaws agape as he and the others witnessed the departure of the *Xythir*.

"Yeah, pretty cool, huh?" Danni McElroy said. She felt a partially masked gasp from Ensign Sato standing beside her, looked at the smaller woman and grinned. Lori Dubauer moved next to Sato and nudged her gently, "Don't worry, she's always like that."

Lieutenant Ma had ignored all the English words, simply echoing Danni, "Cool."

Danni found herself giving the lanky engineer lieutenant a longer, considering look.

In English, she said, "So, Lieutenant, why don't you show us around that hunk of junk you were going to use as a tomb?"

"Huh?" Lieutenant Ma responded automatically. "Why do you want to do that?"

Danni grinned at him and continued in Mandarin, "Because your admiral and my ambassador ordered us to fix it."

Lieutenant Ma gave her a disbelieving look and then, resignedly said in English, "If you'll follow me."

"Lori, Sato, are you two prepared to get dirty?" Danni said, jerking her head to have them follow her.

"Sure thing," Lori said. "I always love looking over ships."

"She was based on your own courier class experimental ship," Lieutenant Ma said apologetically.

"Ooh," Lori said with a grin, "now that'll be even more fun!"

Fun was not how Lieutenant Ma would have described it. Four hours later, it was not even near the top of his list of descriptive words.

"Sir," Lori said slowly when she found one particularly bad weld, "I don't know how anyone let that go. Even on a regular ol' rocket engine, that was gonna fail."

"Lori, our friends don't have all the high-tech gear you get to play with," Danni said diplomatically.

"Lieutenant, this is nothing that cannot be seen with a discerning eye," Ensign Sato said, glancing apologetically to the Chinese engineer. "I imagine your people were working under a tight deadline."

"Yeah, emphasis on the 'dead,'" Danni said quietly. She patted Lieutenant Ma on the arm to take the sting out her remarks. She and he had gotten along so well that she was no longer certain when they were speaking English or when they were speaking Chinese. Or French, for that matter. Lori's French was passable, Sato's was remarkable, and Danni was no slouch, but not as good as she was in Chinese.

"I think perhaps some of the welders need to understand better the nature of their work," Ensign Sato said carefully.

"It's not all their fault," Lori observed sourly. "Remember that about half of the joins are misaligned."

"Pressure test," Danni said to herself. The others looked at her. "Did anyone run a pressure test?"

"Of course," Lieutenant Ma said. "Standard atmosphere plus ten percent."

"How about we recommend that you run it at five hundred percent?" Danni said, glancing to the two ensigns for their opinions.

"Six atmospheres," Lori said, nodding firmly.

"Six atmospheres?" Lieutenant Ma repeated faintly, glancing quickly around the pressure hull. He licked his lips. "Do you normally test to six atmospheres?"

"Make it ten," Danni said. "A good round number."

"Why ten?"

"Because that's what we tested *Voyager* at," Ensign Dubauer told him firmly. "I'm sure that your commanders won't want their ship to be any less capable than ours."

"Test at ten atmospheres and you'll be certain," Danni said, smiling at the Chinese engineer.

Lieutenant Ma met her gaze and smiled back. "I shall make this recommendation to Captain Ren."

CHAPTER SEVENTEEN

Xythir

"*VOYAGER, VOYAGER*, THIS IS AMBASSADOR PICKETT," JIM CALLED AS SOON AS *Xythir* popped out of space a mere kilometer from the smaller ship. "Halt your jump. Prepare to receive a passenger."

Jim smiled to himself imagining the consternation and amazement unfolding on the smaller ship's bridge.

"Mr. Ambassador?" Emily Steele's voice came back with tones of astonishment.

"There's been a slight change, Captain," Pickett said to her. "We're going to run the sled over to you with a VIP."

"A VIP?" Emily said. "You, sir?"

"Captain, I have asked that Admiral Wang of the People's Liberation Army's Navy accompany you on your historic jump to the stars," Pickett told her in full ambassadorese. He appreciated the stunned silence on the other end.

And then, as expected, Steele said, "We will be more than happy to have the admiral accompany us on this historic voyage. We are thrilled that the Xlern have arranged for this to happen and look forward to learning more at your earliest convenience."

"It was a bit of an emergency," Jim admitted cryptically.

"I can imagine," Emily replied with feeling. "I'll have crew standing by at the midships airlock."

"Very well," Pickett said. "I've asked Captain Nexl to let us wait here when you jump, so that we can get a record of your departure for the history books."

"I'll tell the crew," Emily said, "I'm sure they'll be thrilled."

"The admiral speaks French," Pickett told her.

"I'm sure that we've got someone in our crew who can speak either French or Mandarin," Emily allowed.

"Very well, Pickett out."

* * *

Voyager

"So we're getting a supernumerary or another commander?" Mac asked as Emily and he glided down the central shaft toward the airlock. With *Voyager* halted, they had lost their artificial gravity.

"No matter what his rank, he's not giving orders," Emily declared. "He can *advise* all he wants."

"From what Mr. Pickett said, I think this is more a political stunt than anything else,"

Mac said.

"Then you're an idiot, Mac," Emily snapped. "The Chinese are going to want to be in on this, and they'll want in in a big way."

Mac shrugged. "I'm surprised they didn't demand more participation sooner."

"They must have done something to attract this much attention," Emily said. They stopped just short of the airlock where Mick Hsu was waiting, suited up for an EVA. Emily nodded to him, raised a hand above her head and spun a finger commandingly, ordering the life support specialist to turn so that she could double-check his connections.

"Looks good, Mick," Emily said. "Turn around so I can check the front."

Obligingly, Mick turned back. "What's all the fuss, Skipper?"

"You speak Chinese, right?" Mac said to him. Hsu Ya Dong preferred to go by 'Mick'—something to do, perhaps, with his Irish in-laws—but he was undoubtedly Asian in origin. Mac, democratic by nature, hadn't really registered the other's ethnicity, being more interested in ability than origin.

Mick Hsu smiled and nodded in his helmet. "I certainly hope so."

"Well, dust it off, because you're going to be liaison for an Admiral Wang of the People's Republic," Mac told him. "Apparently, that's why we're stopping."

"Neat," Mick said. He nodded to the skipper and stepped into the airlock. Emily nodded back and motioned for Mac to help her close the airlock door. Mick Hsu quickly evacuated the air and opened the outer door. Being careful to lock on his safety cable, he stepped out and onto the ship's side, out of their sight.

Emily punched a comm link. "Radio check, Mick."

"Read you Lima Charlie, Skip," Mick replied jauntily. "I've got the sled in sight, I'm signaling to it. They've replied. They're here. I've got the admiral; we're coming back."

In a moment, Mick and a smaller man wearing a suit marked with the Chinese flag entered the airlock. Mick pulled the outer hatch closed.

"Good seal," Emily said, watching the monitors.

"Good seal," Mick said, after checking the interior readings. He cycled the lock, and a moment later the interior light flashed green. Emily nodded to Mac who started the door moving while Mick pulled it into the airlock.

"Admiral Wang, I'm Captain Emily Steele of the *UNS Voyager*," she said, extending a hand to the smaller man.

Admiral Wang took it, stepped into the ship, saluted her, and said in halting English, "Permission to come aboard?"

"Permission granted, sir," Emily said, snapping him back a crisp salute and smiling at his choice of protocol. She waved to Mick who was coming up behind him. "Chief Petty Officer Hsu will help you out of your suit and see to your needs."

"*Parlez-vous francais?*" the admiral ventured.

"I don't speak French but perhaps my Mandarin is passable, sir," Mick spoke up from behind him in that tongue. "The captain says that I'm to help you get settled in, sir."

"Please tell the captain that I do not want to delay our departure," Admiral Wang replied.

Mick translated this to the captain who replied, "Please tell the admiral that we'd be honored to have him join us on the bridge for this historic moment."

*   *   *

Xythir

">>**I would invite you up to our command deck, Ambassador Pickett, but our displays are not adjusted to your visual range,**<<" Captain Nexl said. ">>**We could arrange a much better view for you here in this room.**<<"

"Thank you, Captain Nexl, here will be just fine," Pickett replied.

">>**After your** *Voyager* **has departed, would you like us to return to Jupiter or the moon of Mars?**<<"

"If you don't mind, I think I'd like to remain here until *Voyager* returns," Jim said. He paused for a moment, adding, "I was thinking they could get a ride with you back to either Jupiter or Phobos which would save time and fuel."

">>**That would be efficient,**<<" Engineer Officer Axlu admitted.

Pickett got the impression from the captain's reaction that he would have preferred Axlu to remain silent.

">>**If you watch the monitor there, you will see** *Voyager* **transition,**<<" Axlu now chimed, pausing to wave its fore mannies toward one monitor. ">>**It is displaying in a format suitable for your eyes.**<<"

"Thank you," Pickett said, glancing at the monitor. *Voyager* was centered in the view, with the whole of her long axis visible. He could see the airlock through which Admiral Wang had recently ventured. A slight nimbus of light emanated from the four semi-circular beams that extended from the rear of the newly built propulsion module. The nimbus extended forward to the front of *Voyager* and then slightly beyond. The light in the front grew brighter and then became a dazzling display of sparks and lightning that ended in darkness.

In a moment, *Voyager* seemed to twist and shrink as it zipped into the enlarging darkness in front of it, a darkness outlined by the nimbus of the star drive.

Then she was gone.

The nimbus vanished with her. There were only stars and the darkness of space where the ship had once been.

"Did it work?" Pickett said.

">>**We'll know soon enough,**<<" Engineer Officer Axlu replied.

">>**In the meantime, Ambassador Pickett, perhaps we could consider the technological exchange?**<<" Captain Nexl chimed elegantly, using all three sets of chime-castanets.

">>**Is there anything we can get you? Do you require refreshment or relief?**<<"

Engineer Officer Axlu said.

"Actually," Pickett replied, "I am afraid that I'm on tenterhooks, waiting for *Voyager* to return."

">>**This word 'tenterhooks' has no meaning in our language,**<<" Engineer Officer Axlu said. ">>**Could you explain?**<<"

Pickett frowned for a moment in thought, then explained how the phrase came from the old process of drying wool. "... so the wool was stretched out to dry on tenter-frames and held in place with tenterhooks."

The two aliens shivered, pressing themselves to the ground as though in pain.

">>**That is a horrible expression!**<<" Engineer Officer Axlu said, his smaller chimes clashing discordantly.

"I am sorry. I meant no offense," Pickett apologized quickly, "I was merely trying to convey my emotional state."

">>**You did it very well,**<<" Captain Nexl replied. ">>**In that regard, I suppose we should wait until you are off 'tenter-hooks' with regards to the return of your ship.**<<"

"Thank you." Jim Pickett ostensibly turned his gaze back to the external display using it as a way to disguise his emotions. The aliens had promised that the Yunuffili star drive would be better and more efficient than the Amuksli drive, but would it allow Earth ships to jump from any orbit to any destination as the *Xythir* had demonstrated by its jump from Jupiter to Mars? Or was there still a better star drive that the aliens were holding in reserve?

What disadvantage would having an inferior star drive impose upon mankind? Could humans still compete? Or was it possible to ignore the interstellar trade and concentrate instead on colonization of new worlds?

In basic economics, Pickett recalled, even the most productive organization could find profit in trading with a less productive organization. The simplest examples of the Production Possibilities Frontier involved two farmers each producing beef and potatoes. The example had it that while one could out-produce the other in both beef and potatoes, it worked to their mutual advantage to let the more efficient producer concentrate on beef while the less efficient one concentrated on potatoes—the combined output was greater than either individually.

So why wouldn't the same basic thinking apply to humans and interstellar trade? Clearly the aliens expected to make a profit from their encounter, regardless of their vague protestations of an accidental encounter. If that were so, then it would make sense for mankind to engage in interstellar trade.

The aliens seemed eager to deal with separate governments, which made sense in that they were hoping that the competition would drive down the cost of doing business. Pickett knew that, given the choice, China and the Euros would happily do anything to gain a competitive advantage in what had to be the biggest market ever imagined. Nor, for that matter, would the U.S., Russia, and all the rest of the world be far behind.

Of course, China might be expected to put its initial efforts in colonization, as it had already invested much in the colonization of Mars, while Russia would be eager to gain any profit it could from any venture. The U.S. would probably hope to find some way to regain its past glory, which might include a combination of colonization and trade.

It was easy enough to envision fleets of starships carrying goods to distant stars.

">>**Ambassador Pickett, we are getting indications of a return,**<<" Engineer Officer Axlu said just a moment before there was a blinding flash on the external monitor and *Voyager* blinked back into view.

"Can you open a communications channel to them?" Pickett asked.

">>**It is done,**<<" Axlu chimed.

"*Voyager, Voyager*, this is Ambassador Pickett aboard the Xlern ship, *Xythir*," Pickett called, hoping that his words would be relayed directly. "Welcome back. You have made history."

* * *

Voyager

"… You have made history," Pickett's voice echoed over the comm link. Emily nodded to herself but she still had to wonder how much better it would have been if the history had been made by mankind alone. *What would it feel like if we'd cracked FTL by ourselves?*

"*Xythir*, this is *Voyager*," Emily said, "we're glad to be back. The journey was quick and uneventful."

"And Alpha Centauri?"

"As I'm sure our friends could have told us earlier, it was uninhabited and uninhabitable," Emily replied, feeling faintly depressed. They had not lingered long at Alpha Centauri, arriving just at the edge of the binary system. Mac and Harry had just enough to train the antenna for a peek at the radio noise—none intelligent—coming from the system and to verify the spectral analysis before Emily, with Admiral Wang's agreement, had ordered them to return. The important thing, Emily knew, was to demonstrate that the Amuksli drive worked.

"But the drive worked and that's the important thing," Pickett replied. "I've arranged a lift for you with *Xythir*. Stand by for docking."

"Standing by," Emily said, turning to Admiral Wang to say within earshot of Mick Hsu, "the alien ship *Xythir* is going to bring us aboard for the return."

Admiral Wang nodded but said nothing. He had been courteous within the limitations of the language barrier but not very forthcoming. He did not go out of his way to ingratiate himself with the crew. Emily had the impression that the admiral spent a lot of his time thinking.

"Where should we bring you?" Pickett called. "We could bring you to Phobos or Jupiter."

"I imagine that's a question for the admiral," Emily said, turning to make sure that

Mick made the translation.

Admiral Wang spoke slowly. Mick listened, then translated, "The admiral asks why it is not possible to use our own drive to do both."

"This is an Amuksli drive, sir," Emily told him. "I'm not sure if you were kept abreast of proceedings but the aliens arrived at Jupiter in the mistaken belief that we had already developed an FTL drive. When they discovered their error, they sought to give us this one with the proviso that we would agree to say that we had developed it independently.

"Our people back at Jupiter are even now being instructed in the science and technology of a more advanced drive system for which we will trade certain technologies of interest to our alien friends."

"And will this new drive be capable of operating anywhere?" Admiral Wang asked through Mick.

Emily smiled. "That's a very good question, sir. One that I think we should ask, but perhaps circumspectly."

Admiral Wang nodded when the translation came back to him. "You do not trust these aliens?"

"Ambassador Pickett does not trust the aliens, sir," Emily said. "I have come to respect his position."

"I should like to meet your ambassador."

"Ambassador Pickett is the ambassador for the United Nations," Emily said carefully, "so he is as much your ambassador as mine, sir."

"Then all the more reason to meet him," Admiral Wang said. It seemed to decide him. "If it is acceptable to you that your personnel remain at Phobos, I would be willing to return to Jupiter and aid in the negotiations."

"Personnel?" Emily said. "What personnel? And why were they left there?"

* * *

Phobos Shipyard

Using the telescope from the observation blister, Danni eyed the hull of the spaceship *China*.

"Ten atmospheres," Lieutenant Ma reported, sounding, to Danni's ears, quite pleased.

"Give it a moment," Danni said. Sure enough, she saw a sudden bloom on the far side of the ship and then—much to her surprise—the front end of the ship split along one seam like a zipper. "Shit! Are you sure we're safe here?"

"You've got your suit on," Lori Dubauer reminded her, straining not to grab the 'scope from her superior. "What happened?"

"She burst," Danni said, pulling away from the telescope and beckoning Lieutenant Ma forward. "She burst at the far end and then split along the seam at the front." She pursed her lips tightly. "Are you *sure* we're safe here?"

Lieutenant Ma needed only the briefest of looks to realize that *China* was nothing more than scrap.

"Lieutenant Ma!" A voice bellowed and all turned to see Captain Ren bearing down upon them. "My ship! What did you do to my ship?"

"I ran the test that the American prescribed, sir," Lieutenant Ma said, moving to one side to expose McElroy and Dubauer to the captain's wrath. "They were concerned about hull integrity."

"It's ruined!" Captain Ren cried. He turned to Danni. "You've destroyed property that belonged to the People's Republic of China!"

"No, sir," Danni said stiffly, "I've merely exposed shoddy construction that would have cost the lives of members of the People's Republic of China."

Captain Ren loomed menacingly, anger flaring in his eyes but Danni met them firmly, moving unconsciously to a defensive stance, while Lori Dubauer moved beside her.

"Sir," Ensign Sato said in the heavy silence, "I think that perhaps you may want to reconsider."

Captain Ren glanced her way with the same look that had quelled dozens of subordinates over the years. The smaller Japanese officer did not so much as flinch. For a moment, the two locked gazes and then Ren backed off.

"It's ruined," he said, glancing at the glittering pieces that slowly drifted toward the observation blister.

"With all due respect, sir, it was already ruined," Danni said. "If it couldn't handle the pressure test, there was no way it would survive in operation."

Ren pursed his lips tightly. The American was right, however much he hated to admit it. That didn't mean someone would not be to blame for this disaster. If he couldn't blame the Americans, then—

"Lieutenant Ma! Explain this!"

"Captain, I regret to tell you that your construction crews simply aren't up to this sort of work," Danni said coming to Ma's defense.

"I was not talking to you."

"Yes, sir, I understand," Danni said. "Even in my Navy, someone would have to take the fall for this disaster." Captain Ren drew a breath to dispute her interpretation but she drove on relentlessly, "The trick, sir, is to make sure that blame falls where it should so that good people are promoted and such disasters do not persist."

"Constructing a ship in space has never been done," Ensign Sato said.

"The ISS," Lori said quickly.

"That was an assembly of pre-fabricated sections," Ensign Sato said. She gave the Chinese captain a half-bow. "Here is the first time that any nation has tried to create the infrastructure required to build many spaceships simultaneously."

Danni raised an eyebrow. Sato was right: while *Voyager* and her sister ship were built on the Moon, they were built in airtight structures, while the Chinese were looking to perfect the more difficult task of actually building ships in the vacuum of space. And, Danni realized, Sato had pointed out something even more fundamental—the Chinese were building not just ships but the process of spaceship building. That would give them a huge advantage in the future. Instead of building one-off units, they were acquiring the skills to build ships in assembly-line fashion. Danni spent a worried moment wondering how hard the Chinese had worked to keep this particular insight hidden from the rest of mankind, but shook it off, realizing that there were more important issues at hand.

"Lori, do you know what they need to do?" Danni asked her junior officer in a quiet voice.

"Probably just better quality control," Lori said. "They had the seams; they just didn't have them right." She shook her head. "To be sure, I'd have to see how they're doing it now."

Danni nodded but waved her words aside as she turned her attention back to Captain Ren.

"The ship's not a total loss, sir," she said to him. "The equipment inside can be salvaged. It's the hull that's a write-off."

"This ship was to be the first to the stars," Captain Ren said bitterly.

"Well, sir, we made sure that your admiral was the first admiral to the stars," Danni told him, trying to sound upbeat, "but I think your ship will have to settle for being the first homebuilt ship."

Captain Ren waved a hand toward the ruptured vessel. "And what would you do with that?"

"I'd salvage it, sir," Danni said. "I'd bring out all your welders and show them what happened, I'd go over the job orders and I'd identify the defects. Then I'd retrain your people to do the job *right*." She made a face. "But they'll need better materials, too, sir. And we don't know if these alien star drives require an entirely new order of materials for their construction."

Captain Ren nodded, still looking mournfully at the ripped hull floating before them. "I am going to have to report this to the admiral."

"Well, sir, that's the good news, he's not here right now, so you'll have some more time," Danni told him cheerfully. "If I may be so bold, sir, I think that the first order of business is to capture any debris that's floating around and then start to salvage the equipment off your ship."

Captain Ren nodded. "Lieutenant Ma, make it so."

* * *

Harmonie

"Jesus!" Captain Lee swore as *Xythir* suddenly reappeared in the displays. "Navigation, do we need to correct our orbit?"

"Nothing major, sir," Commander Milano replied. "Our automatic systems will handle it."

Captain Lee nodded a silent "thank you" and continued his scrutiny of the alien ship. "What's going on?"

"We're getting signs of aspect change, sir," Commander Milano reported. "The cargo doors are opening."

"*Harmonie*, this is *Voyager*. Radio check, over," Captain Steele's voice came over the speakers.

"We read you loud and clear *Voyager*," Captain Lee called back gladly. "Welcome home. How was the view?" To his comm chief, he said, "Relay all this back to Earth, they'll want to know."

"Aye, sir," the comm officer replied.

"The view wasn't bad," Emily said. "We've got Admiral Wang of the People's Republic Liberation Army's Navy with us."

"I'm sure Admiral Tsukino will be glad to see him," Lee lied glibly. He wasn't at all sure how the Japanese admiral would feel about another admiral—and Chinese at that—arriving on the scene. "How did Admiral Wang manage to get aboard?"

"Ambassador Pickett extended the invitation and *Xythir* met us just before we jumped," Emily replied, sounding calm.

Shit, Lee thought to himself, *that must have been some rendezvous.*

"Really?" Lee said aloud. "I was aware that there was some sort of emergency at Phobos."

"I don't have all the details. Ambassador Pickett will doubtless have them," Emily replied.

"I'll be very interested in hearing them," Captain Lee told her.

"How are things going with the Yon?" Emily asked.

Lee chuckled. "I haven't heard anything which is a good sign, I suppose. But remember you've not been gone more than a few days."

Emily laughed. "Actually, I *do* have a hard time recalling that. It seems like quite a number of light-years since we were in Jupiter orbit."

* * *

Voyager

"Skipper, got a moment?" Mac said as he met Emily at the side airlock. *Voyager* was floating free in tandem with *Harmonie*. Admiral Wang had gone over with the first trip on the sled which had been retrieved from *Xythir*. Emily wished that they could afford to build a few more, the cold-jet sleds were quite useful, but even *Harmonie* was beginning to feel a pinch in her supplies. Neither ship had been intended for this sort of long-term construction.

"I've got to meet with the admirals, Mac," Emily said.

"They need to know this, too," Mac said glumly. Emily raised an eyebrow. Mac took a deep sigh and then said in a rush, "We're going to have to scrap *Voyager*."

"What?"

"Harry and I took a set of EVAs after we got back," Mac said. "We can't tell you if it was the gravity drive or the star jump that did it but there are micro-cracks in all the major load-bearing beams." He pursed his lips tightly. "In fact, I'd guess that there are micro-cracks pretty much everywhere."

"The hull?" Emily asked, her voice rising on the last word.

"Our leak rate is up by fifty per cent," Mac told her. He raised a hand to forestall any panic. "That's still a pretty low number—*Voyager* was a tight-built ship—but neither Harry nor I think that's the end of it."

"It's going to get worse?"

"I can't say when," Mac said. "We don't have enough data yet. We're safe for a couple of weeks at the least. But only if we don't stress the hull any more. If we do that ..." he shrugged.

"So, you're saying that our ship is dead?"

Mac nodded. "I suppose if we could find a way to anneal all the cracks, she'd be okay but I don't know of any place where we could do that." He glanced toward where *Xythir* lay in orbit. "Maybe the aliens know something."

"Shit!" Emily said with feeling. She pursed her lips tightly, then, "So you're saying that any ship we build is only good for one round-trip star jump?"

"No, Skip," Mac said. "I don't know when we got the micro-cracks. It could have been from the jump or it could have been from the gravity drive. If it was from the gravity drive, then you gotta remember that we used *that* more than once."

"Doesn't help," Emily said.

"I don't think the aliens have the same problem," Mac said. "Those ships don't look brand new, not that I'm any expert on alien technology."

"And they've jumped more than that," Emily reminded him.

"Yeah."

Emily fumed for another moment then said, "Okay, Mac. You and Harry keep an eye on it. Let me know when you've got a baseline and what that means. I'll let the admiral—the *admirals*—know that we've got a little problem."

Mac snorted at her choice of words and Emily gave him a wry grin before turning to the airlock. Mac sketched a quick salute which she returned before dogging her helmet and cycling the airlock.

* * *

Harmonie

"So there's *another* thing we'll need to trade with the aliens," Captain Lee said when Emily had finished explaining to the senior officers. Pickett had listened to it all in silence.

"Why didn't they tell us?" Emily said to Pickett.

"I don't know," Pickett replied. "It may be that they aren't sufficiently familiar with our construction techniques"—Emily snorted derisively—"or it could be that they were waiting for us to ask."

"It could be simply that they didn't even think of it," Admiral Tsukino suggested.

"It is possible that they wanted to see if we would discover it on our own," Admiral Wang said in French. Admiral Tsukino—who was also fluent in that language—nodded, while Commander Milano translated for the others.

"In the meantime, I think that we should reduce *Voyager's* crew to a skeleton watch," Emily said. The others glanced at her. "We can't risk a catastrophic failure."

The reports of the rupture under test of the *China* had reached them a few hours earlier via gravity comm. Apparently the three officers stranded at Phobos had found the time to help the Chinese rig up a quick and dirty transmitter. Admiral Wang had been quietly impressed and seemed willing to accept both the loss of the ship and the suggestions of the foreign officers in future actions.

"Where would you put the others?"

"I think we should split them between the Yon and the Xlern," Jim Pickett said. He glanced toward Admiral Wang and said in French, "Sir, I would ask you to consider commanding both contingents."

"If I were to do that, I would have to have Hsu as my aide," Admiral Wang replied in the same language.

Pickett nodded, glancing toward Emily and saying in English, "I think that Chief Petty Officer Hsu would be a good choice for the admiral's aide."

"I have no problem with that," Emily said calmly. Mick Hsu was a good man. He and the Chinese admiral seemed to have come to an effective working relationship that was beneficial to all. It wasn't just that Hsu spoke Chinese but also that Mick was solid in his approach to matters, not so much by-the-book as what-it-took. Emily was beginning to think that Admiral Wang was either cut from the same cloth or was the sort of officer who could appreciate that quality in his juniors.

"Excellent!" Admiral Tsukino said. He turned to Ambassador Pickett, "Now that that's settled, what's our next move?"

"I think it's time to start dickering," Pickett said.

"I should like to be consulted on this," Admiral Wang said, "in the name of the People's Republic of China."

Pickett turned to face him directly. "Admiral," he told him coldly in French, "*I* am the representative of the United Nations. That supersedes even the People's Republic of China."

Admiral Wang met his gaze impassively.

"I shall be happy to keep you abreast of developments, just as I continue to do with everyone here and on Earth," Pickett continued, "but I firmly believe that we must present a united front to the aliens or risk finding ourselves destroyed by our own disunion."

"I agree with the ambassador," Admiral Tsukino said, "while I also agree with you, Admiral, that the ambassador must provide us with timely information and listen to our counsel."

Pickett waved a hand. "I've never thought otherwise."

"With which aliens will you negotiate?" Admiral Wang asked.

Pickett smiled. "Both, of course."

* * *

Ynoyon

~**I do not like this,**~ Sa-li-ri-to said when the news was presented to him by the rock-bangers.

>>**I, too, wish it were otherwise,**<< Captain Nexl replied. >>**However, this is not unexpected.**<<

~**They were supposed to be divided,**~ Sa-li-ri-to hissed back.

>>**We are running out of time,**<< Nexl chimed in response.

~**I know,**~ Sa-li-ri-to said. ~**Much profit rides on this.**~

>>**Indeed,**<< Nexl replied. >>**Shall we use your ship or ours?**<<

~**My ship,**~ Sa-li-ri-to said. ~**They are becoming too accustomed to yours.**~

>>**Agreed,**<< the Xlern captain responded. >>**When?**<<

~**Let's rush them, as they have rushed us,**~ Sa-li-ri-to said. ~**Tell them they must come immediately.**~

>>**Very well,**<< Nexl replied. >>**I shall inform my trade officer.**<<

* * *

"Welcome aboard, Mr. Ambassador," Captain Zhukov said as he extended his hand in greeting to the American.

"It's good to be aboard," Pickett said, taking the hand.

"Let's get you out of that suit," Zhukov said.

"I don't want to keep you from your studies," Pickett replied. In a lower voice, he added, "Besides, on my own I've got plausible deniability."

Zhukov nodded and stepped back. "Then, Mr. Ambassador, if there's nothing more you need, I'll get back to my studies."

"And how are they coming?" Pickett said, moving to pull off his spacesuit.

Zhukov gave him a strained smile. "We are learning and our brains have not yet exploded."

"Captain Steele said much the same thing," Pickett reminded him. "She said when it hurt the most, she finally got it."

"Then I hope I shall get it soon for it can't hurt too much more," Captain Zhukov said with a wan smile.

Pickett arranged his suit on the stand that had been built in the fabrication system of the *Ynoyon* and moved toward the doorway that led into the rooms beyond.

"Just remember, sir," Zhukov called after him, "don't let them bite you."

Pickett raised a hand and waved in acknowledgement. "I'm sure that it's considered poor etiquette."

"It hasn't stopped them from trying," Zhukov said, moving off through another doorway to the learning rooms.

It was awfully quiet after the genial Russian had departed. Pickett looked expectantly around, wondering when the aliens would come for him. They'd practically demanded an immediate meeting and now …

A door hissed open and Pickett had a moment's glimpse of a mass of pink, yellow, blue, and green before his eyes resolved it into a collection of Yon and Xlern. He was glad to recognize the three chime-castanets adorning the limbs of Captain Nexl. Beside him was another, unadorned Xlern. And slightly further away were two of the Yon Hydra.

Pickett spent a moment studying the nearer one as they approached.

The Yon slithered. There was no other way to describe their locomotion. The front Yon of the four-Yon Hydra would move much like a snake while the two side Yons would move sideways and the fourth, rearward-facing Yon, would reverse the motion of the forward Yon.

A Yon's skin was pink and yellow, both lurid in their intensity. The Yon kept their heads high, like a cobra ready to strike.

Pickett could sense the veiled threat in the movements. He decided to consider that purposeful. If the Xlern were the "good cops" then the Yon were perfectly cast to be the "bad cops."

In a moment, though, Pickett's perception changed, and he saw the four-bodied Yon Hydra as a graceful dancer restricted by the central bulge that held the four Yon together in one immense being. *What if they had wings,* Pickett wondered to himself, suddenly imagining the ungainly Hydra as a graceful flying thing.

So far, the thinking among the crewmember who'd been dealing with the Yon were that the bulges where they connected were either some form of egg sack or some repository for a huge brain—possibly both.

Two independent Yon slithered as vanguard to the first Hydra and Jim had the sudden feeling that the separate Yon were dumb cousins to the united Hydra. Could the Hydra assemble for a time and then break up? Perhaps long enough to hatch out new Yon?

What would it be like to share minds for only the length of a pregnancy? Would the separate Yon later recall the feeling? Would it be similar to those of a group of humans brought together for some task—like the production of a play or the crewing of a ship?

Would they want to be together again? Would the personalities clash or build?

So far, no one had managed to replicate the genius that translated the sounds of the Yon into human speech. Nor had someone come up with a neat trick like that of Dubauer and Sato in producing the chime-castanets.

"Captain Nexl," Pickett said with sudden inspiration, "please introduce us."

">>**The human wants me to introduce you,**<<" Captain Nexl chimed.

The foremost Yon Hydra stopped, two of its heads turning to Nexl. A moment later, the forward head darted closer to Pickett and then turned to Nexl, opening its mouth to produce a series of blended sounds, more chorus than words.

">>**This is Captain Sa-li-ri-to,**<<" Nexl said. He moved forward and waved to the second Hydra. ">>**This is Trade Officer Xi-ka-ja-na.**<<" He waved a tentacle to the unadorned Xlern, saying, ">>**And this is Trade Officer Ixxie.**<<"

Jim bowed to each in turn. "Please tell everyone that I am glad to make their acquaintance and hope that this is the beginning of a long and fruitful union."

~**I have no desire to mate with that thing!**~ Sa-li-ri-to hissed when the words were translated to him.

">>**Pardon, Captain, but the human did not intend a mating,**<<" Nexl apologized, ">>**Rather he was referring to a commercial transaction.**<<"

One of the single Yon darted toward Pickett, who did a quick sidestep toward Captain Nexl as he said, "I have not been introduced to this one."

~**Neither Is(sa) nor Li(to) need concern it,**~ Sa-li-ri-to said. One of its heads moved to nip at Is(sa).

">>**The single Yon are a lesser intelligence,**<<" Captain Nexl said in explanation.

Pickett looked at the small Yon which had moved back toward Captain Sa-li-ri-to. "Are the single Yon to be considered safe?"

~**They are** *mine*,~ Sa-li-ri-to hissed, its pink irises slitting in anger.

"I have never met your race," Pickett admitted. "Are the individual Yon capable of thought?"

Sa-li-ri-to hissed.

">>**Ambassador Pickett, it is my understanding that they are,**<<" Nexl said.

"Do they have names?" Pickett asked. "On our planet, as you know, we have lesser intelligences with which we share our space. Perhaps you've seen our four-legged cats and dogs on our television shows?"

">>*Old Yeller!*,<<" Ixxie said mournfully. ">>**Captain Nexl, please ask it why they killed the faithful companion.**<<"

Nexl thought of waving his trade officer's plea aside but admitted that he had questions in that regard.

">>**My trade officer recalls a confusing presentation called** *Old Yeller* **and wonders why the beast was destroyed,**<<" Nexl said.

Pickett looked at the alien in amazement and then nodded. "I remember. The dog had contracted an incurable bacterial infection, called rabies, which swelled its brain, causing it extreme pain and confusion. To save the humans from the same fate, Old Yeller had to be destroyed."

~**What is it saying?**~ Sa-li-ri-to demanded.

Nexl ignored the Yon hydra while it explained Pickett's response to Ixxie.

">>**Oh!**<<" Ixxie banged when the captain had finished. ">>**How sad!**<<" Ixxie moved toward Pickett, upper limbs quivering with emotion.

">>**My trade officer understands,**<<" Nexl explained. ">>**Perhaps in the future your species will find a way to eradicate this bacterial infection.**<<"

~**Enough!**~ Sa-li-ri-to hissed, its sideways heads bobbing up and down in their anger. ~**We are not here for this.**~

"Do you know if the individual Yon are subject to similar such afflictions?" Pickett asked.

">>**I shall ask,**<<" Nexl responded, moved by the emotions behind the question and curious itself.

~**What? Why does the human want to know this?**~ Sa-li-ri-to demanded.

">>**It's just asking,**<<" Nexl chimed, moving slightly away from the Yon captain.

"Did the Yon not have time to watch *Old Yeller*?" Pickett asked.

">>**The Yon do not see in the same manner as we do, finding it more difficult to absorb your transmissions,**<<" Nexl admitted.

"Are you referring to the wavelengths of light or the speed at which their brains react to input?" Pickett asked. "Or are you referring to their multi-brain aspect?"

">>**All of those,**<<" Ixxie rapped.

">>**It's also possible that in one of its prior arrangements, one or more Yon of the current Captain Sa-li-ri-to might have seen this presentation and the memory has faded,**<<" Nexl added.

Pickett's raised an eyebrow as he absorbed this revelation. After he had a chance to collect his thoughts, he schooled his expression and said, "Captain Nexl, Captain Sa-li-ri-to, Trade Officers, I'm at your disposal."

">>**He means that he's ready to talk,**<<" Nexl translated, even as he moved to interpose himself between the human and the two unattached Yon.

"Actually," Pickett corrected the Xlern with a slight bow, "I would prefer to say that I'm ready to listen." He paused. "What is it that we can provide in exchange for your various kindnesses?"

">>**I think we have to start with the Pao V,**<<" Ixxie clattered, moving nearer to his captain.

~**Silence!**~ Sa-li-ri-to swore. To Nexl, he added, ~**If you cannot keep your underlings in line…** ~

His words were not translated before Nexl had hastily moved over to his trade officer and bumped him in a harsh interruption.

">>**But he'll have to know sometime!**<<" Ixxie protested, twisting his body from his captain, to the Yon captain, and then to Pickett.

"Captains," Pickett said suavely, "I understand that in our discussions there will be confusion and misunderstandings. This is normal in our first dealings with others."

">>**Thank you for understanding, Ambassador Pickett,**<<" Nexl chimed back, dipping its foreself politely. ">>**Trade Officer Ixxie rattled too quickly.**<<"

"Nevertheless," Pickett said, suppressing a grin, "why don't we start with this 'Pao V.' I'm afraid that it's not something that I can immediately place. Is it perhaps an oriental object?"

">>**No one's quite sure** *where* **it came from,**<<" Ixxie rapped rapidly. ">>**But now that we have it—**<<" He was cut off as both Nexl and the Yon captain bounded toward him; Nexl bumped him and the Yon captain snapped at him with two of its heads.

Ixxie dropped his rocks and bounded back in fright, ending up crouched behind Pickett in a way that reminded him very much of a frightened deer or other similar four-legged creature, albeit a four-legged creature with an additional and somewhat alarming four arms. Pickett had once spent time working with animals and so when he saw the four-headed Yon captain bearing down on him he instinctively raised his own arms in full extension to block access to the frightened Xlern.

">>**No, no, stop!**<<" Nexl clattered loudly.

Both of Sa-li-ri-to's side heads darted towards Pickett's outstretched arms while its fore head lunged for Pickett's face. Pickett waited until the last moment and plunged to the ground, leaving the alien heads snapping at empty air.

">>**ENOUGH!**<<" Nexl clanged all twelve chime-castanets in an assault of noise. He moved itself toward the Yon captain, and with his two fore-pikki intercepted the nearest two heads and twisted them so that they were snapping at each other. One set of fangs snapped on the jaws of the other head and there was a loud hiss and shriek followed by a sudden tense stillness—the pause between fatal blows.

The pause was broken as one of the individual Yon, agitated by all the aggression filling the air, darted forward to attack toward Pickett and Ixxie—it wasn't clear if it had a specific target or was merely acting on instinct.

It didn't get far. Pickett rolled back to his feet, stepped neatly to straddle it, lifted it by the rear of its jaws, and threw it over his shoulders back toward the other Yon.

">>**No!**<<" Nexl clattered loudly, its volume somewhat reduced by its surprise.

The unattached Yon landed in the midst of Sa-li-ri-to's Hydra connection. One of the two unwounded heads moved to attack it but the Yon twisted and snapped its fangs into the body of its assailant.

In that instant, all five of the Yon shrieked in greater agony and then Nexl froze in place, its fore-pikki quivering as it pointed.

">>**No! This cannot be!**<<" Nexl rapped.

As Pickett watched, the great bulge that connected the four individual Yon bodies of the Hydra together flexed and rippled even as the last uninjured Hydra head grappled with the individual Yon to pull it toward the Hydra's four-tailed bulb. With a sickening, slick noise, the bulb or bulge distended, opened, and just as suddenly, the tail of the unattached Yon quivered and opened like a flower—to insinuate itself into the four-tailed Hydra bulge.

At that instant, all the hissing and shrieking stopped to be replaced by a stunned silence.

When Pickett recovered his senses, he said to Nexl, "Do the Yon often create five-headed Hydra?"

CHAPTER EIGHTEEN

"**>>I think it best if we leave,<<**" Nexl tinkled quietly with only the barest of chimes.

"Leave?" Pickett said. He was still watching warily as the new five-headed Hydra writhed to sort itself into a pentagonal shape, the bulge suddenly that much bigger. In spite of himself, he said, "I thought the bulge was a reproductive organ."

"**>>Usually,<<**" Ixxie responded, finding its legs and moving quietly toward its captain. "**>>I understand that in certain instances—<<**"

"**>>TRADE OFFICER!<<**" Nexl boomed in three-part cacophony. Ixxie's upper limbs drooped in what Pickett took as shame. Nexl recovered himself, saying to Pickett, "**>>Ambassador Pickett, I apologize for my painful volume.<<**"

"It has been a trying time for us all," Pickett replied. He nodded toward the five-headed Hydra. "Captain Sa-li-ri-to, I am very sorry that—"

~**Not Sa-li-ri-to,**~ two of the heads, both uninjured, hissed in interruption.

"**>>Not Sa-li-ri-to?<<**" Ixxie clattered. "**>>Are you still captain?<<**"

~**Captain-General,**~ the two heads hissed. ~**Is-sa-to-li-ri.**~

The two talking heads twisted to examine the three injured heads, moving quickly to caress them reassuring before twining their two necks together and then untwining in unison to inspect the much larger five-sided bulge at the center of their new body.

"**>>Captain-General?<<**" Ixxie rapped, his upper limbs moving rapidly, then continuing to move without making sound, in a motion that reminded Jim of someone wringing its hands nervously.

"On Earth it was an ancient title given to one who had responsibilities in excess of merely commanding a vessel," Pickett said, choosing his words carefully. "Captain-General" was the title Cortez had taken when he burned his ships and destroyed the Aztec empire. Pickett nodded to the new Hydra. "Captain-General Is-sa-to-li-ri, I greet you and regret any harm that I may have inflicted upon you in my ignorance."

The two uninjured heads bobbed in what was obviously meant as acceptance. Then one of the heads—the Sa-head—swiveled toward Ixxie and said to the Xlern, ~**Trade Officer Ixxie, tell the human about the Pao V.**~

"**>>Captain?<<**" Ixxie rapped inquiringly to its senior.

"Perhaps if you'd just tell me what the Pao V *does*, I can determine what it is," Jim Pickett offered diplomatically.

Ixxie waved an arm toward the five-headed Hydra. "**>>It does this.<<**"

"It creates violence?" Pickett cried in surprise.

And then his heart stopped. Or so it seemed. Four of Is-sa-to-li-ri's heads swiveled to him, their piercing pink eyes glowing with an alien intellect—and the four jaws opened.

"It creates intelligence," Is-sa-to-li-ri sang in a chorus of angels.

Jim's jaw dropped and his hands fell lifeless to his sides.

"Say that again," he begged.

">>**Please,**<<" Nexl chimed, inching toward the five-headed Hydra.

"The Alien Artefact Pao V creates intelligence," Is-sa-to-li-ri sang.

"I can hear you," Pickett said in awe. His eyes dipped toward Nexl and he asked, "Captain Nexl, do you hear them?"

">>**A most pleasing sound,**<<" Nexl chimed back in fervent agreement. Behind them, Ixxie smacked approval with its bare limbs.

"The Pao V has been found in the histories of many star-faring civilizations," Is-sa-to-li-ri sang. *"Our records indicate that it was on your planet."*

"I'm sure we would have remembered something like that," Pickett said in a small voice, unable to keep the memory of Arthur C. Clarke's famous novels from his thoughts. "It didn't look like some dark rectangle, did it?"

"On your planet, it was revered by one emerging group in their religious texts," Is-sa-to-li-ri sang.

Pickett found that repeated exposure to the angel chorus was allowing him to react more rationally. "Religious texts?"

"In one religion, it was referred to as the Ark of the Covenant," Is-sa-to-li-ri sang.

"Oh, boy!" Pickett swore. "I think I'd prefer it if we continue to refer to it as this alien artifact, then."

"Most civilizations have followed that precept," Is-sa-to-li-ri sang in reply.

"I feel compelled," Jim said, with a moment's pause to wonder *how* he was compelled, "to point out that, to the best of our knowledge, that artifact is not in our possession."

"Of course not," Is-sa-to-li-ri sang with a tone of humor, *"if so we would not have dared contact you."*

">>**It's on Gliese 581,**<<" Ixxie murmured. Pickett glanced toward the Xlern just in time to see him nudged angrily by his captain.

"If that's the case, then I'm afraid we can't give it to you," Pickett said, wondering how badly that would affect everything. "From the sound of things, it was never ours in the first place and we would refuse to go to war with the inhabitants of Gliese 581 simply to supply it to you."

">>**Well said!**<<" Captain Nexl chimed approvingly.

"Indeed," Is-sa-to-li-ri sang, although one of its heads lowered and darted in the direction of the Xlern captain in a possible display of irritation. *"But in this case, it is not the giving that matters, rather it is the relinquishing."*

Pickett frowned for a long time in thought. "Is this some sort of test?"

">>**No,**<<" Ixxie smacked. ">>**It is a legal issue. A question of rights.**<<"

"If you are asking us to relinquish all rights to this artifact," Pickett said, pausing to suck in a breath as he thought rapidly, "then, on behalf of mankind, I hereby relinquish all rights of ownership."

"Ah! Well played, Ambassador!" Is-sa-to-li-ri sang back. Jim noted that this was the first time any of the aliens had referred to him just by his title. *"And now we come to the question of ownership and what that means to your species."*

Pickett nodded and fleetingly wished that they were seated at a table where he could roll up his sleeves in preparation for some serious dickering.

"We shall continue this discussion," Is-sa-to-li-ri sang. *"However recent events require that I permit myself a rest cycle and conference with my inferiors."*

Two of the heads—the two uninjured ones—speared Pickett with brilliant eyes before nodding slowly and turning away to join the rest of the enlarged body as it carefully negotiated its way past the still stunned and silent Yon trade officer.

"Perhaps it's best if we all return to our ships," Jim said to the two Xlern.

">>**Agreed,**<<" Nexl chimed.

"Ixxie," Jim said, bowing to the Xlern trade officer, "would you accept chime-castanets if I could acquire them?"

">>**Is this a trade?**<<"

"I would consider it a gift in recognition of our mutual adventures together," Jim replied. He waved a hand toward Captain Nexl, realizing that the Xlern were more accustomed to reading limb motion over facial expressions, "Captain Nexl, would that be agreeable to you?"

">>**I see no reason not to permit my trade officer devices suitable to its rank,**<<" Nexl chimed quietly.

Pickett smiled at the Xlern captain's judicious response, reading it to mean that Nexl would not object if Ixxie were given the two pairs of chime-castanets accorded an officer—like Engineer Officer Axlu—but not more. He wondered if the chime-castanets were merely affirming a rank structure or enshrining one.

"Very well," Pickett said, moving aside to allow the two Xlern to precede him.

">>**I cannot say for certain,**<<" Nexl said as he moved through the doorway, ">>**but under normal circumstances, a Yon rest cycle would last ten of your hours.**<<"

"Shall we arrange then to meet again at that time?"

">>**I imagine that would be acceptable,**<<" Nexl chimed back. ">>**However, I should caution that more time may be required.**<<"

">>**Five heads,**<<" Ixxie clapped, clearly seeming still awed by the whole affairs. ">>**How smart are five heads?**<<"

"We humans have only the one," Pickett said noncommittally. He wondered if the Yon had ever heard of a committee and if he should be afraid. But—the chorus of angels. He shook his head. Ixxie was right, the danger was that the five-headed captain-general would be that much more intelligent.

Just before Pickett separated from them to head to the room where he'd stowed his spacesuit, he said, "Trade Officer Ixxie, would it be possible to get the list?"

"**>>What list?**<<" Captain Nexl demanded warily.

"The list of technologies and inventions that you wish to trade for," Jim said carefully. "I'm sure there must be a list somewhere, and as Trade Officer Ixxie mentioned this Pao V artifact, I figured that it must know the list of desired items."

"**>>I do,**<<" Ixxie slapped. "**>>As trade officer, it is my duty to make such things available.**<<"

Jim got the impression that the Xlern "said" that as much to him as to his captain.

"I think it would speed things up greatly if I could get a copy," Pickett said. "I hope it includes your wish list as well."

"**>>'Wish' list?**<<" Ixxie asked.

"Some items that were above and beyond your minimum requirements," Pickett said. "I mention it merely because we may wish to trade for other technologies and items as well."

"**>>I understand,**<<" Ixxie said. Captain Nexl turned back from its position in the lead of the two Xlern and stood beside the trade officer in a stance that Jim interpreted as either angry or impatient.

"I'm sorry, Captain Nexl, I don't mean to step on your normal protocols, but given that time is of the essence and the extraordinary circumstances that have cut short our first meeting, I thought it wise to act with alacrity," Jim said. He wasn't sure how well his words translated or even *if* all of them translated, but he was hopeful that his intent came through.

"**>>It *is* what we came here for,**<<" Nexl admitted. "**>>I have no problem with Trade Officer Ixxie providing a provisional list with the understanding that certain items might be considered of greater importance than others.**<<"

"Of course," Jim said, keeping his smile hidden.

"**>>I shall have it transmitted to you when we return to our ship,**<<" Nexl told him.

"Thank you," Pickett said with a small bow, "but if you are as in need of rest as I am, I would completely understand if you were to wait until after you had recuperated."

"**>>Yes, that's probably for the best,**<<" Captain Nexl chimed back, thinking to itself that such a pause would allow time for further reflection—and to pad the initial list.

* * *

Harmonie

"What's this Alien Artifact Pao V?" Captain Lee said as he pored over his copy of the list Trade Officer Ixxie had said. "I've never heard of such a thing."

"It doesn't matter," Pickett said. On his trip back to *Harmonie* he'd spent all his time considering how to handle that particular question.

"How so?" Admiral Tsukino asked, giving Jim a long probing look. "I would hate for our agreement to derail on something we can't possibly provide."

"In this instance, all they are asking is that we relinquish any claims of ownership,"

Jim said. "They told me that they've located this artifact already."

"So why was it the first thing they mentioned?" Emily asked.

"I think it was a ground-breaker," Jim said. "This is something that is easily dealt with; a no-brainer concession on our part. It also allows us to come to an understanding of such basic concepts as ownership and property."

"I don't understand. Why talk about something they *know* we don't have?" Mac said.

"Ever play the card game, Fish?" Jim asked.

"So you think that they're fishing for stuff?"

"No," Jim said. "I think it was a test."

"A test?"

"To see how honest we'd be," Jim said. "To see where we stood on issues of ownership and prior possession."

"Possession?" Emily jumped on the word. "They thought we had this artifact?" Her eyes narrowed. "Why?"

"Where is it now that the aliens are so certain of its location?" Admiral Wang asked in French. Commander Milano translated for the others.

"The aliens have reason to believe that this artifact has appeared on many worlds," Jim said, "including ours."

"Really?" Mac said, digesting this notion with care. "And what does it do?"

Jim Pickett took a deep, slow breath before responding. "They say it creates intelligence."

"So where is it now?" Commander Milano asked, returning to Admiral Wang's question.

"The aliens say that it is in the Gliese 581 system."

"The one we visited?" Mac said. "The one with the radio signals?" Emily added.

"That's the one."

"Isn't that the one that we sent a radio signal to some decades back?" Commander Milano asked.

"Yup," Jim said with a slow nod, "the very same."

"Oh, Jesus!" Mac swore. Pickett shot him a sharp look but managed to keep his mouth closed.

"Didn't the aliens say something about it being dangerous to interfere with a non-starfaring race?" Commander Milano asked.

"Which is why I think we should jump at the chance to renounce rights to this thing," Jim said.

"Any objections?" Admiral Tsukino asked, glancing around the room from person to person until he finally arrived at Admiral Wang. The Chinese admiral was motionless for a moment and then, with a wave of his hand, said, "I shall leave this decision to our United Nations ambassador."

Commander Milano's eyes lit but he provided the translation in a neutral voice.

"Very well," Admiral Tsukino said, "Mr. Ambassador, this is your call."

"We'll give it to them, with our blessing," Jim said, his lips twitching for an instant. "Now, there's some other low-hanging fruit on this list, why don't we clear it as well?"

"You mean like the paperclip?" Captain Lee asked.

"I can't imagine what they might want *that* for," Mac said.

"Ours is not to reason why," Emily said with a shrug.

"I told them that we'd like some additional options so that we might bargain for more," Jim said.

"Like what?" Captain Lee asked.

"Well, given what we've seen with *Voyager*, I think we might want whatever material they're using for their hulls, if it works better than what we can get," Mac suggested.

"Actually, I'd like to get a better drive system," Pickett said. The others looked at him and he expanded, "They've already admitted that the first one—the one on *Voyager*—is inferior, why should we think the second drive is going to be their best?"

"I wonder if they'd be willing to trade their best," Emily said doubtfully. "Maybe their second best."

"Actually, it might be that their ships don't have the best drive," Mac said thoughtfully. Captain Lee raised an eyebrow in a demand for an explanation. "Well, sir," Mac said to him, "they knew they were coming here; I think we all pretty much agree with the ambassador that their line about making a mistake with us is a bunch of bull, so that means they had time to prepare."

"I can see that," Lee allowed.

"Well, if they had the time, why not select ships suited to the task?" Mac asked. He gestured in the direction of the alien ships floating in space. "In which case they'd probably send ships equipped to perform construction and education."

"So?" Jim prodded.

"So there's no reason to think that these ships are anything other than orbiting shipyards and training facilities," Mac said.

"And you typically don't build them with the fastest drives because they don't need it," Emily guessed, giving Mac a firm nod of agreement.

"Also, it would keep us from guessing their full capabilities," Commander Milano added.

"If we pressed, they could say something like: 'You can see what *our* ships can do,'" Captain Lee said, "and we wouldn't be able to argue."

"I agree," Admiral Tsukino said, glancing toward Admiral Wang for his reaction. The Chinese admiral, provided a steady translation by Commander Milano, nodded firmly in agreement then said something in French to the Italian officer who translated, "Admiral Wang agrees. He also says that he is curious as to how the aliens came up with this list."

Pickett smiled. "They've admitted to watching *Sesame Street*, I suspect they 'watched' a lot more than that."

When Giovanni Milano translated this to Admiral Wang, the admiral replied and Giovanni gave his response, "It seems, though, that they want a mix of things that are easy and impossible for us to provide—such as a copy of the Analects."

Pickett nodded. "I was wondering about that."

"How so?" Emily said.

"It seems that they have a complete copy of the Analects—including the 75% that is missing from our histories today," Pickett said. "They also seem to have access to works by Da Vinci—"

"Is that 'The Erotic Works of Leonardo da Vinci'?" Commander Milano asked.

"Yes," Pickett said, continuing, "Aztec life philosophy and the complete works of Giovanni"—here he glanced at the Italian Commander with a hint of a humor at the name—"Antonio Marchi who was, I understand, instrumental—if you'll pardon the pun—in describing the construction of the modern violin."

Admiral Wang spoke and Commander Milano translated, "They are asking for things which are impossible to provide."

"Such as the dodo?" Pickett asked. Admiral Wang nodded when Milano translated. "Actually, I'm given to believe that we could produce a dodo through genetic engineering but," he gave them all a wry grin, "I'm beginning to suspect that we could simply ask our alien friends for a mating pair."

"You think they have one?" Emily blurted in surprise.

"I think they've got everything on this list," Jim replied. "In fact, there are things here that only someone who had observed our planet carefully for thousands of years might have noticed."

And I know why, Pickett thought to himself, careful to keep his face from betraying his emotions.

"In fact, I think the only possible problem areas are those where there's still an active copyright," Jim said. "I think that can be handled simply by reasonable payments to the copyright holders."

"You could simply claim eminent domain," Emily said.

"I'm a bit worried about the biologicals," Commander Milano said. "Providing them with samples of tea, butterflies, and the dodo—if they don't already have it—might provide them with potent weapons to be used against us."

Admiral Wang was voluble in his response when Commander Milano provided a translation of his own words. The Italian colored visibly and translated in a weak voice, "The admiral says that if the aliens wanted to destroy us, they already have the means."

"I agree," Admiral Tsukino said, nodding to Admiral Wang.

"I think, people," Jim began slowly, "that you're all missing the bigger point."

"Which is?" Captain Lee prompted.

"This list," Pickett said, pointing to the display, "is a chaotic hodgepodge of things we consider mostly inconsequential to our economies—and yet the aliens are willing to trade us the stars for these." He continued to make his point, "It's like the English came and offered Manhattan Island for a bunch of glass beads."

"It was the other way around," Captain Lee said.

"*Exactly*," Pickett said, pumping the table for emphasis. "What they're giving is worth far more than what they're asking." He glanced around to see if anyone wanted to argue his point, then continued, "So the question is: why?"

"I presume, knowing you, Mr. Ambassador, that you have an answer," Emily said. "So why don't you take pity on us poor military types and clue us in?"

"Our friendly aliens clearly know more about us than we'd imagined before we met them, right?" Pickett asked. He waited patiently while Commander Milano translated for Admiral Wang. "And they're asking for very specific items, right?"

"Yes," Admiral Tsukino agreed, an edge of impatience in his voice.

"And they want to make profits, they've said so, haven't they?" Pickett asked. No one disagreed. He waved a hand around the room, "So I think that they've already *been* profiting."

"How?" Captain Lee demanded, sitting forward in his chair angrily. "They only just—oh!" Lee slumped back in his seat, his eyes looking at the ceiling as the insight overwhelmed him.

"What?" Emily demanded, looking from the captain to the ambassador and back. "Oh! My god, that's ballsy!"

"Exactly," Jim said. "The aliens have been profiting from us for several thousand years. The reason they have this list, this very little and very specific list, is because that's what they've been selling elsewhere."

"Are you saying that all this is just so they can cover their asses?" Mac said.

"Yes," Pickett told him with a slow nod. "I think that's exactly it."

"Well, I'll be damned," Mac said. After a moment, he started chuckling. "That's pretty cool!"

Admiral Wang spoke rapidly to Commander Milano who translated, "If this is so, Mr. Ambassador, how do we respond?"

"We take them to court and nail them to the wall," Jim said firmly. "They've proven that they live in a society governed by law—if that weren't so, they would never have tried this trick—so we need to bring them before the law."

"Why not just take their offer?" Emily asked. "We'll get a star drive—two of 'em—isn't that enough?"

Pickett looked at Admiral Tsukino as he asked, "Do you think they've acted honorably? Because if they haven't, wouldn't that mean that they're hoping to sucker us? That what they owe us is far more than what they're offering?"

"They're playing us for dupes?" Mac asked.

"I don't know, Mr. Ambassador," Emily said slowly, "I'd hate to lose what we've got."

"And that's the most telling point, Captain," Pickett snapped back. "They're giving us all this stuff practically for free. So how much is this stuff really worth? And how does it stack up against what we should be getting?"

"What do you propose?" Emily asked.

"They want a contract with us," Pickett said. The others nodded, except Admiral Wang who was still getting the translation. "Well, before I entered politics, I stood before the bar and was admitted as a lawyer." He smiled as he added, "I specialized in copyright law."

"Am I hearing you right, sir?" Emily said, eyes going wide. "You want to *sue* the aliens?"

* * *

The White House, Washington, DC

"Is he *insane?*" Admiral Roberts shouted when he heard the news.

"The Russians are going to go nuts!" Secretary of State John Ellington predicted.

"Can we replace him?" Charles Sumner of the CIA wondered.

"Settle down, people," Greg Merritt said, standing up from his chair in the Oval Office to wave everyone back to their seats. When they complied, he said to Ron Grimminger, his Science Adviser, "Ron, tell us what we know."

"I'm not quite sure I can, sir," Grimminger said, shaking his head in confusion. "If you check out your display, you can read the original transmission and appendices."

"Ron …" the president said slowly, only to stop as Grimminger shook his head, an anxious expression on his face.

"Sir, this is more politics than I'm used to," Grimminger said.

"And *high stakes* politics at that!" Ellington swore, shaking his head. "Never should have sent the sot out there."

"We didn't have much choice," Merritt admitted sourly. His eyes twinkled as he added, "Unless you think Ned would have been better?"

There was a restrained groan from everyone in the room. The latest reports were that the vice president remained sedated in a secure cell on the far side of the Moon.

"I'm not sure which is worse," Roberts grumbled under his breath.

"Sir," Brian McPhee, the White House chief of staff said, looking up from his tablet, "what I get from this, I think that Pickett may have a point."

"He's going to piss away the best thing that's *ever* happened to mankind and you think that's a *good* idea?" John Ellington cried in surprise.

"From what he's saying," McPhee said, tapping his tablet for emphasis, "the aliens haven't been dealing squarely with us."

Merritt raised an eyebrow and gestured for him to expand.

"If Pickett's right—and the people out there at Jupiter don't seem to be arguing against him—then the alien dealings with us seem, at the very least, awfully strange," McPhee said.

"Well, what do you expect?" Roberts thundered. "They're aliens! Why *wouldn't* they be strange?"

"But, sir, look at this list," McPhee said, tapping his screen again. "They want the rights to the whoopee cushion, for God's sake!"

"Let 'em have it," Roberts said dismissively. "They're giving us a star drive."

"*Two* star drives," Grimminger corrected.

"So if they want the whoopee cushion, who cares?" Roberts said.

"But Pickett says that the aliens aren't giving us the best star drive," McPhee pointed out. "He thinks that they're trying to pull a fast one on us."

"He's nuts!" Roberts said, shaking his head in disgust.

"This whole thing stinks," Secretary of State Ellington spat. "We've got two admirals out there—"

"Neither of 'em ours," Roberts interjected.

"*Two* captains that are ours," Ellington persisted, "scientists, engineers—everything except someone smart enough to handle the politics." He grimaced. "For *that* we've got a drunken has-been that we scraped up out of some hole on the Moon."

"He was good," Merritt said, shaking his head. "He was a pain in the ass, but he was good."

"Yeah," McPhee agreed in a reminiscing tone.

"So, Brian, do you think he's still good?" Merritt said, spearing his chief of staff with a piercing look.

"And are you willing to bet everything on that one man?" Charlie Sumner of the CIA added.

There was a long silence as everyone pondered the depths of that question. Finally, the president of the United States said, "You know, Charlie, I think I am."

* * *

ESA "Eurocos" Headquarters,
Noordwijk aan Zee, The Netherlands

"Well, it's official: we're going with the American," Annie-Marie Foquet announced to the assembly.

"My government has said the same thing," Konstantin Alexandrov, the Russian liaison officer said.

"Only the Americans would be so brazen as to consider suing our first alien contact," Werner Ulke said with a tinge of admiration in his voice. "If they're wrong …"

"If they're wrong, we still have the knowledge of at least one star drive," Antonio Scarli, the Eurocos Executive Secretary reminded them.

"But we know that this Amuksli drive is the worst and that it causes metal fatigue,"

Werner Ulke said.

"Which wouldn't stop us from using it if we get nothing better," Anne-Marie Foquet said with a shrug.

"I confess I'm a little more concerned with the revelations at Phobos," Konstantin Alexandrov said, carefully eyeing the others for their reactions. Word from the Kremlin indicated that the Chinese preparations were totally unknown in Russia. He'd been instructed to see if the Euros had been concealing their knowledge or if they were just as surprised.

"Given the problems with metal fatigue and the apparent … ah, quality issues described, I don't think we need worry too much," Antonio Scarli replied.

"I disagree," Werner Ulke said. "They've got a significant head start in shipyard operations. It will be hard to catch up if we decide to do so."

"I think the question is moot until the issues with the aliens are resolved one way or the other," Anne-Marie Foquet said. She turned to Alexandrov. "I've been told that the EU will not protest the American approach; have you heard anything from your home?"

Alexandrov grimaced. "I'm not privy to such information."

Liar, Antonio Scarli thought to himself.

"Not that it matters," Alexandrov continued, aware of the suspicion in the room. "We are, after all, over thirty light-minutes away from Jupiter and in no position to directly intervene."

"Especially as 'our' ambassador is attempting to bring the aliens to their courts," Antonio Scarli said. "At which point, the distance will doubtless be measured in light-*years*."

"Not yet, surely?" Werner Ulke said. "I thought his dispatch suggested that he'd start first by attempting to gain access to the aliens' onboard legal library."

"Yes, that's where he'd *start*," Anne-Marie Foquet agreed. Her chief science advisor was a very smart and dedicated engineer but he was not at all versed in the intricacies of *politics*. Anne-Marie could imagine the aliens' response to Pickett's request. She hid a grim smile and sent a silent thought of commiseration off to Jupiter—Pickett would surely need it.

CHAPTER NINETEEN

Ynoyon

"BEFORE I CAN ADDRESS THIS LIST OF ITEMS," PICKETT SAID WHEN HE, NEXL, AND Ixxie met with Captain—no, Captain-General—Is-sa-to-li-ri and the Yon trade officer, Xi-ka-ja-na, the next day, "I think we need to properly lay the legal groundwork under which we can enact our agreement."

">>**That is understandable,**<<" Trade Officer Ixxie agreed. The greenish blue mottled skin of the Xlern trade officer was now brightened by eight blue metal chime-castanets—two for each upper limb pikki.

"So, the first question is one of authority," Pickett said. "I am empowered to enter into a treaty with your star nations on behalf of the United Nations, which I represent. My question is, which one of you is authorized by your governments to enter into treaty with us?"

">>**Treaty?**<<" Captain Nexl chimed, moving nervously. ">>**We merely want an agreement.**<<"

"But all agreements require an understanding of the underlying principles of law," Pickett replied. "There needs to be an established protocol for dealing with complaints or disagreements that arise.

"In our world and in our solar system, the governments have agreed to work together under the aegis of the United Nations through the United Nations Commission on International Trade Law. Surely there is a similar interstellar body with which we can create an accord?"

There was a long silence.

"Perhaps if I could examine your legal proceedings, I could get a greater understanding of how to construct our treaties," Pickett suggested after a moment. "I mean, I have to believe that any agreement we enter into will be recorded somewhere in public archives so that any of your competitors would not be able to unfairly profit from your agreement with us."

">>**Of course,**<<" Ixxie chimed back. ">>**Otherwise there would be chaos.**<<"

"And wherever these public documents are kept, I presume there are also bodies to deal with disputes with regards to these agreements," Pickett continued, "some sort of court, perhaps." He waved his arms in theatric exaggeration for the benefit of the aliens. "I apologize that I don't understand all the intricacies of interstellar law, particularly with regard to your governments, but I really cannot, in good conscience, make any agreement without gaining a greater understanding."

">>**What do you want?**<<" Captain Nexl said after a quick glance to the still strange-looking five-headed Yon. Apparently Is-sa-to-li-ri was willing to let the Xlern do the communicating or, possibly, they were still trying to sort themselves out. It was probably for the best, Nexl thought to himself, as that amazing new voice the captain-general sang was overwhelmingly beautiful.

"I need to gain a better understanding of your concepts of ownership, of copyright, and of intellectual property," Pickett said. He waved his hands in what he had come to suspect was a decent imitation of a Xlern shrug. "I suppose what we humans need is legal counsel. Someone to guide us through the intricacies of your trade law and treaties."

">>**How would you pay for such services?**<<" Trade Officer Ixxie inquired.

"That's an excellent question," Pickett replied. "I'm not quite sure and, if your legal experts are like those on our world, they are highly educated and therefore highly compensated individuals. But I cannot sign anything without being certain that I've done the best for my homeworld and its people. To do that, I either need to become accredited as a lawyer in your legal system or acquire someone who is." He paused dramatically, then dropped his bombshell, "The one thing I particularly want to ensure is that my people are not unfairly exploited."

">>**Exploited?**<<" Captain Nexl chimed softly, glancing toward Is-sa-to-li-ri. ">>**Why would anyone consider that possible?**<<"

"Because of your list of trade items, Captain Nexl," Pickett replied. "A list that implies not only a hefty acquaintance with mankind but the possible exploitation as well." He shook his head. "So, I think we really should get legal representation just to be certain that there have been no … inadvertent appropriations of our intellectual property."

">>**You want our help so that you can** *sue* **us?**<<" Trade Officer Ixxie rapped loudly in surprise.

"Of course not," Pickett replied suavely. "In fact, what we want to prove is that such a thing did not occur." He shook his head. "Some people are concerned, however, that perhaps there might be some … miscommunication owing to language difficulties and cultural differences. I need to be able to prove to those doubters that such is not the case."

">>**I see,**<<" Ixxie chimed softly.

"We shall bring you to our homeworld and put you in contact with the appropriate persons," Is-sa-to-li-ri sang. *"When can you be ready?"*

"Don't you want to wait until the work has been finished on the other drive?" Jim asked.

"We shall stay here, and the Xlern can convey you," Is-sa-to-li-ri sang.

"I'll have to confer with my officers," Pickett replied, "I really shouldn't just *leave*."

"Time is of the essence," Is-sa-to-li-ri sang back. *"Captain Nexl, when can you be ready?"*

">>**After the next rest period,**<<" Nexl replied. Pickett saw that it and Ixxie were both moving from foot to foot in what he decided was a worried shuffle.

"The price for your aid is that you be ready at that time," Is-sa-to-li-ri said to Pickett. *"Is that acceptable?"*

"Absolutely," Jim said. "Quite generous, in fact."

"Done," Is-sa-to-li-ri said. *"Now, I suggest you depart and prepare."*

* * *

Harmonie

"I'd like to have Captain Zhukov," Jim Pickett said as he relayed the events of the meeting to the senior officers in the wardroom aboard *Harmonie* later.

"Why?" Emily Steele said.

"Politics," Pickett said. He looked to Admiral Tsukino. "I'd like Captain Steele, a medic, and one other person." He shrugged. "I think that's the minimum—and the maximum—we should bring."

"Politics, eh?" Admiral Tsukino said, giving Jim a keen look which the ambassador returned levelly. "I don't know what that will mean to the team working on theory—"

"I already spoke with him, Admiral," Pickett interrupted. "He's convinced that Commander Geister could take his place without too much trouble."

"Why not assign Mr. McLaughlin?" Admiral Tsukino asked.

"Lieutenant McLaughlin is already involved here," Emily said, "and he's also acting commander of *Voyager*. While her hull is now suspect, her computers are still fully functional."

"Very well. Captain Steele, would your medic be available?" Admiral Tsukino said.

Emily blinked. "Louise? Sure."

"Excellent, then it's settled," Admiral Tsukino said. "Your team will assemble when you leave tomorrow, Mr. Ambassador."

"My team?" Pickett said. "Who's the fourth?"

"Why me, of course," Admiral Tsukino told him blandly. He glanced to Admiral Wang. "I'm certain that Admiral Wang will manage ably in my place."

"Politics," Jim murmured to himself with a cutting glance toward the Japanese admiral.

"The service is rife with it," Admiral Isao Tsukino informed him blandly.

Pickett snorted. "Very well. If you'll all excuse me, I've got to get ready."

"I'll go tell Louise," Emily said, rising from her seat.

"Admiral Wang, if you'd like me to consult with you, I can give you half an hour now," Admiral Tsukino offered.

"Send word to Nikolai and tell him to get his butt over here," Pickett said to Captain Steele as he left.

"Will do," Emily promised, wondering when the ambassador had managed to get on a first-name basis with *Harmonie's* commanding officer.

* * *

Xythir

"\>\>**I am Communications Officer Exern,**\<\<" the Xlern clicked as it approached the five tired humans in the training room, adding a quick bow of its front limbs. "\>\>**I have been instructed to provide you with a suitable communications interface for your needs.**\<\<"

"Before we decide on that, Communications Officer Exern," Captain Steele replied, "I think we should first complete our arrangements with Security Officer Noxor and Engineer Officer Axlu with regards to our space requirements and usage."

"\>\>**Please wait a moment,**\<\<" Exern responded a bit, its limbs skewing in a set of motions.

"I think it's embarrassed," Pickett murmured to Admiral Tsukino.

"How do you know?"

Pickett gestured. "The arrangement of the limbs, and their motion. The same rules that apply to us seem to apply to them: freeze, flight, or fight."

"Embarrassment usually falls somewhere in the realm of freeze and flight, so the limbs betray a combination of both reactions," Pickett continued, "The upper limbs quiver and go still, the lower limbs freeze and then quiver."

"I think you're right, sir," Emily said with a strong note of approval in her voice.

"I've had less dealings with the Xlern than with the Yon," Captain Zhukov admitted.

"And what sort of arrangements should we make, Captain?" Admiral Tsukino asked in the ancient tones of indulgent superior to overeager junior officer.

Zhukov glanced over to Emily, his eyes dancing. She tossed her head in retort to his non-verbal dig and directed her response to the admiral, "Well, sir, I think at the very least we want to see if we can arrange sleeping quarters, a watch area, a dining and relaxation area, wash facilities, and some sort of head."

"I think," Pickett said slowly, "that if we can impose upon the Xlern, it would be best if we could provide separate living quarters for everyone." He raised a hand to quell the protests of the others, pressing on, "We're all going to be under a lot of stress and I think it would be good mental hygiene to allow us individual downtime." He smiled as he added, "As much as I like all of you, I think there'll be times when I just want to be alone."

"Of course. You know, the Xlern are probably listening in to this discussion," Zhukov reminded him gently. "And would doubtless want to listen into everything that occurs amongst us—"

"Which might not be such a bad thing, sir," Louise O'Reilly injected. Zhukov raised an eyebrow, inviting her to explain. "Well, sir, as a medic, I wouldn't complain if they were able to detect if any of us were in distress."

"And what might be considered a matter of privacy for us might not interest them at all," Emily added in support.

Jim Pickett smiled and shook his head. "Or just the opposite."

">>**We can arrange whatever facilities you require,<<**" Axlu chimed pleasantly, his four legs carrying him quickly over to them. "**>>I am Engineer Officer Axlu, and I greet you.<<**"

"Greetings, Axlu," Emily replied. "I presume you have monitored our conversation."

">>**I have,<<**" Axlu responded, dipping its fore body in a half-bow, half-nod. ">>**If this has given harm, I apologize.<<**"

"Why did you listen?" Pickett asked.

">>**Partly in execution of my duties and partly so that I could better anticipate your needs,<<**" Axlu replied.

"If we were to ask that we not be monitored or that we have areas that are not monitored, would that request be honored?"

">>**I must agree with your Petty Officer First Class Louise O'Reilly,<<**" Axlu responded. ">>**Such behavior might be considered undiplomatic.<<**"

"How so?" Jim asked.

">>**Just as your Petty Officer First Class Louise O'Reilly has indicated, if we do not monitor your condition, we might fail to notice any signs of physical distress before it is too late,<<**" Axlu answered, ">>**and that could create a diplomatic incident.<<**"

"Please call me PO or just Louise," O'Reilly said. "It'll be easier all around."

">>**PO?<<**"

"Short for Petty Officer," Emily explained.

">>**But she is Petty Officer First Class Louise O'Reilly,<<**" Axlu protested.

"Among friends, I'm Louise," O'Reilly said with a grin, "and when I'm on duty, I'm referred to as PO for my rank, O'Reilly for my last name, or just Louise."

">>**This is confusing,<<**" Axlu said.

"It is confusing even between members of our species," Pickett agreed. "I am curious, however, whether you Xlern have the concept of close associates. In our species almost universally we distinguish between people we know well and those we don't."

">>**Ambassador Pickett, I am an engineer officer, this is not my area of expertise,<<**" Axlu responded with obvious reluctance.

"In a crisis, are you ever referred to in a quicker form of address?" Emily asked.

">>**In such an emergency, I would respond to any input,<<**" Axlu answered.

"Well, Engineer Officer Axlu, in an emergency I respond to 'You!' or 'O'Reilly!' but among my friends and acquaintances, I prefer to be addressed as Louise," O'Reilly said. She gave the alien a slight bow. "In the interests of speedier communications and inter-species harmony, I would be happy if you, too, would call me Louise."

">>**If this is your wish, then I shall be honored to address you so,<<**" Axlu replied, adding almost shyly, ">>**Louise.<<**"

Louise dimpled at the alien's reply.

"Would you be offended if we called you Axlu?" Emily asked.

">>I admit that I would find that uncomfortable,<<" Axlu replied. ">>However, in one of Louise's emergencies, I would not object.<<"

"Could we call you EO, as a shortening of engineer officer?" Louise said.

">>What you said does not translate,<<" Axlu responded.

"I suppose that answers that," Pickett said with a sigh. "Very well, Engineer Officer Axlu, I suppose we shall have to wait until greater understanding is obtained before we continue this conversation on social conventions."

">>I would suggest perhaps one of the communications people for such an endeavor,<<" Axlu replied. ">>It is more consonant with their duties.<<"

"Indeed," Admiral Tsukino said dryly.

"With regards to living space, what can you provide?" Captain Zhukov asked.

">>It is possible to extrude any shapes, contours, surfaces, and textures you desire,<<" Axlu replied. ">>If you have specific objects designed, we could replicate them.<<"

"But do you have the space?" Emily asked.

">>Of course. Most of our ship is empty,<<" Axlu replied.

"Is it not inefficient to have so much empty space?" Admiral Tsukino wondered.

">>It is more efficient to have space available when needed than not,<<" Axlu replied. Jim Pickett got the distinct impression that the notion was unsettling for the alien engineer.

A sudden thought struck Captain Zhukov and he blurted, "So if we had the drawings, you could build us anything?"

">>Of course,<<" Axlu replied.

"Of any set of materials?" Emily said, exchanging looks with the Russian Captain.

">>Perhaps,<<" Axlu answered. ">>The materials must be within our supplies, and the sizings and mixtures within the capabilities of our extruders.<<"

"So, Engineer Officer Axlu, if we provided you with the structure for a spaceship, would you construct it?" Nikolai asked, exchanging grins with Emily.

">>I believe that Captain Nexl and Security Officer Noxor might have some concerns with safety and trade issues,<<" Axlu responded, ">>but it is not beyond the ability of engineering.<<"

"Really?" Emily said. "Do you often have call for such construction?"

Axlu was silent for a long moment, twitching from legs to legs before answering, ">>I think that perhaps I should refer that question to Captain Nexl. Or maybe Security Officer Noxor.<<"

"I didn't mean to upset you, Engineer Officer Axlu," Emily said, raising her hands in a placating gesture. "I'm afraid that Captain Zhukov and I were being a bit mendacious and teasing you. I hope you will not take offense."

">>Allowances are paid when new contacts are made,<<" Axlu responded.

"Is that a common saying?" Pickett asked.

"**>>I have heard it rapped often when dealing with new aliens,<<**" Axlu replied.

Pickett glanced to Admiral Tsukino with a raised eyebrow. The admiral responded with a small nod and then said, "Engineer Officer Axlu, how long would it take to produce a set of living quarters to our design?"

"**>>All construction depends upon the volume, density, composition, and level of detail required,<<**" Axlu chimed in response.

Admiral Tsukino looked at the rest of his party before saying, "I think I have the most experience in designing bases. Perhaps I should take the lead in designing this."

"I'm a fair hand with our CAD tools, sir," Emily said. "I could help you with that."

"And our CAD tools can output data that the Xlern can interpret?" Admiral Tsukino asked in surprise.

Emily smiled. "Yes, sir," she said. "It came as a bit of a shock to us, too."

"Presumably the concept of describing three dimensional objects using a relative center is something that all space-faring alien races would have developed," Nikolai Zhukov said.

"Well, with only a sample of two, I'd say that theory is still tenuous," Emily told him, "but, yes, I tend to agree with you."

"Tables and chairs would be most immediately useful," Jim said. To the alien, he said, "Engineer Officer Axlu, how quickly can I gain access to training materials on your legal system?"

"**>>That is a question for Communications Officer Exern,<<**" Axlu admitted with some slight discordance in his chimes. "**>>However, if I were to conjecture, I would say that this should not take long to arrange.<<**"

"**>>Indeed, Engineer Officer Axlu conjectures rightly,<<**" Exern rapped.

"Communications Officer Exern, would it be possible to present you with a set of chime-castanets suitable to your rank and position?" Jim said, acutely aware of the sharp tapping sound of Exern's rocks.

"**>>I would be honored,<<**" Exern replied. Jim nodded, glancing to the others significantly.

"Is there any particular tonal range or chromatic arrangement that you find especially apt?" Emily asked. Pickett's eyebrow twitched in surprise at her question, but he made no other response.

"**>>Of course I can only ask for a number suitable to the rank of officer,<<**" Exern began in reply, "**>>but if it were possible to get them shaded to match my body, I would be much pleased.<<**"

"Give me a moment with our hand sensor and I'll run the specs over to Engineer Officer Axlu for fabrication," Emily said, pulling out the standard laser mapper—something only a bit more complicated than an old-fashioned red LED light.

"**>>That is a sensor?<<**" Axlu asked.

"Of course," Emily said, moving to hold it in her fingers. "It uses a red laser light and some simple reflective algorithms to create a high-resolution construct."

"We've used similar objects for a number of decades," Jim put in. "In fact we started using them first in commerce to read simple encoded information off of merchandise." Barcodes and barcode scanners were ubiquitous.

"We're going to need power for our equipment," Emily said as she checked the reading on her scanner and, satisfied, pocketed it once more.

">>**Power can be supplied,**<<" Axlu chimed back. ">>**That need has been requested previously, particularly by your Lieutenant Danielle McElroy and also by Danni.**<<"

Emily smiled and shook her head. "Those are two names for the same person, Engineer Officer Axlu."

">>**Really?**<<" Axlu replied. ">>**I had not realized.**<<"

"Most of us call her Danni," Louise said.

Emily smiled and nodded. "On our ships, we tend to get very egalitarian."

"On *American* ships," Captain Zhukov replied.

">>**Really?**<<" Communications Officer Exern said. ">>**It is different on your ship, Captain Zhukov?**<<"

"Indeed," Zhukov agreed. "The crew of *Harmonie* is composed of several nationalities."

">>**And that requires a different protocol?**<<" Exern asked.

"We spend a lot of time trying to produce harmonious communications and other interactions," Jim said, motioning for Zhukov to let him handle the question. "In the case of *Harmonie*, I understand that the most harmonious communications required slightly more respect for rank than occurred on *Voyager*." He paused, then asked, "Do you not have that among your species?"

">>**Some elements of the concept are not foreign to us,**<<" Engineer Officer Axlu said. ">>**Particularly when dealing with people from different oceans.**<<"

">>**With all respect, Engineer Officer Axlu,**<<" Exern interjected, ">>**I believe that we should perhaps direct our attentions to the immediate needs of the humans.**<<"

"Indeed," Admiral Tsukino agreed.

">>**Will you require access to the equipment that Ensign Dubauer used?**<<" Axlu asked. ">>**We could bring you to it.**<<"

"That would be very useful," Emily said. In aside to the others, she said, "I'll bet Lori had a chair and table at least."

">>**If you will follow me, then, I shall lead you there,**<<" Axlu said, waving its upper limbs toward the door that led from the training room to the hallway from the airlock.

With a shrug, Jim Pickett indicated that he had no objection so the five humans followed the Xlern engineer who was trailed closely by Communications Officer Exern.

"I've never been in this part of the ship," Emily commented as a door irised open to reveal a large room with a number of objects scattered throughout.

">>**We left it unaltered,**<<" Axlu chimed. Pickett could almost imagine the alien adding, "Pardon the mess."

Axlu led them to one side and halted even as Emily gave a cry of joy and raced forward to a very normal looking chair, desk, and lamp.

"There's power, too!" Emily said, moving to plug her tablet in.

">>**There is a protocol available here to provide a wireless connection,**<<" Axlu added.

"Yes, I think Lori put it on the general—yup!—it's on the general share," Emily said as she fingered her way through the various data folders on her tablet. She clicked on the application and it installed itself. "Good girl, I'm going to have to get her promoted!"

"If you get her to join the UNS, I can guarantee her a lieutenancy," Pickett said.

"I'm pretty sure she'll get the same opportunity where she is, Mr. Ambassador," Captain Zhukov said lightly.

Pickett shrugged at the captain before glancing to see Admiral Tsukino's reaction. The admiral seemed both amused and thoughtful, which provided Pickett with a pleasure that he refrained from showing.

"If you're happy with the connection, Captain, perhaps you'll show me your CAD software?" Admiral Tsukino suggested. Emily glanced over her shoulder at him. "It might be easier for me to rough out the design myself."

Emily's eyes widened, but then she shook her head and clambered out of the chair, gesturing to the Japanese admiral. "Of course, sir, if you please."

Admiral Tsukino gave her a thankful nod as he sat, tentatively positioned the tablet, and ran his fingers over the surface to get a feel for its sensitivity. Satisfied, he started a new drawing then stopped, turning to look up at Emily. "I don't suppose your talented ensign thought to put her designs for this chair and table up on that general share of yours?"

"Hmmm … I'd be surprised if she didn't," Emily said. "Lori's a bit of a pack-rat like that."

The admiral lifted up the tablet and passed it to Captain Steele, who quickly tapped in a few commands and said, "Yes, she did! Should I open them up for you, Admiral?"

"If you please." A moment later, Emily passed the tablet back to him and Admiral Tsukino grunted appreciatively. His eyes narrowing in concentration, he commenced to rough out a quick set of rooms.

"The Xlern seem to like curves, sir," Emily told him as she watched over his shoulder.

The admiral accepted this with a nod, made a few adjustments, and the straight lines of the walls became slight curves. Seeming satisfied, he imported the desk, copied it, and performed a number of transformations, which quickly made it into a bed. He paused for a moment, then looked up at Axlu. "Engineer Officer Axlu, would it be possible to incorporate some of your training monitors into the walls of our quarters?"

">>It would. However, there is an issue with integration between your objects and ours,<<" Axlu answered.

"If we're going to be working together for any length of time," Admiral Tsukino said, glancing meaningfully toward Ambassador Pickett, "then we should probably resolve that issue in the near future."

">>**Long-term arrangements are not settled,**<<" Axlu chimed in answer. The Xlern made some untranslated sounds that caused the humans to exchange surprised glances before he continued with a translatable, ">>**Perhaps I could arrange to have Engineer Apprentice Xover coordinate with …**<<" He paused for moment, ">>**… someone to work on this problem.**<<"

"I'd be delighted to work with Engineer Apprentice Xover," Emily said immediately.

">>**But you are a *captain*!**<<" Exern rattled in surprise.

"We do not concern ourselves very much with rank when it comes to getting a task completed," Jim said.

">>**It is often the same in my engineering section,**<<" Axlu admitted, its chimes seeming smug in their sound, ">>**and especially so in circumstances of great urgency.**<<"

"I'm glad to know that," Emily said. She looked around. "Should I meet Engineer Apprentice Xover somewhere?"

">>**If Engineer Officer Axlu has no objections, I shall arrange for Engineer Apprentice Xover to be ordered here,**<<" Exern tapped in reply.

">>**Do it,**<<" Axlu chimed back. ">>**Have him meet us in Extrusion One.**<<"

"Where is that, Engineer Officer Axlu?" Pickett asked politely.

"Is Extrusion One the location where completed extrusions are deposited?" Emily guessed.

">>**Indeed,**<<" Axlu answered with a dip of its body—a motion that Pickett was willing to bet indicated a level of respect.

"Well, if the admiral would permit," Emily said, pulling her scanner from her pocket, "I could upload these scans to my tablet, set the materials parameters and send them to your extrusion systems so that when we arrived in Extrusion One we would have a set of chime-castanets for Communications Officer Exern."

"That would give us an opportunity to demonstrate that we've got all the interfaces working properly," Nikolai Zhukov said approvingly.

Emily smiled at him. "My thoughts exactly."

Admiral Tsukino ceded the seat to her, and a few moments later she rose. "If I've got it right, you should have the fab in your queue," she told Axlu.

">>**Let us find out,**<<" Axlu offered, heading toward the door that opened into another hallway which had many doors off it.

"May I come?" Pickett asked.

">>**Any who wishes may come,**<<" Axlu said.

Captain Zhukov moved to join them while Louise said, "I'll keep the admiral company."

The three humans and two Xlern took the nearest door out of the hallway. Emily murmured surprise at the vastness of the room and the equipment in it.

"It looks like our extrusion and sintering facilities on a massive scale," Captain

Zhukov said.

"**>>It is one of our facilities,<<**" Axlu answered with what Jim Pickett took to be a certain tone of pride. The engineer moved over to a central unit, flexed his forward pikki in an intricate dance and then said, "**>>Yes, the extruders have the project and have verified it.<<**"

"How long will it take to build?" Pickett asked.

"**>>Watch,<<**" Axlu answered, moving away from the control console and tapping one small area significantly. "**>>The process is started.<<**"

One work bay was lit with a bright red light. They could make out shapes emerging visibly from a floor of metal.

"Does it extrude and sinter?" Nikolai Zhukov asked, impressed at the speed at which the chime-castanets were forming and cooling.

"**>>It does not sinter,<<**" Axlu chimed unexpectedly.

"No?" Emily said, surprised. "Do the Xlern not need to perform sintering operations?"

"**>>We did not consider such operations possible,<<**" Axlu admitted, chiming in what Emily took for chagrin.

"Well, I'm certain we can arrange for some sort of trade," Jim Pickett said breezily, giving Captain Steele an approving nod for bringing that notion into the conversation.

"**>>The process of sintered extrusion is a closely-guarded secret among the Gihendi,<<**" Axlu responded. "**>>I would be surprised if Trade Officer Ixxie and Captain Nexl would not offer a large recompense for such technology.<<**"

Emily glanced toward Pickett, who nodded in recognition of the value of that admission.

"We are not aware of the Gihendi," Zhukov said carefully. "Is there some reason they might be jealous of the sintering process?"

Axlu's chime-castanets clamored in the sound of a choral waterfall which was not translated.

"Is he laughing?" Pickett wondered quietly. Aloud, he said, "Engineer Officer Axlu, your last communication was not recognized by our software."

"**>>I was not communicating,<<**" Axlu admitted. "**>>I was expressing humor.<<**"

"Could you explain, please?"

"**>>The Gihendi are the best engineers in the known galaxy,<<**" Axlu answered.

"**>>Engineer Officer Axlu, that is something left to the captain!<<**" Exern rapped quickly, moving to separate the sturdy Xlern engineer from proximity with the humans.

The lights at the extrusion bay went out, and a set of robotic tentacles moved to the metal objects, lifted them, and moved them to another work bay where, as everyone watched, the chime-castanets were polished and then painted. A moment later, the tentacles picked them up and placed them on a tray while at the control console where Axlu had started the process. A light flashed, and the depression where the engineer officer had pushed to start the process moved upward, indicating that the process was completed.

">>**Go see if they fit,**<<" Axlu clinked in irritation.

The communications officer was not so perturbed that he waited to argue with Axlu. Instead, he moved quickly to the tray, carefully picked up one, then another castanet and, with a deft alacrity, placed them on all four of his upper limbs.

">>**They feel much nicer than rocks,**<<" Exern chimed. In a higher pitch, he continued, ">>**And they have a greater sonic range.**<<"

"Another satisfied customer," Emily said with a grin.

"I can't imagine them extruding our quarters, though," Nikolai said gloomily.

">>**Larger extrusions are conducted in different areas,**<<" Axlu answered with soft chimes.

"How long will it take?" Emily asked.

">>**We could build the volume of your spaceship in less than an hour,**<<" Axlu assured her musically.

"That's impressive," Jim said. "Come to think of it, how long will it take us to get to our destination?"

"Are we going to Siluria?" Emily wondered.

">>**There is no Siluria,**<<" Axlu answered.

"Was there ever a Siluria?"

">>**Not in this time,**<<" Axlu replied.

The humans exchanged glances but said nothing. Instead, Pickett said, "So where are we going?"

">>**That is a question for Captain Nexl, Ambassador Pickett,**<<" Axlu replied. ">>**We should go check with Admiral Tsukino.**<<"

"Doesn't want to talk," Emily surmised.

"Yup," Pickett agreed laconically.

The door opened as they approached it and a third Xlern skittered inside.

">>**Engineer Apprentice Xover reports.**<<"

">>**Follow us, Xover,**<<" Axlu ordered.

">>**Might one ask for introductions?**<<"

"Xover, I'm Captain Emily Steele," Emily said. "We've met. The other two are Ambassador Pickett and Captain Zhukov."

">>**I thought the Russian Captain was aboard** Ynoyon,<<" Xover responded. ">>**Did his brain explode as you had predicted?**<<"

Emily blushed while Nikolai chuckled.

"No, as you can see, the captain is quite functional," Emily said when she found her voice once more. "He was ordered to join us on our trip."

"We are going to consult with some of your legal people," Jim said on a whim.

">>**Are we going to Siluria?**<<" Xover asked, limbs quivering with wonder.

">>**No, our destination is Thraxis IV,**<<" Exern replied.

">>**Thraxis IV? Are we—?**<<" But Xover was silenced by the combined chimes of both Axlu and Exern.

"What do we need to know about Thraxis IV?" Jim asked with a quick glance toward the rest of the party.

">>**Thraxis IV is the nearest legal center,**<<" Exern chimed in response. ">>**It will take us somewhat more than two of your days to get there.**<<"

"Are they expecting us?" Jim asked. "And will they accommodate our gravity and environmental needs?"

">>**Doubtless they will be prepared when we arrive,**<<" Exern asserted.

Pickett and the others exchanged looks; all had noticed the lack of a direct answer.

">>**Engineer Apprentice Xover, Admiral Tsukino is currently designing living quarters for the humans,**<<" Axlu chimed. ">>**You may bring the humans back to him and provide assistance until the designs are complete.**<<"

">>**With pleasure, Engineer Officer Axlu.**<<"

">>**I have other duties to attend but will return when you are ready to begin extrusion,**<<" Axlu said, directing its chimes to Pickett.

"We look forward to seeing you soon," Jim said, motioning for the group to follow Xover. "In the meantime, Communications Officer Exern, is there perhaps someplace where I might begin my preparations?"

">>**Ambassador Pickett might avail himself of the training room,**<<" Exern replied. ">>**I should be honored to lead him there.**<<"

"Thank you," Pickett said. To the others he added, "I'll join you when you call."

The parties split up, Axlu heading out the same door Xover had entered, while the rest followed Xover and Exern until they arrived back in the room with Admiral Tsukino and PO O'Reilly. Pickett followed Exern out and through to the hallway that led to the training room. At her request, Captain Steele attached herself to him.

Inside, Exern made its way over to the display screens, tapped in a number of complex entries with its mannies, and then stood back.

">>**The training system is programmed to respond to your requests,**<<" Exern said. ">>**If it cannot understand your request, it will ask for clarification until it can. If you find that you need to contact me, simply ask for Communications Officer Exern and the system will connect you.**<<"

"Thank you," Pickett said. "You've been most kind."

Exern gave the two humans a semi-bow and departed.

Emily waited until the alien had departed and then turned to the ambassador. "What now?"

"Now, we learn," Pickett told her with a smile. "How good is your legal training?"

Emily pursed her lips and shook her head. "No more than the standard stuff they give undergraduate engineers. We didn't touch it at Command College nor when I was going for my PhDs"

"We lawyers like to keep it all to ourselves," Jim told her with a smile. He moved closer to one of the displays and said carefully, "Please give me the interstellar agreed legal definition for property."

Anything that is said to be the legal possession of a particular entity, the screen displayed in response.

"Define 'legal possession,'" Jim said carefully.

To have possession recognized under law.

"What defines 'law' in the interstellar legal system?"

Clarify: which entity embodies the laws of interstellar legal adjudication or what is law?

"Which entity embodies the laws of the interstellar legal adjudication?"

The Silurian Multiverse Court is the highest legal entity in all the known multiverse.

"We keep running into this Siluria," Emily murmured.

"And Axlu said it didn't exist at this time," Pickett replied, carefully laying a finger alongside his nose to indicate that it was something they should keep between themselves. "I imagine all our questions will be reviewed and flagged under certain circumstances."

"I wonder what sort of privacy is guaranteed under interstellar law," Emily murmured.

Privacy is a fundamental right of the Silurian Concordance, the screen displayed.

"Define a legal agreement and a legal contract," Jim said with slightly more volume.

After the display responded, Pickett moved on through the basic elements of interstellar contract law, copyright law, patent law, and interstellar trade agreements. Somewhere along the way, Emily squatted on the floor and Pickett, after an amused glance, joined her.

They were into the sort of arcane definitions that, judging by his expression and his rapid-fire speech, Ambassador Pickett loved, when the door irised open, and Captain Zhukov entered, carrying two chairs.

"We voted and thought you should have the first," Nikolai said to the surprised Americans. "How is it going?"

"Jim asks the questions and the wall answers," Emily said as she relieved the Russian of one of the chairs and set it behind the ambassador. Pickett nodded his thanks, stood, rubbed his sore behind, and gratefully sat upon the chair.

"They're not very comfortable," Nikolai apologized.

"Better than the floor," Pickett said quietly before returning his attention to the display.

"How accurate is this information?" Zhukov asked, moving to peer at one of the further screens.

"Do you mean in translation?" Pickett asked with a slight emphasis on the last word as he jerked his eyes toward the ceiling in a reminder that they were being observed.

"That's what I was thinking," Zhukov said slowly, even as he shook his head to give the lie to his words.

"At the end of the day, everything depends upon trust," Jim said. "We have positive proof that the Xlern can provide some of what they claim. We'll have to trust to the rest."

"I thought that lawyers were paid to be skeptical," Emily murmured.

"Lawyers are; ambassadors are paid to get results," Jim replied.

"How are the quarters coming?" Emily asked.

"Admiral Tsukino asks if you would check on his design," Zhukov replied. "I can keep the ambassador company."

"Very well," Emily said, glancing to Pickett for his reaction. The ambassador smiled and waved her out.

"What are standard remedies for failure to fulfill a contractual agreement?" Jim asked as Emily left the room.

* * *

"We'll get carpeting laid in tomorrow," Emily said, as she led a weary Pickett to their newly extruded quarters. "As for sleepwear, well, the aliens aren't very good with such synthetics so we've got something akin to a cross between rayon and wool."

"Charming," Jim replied. "We should have thought to bring our own bedding."

"Xover was almost beside itself with apologies," Emily said, shaking her head in memory, "and Axlu was worse. Louise was able to provide them with some raw cotton but they're stumped at how to extrude it or replicate it. Apparently, it's not the sort of thing they've dealt with before."

"So how do the Xlern sleep?" Jim asked as he entered into the double doors of the extrusion's airlock. "And why the airlock?"

"I think Admiral Tsukino finagled it," Emily said. "He challenged the aliens on their ability to build a proper ship and said that airlocks were a prime requirement."

"Hnh," Jim grunted. They cycled through the second door and Pickett's eyebrows rose. "Nice."

"Rooms for everyone, a galley, a wardroom, a meeting room, and interfaces to the *Xythir's* system in each room," Emily recounted.

"All the comforts of home," Jim agreed.

"Well, except for the sheets, blankets, towels, and other fabrics," Louise O'Reilly said as she moved from one room into the hallway, attracted by the sound of voices.

"What about food and water?"

"Water they've provided, both hot and cold," Emily told him. "As for food, well, we'll be living on our rations for a while."

Rations, in this case, were the standard emergency fare noted throughout all navies for inedibility.

"I suppose we don't want to try Xlern cuisine," Jim guessed.

"We haven't had that conversation yet," Admiral Tsukino said, entering the hallway from a different room.

"At a guess, however, the answer would be no," Emily said.

"How did it go, Mr. Ambassador?" the admiral now asked.

"Well," Jim said, rubbing the back of his neck with one hand, "if tiring."

"Why don't you tell us in the wardroom?" Admiral Tsukino said, waving toward another doorway. "Captain Zhukov is brewing us some tea." He shook his head as he added, "No milk, however."

"Something warm would be nice," Pickett agreed, gesturing for the admiral to lead on.

Tea was served in very bright stainless steel cups. The heat was such that only Louise's sacrifice of a number of gauze bandages allowed anyone to hold them.

"So what did you discover?" Admiral Tsukino asked when everyone had had a chance to taste their tea.

"The law is an ass," Pickett said. "Apparently, it's an interstellar ass."

"So not much different from home?" Emily said.

"Not much at all," Pickett replied, his brows creased. "I shall be very interested in seeing the courts of Thraxis IV."

"Do you need to learn more?" Admiral Tsukino asked.

"No, actually, I'm going to need some time to gather my thoughts," Jim said. "Do we have any paper and a pen or pencil?"

"Pardon?" Emily said, brows rising.

"I'm a bit old-fashioned when it comes to preparing a brief," Pickett said with a dismissive wave of his hand. "It's nice to get close to things."

"I think we could get the Xlern to provide us with an equivalent," Captain Zhukov said carefully.

Pickett shook his head. "I'm not sure that's a good idea."

"I think I could get you something, sir," Louise said. "It might be a bit hodgepodge, though."

"Show me what you've got and we'll see," Pickett told her with a thankful smile.

"Let me go see what I can do," Louise said, moving her cup to the center of the table and rushing out to her quarters. She was back in five minutes. "I've got some stickies and a pen."

"Excellent!" Pickett said, gladly receiving the proffered supplies. He took the first sticky and wrote, *Not secure.*

He stuck it on the table where the others could read it. They all nodded. Satisfied, he wrote another note, pulled it off pad of stickies and passed it to Admiral Tsukino. It read: *Siluria.*

At Pickett's gesture, the admiral passed it around the table.

Thraxis IV? read the next note.

"Well, it will be interesting to see what life is like on an alien planet," Admiral Tsukino said aloud, even as he passed on the second note.

"I'm going to be quite interested to see how their local economy works," Pickett said in agreement.

"Do you suppose they have factories there?" Emily asked.

"Or is it all just administrative?" Pickett countered. "I can't think of any one of our cities that concentrates on just one thing."

"But we're not aliens," Zhukov pointed out.

"True," Jim agreed, "and the demonstrated extrusion capability of the Xlern might obviate the need for factories."

"I doubt it," Emily said. Admiral Tsukino glanced her way, questioningly. "Well, for some things there will always be economies of scale."

"So the local economy will be interesting," Pickett agreed. "As will whatever agriculture and trade that occur."

"I wonder if we could get a tour of their space yards," Emily said. "Clearly, if there is interstellar trade, they've got to have places where they store and distribute goods. We'll want to know the best way to integrate our goods into that trading system."

"Indeed," Captain Zhukov agreed. "I suppose all of us won't be needed all the time we're dealing with the legal system."

"Agreed," Admiral Tsukino said. "In fact, I rather imagine that three of us could find some way to more profitably spend our time."

"With all due respect, sirs," Louise spoke up, "I'd like to have a chance to look at their medical system. I can't imagine that the Xlern have conquered all disease, and I'm quite curious about their biology. I'm also concerned about the possibility of cross-infections."

"Good point, PO," Jim said. "I think that should be something we emphasize during our next meeting with the Xlern."

"I could combine it with my conversation about developing suitable fabrics," Louise said with a smile.

"I rather suspect you could, PO," Pickett said with a deep appreciation in his tone.

"Thank you!" Louise said. To her captain, she added, "We try."

*   *   *

Thraxis IV

">>**We should be arriving on the ground shortly,**<<" Security Officer Noxor assured the humans. ">>**We have arranged it so that the gravity is no more than your Moon's standard.**<<"

"Can we get an exterior view?" Ambassador Pickett asked.

">>**We are nearly on the ground,**<<" Noxor temporized.

"I understand the need for security, but as long as we're in the atmosphere, I doubt that we will be able to obtain star positions sufficient to reveal the location of this planet," Pickett told the security officer soothingly.

">>**It was not for that reason—**<<"

"Please, it's a medical issue," Louise interjected. "Some of us suffer from minor claustrophobia which is exacerbated in times of stress."

">>**I had not realized,**<<" Noxor said as the viewports went active.

"It's more brown than I would have thought," Jim commented as he looked through the viewport nearest him.

"Is this corrected for our eyesight?" Louise asked. A moment later, the view changed and got somewhat brighter.

">>**Apologies,**<<" Noxor said. Pickett got the impression that the security officer, a professional paranoid, found it nearly painful to make such a concession.

"Allowances must be made in first contacts," Pickett said.

"Are there many crops grown here?" Emily asked, craning close to her viewport. "And where would we see them?"

"Would any be edible for us?" Louise added, guessing that this approach would get past Noxor's security-minded thinking.

">>**That question would be best asked of the trade officer,**<<" Noxor clicked back. He had been the last officer to—reluctantly—adopt the human-made chime-castanets.

"I would have thought the question to be one of equal importance for security," Nikolai Zhukov spoke up, looking surprised. "After all, I imagine it would be considered a security breach if one of us ingested something fatal."

">>**Possibly more of a trade issue,**<<" Noxor responded after some moments of untranslatable movements, which Pickett took for agitated thinking. ">>**I can inquire if you wish.**<<"

Pickett gave Louise a quick nod and the medic, always quick on the uptake, said, "I think it would be very important to ensure that we have an adequate supply of food."

">>**You brought foodstuffs with you, surely?**<<"

"We did, but they are of the emergency variety and we are not certain if they will outlast our visit here," Emily said. "It's always wise to have a backup."

"And better to have something tasty," Admiral Tsukino agreed. The bulk of the rations they had were from *Voyager*. They were targeted for American tastes, but after several days of such fare, Isao would happily kill for the simplicity of a clean miso soup.

"Don't you have different preferences among the Xlern?" Pickett asked, suddenly curious. "I would assume that several regional dishes would dominate various seas."

">>**There is a large disagreement between the value of land- and sea-food,**<<" Noxor admitted.

"Which do you prefer?"

">>**I wasn't finished, Petty Officer First Class Louise O'Reilly,**<<" Noxor rapped back somewhat testily. ">>**For myself, I find that a nicely charred nishak steak with umdoo sauce is worthy of attention.**<<"

"How did the translators manage 'nishak' and 'umdoo'?" Pickett said, glancing to Emily.

"Admiral Tsukino linked our translators into the Xlern computers—"

"How?"

"Well," Admiral Tsukino admitted slyly, "it wasn't that difficult. It was easy enough to gather that their computers would have started with a base eight counting system."

"The admiral is being modest," Nikolai said. His lips twitched as he told the admiral, *"Watashi wa nohongo wo hanashimasu."*

"Ah sō desu ka?" Pickett asked, smiling at the admiral.

"Koko de daremoga nihongo o hanasu nodesu ka" Admiral Tsukino asked.

"No, I don't," Emily replied. "Nor does Louise unless she's been taking a correspondence course recently."

"No, Captain," Louise admitted. "I wonder if our alien friends might come up with a universal translator for us."

"We're about to land," Emily said, pointing to the window. The view had changed to a dirt landscape that was mostly barren, except for several small upright objects in the distance.

"Is this their spaceport?" Pickett asked in wonder.

"I believe it is," Emily said, peering intently through the window until it was obscured suddenly and they entered shadow.

">>**We are entering our docking station; please wait for egress,**<<" Noxor informed them.

The hatch hissed open. Noxor moved forward, twitched and chimed a few messages with the downside Xlern and the pilot, then said to the humans, ">>**We are ready to depart.**<<"

"Gear up, folks," Emily said, hefting a pack on her shoulder.

At Pickett's suggestion, each of them carried enough food, clothes, and supplies for a week. Noxor had promised that water would not be an issue and that the power points supplied on the *Xythir* would also be supplied at their quarters and in the courts.

It was Louise who summed up their feelings as she muttered, "'For what we are about to receive …'"

CHAPTER TWENTY

"SAY WHAT YOU WILL, BUT WE COULD NEVER HAVE GOTTEN THIS FAR WITHOUT the Xlern," Jim Pickett said as he relaxed in their planet-side quarters later that evening. He glanced meaningfully at the ceiling and walls, raising his eyebrows to draw everyone's attention: the rooms were undoubtedly bugged, "for your safety," as Axlu had said not too long ago.

"Absolutely," Admiral Tsukino agreed. "They've been more than kind to us."

"Those who demand security over freedom deserve neither," Emily said, her lips twitching as she registered her understanding.

"Regardless of our security, I still maintain that the Xlern's—and the Yon's, for that matter—treatment of us has been outstanding," Jim repeated. "I look forward to seeing more of their civilization and hope that we can come to a mutually beneficial accord."

"I agree," Emily said. "Just think of how selfless they were in equipping *Voyager* with that gravity drive—"

"Although it seems to have been a troubling gift," Admiral Tsukino reminded them, "given all those structural problems it possibly created."

"The jury's out on that, sir," Emily said. "It could just as easily have been that Amuksli drive of theirs."

"Doubtless they will be able to trade us a technology that circumvents the issue," Nikolai said.

"Another thing to trade for," Jim said, "I've already got it on my list."

"Well, Mr. Ambassador, if you don't mind, I think it should be my priority to see to our maintenance requirements," Louise said. "I'd like to secure a decent source of nutrition—preferably several—and then I'd like to gain an understanding of what sort of medical facilities we can count on while we're here." She held up a hand as her superiors started to respond, adding, "It's not that we aren't all very healthy, but accidents do happen."

"Just consider Commander Reynaud," Nikolai said.

"*That* accident will not happen here," Emily said.

There was a slight silence as the men of the group absorbed this, then Admiral Tsukino said, "I imagine I'll be accompanying the ambassador but—"

Emily forestalled him with an upraised hand. "We should operate in pairs at the least." Admiral Tsukino nodded after the slightest glance at the American captain to remonstrate her for interrupting a superior. "But we're an odd number, so I guess that Nikolai and I should accompany Louise on her rounds."

"Very well," the admiral said. "I would wish that we could spread out and cover more ground."

"There's a lot to learn," Jim said, "and we don't know how long we'll be here to learn it."

"Surely we'll come back?" Emily asked. She gestured to the city beyond them, "I mean, this is the center of their legal system, so this must be a fairly moderate trade center as well."

"One would imagine," Jim said.

"I suppose that's something we should consider while we're making our rounds," Nikolai said, glancing to Emily for confirmation.

"Indeed."

"Well," Jim said, "I think we'd best see if we can get any sleep before the morning."

"If you're having problems, come see me," Louise said. "I don't like issuing 'em, but I've got a few sleep aids."

The others nodded and filed off to their individual rooms. The layout, they had pleasantly discovered, was a recreation of the quarters the admiral had designed aboard *Xythir*. Security Officer Noxor had admitted that the plans had been re-used under the belief that the humans would feel more comfortable in a space of their own design.

At least, Jim thought as he pulled on his pajamas, they had managed finally to get the fabrics right. He slid under the warm almost-wool blankets and into the almost-cotton sheets and found himself wishing they'd managed to better communicate the varied requirements for a decent pillow. In the end, he bunched up a pair of almost-towels and slipped them under his head.

*   *   *

"They seem to use a lot of robots in their work," Emily commented to Louise as Security Officer Noxor guided them to their destination. She pointed out the window of their vehicle to the surrounding fields.

"I wish we could see over those hills," Nikolai said. The spaceport was in a valley with hills on three sides and an ocean on the fourth. It reminded Emily of Los Angeles in some ways.

"There aren't many buildings," Emily said as she put her finger on the difference between this spaceport and the West Coast metropolis.

"Maybe they're underground," Nikolai suggested. He stared out the window on his side of the vehicle and shrugged, looking thoughtful.

"Security Officer Noxor, what is our destination?" Louise asked carefully.

">>**You had requested a location where you could obtain foodstuffs,**<<" Noxor chimed back.

"And that is our destination?" Nikolai asked.

">>**We are going to the interstellar marketplace,**<<" Noxor replied.

"How will we pay for our goods?" Emily asked.

">>**Captain Nexl has provided me with a credit chit,**<<" Noxor said. ">>**We will add it to your costs.**<<"

The vehicle slowed, moved to the side of the road and stopped, the canopy rising to let the passengers disgorge.

"**>>Please follow me,<<**" Noxor ordered.

Emily had a moment to smell hot, dry dust, and then her senses were overwhelmed with a range of spices and scents, some familiar, some not.

"**>>Your basic sustenance levels have been entered into the international registry,<<**" Noxor informed them. "**>>We will obtain a detector here.<<**"

It led them up a ramp to a deserted room. It looked like it would hold a large crowd, and there were a number of windows at the far end, openings to back offices. Only one window was open and there was a—

"Which species is this?" Emily asked, looking at the new alien in surprise.

"**>>It is a Gharm,<<**" Noxor replied. "**>>Not a life-form but an appendage of a computing entity.<<**"

"It's a robot?"

"**>>That would be a poor description,<<**" Noxor responded with a tone of pique, almost like a sniff, "**>>but your language is lacking in nuance.<<**"

"I do believe we've been dissed," Louise said in low, amused voice to her captain. Emily flicked her hand in a let-it-go gesture.

Noxor moved forward to the Gharm and rapped on the counter for attention, chiming, "**>>Detectors for the humans.<<**"

"**>>Sustenance or damage?<<**" came the response.

"**>>Sustenance,<<**" Noxor clicked in reply. Emily could see the way Noxor seemed to hop from foot to foot and decided that the Xlern was both irritated and embarrassed at the question. She didn't need to look at the other two to know that they had caught on to the implied threat in the Gharm's question.

"**>>Number of detectors?<<**"

"Five," Louise said, glancing to see if the Gharm reacted to her words.

"**>>Unknown form of communication—<<**" the Gharm began, then suddenly, "Communication identified as human language known as English. Five is a number. Assumption: five sustenance detectors required."

"We'd also like five damage detectors," Emily spoke up quickly. "And I am curious, how did you learn to speak our language?"

"Centercomp is repository for all contact information," the Gharm replied. "Original data obtained—"

"**>>Stop!<<**" Noxor boomed loudly. "**>>Restricted information.<<**"

"Restricted?" the Gharm responded.

"**>>Trade in progress,<<**" Noxor rapped, all its limbs swaying rapidly.

"Wow, it's pissed," Louise commented in an undertone.

"We do not need to know now," Emily said. "Can we have the two sets of detectors? Could you color code them green for the sustenance detectors and red for the damage detectors?"

"Done," the Gharm said. A moment later it handed out two clear bags with small objects inside.

Emily moved forward and took them, opening the bag with the green objects and handing them out to the others. She pocketed a red damage detector and passed two over to Nikolai and Louise, who also pocketed them.

"How do they work?" Emily asked. Then, realizing the broadness of the question, she hastily added, "How do we know if they have detected something?"

"The detectors emit audible and visual cues," the Gharm replied. "The cues are set to the standards for human English."

"And those cues would be?" Emily asked. She got the impression that Security Officer Noxor was sitting hard on its temper.

"A green light and a warm tone for the sustenance detector," the Gharm said. "Additional nutritional and preparation information available upon request in various formats, including audible."

"And for the damage?"

"A warning blare and red light," the Gharm said. "The louder the tone, the brighter the light, the greater the danger."

"Excellent," Emily said, "very well designed for humans."

"Pleasure," the Gharm responded. "Do you require anything else?"

"What else could you provide us with?" Nikolai asked, even as Noxor started herding them to the door.

"Infinite response required, time unavailable," the Gharm said.

"Well then, we'll have to wait until another time," Nikolai said. "It was a pleasure interacting with you."

"Pleasure," the Gharm said.

They were at the exit when Louise turned and rushed back to the window. "Wait a minute! Would it be possible to get a guide or a map?"

">>**It is forbidden!**<<" Noxor boomed furiously.

"Why?" Louise asked. "If we get separated from you, wouldn't it be useful for us to find our way back?"

">>**You will not get separated.**<<"

"But it's a marketplace!" Emily objected. "It must be crowded and full of life! One of us could get detached or separated easily. Wouldn't that be a security nightmare?"

">>**It is not crowded.**<<"

"How do you know?" Nikolai wondered.

">>**I know**<<," Noxor replied. ">>**Come.**<<"

"Oh, yeah, it's pissed," Louise said as she rejoined the others.

">>**This way,**<<" Noxor chimed, leading them back down the ramp. They turned right, away from the street entrance and through great doors.

For protection, almost instinctively, the three humans bunched together behind the small alien. As they crossed the threshold into the great trading hall, Emily stopped in wonder.

"This place is dead."

* * *

"Huh," Jim muttered to himself as he and Admiral Tsukino were led down brightly lit hallways with multiple iris-doorways on either side.

Admiral Tsukino raised an eyebrow, encouraging further discourse.

"Not many people around," Pickett expounded. To their guide, Security Apprentice Doxal, Pickett said, "Is this early?"

">>I would not know, Ambassador Pickett,<<" Doxal replied. ">>That is outside my area of expertise.<<"

"Trade Officer Ixxie," Jim said to the other Xlern accompanying them, "is this normal?"

">>I am not sure what you mean, Ambassador Pickett,<<" Ixxie chimed back.

"I would have expected to see some other life-forms in these halls," Jim said, waving a hand, "and I don't know how good these doors are sound-proofed, but I would imagine we'd hear something from the other side."

">>I could ask,<<" Ixxie offered. He paused at a door and swiped the plate to open it. The door irised open to reveal a small room. ">>This is a briefing room. You and the admiral can conduct your research here.<<"

"When can I present my credentials?" Jim asked.

">>Pardon?<<"

"My credentials, when can I present them to the appropriate authorities?" Jim said. "I need to be sure that we have established legitimate contact and established a basis for trade."

">>I shall ask,<<" Ixxie responded. ">>I shall leave you for the moment to deliberate.<<"

The two aliens backed out of the room and the door irised closed. Out of habit, Admiral Tsukino went to the door and pressed the plate that opened it. He made no comment when the door failed to open.

"I'm sure they'll have a good reason for that when we mention it," Jim assured him.

"Undoubtedly," the admiral agreed. "And now? What do we do?"

"Look around," Jim said. "There's nothing else to do until we can meet with someone with authority."

It took them less than five minutes to exhaust their attentions on the room. They returned to the table—identical to the ones that they'd had on *Xythir* and sat in the similarly identical chairs.

Jim pulled out his tablet and glanced through the briefs he'd written up. Admiral Tsukino, after a moment watching him, drew out his tablet, and started reading also.

"I'll give them thirty minutes," Jim said as he scrolled through another page of notes. "And then?"

"Then I'm all for testing how strong these chairs are against those iris doors," Jim told him with a slight smile.

"It would be an interesting experiment," the admiral agreed blandly.

* * *

"Well, sirs, here's the thing, we might have been shopping in the local supermarket," Louise O'Reilly said as she placed the evening meal on the table of their wardroom. "I've got spaghetti and salad complete with what appears to be a reasonable shredded parmesan."

"Meat sauce?" Jim said as he looked at the bubbling bowl in front of them.

"Maybe it's soy but I couldn't tell," Louise said. "Our little greenies gave me a nutritional breakdown but got awfully quiet when it came to a precise source."

"We've stocked up with grains, meats, fruits, vegetables, pretty much anything a healthy American might want," Emily added. She nodded toward Admiral Tsukino, "Even miso soup."

"Not exactly what I'd call typically American, but I'm glad," Admiral Tsukino said, ostentatiously filling his bowl with noodles and topping it with spaghetti sauce.

"Any wine with that?" Jim asked wistfully.

"Oddly enough, no, sir," Louise said. "It appears our selection didn't go that far."

"Must be some planet, though, to have a whole market devoted to human foods," Jim said testily.

"Yeah, that is interesting," Emily agreed, "except that I got the impression that the market was supposed to be interstellar."

"Perhaps they decided to showcase human food in our honor," Admiral Tsukino suggested.

"Under similar circumstances, I think we would also display our culinary specialties as well, in the hopes of opening up new markets," Jim observed. "You know hot dogs—"

"Got them!" Louise interjected.

"—and hamburgers—"

"Got them, too!"

"Apple pie?" Jim asked.

"Oddly enough, no," Emily said. She glanced toward Louise. "You'd think that would be on their list."

"I suppose they can't make everything," Louise allowed with a shrug, "and apple pie is pretty complex, requiring eggs, and flour and all sorts of stuff ..." She broke off thoughtfully, then said, "You know, I don't think I saw any eggs there."

"I'd be very surprised if they had those," Jim allowed. After a moment, he added, "Probably no fish, either."

"Yes, sir," Louise agreed, frowning thoughtfully.

"There might be some things that they find distasteful," Admiral Tsukino allowed.

"What was surprising is the total lack of anything *but* human foods," Emily said, "and, for that matter, they were all American cuisine."

"Well, for what we are about to receive," Jim said, dipping a fork into his bowl. He took a bite and groaned in pleasure. "That's very good!"

"It's missing something, isn't it?" Admiral Tsukino asked.

"No onions," Louise said. "Nor mushrooms. Garlic, though."

"I suppose beggars can't be choosers," Emily said, taking another bite of her salad. "The salad is good."

"Only an oil and vinegar dressing," Louise apologized.

"Yeah, they were very sorry that we didn't want to buy their ranch dressing," Emily recalled.

"And who was they, Captain?" Admiral Tsukino asked.

"Gharm, mostly," Emily said. "In fact, I think the whole floor was serviced by Gharm."

"Gharm?"

"Noxor said that they are robots working for Centercomp," Emily said carefully. "They looked very much like a robotic version of what you'd get if you crossed a Xlern and a Yon."

A momentary shudder swept through the room, dismissed silently.

"Interesting," Jim said after he'd recovered. "Perhaps the Gharm are designed to be multi-functional—usable by both Xlern and Yon computer systems without alteration."

Nikolai paused with his fork mid-way to his mouth, then nodded. After he'd swallowed, he said, "That would be efficient."

"If true, however …" Jim said, letting his voice trail off.

"And how did your day go, sir?" Emily said when it became apparent that the ambassador would say nothing more.

"It went very well," Jim said. "Admiral Tsukino managed to get himself to level seven on his Sudoku Challenge and I beat the computer at chess four times." He frowned, then added, "I hope tomorrow will be more productive."

"And if not …?"

"If not," Jim said with a sigh, "then I think it will be time to take a more assertive position."

"We are guests," Admiral Tsukino said slowly.

"We are here to make a deal," Jim replied. "It is not possible to deal unless there is someone to deal with."

"What are your plans for tomorrow?" Admiral Tsukino said to the others.

"I thought, sir, that the plan was to visit their medical facilities, if possible," Louise O'Reilly replied, keeping her voice free of the tone that countless noncommissioned officers used to remind their superiors of what needed doing.

"I think, PO," Admiral Tsukino said in measured tones, "if you don't mind, I'll accompany you."

"I could keep the ambassador company," Emily offered. There was a moment's tension as the others considered this—allowing the two Americans to be solely responsible for negotiations—then Admiral Tsukino shrugged.

"I can loan you my Sudoku app."

* * *

Harmonie

Admiral Wang led the meeting. Captain Lee represented *Harmonie*, while Mac was there for *Voyager*. But the stars of the meeting were Commander Karl Geister and Lieutenant Peter Murray, representing the theory and practical teams that were aboard the Yon ship.

"And you're certain about this?" John Lee asked Peter Murray, after he and Geister had finished their reports.

"Yes, sir," Peter Murray told him. "We're certain we've got a good grasp on the theory, and the practical side of things aren't really all that difficult." He shrugged. "In fact, they are less demanding than the leap to produce the Amuksli drive."

"Not really a surprise," Mac said. Admiral Wang glanced at him. The Chinese admiral was a master of the impassive look, but John McLaughlin had decided that he was basically a technocrat at heart, not a political appointee. The admiral, John thought to himself, knew how to lead without being overbearing. The law of averages demanded that the project get at least one bad commander, but so far Jupiter seemed blessed in picking only winners. Even Captain Lee, whom Mac had previously regarded as something of a stick-in-the-mud, had proved himself capable of allowing others more gifted to do their job—and he was man enough to give credit where credit was due.

"The first leap is the hardest, usually," Mac explained.

"I agree," Admiral Wang said, his words being echoed in English translation by Mick Hsu. The admiral glanced at Lieutenant Murray. "And how long will it take to produce a working prototype, given *Voyager* is no longer available?"

"A week," Murray declared. Anticipating their surprise, he continued, "That's assuming we can cannibalize the *Voyager* for instrumentation and controls. The aliens have some truly marvelous extrusion systems and, when you get down to it, the bulk of the living quarters of any ship is fundamentally some sort of hollow structure."

"They say they can build a ship in a week?" Captain Lee repeated, not quite trusting his ears.

"We could build equipment to do that, sir," John McLaughlin said. "In fact, if anyone will listen to me after this, I'd recommend that we consider setting up extrusion facilities on the Moon and Phobos—they're probably the best locations we've got."

"What would that entail, precisely?" Admiral Wang said. Then he allowed a frown to cross his expression, adding, "Please do not answer at the moment but rather when there is time."

"Actually, sir, you've got Ensigns Dubauer and Sato there now. They could probably get your people pointed in the right direction," Mac told him with a shrug. "It's not something that happens in a week, though. I imagine it'd take months to get such a facility fully operational."

"And you'd loan them that long?" Admiral Wang said in surprise.

"They're not mine to loan, sir," Mac replied with a shrug, "but I imagine there's going to be a lot of international cooperation going around, and as they're there in the first place, it might be a good idea to suggest it to a higher authority."

"Ensign Sato is employed by the Japanese Space Service," Lieutenant Fukui reminded them.

"And Lori Dubauer is U.S. Navy," Captain Lee said in oblique agreement. To Admiral Wang, he said, "I can put in a request when we send the next communiqué Earthside."

"That won't be necessary," Admiral Wang replied blandly. "I think we should wait until the first jump of this new ship—and what shall we call it?"

"Speaking for the U.S. Navy, sir, I think we're willing to take your suggestion," Captain Lee told him diplomatically.

"I'd say the same for Europe and Russia," Karl Geister added.

"If I may, sir," Mac spoke up, "I'd like to reserve the obvious United States Navy name for a future ship."

Admiral Wang looked at him for a moment as he thought, then nodded. "I imagine that *would* be a point of pride," he allowed. He sat back and then leaned forward again. "If this doesn't sound too presumptuous, how about we christen her *Unity*?"

"Works for me," Mac said, glancing around the table. "I suppose the other question is who will command it?"

"Given that most of the equipment is going to be cannibalized from your ship, Lieutenant, I'd say the answer is obvious," Captain Lee told him with a bland smile.

"You *are* currently the only official representative of the United Nations Navy, Lieutenant," Admiral Wang agreed.

John McLaughlin sat back in his chair and blew out a sigh. "Oh, boy."

* * *

The White House, Washington, DC

"The stock market is down 10%, consumer confidence has plummeted—everyone's holding their breath," Brian McPhee said as he surmised the current situation to the group gathered in the Oval Office. "And people are beginning to wonder what's up with the vice president."

"I thought we told them," President Merritt replied testily.

"We did but his supporters are agitating against us," McPhee replied with a grimace.

"Well, they can just wait, we've got bigger fish to fry," President Merritt reminded him.

"The biggest worry, frankly, is that this whole United Nations Navy that Pickett sprang," John Ellington opined. "People are afraid that our navy is going to defect wholesale."

"I thought we made it clear that that didn't happen," the president snapped.

"We did, but then this Chinese admiral tells us that the first *working* interstellar ship is going to be a UN ship," Ellington replied unhappily.

"And people see that as a slap in the face to our national pride," Anne Byrne, the White House press secretary added.

"We're going to stress that while it's got an international crew, Captain McLaughlin is an American," McPhee said. "That seemed to play well with test audiences."

"So what's going to turn things around?" Greg Merritt said, scanning the faces of his cabinet.

"That's hard to say," McPhee admitted with a sour look. "We're never going to appease those of Alquay's party who want things back to the way they were. Industry's scared the aliens will out produce it and, contrary to everything, people are still afraid the aliens will invade and destroy us all."

"That's nice, Brian, you told me what's happening but *not* how to fix it," Merritt snapped. "Who's got that answer?"

"The best bet, sir," Ron Grimminger, the White House science advisor, said into the silence, "is if we can somehow show we're smarter than these aliens; that we can beat them at their own game."

"That'll be some trick!" George Morgan, secretary of defense, groused. "How would that work, do you think? Will they just give us everything and run away?"

"Even that wouldn't work," McPhee said glumly. The others turned to him. "What has to happen is that we show these guys that we're not only as good as they are but *better*."

"There's more to it than that, Brian," Greg Merritt said, his lips pursed. The others looked at him. "No matter what happens, this is a game-changer. Things are never going to be the same. We *know* there are aliens; we *know* they've got star drives. Our people have to start looking forward to a future with aliens, a future with interstellar ships, and all that will mean."

"What will it mean, sir?" Brian McPhee asked him somberly.

"It'll mean that we're going to have a whole new set of rules to learn before we can expect to win," President Merritt replied.

"And the one guy out there learning them is the drunk we left stranded up on the Moon," Navy Secretary Elijah Wood muttered sourly.

"Yeah," Greg Merritt said with a snort, "lucky us."

He sat back at his table and stared up to the ceiling for a long while. Then, when he leaned forward again, there was a new light in his eyes.

"Annie, listen carefully," he said to his press secretary. "This nation was founded by those who dared cross great distances, risk great dangers, people who were willing to boldly risk all. As Americans, we are proud to be at the forefront of this new frontier and we will lead the way into this new world … these new *worlds*, bringing with us the hopes, dreams, and faith that our forefathers bestowed upon us. People of America, this is a new day. This is the dawn of a great adventure, the sort of adventure that led the down-trodden to a new land, the sort of adventure that will bring Americans to new worlds, new heights, new frontiers, and new glories …"

The others leaned forward in their chairs like moths to a flame as the president continued drafting his greatest speech.

* * *

Xythir

>>**Captain Nexl, we have a report from the** *Ynoyon*,<< Communications Officer Exern reported.

>>**And?**<<

>>**The stumblers are building their Yunuffili ship.**<<

>>**They are ahead of schedule!**<< Captain Nexl rapped harshly.

>>**The** *Ynoyon* **reports they are three weeks ahead of schedule. Their captain; requires you to expedite,**<< Communications Officer Exern reported. >>**Their captain requires a response.**<<

>>**And what else can I say?**<< Nexl demanded. >>**Tell them that we will move things up.**<<

>>**I had always thought that the stumblers would prove adept,**<< Communications Officer Exern observed as he prepared the response, >>**but I would never have guessed** *how* **adept!**<<

>>**It only moves time forward, Communications Officer,**<< Captain Nexl responded. >>**Our plan remains.**<<

>>**It shall be a relief to be freed of our burden,**<< Exern agreed.

>>**Indeed,**<< Nexl responded. >>**When you're done with the message, send a chime to Security Officer Noxor, informing him of the increased pace.**<<

>>**It shall be done, Captain Nexl!**<<

* * *

Thraxis IV

"Finally!" Jim Pickett swore as he and Captain Steele were escorted into a new room. The doors irised wide and Noxor led the way. Both would have preferred to have Trade Officer Ixxie with them, but apparently the two decided to switch off that day. "This is going to be something."

They both stopped as they entered the room. Emily turned to him and said, "Was this the something you expected?"

"It looks straight out of a Perry Mason episode," Pickett said, eyeing the wooden benches, the low railing separating the spectators from the actual chamber, the raised platform and the judge's chair. Pickett glanced around. "But this is *definitely* not a trade legation or anything of the sort."

He turned to the alien. "Security Officer Noxor, I wonder if I was sufficiently clear in my request to present my credentials and established diplomatic relations."

">>**We need a contract,**<<" Noxor replied. ">>**This is where contracts are signed.**<<"

"Not even on TV," Emily murmured.

Jim Pickett turned around and headed back to the iris-door.

">>**Where are you going?**<<" Noxor called after him.

"Out!" Pickett called over his shoulder. With a start, Emily jogged to catch up with him. The door closed before the alien could follow them.

"Quickly," Pickett said to her, "knock on every door until you find someone. You take the left; I'll take the right."

They raced off, pausing only long enough for the doors to iris open and check quickly inside before moving to the next room.

">>**Wait! Halt!**<<" Noxor cried at them. ">>**Come back here!**<<"

Pickett waved but did not pause. They reached the end of the hall and the last door set in the middle.

">>**Don't go there!**<<" Noxor boomed after them.

Pickett ignored him, pressing the plate next to the door. It irised open and they stepped through.

"Wait a minute!" Emily cried. "I've been here! This is the marketplace!"

"Come on," Pickett called, racing past her, "run!"

They ran across the now empty marketplace to the far side.

"Did you go through this door?" Jim said as they reached the end.

"I can't be sure," Emily said, panting. "I don't think so."

Pickett pressed the plate and they stepped through, Noxor following far in the distance.

On the far side they halted, eyes wide with astonishment.

"Captain! Mr. Ambassador! What are you doing here?" Louise O'Reilly cried.

">>**Where is Security Officer Noxor?**<<" Trade Officer Ixxie asked.

"Where is this place?" Pickett said.

"We're at their medical facilities," O'Reilly replied. "Where did you come from, sir?"

"We just came through the marketplace," Emily told her and the others. "Before that, we were in the courthouse."

"This is a scam," Pickett declared.

"Pardon?" Louise O'Reilly said.

"Movie sets; the court room was straight out of Perry Mason," Pickett said. "And you know about the marketplace."

"Perhaps they built them to make us feel at home," Nikolai Zhukov suggested.

"I'd buy that except then you'd expect them to negotiate with us, to let me present credentials," Pickett said, shaking his head. He looked for and found what appeared to be a normal plastic chair, the sort commonly found in hospitals in old television shows. He took a seat and put his head in his hands.

"Sir?" Emily said. When he didn't respond, she said, "Jim?"

Pickett looked up and then sprang up from his chair, sending it skittering across the floor away from him. "It's a scam," he said. "They must have hoped that we'd be so eager to sign that we wouldn't stay long—"

"Then why didn't they meet us yesterday?" Admiral Tsukino wondered. "We spent the whole day waiting."

"I think I threw them off with my diplomatic credentials," Jim said. "Try as they might, they couldn't find that in any TV show—"

"Sir," Louise O'Reilly began slowly, "that seems a bit *much* if you don't mind my saying."

"Is it?" Pickett mused. "Let's see …"

He turned as Security Officer Noxor entered the room.

"Nope, no guns," Pickett said, pointing at the alien. "Didn't you get the impression that the security officer was a bit paranoid?"

"It's his job," Emily explained. Then she frowned. "And he's not doing it."

"Nope," Pickett agreed with a smile, "he certainly isn't." He turned to Louise. "Which means, PO, that I'm right."

"The aliens are scamming us?" Louise said in amazement. "Why?"

"*That*, PO, is the multi-trillion-dollar question," Pickett told her with a smile. He turned to Noxor. "Security Officer Noxor, I demand to speak with Captain Nexl immediately."

"**>>Captain Nexl has requested that you and your party return to the** *Xythir* **as soon as is convenient for you,<<**" Noxor replied. "**>>Captain Nexl has authorized me to<<**"—he paused and seemed to continue only with difficulty—"**>>apologize for our recent actions.<<**"

"Apologize?" Pickett said, scowling, "I should think so!"

"**>>As indicated, Captain Nexl has authorized me to apologize on behalf of the Combine and to assure you that this was a necessary step in negotiations,<<**" Noxor responded.

"Necessary? How?"

"**>>Captain Nexl has informed me that he will explain at the appropriate time,<<**" Noxor replied. "**>>If you will accompany us, we will return to your quarters so that you may retrieve your equipment before we board** *Xythir*.**<<**"

"You hold us hostage to your ship, Security Officer Noxor, a position which I find an intolerable insult among equals," Jim swore. "It is hard to imagine that we are getting a fair deal under such circumstances!"

">>**Please,**<<" Noxor responded, seeming quite distraught.

"I think, Mr. Ambassador," Admiral Tsukino said in a soft voice, "that we should do as requested."

* * *

Xythir

">>**Captain Nexl will be here shortly,**<<" Engineer Officer Axlu said as the group gathered outside their quarters. ">>**Captain Nexl apologizes for the necessary ruse and says that all will be revealed at the appropriate time.**<<"

"He sent Axlu and Xover to placate us," Pickett observed sourly. "We had Noxor and Ixxie to intimidate us."

"Should we consider ourselves your prisoners, then?" Emily demanded.

">>**Prisoners implies either illegal activities or a state of hostility,**<<" Axlu responded. ">>**Neither exist in our thinking.**<<"

"If we're not prisoners, then I'd like to speak with Admiral Wang and Captain Lee aboard *Harmonie*," Admiral Tsukino replied.

"And *I* would like a direct link to the White House," Pickett demanded.

">>**Is not that the capital of one nation and not of all?**<<" Axlu asked.

"It doesn't matter; the information will be relayed," Pickett spat out.

"Mr. Ambassador," Emily said, moving to lay a soothing hand on his shoulder.

Jim Pickett jerked his shoulder away in a display of anger. "Either we communicate with whom we wish, when we wish, or we must consider ourselves your prisoners. If we are prisoners, I am unable to enter into any negotiations with your Combine."

"And what is this Combine?" Nikolai Zhukov added. "Why was this not mentioned earlier?"

">>**These are not questions I can answer,**<<" Axlu replied. ">>**I can tell you that your people have succeeded in grasping the theory and technology required to produce the Yunuffili drive and have begun to extrude the hull for their new ship.**<<"

"Really?" Emily said, glancing toward Nikolai. "And how soon will this ship be ready?"

">>**Less than a week, I understand,**<<" Axlu responded. ">>**I have been told that your Lieutenant McLaughlin will be in command and that the vessel will be christened** *Unity*.<<"

"You have not answered me," Pickett said. "Will I be permitted to speak to the president of the United States?"

A door irised open and they all turned to view the new entrants. At the forefront was

Captain Nexl with its three sets of chimes. ">>**If you will follow me, I will bring you to our bridge,**<<" Nexl chimed, bowing forebody and forelimbs graciously.

"Will we all fit?" Nikolai asked, gesturing both to the whole party and then to their height.

">>**It would be uncomfortable, perhaps two of you would be willing to accompany me?**<<" Captain Nexl responded.

Pickett exchanged a sour look with Admiral Tsukino. The Asian's impassive response left the issue in the ambassador's hands. "Very well," Jim said. "Admiral Tsukino, do you wish to come?"

"I'd enjoy seeing the command deck of this ship, yes," Admiral Tsukino replied. He glared at Axlu for a moment then, added, "Provided that Engineer Officer Axlu will, on his honor, guard the safety of the others."

">>**I assure you, Admiral, that your people will be as safe as the rest of us,**<<" Captain Nexl chimed back.

"And how safe is that?" Nikolai asked.

">>**Not as safe as we would like,**<<" Captain Nexl admitted.

"When we get to the bridge, perhaps you'll care to explain this entire charade, Captain Nexl," Jim said.

The little eight-limbed alien seemed momentarily to flatten himself in a deep bow. ">>**Believe me, Ambassador Pickett, it shall be as great a relief to me as to you.**<<"

"What he doesn't say is why it'll be a relief," Emily muttered, as Pickett and the admiral followed the alien captain through the iris-door and out into the hallway.

* * *

">>**The journey will take a number of minutes as we must traverse half the distance of the ship,**<<" Captain Nexl said as he led them into an elevator.

"Does this give you enough time to brief us?" Jim said, taking that revelation in stride.

">>**Time enough to start,**<<" Nexl returned. He paused for a moment and then gave Jim a half-bow. ">>**You are correct in guessing that** *Thraxis IV* **was a 'scam.'**<<"

"Then you admit to negotiating in bad faith!" Admiral Tsukino said.

"Actually," Pickett said with a sour look, "we never *started* negotiations." His look darkened as he added, "Which, in itself, was bad faith."

">>**But you figured it out,**<<" Captain Nexl said. ">>**Which was required.**<<"

Pickett's brows furrowed as he considered that. "It was a test?"

">>**I think you would more correctly call it a validation,**<<" Captain Nexl replied. ">>**We proved to ourselves that you would not be willing to negotiate under unfavorable circumstances.**<<"

"I don't understand," Admiral Tsukino said, glancing to see if the ambassador had any ideas.

"I think, Admiral, that our friends wanted to prove that we were competent to enter into an agreement," Jim said, "which implies that there is some level of oversight into such dealings."

">>**It has been the cause of many grave injustices when first contacts are made,**<<" Captain Nexl chimed in agreement.

Admiral Tsukino nodded.

"If their legal system is sufficiently just, we could later sue for reparations," Jim surmised. He glanced toward the small alien captain. "And those reparations would not only be hefty but would probably include a bar from future trade."

">>**At the extreme, lives have been forfeited,**<<" Nexl chimed.

"That seems excessive," Jim said. His lips twisted upwards. "Did they have bad lawyers?"

">>**No,**<<" Captain Nexl chimed, ">>**they had honest lawyers.**<<" It paused to let the two humans absorb that for moment. ">>**In most cases, new alien species have proven to be the source of much innovation and invention. The addition to the intergalactic has been overwhelmingly positive.**<<"

"Right," Jim said.

"Winners refine, losers innovate," Admiral Tsukino murmured.

"Pardon?" Jim said.

"It is one of the lectures I gave at the Academy," Admiral Tsukino explained. "It's invariably the case that those with little or nothing to lose are willing to take greater risks. In war, this has translated to huge innovations."

">>**Such as your armored warfare in your Second World War,**<<" Captain Nexl chimed in agreement.

"I thought you were a trader," Jim said, giving the alien captain a suspicious look.

">>**Traders are often at the forefront of trade disagreements,**<<" Captain Nexl reminded him.

"And many traders hold reserve commissions in their military," Admiral Tsukino noted.

"So they can be eyes and ears," Jim murmured. He blew out a sigh. "I was kinda hoping that aliens would be above such politics."

">>**Politics deals with people,**<<" Nexl chimed back, adding an undertone of amusement, ">>**and all aliens consider themselves 'people.'**<<"

"So it's actually *worse*?" Jim groaned.

">>**It is somewhat more challenging,**<<" Captain Nexl admitted, ">>**but in my own experience it has also been more rewarding.**<<"

"Yeah, I always preferred working on trade deals than elections," Jim admitted. He pulled himself together. "So we're going to the real place now? And then what?"

">>**That is where things will get difficult,**<<" Nexl chimed.

"Because you pulled this little scam of yours," Jim said.

"I'm sure we'd be willing to forgive them their subterfuge, given how they helped our people in that medical emergency," the admiral declared.

"Not that scam," Jim said, shaking his head and waving a hand around them, indicating the ship and everyone in it, "*this* scam!"

">>**Which is?**<<"

"You tried to play us," Pickett said. "You tried to convince us that we had to go along with your invented emergency, but all along you were playing for different stakes, weren't you?"

Nexl's four upper limbs slowly fell to his sides, very much like a guilty child trying to make himself small and unseen.

"When all along you'd stolen from us and you had a list of *exactly* what you needed from us to get you off the hook for intergalactic copyright violation," Jim declared.

Nexl lifted his two fore-pikkis and chimed feebly in something untranslatable.

"But *that's* not even the real scam, is it, Captain?" Jim persisted.

The door irised open and Captain Nexl moved feebly unto the bridge. Jim Pickett followed on its rear limbs.

"Very perceptive Mr. Ambassador," Is-sa-to-li-ri, the five-headed Hydra Captain of *Ynoyon*, said as it moved toward them and away from the two other cowering Xlern. "And just what *was* our real scam?"

"You're not singing!" Jim declared, looking around the crowded room. There were separate areas which he was certain would be for navigation, communication, weapons, and propulsion but he had no way of distinguishing one from the other. There was a large display on one wall, which at the moment seemed to be filled with slithering symbols. Pickett ignored them after idly deciding that they might be a form of Yon writing.

"It presented an unfair advantage," Is-sa-to-li-ri said. "What you are hearing is a modulated system based on the Gharm's Centercomp."

"Which any of you could have used all along," Jim said, lips pulled tight in anger.

"We could," the Yon captain allowed. "And if so, we would not be here before you now." It paused for a moment, two of its heads swiveling to join the third in giving the human their full attention while the two rearmost heads idly flicked and hissed in the general direction of the Xlern. "Our species is the result of some very amazing serendipities."

Jim froze as his brain raced ahead to a conclusion that had been slowly building over the past several days. "When did the Pao V artifact leave your home world?"

The two side heads snapped around to gaze directly at him, frozen in surprise, while the middle head wagged slightly.

Pickett turned his attention to Nexl. "Did it go to your world then?"

"The Pao V?" Admiral Tsukino repeated.

"On Earth it was called the Ark of the Covenant," Jim said.

"That was only one of its forms," Is-sa-to-li-ri replied. "The Pao V is one of the most closely guarded secrets in the known multiverse."

"So why did you tell us about it?" Jim asked. And then he blew out a sigh. "Holy shit, Gliese 581!"

"Mr. Ambassador?" Admiral Tsukino said.

"Admiral, that's it!" Pickett said. "That's *why* the whole scam! That's why it's so easy to give us everything!" He banged his fist against his head, then lowered it so that he could bite his thumb in concentration. When he looked up again, his eyes were burning bright and locked on Is-sa-to-li-ri. "Does this happen every time? Does the Pao V create intelligent species on every planet?"

">>**It is not always successful,**<<" Captain Nexl chimed. He shuffled slightly toward Jim and Is-sa-to-li-ri.

"How?" Admiral Tsukino asked.

"Not all black holes are old," Jim guessed. "Or maybe just neutron stars, I don't know."

"Fire is one of the common elements," Is-sa-to-li-ri said. "And all species who play with fire learn that it can burn."

"We sent a goddamned message to Gliese 581!" Jim cried. "And they got it!"

"We got it," Is-sa-to-li-ri told him.

"And *that's* why you came!" Jim cried triumphantly.

"Why does the message matter?" Admiral Tsukino asked, glancing from Pickett, to the Xlern, and then to the Yon in hopes of enlightenment.

"There are rules against contacting a species that doesn't have interstellar flight," Jim said. His brows furrowed and he said to Is-sa-to-li-ri, "You've been monitoring our communications for a long time, haven't you?"

">>**Ever since your first transmissions were detected,**<<" Captain Nexl agreed.

"But *they* contacted us and we don't have interstellar flight," Admiral Tsukino blurted.

Jim turned to him, his expression bleak. "But Admiral, there are exceptions to every rule." He didn't wait for a reply, before turning to Is-sa-to-li-ri, "And those exceptions are usually for extraordinary circumstances."

"And come with grave consequences," Is-sa-to-li-ri agreed. Then their three forward-looking heads converged for a moment to form a strange triangular array before moving apart again, the middle one still nodding slowly as the alien Hydra said, "Sometimes also with serendipitous results."

"We were lucky," Jim said. He narrowed his eyes. "There's never been a five-headed Yon before, has there?"

"Never," Is-sa-to-li-ri agreed, "but I expect only to be the first of many." Their forward-looking heads again bracketed Jim with their gaze as the Yon's tone grew amused, "If nothing else, Jim, you'll have a job as a Yon tosser."

"If I do, I'll want hazard pay," Jim replied without hesitation. He had the distinct impression that the Yon Hydra was amused by his response. Then a new thought struck him. "Were you here all this time?"

"No," the Yon captain replied, "I only arrived when Captain Nexl called."

"Which means that you took less than a day to get here," Jim surmised. "Which means that even that super drive you've taught us how to make isn't the best."

">>**Well, naturally,**<<" Captain Nexl replied, seeming shocked at the notion that they'd provide the best star drive for free.

"So you're here," Jim said, returning to the latest subject. "Does that mean my people are here with that new ship of theirs?"

"No."

"When will they get here?" Admiral Tsukino asked.

"They aren't coming here," Is-sa-to-li-ri replied.

"I thought you said they had built the new drive," Jim said, turning his attention back to the Yon captain.

"They have," Is-sa-to-li-ri said. "And they are now on their maiden voyage." Its two outer heads executed a set of gyrating maneuvers and Jim thought that it seemed like the yellow-pink heads with the gold yellow eyes were amused in an I've-got-a-secret sort of way.

">>**We're going to meet them,**<<" Captain Nexl said.

"They're going to your capital or wherever your main intergalactic law courts are," Jim guessed. "We'll just happen to meet them when they make their debut to the whole galaxy."

"Multiverse," Is-sa-to-li-ri corrected almost absently. "But yes, that is the plan."

"Lucky for you," Jim said.

"Ambassador Pickett, if there's one thing we've learned across the times, it's that only the lucky survive," Is-sa-to-li-ri told him. "Once there, we'll be able to guide you through the accreditation process and enter into a proper legal contract including trade and reparations."

"Well, I hope you guys have good lawyers," Jim told them with a toothy grin.

"Why?" Is-sa-to-li-ri asked in surprise.

"Because," Jim said, his grin expanding, "before I entered politics, I was a lawyer." He paused for a moment. "And I'm going to take you to the cleaners."

CHAPTER TWENTY-ONE

"OKAY, WE'RE READY," ACTING LIEUTENANT-COMMANDER JOHN McLAUGHLIN of the United Nations Navy told the People's Liberation Army's Navy Admiral Wang. *Unity's* bridge was immense compared to any ever before controlled by men in space. Mac was glad of the room, partly the result of his own decision that the ship should be built with upgrades in mind—he had a notion that *Unity* might find itself engaged in exploration in the near future, and he wanted *lots* of room for the sensors suites he was hoping Ambassador Pickett—or at least Admiral Tsukino—would acquire from the aliens.

Unity was also built with politics in mind, so Mac had been careful to design in a special station for superior officers, as well as an admiral command deck and spacious quarters. Or, if not an admiral, then an ambassador.

Of course, at this moment, the admiral was making use of the extra seating that had been built into the command bridge so that he could view events firsthand.

"Very well, you may proceed," Admiral Wang said, his words ably translated by Mick Hsu.

Sergeant Yin was not in evidence, having been asked to hold himself in readiness down in the second command deck. It was something of a sop to his pride, Mac guessed, but it was also not a complete sinecure. The Sergeant would never equal Mick Hsu in his ability to understand or manage complex engineering systems, but the Chinese sergeant was able to learn how to perform rote tasks at speed and was not so prideful that he couldn't accept his status.

"Engineering, this is the captain," Mac said, still feeling odd about identifying himself that way. Admiral Wang glanced in his direction, and Mac had the feeling that the Chinese admiral had read his emotions, but he said nothing.

"Engineering, Lieutenant Murray," a clipped English voice responded.

"Ready when you are, Pete," Mac told him.

"I feel obliged by past history to try on a Scots accent and inform you that our propulsion systems are not able," Murray quipped, "but I'm no good at a Scots accent, and your guess is as good as mine about the engines."

Admiral Wang said something as Mick Hsu kept up his rapid-fire translation, and Mick laughed and responded before explaining to his skipper, "The admiral was just telling me that he grew up on *Star Trek*."

Mac grunted in agreement, then flicked open the comm unit. "*Harmonie*, this is *Unity*, we are prepared to translate."

"*Unity*, this is *Harmonie*," Commander Milano's Italian-accented voice came back immediately, "acknowledged."

"Good luck and Godspeed," Captain Lee's voice added on the transmission.

Mac looked over the panels one more time, then said, "Engineering, you may translate *now*."

* * *

Harmonie

"We've confirmed that *Unity* has gone," Commander Geister told Captain Lee.

"Captain! The aliens!" a new voice burst out. It was Lieutenant Cohen. "They're gone!"

Captain Lee brought up the display on his monitor and swore silently. A moment later he said, "Very well, make a note in the log and add it to our transmission to Earth." He stared at the display even as he worked to project the calm that was required of a commander. A moment later he added, "Let the science modules know and see if they've got anything they want to report."

"Aye, sir," Lieutenant Cohen replied in a small voice. Captain Lee turned to look at the lieutenant and nod significantly to the other crewmen. Cohen started as he caught the captain's silent rebuke and nodded, lips tight. "I'm sure they're probably just as curious as we are," he added in a more positive tone.

"Well no one was expecting it," Lee said, "but all our instrumentation was tuned for *Unity's* departure, so maybe we'll pick something up on the *Ynoyon's* movements, too."

Well, Captain Lee thought to himself, *it's just gotten mighty lonely up here. Still,* Harmonie *has a mission, a crew, and the fuel necessary to complete it.*

Captain Lee sat back in his seat and closed his eyes for a moment. When he opened them again, he stood up, stretched ostentatiously, and said, "I'm going to my quarters."

"Aye, sir," Commander Milano, the designated officer of the watch, replied, "I have the conn."

* * *

Xythir

"Well, where are they?" Jim Pickett demanded as he paced in front of the large viewing screen.

"They will come," Is-sa-to-li-ri assured him.

"Do you mean the *Unity* or the greeting party?" Emily Steele asked. Jim and Admiral Tsukino — who was now going by his first name, Isao, at the request of Is-sa-to-li-ri—had returned to the quarters module and given the news to the others. The alien and the admiral seemed to have developed an understanding when Pickett wasn't watching. After the dust had settled, Pickett had decided not to report back to Earth immediately, preferring to wait at least until the *Unity* arrived.

Now that the ship was due to arrive, Jim and Emily were up on the command deck while the others took what rest they could in preparation for what the aliens insisted would be a rather momentous occasion.

"Don't you get new species all the time?" Isao had asked Is-sa-to-li-ri.

"No," the Yon Hydra had replied, "about once every five or six thousand of your years when we're lucky."

"And when you're not lucky?" Jim had asked.

"We get another black hole or neutron star," Is-sa-to-li-ri had replied bleakly. "Which is why we were glad you were lucky."

">>**Sensors report a growing ripple,**<<" Engineer Officer Axlu now reported.

"Is that our ship?"

"Probably," Is-sa-to-li-ri replied. "There is no way to determine origin until after translation."

*   *   *

Unity

"Transition complete, all systems normal, Admiral," Mac reported as soon as he was sure everything was properly in hand. "Scanners activated."

"We've got a positive ID on the star," Ensign Sally Norman, another convert to Ambassador Pickett's impulsively created United Nations Navy, reported. "It matches the signature we were given by the Yon."

"We're picking up transmissions," Midshipman Saxon reported in a pleasant English accent.

"Pete, how are we standing with the engines?" Mac called over the comm.

"Ready when you are, set for return to Jupiter orbit just as ordered," Peter Murray replied. With a tone of awe, he added, "Mac, this ship is *built!*"

"Yeah," Mac agreed with a deep sigh, "that she is."

Admiral Wang said something and Mac looked toward him, waiting for Mick Hsu to translate, "She is the first of many, but I hope she is the last not built by humans."

"I agree absolutely," Mac replied with feeling. "I'm thrilled as punch that the eetees decided to let us have this technology, but I'll be a *lot* happier when we can build it all ourselves."

Still, much of the internal equipment and life support was gear cannibalized from *Voyager*. Idly, Mac wondered what would happen to that hulk. The micro-cracks were sufficient to render her nothing more than a museum piece. She'd done her job well; she didn't deserve to be scrapped. Idly, Mac entertained the notion that a bit of this extruded alien material might not be all that was needed to return the basic hull to space-worthiness. It might make a nice run-about for someone, say a peripatetic explorer with a crew crazy enough to follow her anywhere. Although—

"*Unity, Unity,* this is Captain Emily Steele aboard the *Xythir,*" a voice piped up over the comm system. "We'd like to be the first to congratulate you on your amazing voyage."

"Sonuvabitch!" Sally Norman swore, stealing the words before Mac could use them himself.

"*Xythir*, this is *Unity*, thank you very much," Mac replied with a baleful glance toward Norman.

"On behalf of the Xlern/Yon Combine, we'd like to welcome you to Nervashun, the galaxy's legal center," Ambassador Pickett spoke up over the link. "I understand that Admiral Wang Banai is aboard. I'd like to invite him and you, Captain McLaughlin, to join us on *Xythir* where we'll meet up before going planetside."

Planetside? Mac thought in alarm.

"Still think that uniform was a good idea, sir?" Ensign Norman murmured from her seat at the navigation console.

Mac kept himself from growling at her.

"Mr. Ambassador, if you give us a few minutes to sort things out here, we'll be happy to join you," Mac said, glancing toward Admiral Wang for agreement. "I'll have Mick Hsu join us, if you don't mind."

"The more the merrier," Pickett agreed blandly. "Oh, by the way—"

"Jesus!" Sally Norman swore in surprise. She recovered quickly. "Sir, I've got a new contact, massing twenty-three plus megatons and—" she broke off and swore again "—it's the *Ynoyon*." Sally shook her head as she added, "They're about two kilometers off our port side, sir."

"Hotshots," Peter Murray muttered.

"I was about to say," Pickett continued, "that the *Ynoyon* will be joining us." He paused for a moment perhaps in silent apology. "Please come aboard as soon as possible. We've got a lot to discuss and very little time."

Admiral Wang said something in Chinese and Mick Hsu sniggered. Mac glared at him, and the chief colored, explaining, "The admiral says that the aliens seem to relish grand entrances and short fuses."

"Yeah," Mac said, glancing toward the nav display with the huge alien ship clearly in view, "I get that, too."

* * *

Descent to Nervashun

"We need to get these, too, sir," Mac said to Jim Pickett as they watched the view from the ports of the shuttle which was silently and descending quickly into the alien skies.

"Absolutely," Jim agreed. He tapped his shirt pocket, adding, "It's already on the list."

"Is it a big list?"

Pickett smiled and shook his head. "Just a big bill, son, that's all we need to start with."

"I still say I'd be more use going back to Jupiter than coming down here," Mac muttered. He glanced out the window again. "Not that I'm complaining about the view."

"As soon as we're done the preliminaries, I'll let you go, Mac," Jim told him. When he saw the newly-minted commander's relief, he added, "But you're to come right back after you've reported and *whatever* you do, you're not to go to Earth."

"Phobos, but not Earth," Mac said with a nod. "You already said that."

"It bears repeating," Jim said. He looked away and found Emily Steele's piercing blue eyes gazing at him. He smiled at her but she gave him a pinched look and a shake of her head—she could guess what he must be going through at the moment.

">>Two more minutes,>>" Captain Nexl chimed in warning.

"Okay, everyone, this is the day we get out of kindergarten," Jim said, turning to the collected people in the spacious cabin. "We need to be on our best behavior and remember that we are not being threatened."

"Of course, just because they look like the Devil himself doesn't mean we should be afraid," Nikolai Zhukov remarked.

"Yeah," Pickett agreed. "And don't forget, according to Captain Nexl here, they're more afraid of us than we are of them."

"I still can't believe their sun," Mac muttered, as they broke through the clouds to be bathed in an unnerving red glow.

"Theirs is a more active world than ours," Jim reminded everyone.

"Which is why they can manage the seven limbs," Louise O'Reilly said. Despite Pickett's pleas, the PO had refused her offer of a commission into the fledgling United Nations Navy, just as she had refused Captain Steele's offer of a commission as ensign.

"I'm happy the way I am," O'Reilly had told the both of them. Emily had promoted her to petty officer, regardless, saying, "You've earned it just on this experience alone, Louise, so I'll have no argument on that score."

">>**One minute,**<<" Captain Nexl reported.

"Okay, everyone, remember that they're going to be gawking at us just as much as we're going to be gawking at them," Jim said. "If you get too overwhelmed, just get close to Xover or Ixxie and they'll get you out."

The two Xlern were wearing special brassards which crisscrossed over their bodies.

"Remember that Security Officer Noxor and Security Apprentice Doxal are our bodyguards," Jim finished as the shuttle bumped gently onto the ground. "We're to stick with them, not just for our safety but because they understand the environmental limits."

Nervashun, unlike Thraxis IV, was a full planet with a gravity somewhat less than Earth's—far greater than Pickett's body could handle and so he in particular had to be careful to stay within the bounds where gravity was controlled.

">>**Hatch secured. Equalizing,**<<" Engineer Apprentice Xover reported. ">>**All systems correct. We may exit.**<<"

"Captain Nexl, what's the correct order here?" Jim asked. "Should I go first, or you?"

">>**Security Officer Noxor will lead, followed by Security Apprentice Doxal,**<<"

Nexl responded. ">>**They will let us know when to egress.**<<"

It had been agreed, after a hasty consultation with all the captains and admirals, that Is-sa-to-li-ri would not descend with them. The Yon was their reserve and wished, if possible, to preserve news of its five-headed existence until the appropriate time.

A moment later, Nexl chimed, ">>**They are ready. Are you?**<<"

"Showtime, folks!" Jim called over his shoulder as he stepped briskly out of the shuttle and into the walkway that led into the spaceport proper.

Jim emerged into a large room, quite unlike most airport gateways and more like the rooms on Earth specially built for receiving dignitaries. But it was not the room that caught his attention, it was the aliens. And their noise.

It seemed that some inkling—at the very least—of their world of origin had leaked, or been leaked, because Jim found himself looking at all sorts of strange attempts to re-create an Earth-style greeting and welcome. Some were simply large banners amusingly misworded such as "Earthman home come!" and "New world founding!"

Jim nodded, waved, and bowed as he felt appropriate even as Noxor and Doxal formed a strangely formidable bow wave in front of him. The crowds parted easily enough. Jim found himself and the others bustled onto a simple gravity craft that silently led them off through the building and out into a special area which screamed "Customs and Security."

Apparently, their arrival had been cleared already. Even so, the humans were sent through some form of de-lousing or similar bright light zone. Afterward they were escorted into a bubble-domed grav-car and led on the alien version of a ticker-tape parade to a huge building at the outskirts of what appeared to be an enormous metropolis, dwarfing the late New York City in height, grandeur, area, and style.

The grav-car docked, and Jim followed Noxor and Doxal out and into a waiting area, which was separated from the rest of the building by a transparent bubble.

">>**It is necessary for your safety from bacteria and other microscopic organisms,**<<" Security Officer Noxor rapped.

Jim got the impression that the Xlern wasn't quite sure whom the wall was protecting from whom—or what.

He knew that before any negotiations or treaties could occur, he had to present his credentials and have them accepted by the Star Council of Nervashun. The Star Council, Nexl assured him, was an interstellar body similar to Earth's United Nations.

Jim had carefully created his credentials, using chosen words from the many correspondences he'd received from Earth. There had never been an Ambassador Extraordinary and Plenipotentiary sent from the United Nations before and, Jim suspected, there were probably still some very vociferous arguments over whether that had *actually* happened or whether the United States had pulled a fast one on the rest of the world, to which said "rest" were only now beginning to understand.

The finished document looked like nothing Jim had ever seen before, partly because it was printed on the Xlern extruders. In fact, the formal "paperwork" was secondary to the official electronic transcripts which were provided by the Xlern, and included extensive notes on the human technology and possessions.

">>**Let's hope they don't decide to incinerate us,**<<" Captain Nexl now chimed quietly.

"It would rather put a damper on the festivities," Jim agreed. "Also, I'd have to believe that your ambassadors—Xlern and Yon both—would have greased the wheels sufficiently ahead of time, or we wouldn't have gotten this far."

Still, it was strangely comforting to know that the little eight-limbed Xlern was having as much stage fright as Jim himself.

">>**We are moving to the center,**<<" Nexl chimed even as Jim felt the slight tug that informed him of their platform's departure from the surface.

"It looks like something out of *Star Wars*," Emily Steele muttered as their circular platform noiselessly moved into the center of a huge semi-spherical room. On all sides, they could see various alien representations and empty spaces where the representatives were absent on other business or elsewise engaged.

"How many?" Jim asked, partly out of curiosity but partly to give the others something to consider.

There was a silence for a moment and then Admiral Tsukino said, "At a rough count, there is room for a thousand different delegations."

">>**Not all of them are full,**<<" Captain Nexl chimed.

"Are they saving us a spot?" Captain Zhukov asked.

"I think that's what we're going to find out," Jim said.

">>**The central speaker will pose the question,**<<" Nexl chimed as their platform slowed and hovered just slightly below and off the center of the huge chamber.

"Ambassadors, we are convened to examine the credentials of one James Earl Pickett, Ambassador Extraordinary and Plenipotentiary for the United Nations of the planet Earth and its colonies in the solar system known to them as Sol," a voice spoke up in a pleasant contralto. "What say you?"

"I am given to understand that there are irregularities in the contact, some of which are identified with members of the Xlern and Yon under limited combine," a thin, reedy voice spoke up.

"Ambassador Yargan Isnuvla of Gihendi Prime," a different voice spoke in an undertone.

">>**The Centercomp is translating and identifying,**<<" Captain Nexl informed them.

"Who are the Gihendi?" Jim asked.

">>**They make the Gihendi jump drive, the best in the known galaxies,**<<" Engineer Officer Axlu chimed.

">>**They want the paperclip,**<<" Trade Officer Ixxie added.

"The paperclip?" Emily Steele exclaimed. "Why on Earth?"

"**>>Nothing to do with Earth,<<**" Axlu replied tersely. "**>>Most believe that it's got something to do with their drive but they won't say what.<<**"

"A paperclip is part of the most advanced star drive?" Nikolai said in wonder.

"**>>We believe that they modify the original shape,<<**" Axlu responded, "**>>but no one is certain.<<**"

"**>>Mr. Ambassador, they are waiting for you,<<**" Captain Nexl chimed.

Jim took a deep breath and stepped close to the edge of their platform. He felt, rather than heard, Captain Steele and Captain Zhukov advance on either side of him in unsolicited solidarity.

"I greet you," Jim said. "I greet you on this day which I never in my entire existence hoped to see.

"I greet you for my people, for those who have lived and died to bring our people the stars," he continued. "I greet you for those who find this one moment to be the single most terrifying event of their lives; the worst of all their fears.

"I greet you in the name of a world still divided, a world striving to build its first colonies, to understand its solar system.

"We are a young people and we have made mistakes. I hope we will make more mistakes—for the one thing our history has taught us is that only those who make mistakes can learn from them.

"We were contacted by first the Xlern ship *Xythir* and then the Yon ship *Ynoyon* after our first fusion powered ship reached the nearest of the four gas giant planets in our solar system and just as our first antimatter ship was readying for its maiden voyage. We were informed that we were contacted in error, that the combined signatures of our two different ships appeared to give off the signal of a star drive."

Jim paused for a moment. "We never believed that to be true. We were offered the technology and science behind not just one but two star drives on the proviso that we claimed to have invented the first ourselves and traded with the Xlern-Yon combine for the second." Jim allowed himself to smile. "Our alien 'friends' had a little list of items they would take in trade for their munificence.

"We never quite believed them even when, as a token of their intentions, they provided us with an emergency propulsion to return one of our sick personnel to our moon where she could receive proper medical care.

"Even then, we knew that we were at their mercy," Jim continued. "And now we are at your mercy. We are a new species; we have been given the stars; we are ready to engage in this wider realm, but we will only do so if we find that there is a rule of law here that we can rely upon to provide judgement for our grievances."

"We have a full briefing," the Gihendi ambassador said. "We are not concerned with legal proceedings here."

"Pardon me, Ambassador, but on my world, all matters involve the law," Jim interrupted quickly. "The question first and foremost to be answered is whether this body will accept my credentials and admit me as a member. Only then can legal issues be considered. We *must* have an established relation with the rest of the stars."

"A vote has been called for," a contralto voice spoke again. "Is there further discussion?"

"What guarantees can you give?" the reedy voice of Ambassador Isnuvla asked.

"You have seen our histories," Jim said. "You must be able to judge us in comparison with your own integrity and respect for the rule of law." Jim waved his hands toward Nexl and the rest of the Xlern. "The Xlern have brought us here after first bringing us to Thraxis IV—"

"This is known," the contralto voice informed him.

"An old trick, well known amongst thieves and traders," a deep, booming voice added.

"Ambassador Iv Chaluskera of Nurq," the computer voice informed them.

"Not unknown among humans, either," Jim admitted, "but not respected nor considered legal."

"It is not legal here," Iv Chaluskera boomed. "You are right to request recompense."

"A vote?" the contralto voice asked again.

"Council President Leniana Murqt," the computer voice informed them. Jim wondered why it hadn't told them before. "The vote is called. The tally is in."

"Ambassador James Earl Pickett," Leniana Murqt's contralto said, "you are welcome among us. May your world and worlds prosper and find justice."

"Thank you, Council President," Jim said, bowing slightly. "It is an honor to be among you." He paused a moment. "I thank you for your time and look forward to making acquaintances with all. For the moment, however, I believe that I need to learn of your customs and should therefore retire."

"We have consulted our records," Murqt responded, "and this is not abnormal. We shall be glad to provide you with any assistance you require."

"Thank you, again," Jim said with another bow. "I do not wish to delay this august body in further deliberations." He stepped back from the edge of the platform.

A wall of sounds, lights, and movement welled up around them as their platform did a slow gyration around the large chamber and then returned to their origins.

">>**They were cheering you,**<<" Captain Nexl chimed with no lack of pride.

">>**And they're hoping that you will take us to the cleaners,**<<" Trade Officer Ixxie mourned.

"I suspect they were cheering you and the Yon as much, Captain Nexl," Jim said. To Ixxie, he added, "We promise to be fair and honest."

"You have a request for audience, Ambassador Pickett," the computer voice told him.

"From whom?"

"Council President Leniana Murqt and Ambassador Yargan Isnuvla of Gihendi Prime," it replied.

"Can they meet us in person?"

"Our protocols have cleared you for contact," the computer responded.

"Computer," Emily Steele spoke up, "do you have some name or some appellation we can use?"

"Some people like to call me Prime," the computer responded.

"Prime?" Jim mused. "And what would your powers be, Prime?"

"I am the primary computer for the Council here on Nervashun," Prime told him.

"So Prime seems like a suitable name," Admiral Tsukino murmured.

"Very well, Prime, please let them know that we would be happy to meet them," Jim said.

A moment later, a side of their transparent bubble bulged and pressed out to meet a wall that immediately became transparent and then popped to create a corridor.

"For what we are about to receive," Louise murmured as two figures moved toward them.

"Bozhe moy!" Nikolai swore under his breath as the first figure became discernible. It was taller than any of the humans by about a meter, garbed in red and black cloth, which wrapped its arms and torso and obscured its legs. A belt of silver was wrapped around its midriff, but, of course, it was the horns that caused Zhukov's comment.

"It has no tail," Emily noted.

"It is rumored that my people interacted with yours before your recorded history," the contralto voice of Council President Leniana Murqt came to them. Her mouth opened sideways rather than top-to-bottom like a human's, and her eyes were multi-faceted, each of the seven segments gleaming a slightly different shade of red. The "horns" at the top of its "head" were oddly elegant. Jim recalled from Nexl's briefing that the horns were really another pair of manipulative limbs.

The top of the Nervashun's head was rippled, not quite with grooves nor with scales but something in between, while at the sides Jim could make out the iridescent disks that marked its tympani—eardrums for the Nervashun.

"It entered our racial memory," Emily said.

Jim stepped forward. "I am James Earl Pickett."

A hand and horn extended in his direction. "I welcome you to my world and our alliance."

"Alliance?" Jim said, raising an eyebrow. "There are others?"

"Of course," Murqt replied. She gestured out and around, indicating the heavens above them. "In this galaxy and many others nearby, we are the primary alliance. Beyond that, however, there are other alliances."

"Are any of these alliances at war?" Captain Steele and Captain Zhukov said simultaneously.

"War is an extension of politics," Jim said quellingly. "It is not different among the stars, is it?"

"No, it is not," a thin reedy nasal voice responded. The second alien was hovering on its own platform. It was a little over twelve inches high.

"**>>I did not have a chance to introduce you,<<**" Captain Nexl chimed apologetically. "**>>I did not think we would meet a Gihend today.<<**"

"And you have not," the reedy voice replied testily. As if in response, the air behind the small alien shimmered and Jim suddenly realized that there were many more—at least a dozen—shimmering flying Gihend behind the first. "We are Isnuvla, Yargan is Our Voice."

"You are a hive mind?" Admiral Tsukino said, moving forward and peering intently.

"That is a poor description," the thin voice of Yargan responded.

"You have the advantage over us, kind beings," Jim said carefully with another slight bow. "We are only coming to grips with the notion of the Council and this alliance. And yet we are also having to comprehend new and diverse life-forms and ways of being."

"We do not mean to overwhelm you," President Murqt said. "Yargan and I merely wished to offer our congratulations and whatever services you might need."

"If you're looking for a good lawyer, talk to Murqt," Yargan squeaked. "If you're looking for a good engineer, talk to us."

"Paper clips?" Emily said, moving forward, peering at the group of Gihendi. "Why paper clips?"

Yargan's head swiveled toward her, and it opened its mouth, revealing two rows of silver-sharp teeth. "Do you have any?"

"Ask if they know knitting, Voice," another reedy Gihend said. "We would pay to know that. Manifold theory, cross-dimensional analysis …" Its mouth snapped closed, and it swirled on its platform in what appeared to be rapturous joy.

"The Gihendi find mathematics and shapes…amusing," President Murqt said.

"I think I would have chosen a different verb," Emily said, eyeing the swarm of Gihendi with renewed interest. "And among my people, there are those who would agree with them." She thought of Mac and Lori Dubauer.

"Did you bring any?" the little ecstatic Gihend demanded, eyes wide and teeth gleaming.

"Doquoi, be hush," Yargan squeaked. "The humans do not understand that only the Voice speaks with authority."

"Ask then! Ask!" Doquoi chirped in irritation.

"This must wait for another time," Murqt said. "Our new ambassador is overwhelmed and needs to establish an order and embassy, is that not so?"

"It is among my plans," Jim admitted evasively. "I also think we must begin legal proceedings at the earliest possible opportunity. If the alliance is similar to our United Nations, legal proceedings can be time-consuming."

"You will find allies where you need them," Murqt replied. "In fact, I was going to suggest a legal firm—"

"**>>Guhorqt!<<**" Captain Nexl chimed in what appeared to be horror.

"Yes, I was going to recommend the firm headed by Naliash Guhorqt as being well-versed in these sorts of … imbroglios," President Murqt admitted.

"I was going to suggest the same," Yargan added. "I was also going to suggest the domicile firm of Levash and Gorgqun as fitting to ambassadorial needs."

"I also need to open a line of credit with one of your monetary establishments," Jim said.

"Of course," President Murqt agreed suavely.

"Teach us to knit; we give you gold!" Doquoi squeaked.

"Actually, given the strange circumstances and our belief in your positive outcome," Yargan squeaked, "we were going to suggest that we could provide you with a line of credit based on your word alone."

">>**Take it! Take it!**<<" Trade Officer Ixxie chimed quickly. ">>**The Gihendi** *never* **make such offers.**<<"

Jim glanced toward Admiral Tsukino, who returned his look impassively.

"Very well, Ambassador Isnuvla, we accept your generous offer and, on my word as ambassador from Earth, I promise to repay you at the earliest possible time."

"Good!" President Murqt said. "And now that that's settled, if you wish, we can dismiss these Xlern—"

"Pardon, President Murqt, but that won't be necessary," Jim told her with a slight bow. "I need to converse with them on legal matters and consult on others."

"I see," Murqt replied, her horns twisted slightly. "Well, if you've matters in hand, we shan't detain you any longer."

"Thank you," Jim said. "And if you could, would you please ask the law firm you recommended to contact us when we're settled?"

"Indeed," the council president said with a slight bow and horn-bobble.

"One more thing, President Murqt," Jim said. "I'd like to have our ship, *Unity*, return to Earth. I have dispatches I'd like to send."

"I shall inform planetary security," President Murqt responded. "For the time being, we will extend them diplomatic immunity as a courier."

"My thanks," Jim said. The Nervashun give him a slight nod and turned to head back the way she came.

After they were out of earshot, Louise muttered, "If that's a female of their species …"

"Yes?" Jim prodded when she trailed off.

"I was just wondering how they mated," Louise admitted.

">>**I am told it involves locking horns,**<<" Trade Officer Ixxie chimed in response. ">>**It is, by the way, something of a** *faux pas* **to refer to an impasse in the same way.**<<"

"Indeed," Jim said, his lips quirking upwards. "I imagine we shall make it a point to avoid locking horns with our hosts in either way!"

* * *

The White House, Washington, DC

"People of the Earth, of the Moon, of Mars, of our solar system, tonight I greet you with the greatest news that a person has ever had to give," President Merritt said as he spoke into the cameras that would beam his words around the planet, and out to the stars. "You have heard, of course, that we are not alone in the galaxy. That there are intelligent species—thousands or more—who are traversing our galaxy and others.

"That two of those star-faring alien species have contacted us at Jupiter and taught us how to build our own star drives."

He paused dramatically.

"Today, we have received confirmation from the United Nations Ambassador Extraordinary and Plenipotentiary, Ambassador James Earl Pickett, that we have been admitted into the Alliance of Star Nations of the greater Milky Way galaxy.

"People of Earth, we are not alone. We have allies. We have friends. And we will soon have our own worlds to colonize, new frontiers to explore, and new partners with whom to trade.

"Ambassador Pickett has assured me that we will not be paupers in this new universe, that we will not be beggars or second-class citizens. He has asked that we formally recognize the United Nations Navy as our interstellar navy, tasked with providing customs and security services to all nations that engage in star trade, and I, and the Congress of the United States, have formally agreed. We ask all nations to also agree. Our individual states will continue as before and not be hindered in their exploration of space or establishment of trade, but just as they recognize the United Nations as the authority for handling trade and legal disputes, we ask that they recognize the United Nations Navy as mankind's navy.

"The rest of the details will be worked out in the United Nations, I am sure," he said, "but today I can promise you that we are safer, more secure, stronger, and bigger than we've ever been in the history of mankind.

"Thank you, God bless you, and good night."

* * *

People's Liberation Army shipyard, Phobos

"Phobos, this is *Unity*," Admiral Wang called in Chinese. "We request immediate docking."

"Unknown ship, this is Captain Ren of the People's Liberation Army's Navy, request denied."

"Captain Ren," Admiral Wang responded in a tone distinctly chilly than before, "you will let us dock immediately. You will have the foreigners and Lieutenant Ma ready to embark upon our docking."

"Admiral?" Captain Ren Wenwu said in a much smaller voice. "I—I had—"

"Docking instructions, Captain," Admiral Wang cut across him. To Mick Hsu, he added, "He was always an idiot."

Mick merely nodded, saying nothing. He had heard the admiral's lengthy and heated discussion with Beijing and had guessed that Admiral Wang might shortly appear in UNN garb ... which would be Beijing's loss. The admiral, Mick had decided, was much more of a bureaucratic paper-pusher than, say, Admiral Tsukino, but he had stars in his eyes just the same. Prickly, difficult, probably a back-stabber, but good enough to work for; he'd get results.

Mick had been watching Jim Pickett since they'd first started their mad, insane, antimatter-powered streak from the Moon to Jupiter. Mick Hsu was pretty certain that Jim Pickett had learned to play things close to his chest from the time he was old enough to toddle. Admiral Wang, if Mick was right, was going to find himself ensconced on Nervashun—and loving it.

* * *

"Mac!" Danni McElroy cried as she crossed through to *Unity's* spacious docking level. He lowered his head and indicated the rank on his shoulder and she stopped herself, "Commander McLaughlin, this is a surprise!"

"It is indeed, Lieutenant," Mac told her. "You ready for the ride of your life?"

"I've *always* been ready," Danni told him. She saluted him, and he returned it as was required for entering a ship. She stepped aside as Lori Dubauer and Ensign Sato followed and, in turn, widened their eyes in surprise, then recovered and issued sharp salutes in turn.

"Good to see you two!" Mac said, extending his hand to each in turn.

A final figure swam down the connecting tube between *Unity* and the Phobos shipyard. "This is Lieutenant Ma, sir," Danni said, moving to stand next to Mac. "He's good stuff; you'll like him."

Lieutenant Ma came to a halt, looking confused until Danni jerked a hand toward Mac. Then the Chinese lieutenant snapped to attention and saluted.

"Mick," Mac called over his shoulder as he extended his hand to the still-confused lieutenant, "tell him we don't bite."

"Much," Danni added softly.

"Is Lieutenant Ma familiar with the standard docking procedures?" Mac asked her.

"Yeah," Danni said.

"Mick, tell the lieutenant he's in charge of getting us free of the station and prepared for jump," Mac said to the chief. "As soon as you two are done, you're to report to the admiral—I mean, to Admiral Wang."

"Aye, sir," Mick Hsu replied, sketching a quick salute before beginning a rapid-fire exchange with Lieutenant Ma. "Can I tell him where we're going?"

"Sure," Mac said, gesturing for the others to follow him. "And get him bunked down in officer country."

"Effete snobs," Mick murmured in a voice that was intended to be ignored.

"That's officer effete snobs," Mac corrected without turning.

"Where are we going, sir?" Ensign Sato asked as they entered what appeared to be a standard Xlern lift. "And how big is this ship?"

"She's a megaton in mass and built for a crew of two hundred," Mac told her. He waved around the place. "We're a bit short-handed, but as most of those are survey and exploration slots, we mostly manage."

"So we're going to be busy," Danni McElroy guessed.

"Just now we're going to Nervashun to meet up with the ambassador," Mac told her. "We've got Captain Lee, Commander Geister, Commander Milano—pretty much every warm body we could scrounge up."

"Why, sir?" Lori Dubauer asked. "You've got enough to man this ship, you said so already."

Mac smiled at her knowingly and then gestured for them to follow him as the lift stopped. "This is officer quarters. Maps are on the walls and the computer answers to questions in any language we know."

"I hadn't expected *that*," Danni said.

"A gift from the Gihendi," Mac told her. "Apparently they *really* want to get to know us."

"Gihendi?"

"They look like a cross between a wasp and a pixie," Mac said. "They have hive minds and they love topology."

"Oh, just your sort of folk, sir!" Danni said brightly.

"And yours, Lori," Mac said to the young ensign whose eyes had never stopped sweeping around the ship. "And Sato's, too, unless I miss my guess."

"So we're going to play catch-up again?" Lori Dubauer asked.

"Only until we learn enough to start playing catch-us-if-you-can," Mac replied, tapping the side of his head. "Jim says that we're going to give these aliens a run for their money, and I'm inclined to agree with him."

"Really?" Danni asked, eyes wide. "Do you really think so?"

"Yes, Lieutenant, I do," Mac said. "Now, get your gear stowed—your quarters are marked with your names—and then let me show you the bridge."

"Sir? I'm not sure that Captain Steele would—" Danni began, obviously uncomfortable with the direction he seemed to be taking.

"I've got your orders here," Mac said, tapping his chest. "You, Lori, Sato—hers from her admiral—you're all seconded to me and *Unity* until we reach Nervashun." He smiled at them. "It won't take long, but we want you to get a bit of a feel for the ship while we can."

"Okay," Danni said with relief. "I just didn't want—"

"The last I want to do is step on anyone's loyalty," Mac cut her off. "But for the moment, you're under my command, just as I follow the orders of Admiral Wang—"

"Admiral Wang?"

"—and he is following the directions of Ambassador Pickett," Mac finished. "Get your gear stowed, people."

A few minutes later, they stepped out onto the bridge of *Unity*.

"All ready?" Captain Lee asked as Mac approached him.

"That, sir," Mac told him with a smile, "is up to you."

"Me?"

"Orders, sir," Mac said. "Everyone is to get as much bridge time as possible. It means, sir, this ship is yours until we get to Nervashun."

Captain Lee moved closer and said in a quiet undertone, "I don't know what to do."

"Welcome to the club, sir," Mac told him. Then he added, "It's not hard, just tell navigation to prepare to jump, check with engineering, and issue the order."

"So, pretty much like on any ship," Lee said.

"But a hell of a lot faster, sir," Mac agreed. He gestured to the command chair. As Captain Lee stepped toward it, Mac came to the side and murmured, "I'm here if you need me."

"Appreciated," Captain Lee said, seating himself, his spine straight and eyes swiveling to every part of the bridge. "Feel free to make any suggestions, Commander."

"Aye, sir," Mac replied, hiding his relief. He'd been a bit sore when Admiral Wang had sprung this plan on him, but he'd become resigned to it—and while Captain Lee was more stick-in-the-mud than Emily Steele, Mac knew that he was also smart enough to know when to ask for help and officer enough to only ask when necessary.

"Navigation," Lee now said, "is our course set?"

"Aye, sir," Lori Dubauer replied, having received her own crash training.

"Communications, our compliments to Phobos and we're ready to depart," Lee said. Beside Admiral Wang, Sergeant Yin muttered a translation. The admiral opened a comm link and said something quickly in Chinese. A moment later, Sergeant Yin said to the captain, "They wish us a good journey, Captain."

"Very well," Lee said. "Thrusters. I want a good five kilometers separation."

"Ten, sir," Mac murmured.

Lee accepted that with a nod but said nothing until the propulsion chief said, "Five kilometers, sir."

"Okay, give us another five for luck," Lee told him, then looked at his armrest comm link and punched up a new connection. "Engineering, how are we for translation?"

"Lieutenant Ma says that all systems are on line, sir," Mick Hsu's voice came back quickly.

"Navigation?"

"Course set and locked, sir," Lori told him.

"Very well. Translate," Captain Lee said as if it were something he'd done countless times.

A moment later, *Unity* disappeared from the solar system.

CHAPTER TWENTY-TWO

Earth Ambassador's Residence, Nervashun

"AH, THE PAO V!" JAVASHTAN KATZ, SENIOR PARTNER AT GUHORQT, KATZ, AND Gevistansh, said with the gargling chortle that indicated, for the Nervashun, laughter. "I see now the bottom of their plan."

"Yes, I rather thought they called that out in bright lights," Jim said with a small smile. "I take it that we've been handed what we on Earth would call a hot potato."

"If you mean something that is hotter than the sun, denser than black holes, and more lucrative than the diamond stars of Jivax IX, then I would agree with you," Javashtan— "call me Jav"—replied.

The rest of the aliens' list had been quickly sorted out for possible licenses, complete with suggested royalty and reparation payment plans—plans that left Jim smiling more and more every day. Jav was no less enthusiastic.

"Of course, they're a Combine, so they've limited themselves," Jav had said, meaning the Xlern and the Yon. "In fact, I'm pretty sure that's what they intended in the first place."

"Why?"

"Well, your hot potato," Jav said with a remarkable shrug of his upper arms.

"Let me guess: if they didn't hand us this hot potato, then they'd still have it," Jim said. "So they cobbled up their story, got us pulled into the Alliance, and now we're going to be the **ones** to deal with the next batch of newcomers."

"Exactly," Jav agreed. "Pretty shrewd of them when you think of it."

"This sort of thing happens a lot, right?" Jim said. "Each emerging intelligence gets to bring on the next intelligence?"

">>**It's more than that,**<<" Captain Nexl chimed. ">>**It was no accident that your planet sent a signal to Gliese 581.**<<"

The Nervashun lawyer had been shocked when Pickett had insisted on having Nexl sit in on the proceedings—at least until he had understood *why*, and then he'd been positively gleeful.

"That's happened before?"

">>**Yes.**<<" Nexl chimed in response.

"More than once?"

">>**Most times,**<<"

"Is it connected with the Pao V, then?"

">>**We think so.**<<"

"Huh," Jim said and then shrugged. "All the more reason to continue as planned."

">>**Your proposal has surprised Is-sa-to-li-ri,**<<" Nexl rang back.

"What is Is-sa-to-li-ri?" Jav asked.

"My star witness, if need be," Jim said. "And no, I'm not worried about client privilege here; you're on a civil case." To Nexl, he said, "And I'm ecstatic to learn that I've managed to surprise them."

"Is-sa-to-li-ri," Jav murmured to itself. A moment later, its yellow slits narrowed along their vertical axis—the Nervashun version of narrowing its eyes. "Wait a minute, are you trying to say that there is a five-headed Hydra?"

"Privileged information," Jim told him, tapping the side of his nose. "If there were, why would that be of interest?"

The red-skinned alien caught on fast. "Well, we know such things are impossible; the angular displacement alone is theoretically possible, but the dangers in tampering with an extant four-headed Hydra make it completely beyond the realm of possibility."

"So, let's pretend," Jim said, not bothering to explain his part in the aerial insertion of the fifth head. "Why would it matter?"

"It is known that Yon intelligence increases geometrically with the number of individual Yon united," Jav said. "Where four are sixteen times more intelligent than one, five would be thirty-two times more intelligent—they would be easily near the top of the intelligence scale for certain things." It paused for a moment. "Not quite up with the Gihendi, whose hive mind can occasionally reach several thousand times normal intelligence, but probably with fewer incidents of psychotic episodes and paranoid schizophrenia."

"When you have a lot of points of view, it becomes difficult to focus," Jim guessed with a nod. "We've seen that occur in some of our more intelligent humans, too."

"I'm sure," Jav agreed, "but to date, none of your renegades have managed to destroy planets."

"Not for want of trying," Jim said, "although I imagine now that our scope will increase it might be a possibility."

"A lot of our wars have been fought to contain such deviants," Jav said.

"As have ours," Jim said. "I gather you are implying that the greater the intelligence, the greater the potential scale for destruction."

"Ignorance shouldn't be discounted," the Nervashun lawyer observed.

"Yeah, the sort of things that makes a diplomat's life," Jim agreed sourly. "But if there's a downside to great intelligence, there's also an upside."

"With the Yon, the upside is a greater understanding, as well as increased language and social skills," Jav guessed. It shrugged, a movement that, alarmingly, also including its horn-limbs. "The intelligence will translate to greater trading skills, and possibly to greater mathematical ability—something the Gihendi would not appreciate." The lawyer shook its head. "For my people, it would disturb the current order of things."

"I had noted that the Nervashun like stability," Jim said carefully.

"Let's just say that we've found the opposite to be the cause of more excitement than we generally appreciate," Jav corrected.

"I imagine that a single five-headed Yon wouldn't upset the balance of power too much," Jim said. "The real problems would come if this were to become something more widespread."

"Yes," Jav said, squashing its lips in a vertical line. "I imagine Council President Murqt and others would pay a great deal to see that any occurrences are limited in number."

"Well," Jim said airily, "that's something to consider if it ever becomes a problem." He looked toward Nexl. "In the meantime, counsel, do you believe we are prepared to proceed?"

"I've got the documents drawn up," Jav replied. "I understand," the two eye slits widened with joy, "that the Xlern-Yon Combine have registered no objections to the terms. So, it is only a matter of getting the appropriate signatures on the agreement."

"Excellent!" Jim said. Things had gone better than he'd hoped and looked to go even better than—

"We need Captain Nexl, his trade officer, and Captain Sa-li-ri-to and his trade officer to affix their marks in person at the court registrar and then we'll file the agreements," Jav said happily.

"Ah," Jim said. He was afraid there might be a catch. "That might be a little more difficult than—"

"I thought you said they were in agreement," Jav said, sounding—and looking— suddenly less like a lawyer and more like an angry red-skinned devil-shaped … devil.

"They are," Jim said. "The trouble is that the Yon captain is rather, uh …"

">>**Indisposed,**<<" Captain Nexl suggested.

"Overburdened," Jim essayed.

"Over-headed, perhaps?" Jav said. "I take it then that your question earlier was not quite so academic as I'd hoped. Am I right in guessing that we now have to handle the acceptance of this Is-sa-to-li-ri as the legal heir and representative of Sa-li-ri-to?"

"That won't be a problem, will it?" Jim asked hopefully.

The Nervashun's horns went straight out for a moment and then curled inwards, drooping almost to touching the furrows of its skull. "An inheritance case," the Nervashun moaned. "A *Yon* inheritance case!"

"That bad, eh?"

"Worse." A moment later, Jav rose from its seat. "Although, given the effects of the Pao V, nothing I should not have assumed." It turned toward the exit. "I'm going to have to consult with the partners."

* * *

Unity

"We're taking the shuttle down," Mac informed Danni as he, Admiral Wang, Lieutenant Ma, Mick Hsu, and Ensigns Dubauer and Sato looked at him. "Captain Lee will get the ship tucked into orbit and then I'll swap with him."

"Is there much need for a watch in orbit?" Ensign Sato wondered.

Mac shrugged in response. "I don't know, but it gives Lee and his crew time to work in the simulators, if nothing else."

"And run passive sweeps with everything we've got," Danni McElroy added urgently.

Mac smiled at her. "You just keep trying to teach us how to suck eggs; we'll learn someday."

The young lieutenant went nearly as red as her hair.

Mac put an arm on her shoulder and she looked around. "Really, Lieutenant, you know that the only stupid question is—"

"—the one that's not asked," Danni finished, feeling a bit less sheepish.

"And you're right, this should be a gold mine for us, even on passives," Mac assured her. "So far we've got positive IDs on about thirty different ship types and we've got a field that includes thousands."

"I wish we could deploy some drones."

"We don't have any and until we've had a chance to see how *our* sensors deal with them, I don't want us to spook any of our new 'friends' unnecessarily," Mac replied.

"Aye, sir," Danni said. "I suppose that would come under the category of 'a bad thing.'"

They clambered aboard, Mac waving her toward the cockpit. "You're to fly co-pilot on the way down and pilot on the way up, LT."

"What?" Danni cried in surprise. "But, Skipper, I'm not qualified."

"Learn fast," Mac told her with a shrug. When she looked ready to continue her protests, he added, "You're taking an antigravity ship into a gravity well, how hard can it be?"

Danni sighed and turned to the cockpit. In the pilot's seat, she found Sally Norman, dressed in her fetching new United Nations Navy uniform.

"I heard, ma'am," Sally told her with a smile. "The skipper's right, it's not hard." She gave Danni a quick overview of the controls, then handed her the pre-flight checklist. Danni found it to be simple, sensible, and not so confusing. Sally caught her growing relaxation and said sympathetically, "As Captain McLaughlin said, ma'am, given what we're doing, the flight controls aren't too different from a powered craft."

"What about emergency procedures?" Danni asked. In everything, it was the emergency procedures that were the most involved and demanding.

"We've got the checklist," Sally told her. "At some point, as with everything, you get down to 'kiss your ass goodbye.'"

"I'd prefer to avoid that," Danni said, moving through the rest of the checklists to the emergency procedures.

"The computers are pretty good. They can do all this by themselves," Sally said. "Mac is insisting that we do as much on manual as we can."

"Sort of pre-emergency training," Danni guessed.

"Exactly!" Sally agreed. Then her tone changed and she said, "Departure checklist."

"Roger," Danni said, all business. "Door seals."

"Check."

"*Unity*, this is *Unity-1*, prepared to detach," Danni called over the comm.

"*Unity-1*, clear for detach," the crisp English voice of Midshipman Saxon returned efficiently.

"Detach," Sally said.

Danni marked it on the list, moved to the next item. "Confirm detach."

"Detach confirmed," Sally said just as Saxon called, "*Unity-1*, we show a clean detach."

"Cold jets to 3 meters," Danni said.

"Roger, moving to 3 meters," Sally replied.

They worked through the checklist, moving to contact Nervashun Approach and acquire a beacon and coordinates for their landing pad, then on to the descent at a slow and steady three kilometers per minute. They broke through into the stratosphere, slowed to a more leisurely six hundred meters per minute, before finally switching to a controlled descent at a steady one hundred and sixty meters per minute, then. They slowed, to a crawl just a few meters above the pad and landed without a bump.

"Contact lights," Danni called out, completing the landing checklist.

"Arrival checklist," Sally ordered.

"Roger, arrival checklist," Danni responded. "Contact arrivals on channel 73."

"Nervashun Arrival, this is *Unity-1* safely down on landing pad twenty-three," Sally commed calmly. "Request docking spaceway and power connections."

"Understood. Initiated," a bored voice returned. "Your personnel are cleared for departure; your systems are connected. Set sleep mode to automatic."

"Negative," Danni called. "*Unity-1* is not prepared to enter sleep mode at this moment, request a delay."

"State nature of delay."

"Our personnel are still aboard," Danni replied.

"Very well, you may engage sleep mode on departure," the bored voice replied. Before it cut the communications link, Danni heard some mutterings from the controller which she guessed would translate to something like "Tourists!"

"Hatch secured," Mac called from the cabin. "Connections green; everyone out!"

"Last one out call out," Danni called over her shoulder. She found Sally Norman eyeing her with interest. "Sorry."

Sally shook her head. "Don't apologize. You just made me realize the difference between an amateur and a professional."

"You were always a professional, Sally."

"I guess I just don't have your experience."

"That," Danni told her with a smile, "comes with experience." She pointed to the ship they'd just landed. "And it seems to me that you're getting enough of that now."

They unbuckled their belts and moved out of the cockpit, suffering a moment of confusion as the precedence of pilot warred with the precedence of rank. Danni laughed as she let Sally wave her out first and evened things up by ensuring that Sally went through the hatch first while Danni stayed behind to engage the automatic sleep mode.

Lights throughout the ship flickered off, and the sound of the air conditioner wound down as she made her way down the jetway and into the arrivals hall proper.

Mac was waiting for her. "Good job, Lieutenant."

"Thank you, sir," she told him. With a smile, she added, "It was a piece of cake, just like you said."

"And no more exciting than *Voyager's* first flight," Mac agreed with a chuckle.

* * *

"I don't like it one bit," Emily Steele said as Pickett outlined his plan of action to the collection of officers and noncoms assembled in the embassy's main conference room. "You could get yourself killed!"

"Captain, I appreciate your sentiment, but I am, and always was, expendable," Pickett said.

"I have to agree with the captain," Admiral Tsukino said. He glanced to Admiral Wang and noted with pleasure that the Chinese admiral nodded in agreement.

"Da," Captain Zhukov added staunchly.

"They're right, sir," Danni McElroy spoke up from the rear seats. "You can't risk it."

"I'm not sure we have much choice," Jim said. "It was risky the first time, but we know of no one else who succeeded. And the success of our mission rests on this."

"I agree with your fellow humans," Jav said, speaking from the seat beside him. "I am rather pleased to note that they seem to have grasped the import of your position more fully than you."

"Pardon?"

"Ambassador Pickett," Emily said, rising from her chair, "Danni's right. You're the one who brought us all here, you're the one who pulled off this whole big scam—"

"It's not a scam!"

"It's a scam, sir," Danni said flatly, smiling at him, "and you're the only one who could have pulled it off." She waved a hand around the room, indicating the walls and the world beyond. "We're on a *new* world. We've been *admitted* to a galaxy-wide league of aliens. You did that. It was you who convinced everyone—presidents, generals, admirals, captains, even"—her hand stretched out toward McLaughlin—"sour old engineers, that it was possible, that it was doable, and that they could do it."

"Danni's right, sir," Mac said, rising to stand alongside her. "You've got to give this job to someone else." He paused a moment, then added, "In fact, I think it's high time you did a whole bunch of delegating."

"I plan to, Mac," Jim told him with feeling. "In fact, I plan to hand this all off to someone—"

"No!" The shout was unanimous and it shocked James Earl Pickett to silence.

"You were right to say that this isn't easy," he told them in a husky voice. "I'm proud to have your support"—he glanced around the room—"all of you but, ultimately, if this is to succeed it can't rest on just one set of shoulders."

"Exactly," Danni said with feeling. "So why are you so damned determined to put it on yours?" As an afterthought, she added, "Sir."

"I'm not," Jim said, "and I think if you look at this room, you'll notice that I haven't."

"You're avoiding the issue, sir," Nikolai Zhukov told him. "You know full well that it was you who built this team and welded it, however imperfectly, into the first interstellar organization of mankind." Zhukov shook his head. "That is an incredible feat and one requiring abilities not given to many."

Admiral Wang nodded firmly and dictated a response to Mick Hsu. "The Russian captain speaks the truth."

"Okay," Jim said. "That doesn't change things. I'm still the only one who pulled this trick off, and we *need* to do it again, in front of the whole Council, or we're going to spend years in the courts fighting over the Yon inheritance rules and against a growing opposition." He closed his eyes and sighed. "We could fall on this one issue."

"Yes, sir," Danni said in a chipper tone. "We got that. We also know that we could have failed on any *one* other issue in this long line of issues." She raised her head and met his eyes. "Seems to me, sir, that what you need is a snake-wrangler."

"I suppose we could send back home …"

"Pardon sir, but if you want a snake-wrangler, why go so far?" Danni interrupted him.

"Do you know any, Lieutenant?"

"It wasn't in my records, sir," Danni told him softly. "Because I thought it'd get me profiled out of the service before I could get in—"

"Are you saying that you had snakes?" Mac interjected in surprise. "I never would have taken you for a—"

"Actually," Nikolai Zhukov stood up slowly, "she's not the only one."

"*Et tu, Brute?*" Emily Steele said, raising her hand. "I was a bit of a coward. I only kept corn snakes."

"So, Mr. Ambassador, it seems that you have no less than *three* alternatives," Danni said, "and all you had to do was ask."

Jim bowed his head for a moment and raised it again, smiling at the red-haired lieutenant.

"I am suitably chastened, Lieutenant," Jim said. "And seeing as we're now moving on to asking … I have a short list of recommendations and positions that need filling."

Danni's eyes widened. "Oh, no!"

"In particular," Jim continued, his smile broadening, "beyond chief Yon wrangler, I find myself desperately in need of a communications officer—"

"Damn!"

Pickett nodded in reply and swiveled his head toward Ensigns Sato and Dubauer. "I'm also in need of some savvy technical people to fill out our trade and science mission—"

"Sir!" Lori Dubauer cried in protest, her eyes turning beseechingly toward Captain Steele.

"Don't look at me, Lori," Emily told her, "I've been bought and paid."

"Ma'am?" Lori squeaked.

"You'll see," Emily said, glancing back toward Ambassador Pickett.

"I'll need a medic and food specialist," Jim said, turning to Louise O'Reilly, who merely nodded. "Admiral Wang has consented to be our primary military attaché and on-site representative for Chinese affairs." He glanced toward Mick Hsu. "Mr. Hsu, if you would, I would request that you join our staff as translator and technical consultant—"

"Sir?"

"I have it in mind that this will be a very broad-based establishment," Jim told him. "While we will adhere to a chain of a command, we will also insist upon open lines of communications. Admirals Wang, Tsukino, and myself are agreed that you are a distinct asset in numerous areas. We'll keep you busy, but we won't give you busywork."

"Sir," Mick began slowly, turning slightly to include Admiral Wang in his gaze, "I'm an American. I'm Navy. My first loyalty is to my country."

"Actually, Mick, your first loyalty had *better* be to your species," Emily told him. Her tone mellowed as she continued, "But I understand what you're saying. We're not asking you to break your oath or act in any way contrary to your beliefs. We think that your honesty and faithfulness will be an asset. Admiral Wang has made it clear that he understands where your loyalties lie and will respect them."

Admiral Wang added something in Chinese and Mick Hsu replied in the same language before turning to Pickett and saying, with a shrug, "What can I say? It'd be an honor, sir."

"What about everyone else?" Danni asked.

"Well, we've got some plans," Jim told her, "but until you do your Yon wrangling trick, there's no point in rolling them out."

"Actually, Mr. Ambassador," Javashtan Katz interrupted diffidently, "I think that, for your demonstration to succeed, you are going to need slightly more than one 'Yon wrangler'—as you so quaintly phrase it."

* * *

Alliance Grand Assembly, Nervashun

"Really, Mr. Ambassador, this is most unusual," Council President Murqt protested. "At our first meeting you had suggested that you would need time—"

"I beg your pardon, Madame President but the need is urgent," Jim interrupted her with a low bow from the edge of their floating platform. Instead of supplicating from their assigned enclave near the bottom of the huge hemi-spherical assembly hall, Jim and Javashtan had arranged—mostly through the offices of Guhorqt, Katz, and Gevistansh and no small amount of political pull—to get them on the floating platform upon which they'd first appeared. "It pertains to resolving certain civil matters but also impinges upon this august body in a way which I believe demands their urgent attention."

"Really?" Murqt asked dubiously, "and how is that?"

"If I may," Is-sa-to-li-ri stepped forward from the group of Yon that had clustered tightly together on the platform, "I believe I may address that."

"Who are you?" Murqt asked.

"I am Is-sa-to-li-ri of the Yon," it sang. There was a muted gasp and then a huge roar as the various emissaries realized that the Yon's song had come to them before the translation. In fact, Jim realized, the Centercomp Prime hadn't even provided a translation. He wondered idly if this was because Prime itself was shocked or because it realized its services were unnecessary.

Murqt recovered quickly, Jim noted with approval. "And how does this impinge upon your civil suit, Ambassador Pickett?"

"The five-headed Yon now known as Is-sa-to-li-ri was formerly the captain of the Yon trading ship, *Ynoyon,* and their signature is required for our contract," Jim told her.

"I see," Murqt said easily. "The normal procedures require that the Yon certify that this entity is the sole inheritor of the entity previously known as Sa-li-ri-to." She paused. "That doubtless would take some time. I imagine you wish to petition the Assembly for speedier recognition."

"We object!" a voice came loud and stridently through the air.

"Ambassador To-me-lo-ka of the Yon," Prime informed them.

"You cannot object, you are beneath me," Is-sa-to-li-ri sang back.

"Hey!" Jim cried, turning angrily toward the five-headed Hydra. "Diplomatic, remember?"

"They are nothing," Is-sa-to-li-ri sang back.

"You need to control yourself or you're going to get us all killed," Danni said to the Yon.

"I withdraw my objection," To-me-lo-ka said in a surprisingly small voice. "I move to recognize Is-sa-to-li-ri as rightful heir of Captain Sa-li-ri-to."

"He is awed by my mightiness," Is-sa-to-li-ri said smugly to Jim.

"With all due respect, Yon, you're getting big-headed," Danni murmured.

"I warned you," Jav muttered to Jim. "The Council will want to vote on this."

"Yeah," Jim agreed, "I'm sure they will." He turned back to the others in his group. "I think it's time for the finale."

"Are you sure?" Danni asked, eyebrows raised.

"Yeah," Jim said. "Madame President, as a *bona fide* of our claim, I would like now to show how it is possible to create a five-headed Hydra."

"This is a not a circus!" President Murqt swore. "We do not need such demonstrations at this moment."

"On the contrary, Madame President, I'm concerned with the balance of power," Jim told her. He nodded to the others. "My people have volunteered to perform their part in this and the Yon have volunteered for their part, including Is-sa-to-li-ri." He waved a hand toward the five-headed Hydra, which responded by lowering three of its heads in acknowledgment. "We believe that it is important that everyone understand the requirements and challenges so that we may all correctly assess the implications of this new, higher intelligence."

Is-sa-to-li-ri, which alternated between being imperious and humble, had raised no objections when Jim had outlined his plan. Jim wasn't so sure, on the great stage of interstellar affairs, if the Yon wasn't having second thoughts. He meant to present the Yon and everyone else with a *fait accompli*. After that, he figured he'd find some way to proceed.

Three four-headed Hydra moved into separate groups, accompanied by two single Yon and a single human.

They moved in a ballet of sorts, something that Danni had hastily choreographed from the visuals that the Yon had provided of "Pickett's Last Grab"—as Danni had humorously labeled it.

The three groups were arranged in the points of a large triangle. The humans moved toward the points, charging toward each Yon Hydra. At the same time, the individual Yon, the *geas* Yon, understandably took defensive positions in front of their controllers.

"Now," Jim called in a voice that was not loud but carried.

Danni McElroy, Nikolai Zhukov, and Emily Steele charged toward their respective Yon Hydra. As individual Yon snapped at them, they turned, grabbed their assailants behind the jaws and threw them over their heads in near-perfect replica of Jim's own move.

"What is the meaning of this?" President Murqt demanded.

"You are assailing Yon Hydra!" To-me-lo-ka cried.

Then: silence.

Three Yon snapped at their betters. Three Hydra moved to defend themselves—and three four-headed Yon Hydra found themselves locked on by a fifth Yon.

Their bulges streamed opened, seamed together, and fused while the Hydra screamed in surprise and rage.

The humans withdrew even as Is-sa-to-li-ri sang, *"Welcome."*

A moment later, the three new five-headed Hydra sang back, *"We greet you."*

Pandemonium broke out.

Danni, Nikolai, and Emily, all slightly breathless, converged on Jim Pickett.

"Well," he said, "it's just as exciting to watch as it is to do."

"Really?" Danni said. "I thought I was gonna die."

"Yeah, that's how I felt when I did it."

"Was it worth it?" Emily asked, gesturing to the lights and sounds of the frenzied Assembly.

"One five-headed Hydra is a problem," Jim said in reply. "Five five-headed Hydra is a balance of power."

"Five?" Mac said, looking at the three new Hydra. "I only see four."

"Ah," Jim said, "that's because we haven't yet offered this trick to the ambassador and his geas Yon."

"As a courtesy, no doubt," Jav said, its horn-limbs quivering in amusement.

"Exactly," Jim agreed. He moved toward the edge of the platform and spoke up. "Madame President, I move that the Yon Is-sa-to-li-ri be recognized as the rightful heir of Sa-li-ri-to."

"The Assembly has been asked to recognize this," Prime said. "The Assembly … is in some disarray."

"You!" President Murqt shouted, her platform flying down toward theirs. "Get out of here, take your ruling and leave!"

"Thank you, Madame President," Jim said with a bow, and gestured for the others to move back toward the center of the platform.

"We Yon are grateful for the kindness you have provided," Is-sa-to-li-ri sang.

"Are they talking to us or the president?" Danni wondered.

"Both, I think," Emily replied. She turned to Pickett. "So what now, Mr. Ambassador?"

"Now," Jim told her with a smile, "we talk about those *other* arrangements."

Chapter Twenty-three

"So, is everyone in agreement?" Jim said as he gathered the officers and noncoms together for one final meeting.

"I believe so," Admiral Tsukino said, glancing to the others, "although I must say, sir, that I had never expected—"

"You were the natural one for the position, Admiral," Admiral Wang interrupted him in quite passable French. "I'll remain here until I hear differently." His expression changed somewhat, and the others exchanged knowing looks: while his superiors may wish otherwise, Admiral Wang had positioned himself both politically and physically as to be nearly unassailable. And, as Jim had guessed, the new order appealed more to the admiral than the old. "Of course, I'll keep an eye on those ships which we can't currently crew and dispatch them as soon as possible to their respective nations."

"Or we'll come up with more recruits for the UNN," Jim said.

"Doubtless so," Admiral Wang agreed. It was an open secret that Admiral Tsukino would be resigning his commission, having in his pocket a commission from Ambassador Pickett. Jim wasn't sure that Admiral Wang wouldn't soon ask for one of his own—the Chinese admiral was clearly thinking along those lines, but still had not quite decided where his ultimate loyalties lay. Besides, Jim thought, there was a lot of room for a mercantile navy, too.

"Captains Zhukov, Lee, and Steele should be reporting in on Earth any moment now," Jim said. "I imagine that'll cause quite a stir."

"In the meantime, Mr. Ambassador, we should discuss our exploration strategy and how we'll present it to the UN General Assembly," Danni McElroy reminded him.

"Yeah," Jim said with a heavy sigh. Then he brightened. "Of course, my work here will mean that I'll have to delegate …"

Danni groaned and then caught herself. "I imagine Captain McLaughlin will be able to spare some time for *Unity* to pay a little visit."

"Actually," Admiral Tsukino said with a chuckle, "I expect everyone will be too busy playing with their new toys to spend much time listening to the General Assembly."

Jim smiled. "Yes, I rather expect so."

"Hah!" Danni McElroy snorted. "That's what you *planned*!"

"Well," Jim said, "when all's said and done, I'm glad that Emily won the toss."

"If I recall, sir, you used a two-headed coin," Danni remarked.

"Perhaps so," Jim said. "At any event, she'll be reporting in just about now."

* * *

The White House, Washington, DC

"This is the White House. How may I direct your call?" Operator Lucy Grimes said wearily, some two hours before the end of her long and grinding shift. Cranks, crackpots, idiots, those were the usual for her.

"This is Captain Emily Steele, and I'd like to speak to the president," a rich warm voice replied.

"Captain Steele?" Lucy said. The name sounded familiar. "You need to go through the department of defense."

"That's a bit difficult, and I'd prefer not," the captain replied. "If you'd just mention my name to the president or any of his staff, I'm sure they'll want to hear from me."

"Captain, the president is a very busy person—"

"It's just that I don't want to get shot at," Emily said. "I'm not quite sure how good our defensive mechanisms are, you see, as this is only as shuttle."

"A shuttle?" Lucy repeated. She pressed a button, and her call was relayed to security. "Captain, where is this shuttle and why are you worried about getting shot at?"

Lucy was certain that her words had alerted the Secret Service.

"I'm about a hundred miles out and on a direct course," Emily replied. "Oh, dear! You've raised your defenses. Would you *please* put me through to the president?"

"Captain Steele, this is Agent Matthews," a new brash voice cut in, "where are you and what is your business?"

"I'm about seventy miles out," Emily replied, "and I wish to report to the president. Ambassador Pickett sent me."

"Ambassador Pi—Wait a minute! Are you from Mars?" Lucy said, punching her call through to the press secretary. "Anne? We've got a Captain Steele for the president. She says she's on some sort of shuttle."

* * *

"Mr. President, Captain Steele!" Anne Byrne said, rushing into the Oval Office with her phone in hand.

"What?" President Merritt said. "Where?"

"On the phone, sir," Anne said, handing it over.

"Captain Steele, this is President Merritt," Greg Merritt said, motioning for Byrne to stay and record the conversation. "Where are you?"

"Sir, as I've said, I'm inbound at forty miles," Captain Steele replied. "I've got the vice president with me, we picked him up on the way, and we've got some important business—"

"Captain Steele, where are you coming from?"

"Well, sir, the Moon was our last stop before we entered orbit," Emily replied. "As I said, we picked up the vice president and now we'd like to land."

"Land where?" Elijah Wood asked, grabbing the spare phone from its cradle as he rushed into the Oval Office along with the rest of the cabinet.

"I figure, sir, that we could land where you put Marine One, if that's all right," Steele replied. "That's what vice president Alquay has requested."

"This is highly irregular, Captain Steele," Wood said in a scathing tone.

"Oh, sir, this is nothing," Emily replied.

"Nothing?" President Merritt repeated.

"Yes, sir," Emily replied. "We're coming down to final now, sir. Are we cleared to land?"

"Radar has a large craft on a direct descent to the White House lawn," Joel Roberts reported, looking up from the tablet that was bathing him in a red light. "The boys in ADA say they've seen nothing like it—"

"Sir!" George Morgan spoke over him. "NORAD is reporting multiple large targets in orbit with small craft descending—"

"Mr. President, everything is fine, I promise," Emily Steele said soothingly. "Anything in U.S. airspace is friendly."

"How do you know that, Captain Steele?" Admiral Roberts demanded frostily.

"Well, sir, because they're under my command," Emily replied calmly. "Admittedly, I had to borrow some alien crew—"

"What, Chinese?" Admiral Roberts cried hotly. "Young lady—"

"Joel, shut up," the president said, glaring at the admiral whose breath puffed away in one defeated glare. "Captain Steele, you say you command these ships?"

"Yes, sir," Emily said. "I've got the one that's right over the capital, and Captain Lee has the other one right next to it, they're the largest."

"And who owns these ships, Captain?" John Ellington demanded. "Are you making us captives?"

"Captives?" Emily sounded genuinely surprised. "Oh, no, sir! Not captives."

"Then what?" Greg Merritt demanded.

"These are our ships, sir," Emily said. "I can explain it all better when we meet but ..." She was silent for a moment, and then said, "You probably know that I'm no longer the captain of the *USN Voyager*."

"Yes," Merritt replied, "we'd heard. You have a new ship?"

"Yes, sir," Emily said, her voice full of pride, "Captain Lee has the *United States Starship Constitution*, sir."

"A *starship*?" Ellington gasped.

The president waved him to silence. "That's a proud name," the president said. "And you, Captain? What is the name of your ship?"

"The *United States Starship Enterprise*."

The End

ABOUT THE AUTHOR

Todd J. McCaffrey is a U.S. Army veteran, a cross-continent pilot, a computer geek, and a *New York Times* bestselling author.

He feeds his weirdness with books, large bowls of popcorn, and frequent forays to science fiction conventions. He is the middle son of the late Anne McCaffrey and is proud to list among his credits eight books written on Pern—including five collaborations.

His website is: http://www.toddmccaffrey.org

ACKNOWLEDGEMENTS

It all started over 30 years ago when Mum's then-lawyer, the famous Jay Katz ("the Katz who defends dragons") mournfully asked, "Why doesn't anyone write a science fiction book about a lawyer?"

Naturally, I couldn't resist the challenge. But life, kids, and stuff all intervened. I found the first 30,000 words nearly 30 years later when I was looking to free up room on my computer. And I read it and thought, "Hmm... I can finish this!"

I'd like to thank all my alpha and beta readers for their insights into the book which made it better and reduced the number of errors significantly.

The amazing Mike Resnick provided most affable support on the finished product and the praise and encouragement from Jody Lyn Nye and Bill Fawcett convinced me that I had a winner on my hands.

Speaking of winners, I'd like to thank the Winner Twins, Brit and Brianna, for all their support and encouragement.

I'd like to thank Jeff Weiner for creating the marvelous cover.

Any mistake you find are all mine.

Made in the USA
Monee, IL
08 September 2021

b17ad99c-dc49-43d0-9e38-131c61908574R01